The Rescuer

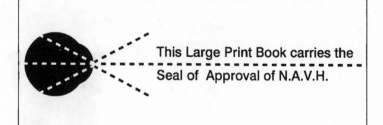

The Rescuer

Book Six – The O'Malley Series

Dee Henderson

Walker Large Print • Waterville, Maine

Published in 2006 by arrangement with
Multnomah Publishers, Inc.

The text of this Large Print edition is unabridged.
Other aspects of the book may vary from the original edition.

Set in 16 pt. Plantin by Elena Picard.

Printed in the United States on permanent paper.

ISBN 0-7862-6319-9 (lg. print : hc : alk. paper)
ISBN 1-59415-030-3 (lg. print : sc : alk. paper)

"I came that they may have life,
and have it abundantly."
John 10:10

As the Founder/CEO of NAVH, the only national health agency solely devoted to those who, although not totally blind, have an eye disease which could lead to serious visual impairment, I am pleased to recognize Thorndike Press* as one of the leading publishers in the large print field.

Founded in 1954 in San Francisco to prepare large print textbooks for partially seeing children, NAVH became the pioneer and standard setting agency in the preparation of large type.

Today, those publishers who meet our standards carry the prestigious "Seal of Approval" indicating high quality large print. We are delighted that Thorndike Press is one of the publishers whose titles meet these standards. We are also pleased to recognize the significant contribution Thorndike Press is making in this important and growing field.

Lorraine H. Marchi, L.H.D.
Founder/CEO
NAVH

* Thorndike Press encompasses the following imprints: Thorndike, Wheeler, Walker and Large Print Press.

Prologue

Paramedic Stephen O'Malley drove north from Chicago the night of June 25, leaving behind life as he knew it. The wipers pushed rain off the windshield, but even on high they gave a clear view of the road for only a few seconds. Cars ahead were visible as red diffuse taillights that occasionally brightened as drivers touched their brakes.

A semi with a trailer rolled past him, throwing water up in a sheet across his windshield. For several seconds he was effectively blind as the wipers struggled to shove the water off. As the deluge cleared, the semi pulled over into his lane. The trailer crossed too far and went into the edge of the roadside. Gravel peppered his car. Stephen immediately slowed, trying to avoid an accident.

He didn't want to die on a stretch of highway tonight. One funeral in a day was enough. It had been overcast at his sister's graveside this morning. By the time the O'Malley family dinner broke up, a heavy drizzle hung in the air. He should have known the weather would turn into a thunderstorm during his drive.

Stephen reached down and changed the radio station, looking for talk radio and a distraction. The oak casket he'd helped carry from the church to the waiting hearse and then to the graveside had been too light. Even with the weight of the casket, it was impossible to hide the fact Jennifer died a shadow of herself. She'd lost a hard fought battle with cancer, convinced until the final weeks that God would work a miracle and heal her. A senseless faith. Stephen shoved a button on the radio to change to a different station. He wasn't going to think about Jennifer. He'd just start fighting tears again.

Wind gusts struck the driver's side of the car. Stephen spotted a blue exit sign advertising gas, food, and hotels and hit the turn signal. He needed a break. If he planned to drive all night, at some point he would need a full tank of gas and something cold to drink. It might as well be now.

He chose a gas station with a canopy over the pumps and a general store for supplies. He topped off the gas tank, checked the oil and fluids, then went inside to pay. The place was deserted but for one other person paying at the register and the sound of a radio announcer listing sports scores.

He wasn't hungry, but food would help keep him awake. He stopped at the self-serve counter in the center of the store under a sign advertising chili by the pint. He could hear Jennifer reminding him about the inevitable heartburn. He shook his head and moved past the kettle.

He had a choice between a Polish sausage spinning on a heat rack that looked as if it had been there for hours or a cold deli sandwich that he couldn't identify. He slid open the cover, used tongs to pick up the Polish, and stuffed it in a hot dog bun. Onions, pickles, and hot mustard made the meat disappear. A store special offered the drink for an extra fifty cents. He tugged a large blue cup from the stack, set it under the dispenser, and was generous with the ice. The Diet Pepsi was sputtering with air so he added regular Pepsi to fill the cup. At least the plastic lid fit. He tucked a straw in his pocket.

The clerk rang up the items. Stephen added a newspaper to the stack.

"It's a bad night for driving. They're saying this rain will get worse before it gets better."

Stephen pulled bills from his wallet. "At least there's less traffic." He pulled change from his shirt pocket, and as he did so green M&M's tumbled into his hand. For a moment Stephen simply looked at them. He rubbed his thumb across the chocolates, turning two of them over. Ann's son Nathan had been sitting on his lap after dinner, having M&M's for dessert. The child provided a welcome distraction from the solemnity of the funeral meal. Nathan had picked out the blue ones for himself and shared the green. Stephen hadn't even realized. *You're so precious, little man.*

Stephen slipped the M&M's back in his pocket. Jennifer would have been pleased to know that Ann had brought her two children to join the dinner. It was a meal where the boys had to be on their best behavior, but they didn't grasp — nor should they — the reality of death and the loss it brought. That empty chair at the table where Jennifer had once sat haunted Stephen through the meal. The boys' presence had indeed been a welcome distraction.

Life went on.

He took the receipt and nodded his thanks.

Wind whipped the bag as he stepped outside. He turned his shoulder into it and walked to his car. He tossed a roll of paper towels on his jacket in the backseat. The

Emergency Medical Services patch on the left sleeve had come up in one corner, and the EMS logo on the back of the jacket was encircled with fluorescent orange tape rubbed nearly through in spots.

He had grabbed the jacket out of habit rather than need. The leave of absence from his paramedic job was open-ended. His boss avoided accepting his resignation, and Stephen had conceded the theoretical possibility that he would change his mind.

He had spent a lifetime rescuing people. The last few months had left him with the certain knowledge that he couldn't carry the weight anymore. He didn't want his pager going off. He didn't want to face another person injured, bleeding, and trying not to die. Stephen was done with it. The profession that had been his career for the last decade no longer appealed to him.

He parked near the exit so he could note down the gas, mileage, and date. Where was he going? He picked up the map, studying it in the dim overhead light. He was driving north, with no particular plan except to be out of the state by morning. He just wanted — no, needed — some space. The decision had been coming for years.

What would his family be saying right now? "He's hurting . . . give him space . . .

let's call him tomorrow." Kate had nearly strangled him when she asked him not to go, or to at least let her come along as navigator. As if she could navigate any better than he could. Outside the city she was notorious for getting lost. He smiled as he chose the road he'd take, then folded the map. If it wasn't for the fact she was married, he would have said yes just for the pleasure of her company.

The bond between the seven O'Malleys went deep. At the orphanage where they had first met, family was nonexistent. They had chosen to become their own family and decided on the last name O'Malley. Now with Jennifer's death there was an undercurrent of fear that the bond between them would change in unpredictable ways, would not hold.

Maybe he was the first sign that it was breaking.

He was thirty minutes away from family and already wondered what he was doing. He rubbed the back of his neck. He could turn around and go back. His family wouldn't pry that much. They'd just swallow him back into their fold and do everything they could to try to help him.

He couldn't go back. He loved the O'Malleys. He just didn't think he could handle being around them for the next few months. He was the odd man out. They were all couples now and he was still unattached. They had all recently come to believe in God, and he didn't want to explore the matter. They said Jennifer was in a better place, talking about heaven as if it was real. Maybe it was, but it didn't change the fact that his sister was gone.

For all his discussions with Jennifer about the subject before she died, the reality of her absence overrode any comfort that nebulous concept of heaven gave.

He pulled back onto the highway. He was going to drive and see the country until he found a sense of peace, and if it took a year, then so be it.

The flashing lights in the rearview mirror caught his attention — the blue and red medley bright in the rain — and then the sound of emergency sirens reached him. Stephen pulled to the right lane. The word *ambulance* on the front of the vehicle grew larger as it approached.

The vehicle rushed past.

Ten minutes later highway traffic began to slow, and then both lanes of cars ground to a halt. Stephen eventually reached the spot where a cop was directing traffic to the far left lane. The ambulance, lights still flashing, was angled in ahead of a fire engine crowding the right lane.

A trailer that had broken free from a semi lay overturned in the road and a smashed-in car had taken a nosedive into the ditch. Through the rain he could see the firefighters working to extract a passenger from the car. *Remove the window before you force that door.* The frame was crumpled to the B-Pillar that went from the undercarriage to the roof and provided structural support for the door frames. If the firefighter popped that door before he took care of the window, they would be working on an extraction while kneeling in shattered glass.

He should stop and offer to help. Stephen didn't act on the fleeting thought. He knew what to do — they probably did too — and if they didn't, they had to learn somehow. Most rescue skills came from hard-won experience. He couldn't rescue everyone in the world who got into trouble. He had tried and it about killed him.

The cop finally signaled his lane of traffic forward. Stephen made one last assessment of the wreck as he slowly passed by. In another lifetime he'd written the book on vehicle extraction. The paramedics were bringing in the backboard and just about had the victim free.

He turned his attention back to the road.

He owed Jennifer. She had asked that he be happy, settled, and at peace with life. She had pushed her version of a solution — encouraging him to settle down with Ann and to come to church, but he wasn't able to believe as she longed for, and she hadn't lived long enough to see him settled down, even if he'd been inclined to do so. He had let her down. And it hurt.

Jenny, I already miss you something terrible. Why did you have to die?

Silent tears slid down his cheeks, and he wiped them away.

He pulled out a bottle of aspirin from the glove box and dumped two tablets into his left hand. He popped them in his mouth, grimaced at the taste, and picked up his soda. The sides of the cup were sweating and the paper was getting soft. He took two long draws on the straw to wash down the tablets.

His phone rang for the fourth time. Stephen looked over at it. He had a feeling the caller wouldn't give up, so he flipped the phone open with one hand. "Yes?"

"Stephen?"

Meghan Delhart's voice was like the brush of angel's wings over a bruise, a tender balm to a painful hurt. His hand

15

tightened on the steering wheel and he glanced in the rearview mirror to make sure he could slow down without causing problems for someone driving too close to his car. He dropped his speed another five miles per hour. "Hey there, beautiful." Meghan had been at Jennifer's visitation last night.

"You were on my mind and I took a chance you'd still be up. It sounds like you're on the road somewhere."

"Just driving, thinking." She would understand what he didn't say. There had been nights when she walked out of a shift as an ER nurse not sure whether she wanted to go home, let alone back to work. He'd often played checkers with her on the ambulance gurney while he followed up on the patients he'd brought in.

If anyone had a right to complain about life, it was Meghan. She'd run away for a year in her own way after her car accident and its aftermath. She retreated to live with her parents and told friends not to visit. She went away to lick her wounds, and when the year was over, she came back at peace, with no signs of how hard the transition had been. He envied her strength. If Meghan could adapt to the tragedies that came in life, so could he. Jennifer was gone. He had to live with it.

16

"How far are you planning to drive?"

"Until sleep says find a hotel." He changed the radio station he was listening to. "I took a leave of absence from work."

She let that sink in. "That might be good."

He rolled his right shoulder. Good, bad, it just was. He didn't have the emotional energy to handle the job right now.

"Are you driving through rain? The storm is getting close here."

"Wind driven rain," he confirmed. "Where are you staying?" She'd come into town for the funeral, so she must still be in the area.

"I borrowed the keys to my grandparents' vacation place in Whitfield."

Whitfield . . . he finally placed it on his mental map. She was about twenty minutes northwest of his position. The storm must be tracking her direction.

"I have a love-hate relationship with storms."

He heard the tension in her voice. "I know," he said gently. About all she remembered of the night of her accident was the lightning and the thunder. The majority of her prior week — and most of the following several days — had been wiped out of her memory and never returned.

17

"You okay, Meghan?" He was reluctant to get pulled into it tonight, but the fact that she wasn't asking drew the words out.

At twelve she had worn reading glasses, her nose often in a book, and had a habit of mixing up her *r*s and *w*s when she tried to speak fast. She was one of his first friends from the neighborhood around the orphanage, an endearing one in an embarrassing kind of way for a preteen boy teased about hanging out with a girl by his friends. He hadn't realized until he spotted her across the room last night just how much he missed her.

"I'll be okay when this storm blows over." She turned her radio to match his station. "I'm going back to Silverton tomorrow. Dad is coming in to pick me up."

"Do you want to go tonight? I'll give you a lift if you like."

"I don't need rescuing, Stephen."

He smiled. "Maybe I do."

She was quiet a moment. "You wouldn't mind?"

"I wouldn't mind."

And as she hesitated, he hoped she would say yes. Meghan was one of few outside his family who he fully trusted to understand his mood on a night like tonight.

"Yes, I'd appreciate a lift. I'm already

packed, and I won't be able to sleep with this storm overhead."

"Then I'm on the way." Stephen picked up the map to figure out how to get off this highway and over to her area.

"Would you like coffee or tea?" Meghan asked.

"I'd love a cup of your tea with honey and cinnamon."

"It will be waiting. I'll turn on the driveway lights and leave the back door unlocked. Come on in so you don't get drenched."

"I'll be there soon."

He set down the phone. Meghan had talked him out of running away once before. He doubted she could do it again, but he at least wanted to say how much he appreciated her coming to town for the visitation. They were friends, and destined to always be just friends given he hadn't been smart enough to settle down with her when he had the chance — and life rarely gave second chances.

His life was littered with *if onlys*.

He would give Meghan a lift home and then continue with his drive. If he let himself start grieving the past, the pain would never end. One of those *if onlys* had nearly cost Meghan her life.

One

Friday, August 16
Chicago

Stephen parked the ambulance next to a police squad car in the parking lot across from
the county building and confirmed his location with dispatch. He'd dropped off his
partner Ryan at the gym down the street to
take a much needed shower. A happy drunk
staggering home at 6 a.m. had lost most of
his last beer across Ryan's shirt. It already
had the makings of an interesting Friday
shift.

The heat hit him as he stepped from the
vehicle. It was a day that would send tem-
pers flaring somewhere in the city, and his
squad would be sent to patch up the results
of the inevitable fights. Stephen hoped they
didn't get a DOA run: He'd had enough
dead-on-arrival calls to last the year. He
spent his days dealing with car accidents,

heart attacks, gunshot victims, and drug overdoses. He didn't need some rookie cop trying to comfort the family calling him out to a victim with no pulse whose body was cold and stiff. This job wore at him enough without adding the strain of having to tell people they were looking at a corpse.

Stephen shoved his hands into his pockets and tried to force himself out of the morbid mood. Last night's dispatch to a man who had died hours before lingered in his mind like some dark dangerous cloud. Being a paramedic might be a noble profession, but it didn't run to being a chaplain. He didn't need crying kids and angry spouses shouting at him to do something when it was obvious there was nothing he could do. The voices had haunted his dreams last night.

What he really needed was a vacation, a nice long pedestrian vacation where no one paged him or, for that matter, knew him. The decision resonated, and he made a mental note to force some time off into his schedule. He loved his job, but there were days he wanted to walk away from it.

Stephen entered the restaurant on the corner and paused in front of the display of pastries and donuts to glance around the tables for his sister Kate. Cops hung out here.

He eliminated those in police blues and looked at the remaining ladies. Kate rarely looked like the cop she was. As a hostage negotiator, she tried to downplay any sense of being a threat to the person she was trying to convince to surrender. He didn't see her and was surprised that he had arrived first.

Stephen waved good morning to the owner and walked to Kate's favorite table in the back of the restaurant. She preferred to sit with her back to the wall so no one could come up behind her.

He ordered a sunrise special for himself and, since Kate was a creature of habit, ordered blueberry pancakes and coffee for her. He'd learned to eat early and well as time for lunch in his job was never a given. He turned up the sound on his radio. Kate was rarely late unless she was out on an assignment somewhere. There had been too many close calls with her lately. The last thing he needed was his sister getting herself shot.

He was on his second cup of coffee when she arrived. Kate wore jeans and a pale blue shirt and carried a folded newspaper under her arm. He rose and pulled out the chair for her. She had been out in the sun this morning — the beginning of a sunburn was showing on her face and she had the glow of sweat on her skin. Since she hated early mornings, he guessed she'd been on a call somewhere in the city.

He could feel the heat coming from her back as she took her seat, and the sun had lightened a few more strands of her hair. He was constantly tugging a baseball cap on her to keep her from getting sunstroke on the job. She tossed her newspaper onto the table. "Thanks."

"I'm glad you could make it." Stephen sat back down. "I already ordered for you."

"Great. I needed this break." Kate dipped a napkin in her glass of water and used the wet corner to clean her sunglasses. "The heat is getting to people. We had an incident at a manufacturing plant this morning, and I spent two hours leaning in a window to have a conversation with a guy."

He pushed five sugar packets across the table for her coffee. "Did it end okay?"

She glanced up and smiled at his question; he had to smile back.

"It was the usual supervisor–employee fight that just kept building until they threw a few punches and then the employee pulled a gun." She set down the sunglasses. "He talked with his kids and apologized for a fight with them the night before, released

23

his supervisor, then gave himself up. The gun turned out not to be loaded. I would have resolved it in an hour, but the supervisor wouldn't keep his mouth shut. Even *I* felt like hitting the guy at one point, so I can understand how the fight got started."

She dumped four packets of sugar in her coffee, tasted it, and added a fifth.

"You're going to make yourself hyper drinking that."

"Sugar is my one vice and I'm sticking to it." She propped her elbows on the table, steepled her fingers, and pointed at him. "Your call this morning was a surprise. What's happening, Stephen?"

"I need a favor."

She tilted her head to the side. "I'm always good for one."

"It's not difficult — I need you to meet Lisa at the airport for me tonight. She's carrying bones back with her and needs an extra hand." Their sister Lisa was a forensic pathologist for the city coroner's office. She'd been working for weeks to figure out how a Jane Doe had died and decided it was time to consult the experts at the Smithsonian. It got a little complex explaining to airport personnel and taxi drivers why she was hauling around boxes of bones.

"Sure, I'll meet her. Have you got other plans?"

"A date."

Kate's expression shifted from amusement to interest. "A good thing to have on a Friday night. Do I know her?"

"Maybe . . . Paula Lewis. I've had to cancel on her twice when a dispatch held me up, and it hasn't been easy to get her to say yes again. I'm going to make it up to her tonight."

"Paula's a nice lady, if you like doctors."

He smiled at the qualification. "Very nice." Their sister Jennifer was a pediatrician and therefore an exception, but beyond that Kate did her best to avoid those in the medical profession and their inevitable work-related conversations.

The restaurant owner brought their breakfasts and paused to chat with Kate. News affecting the city in general and the police department specifically was debated here long before it reached the watercooler at the precinct.

Stephen spread jelly on his toast and listened to his sister's intense talk about work. Kate was the heart, soul, and passion of the O'Malleys. When someone in the family needed an advocate, she was the one they turned to.

He couldn't imagine life without Kate in it. Having lost his little sister Peg in a drowning accident and his parents in a car accident by the time he was eleven, he'd been convinced at an early age that he was destined to lose people he cared about. He'd been feeling pretty grim at Trevor House until Kate came crashing into his life. She had practically dared him to try to get rid of her. Her tenacious leading with her chin, her I'm-in-your-life, deal-with-it attitude had slipped under his guard like nothing else ever could. He loved her for it.

The conversation broke up and Kate turned her attention to her breakfast. "So what have you been up to lately besides convincing Paula to give you another chance?"

He opened his shirt pocket and tugged out a checker piece he had carved. "Another one for your collection." They would have enough to play a game soon.

She studied both sides of the checker. "You're getting really good at the detail work."

"The whittling is a challenge. It's certainly tougher than hanging drywall." On his days off he gutted and remodeled old homes. He enjoyed the carpentry work. It didn't wear at his emotions the way being a paramedic did.

She tucked the piece in her pocket. Kate's eyes narrowed as she looked over his shoulder.

He knew better than to turn and look. Her face turned impassive. At her simple shift-to-work mode, Stephen slid his plate aside. The more impassive she got, the more dangerous she was. "Cool off, Kate."

Her gaze met his and the anger in her eyes had him leaning back. "That cop nearly cost me a child's life."

"You look like you're ready to deck him."

"Maybe serve him my breakfast in his lap." She picked up her water glass. "We had a custody blowup last week. A dad took his daughter from school during recess and holed up at his place, threatening to kill her rather than let his wife have custody. I got called in. That patrol officer nearly gave away the SWAT team position when he decided to get some media airtime and describe what had happened and his role in it."

"Not everyone avoids media like you do."

"He's not a rookie; he knows better."

Stephen reached over and loosened her fist. Whoever made the mistake of thinking Kate was not a cop down to her marrow didn't understand what drove her. Justice for her was very black and white. "Let it go."

27

Peg's drowning had driven him to be a paramedic, and Kate had also made the decision to be a cop at an early age.

"You're right. He's not worth it." Her tension turned to a hard smile. "He's a little out of his normal patrol area. He probably has a meeting with my boss to discuss the incident. He won't feel like stopping to eat afterward."

Stephen smiled. "That's better. Your optimism is back."

"It's going to be one of those Fridays. I can feel it."

"I hope you're wrong."

His radio sounded. Stephen pushed back his chair and stood. He set money on the table and leaned over to kiss Kate's cheek. "I've gotta go. See you around this weekend."

"I want to hear about this date, Stephen."

Knowing the O'Malley family grapevine, it would be common knowledge soon after it was over. "As if I could keep it from you. Stay safe, Kate."

"I'll do my best."

Stephen headed back to the ambulance. He stayed in Chicago because of Kate. He didn't bother to tell her that, but she probably already knew. Someone needed to watch her back, and their oldest brother Marcus who normally filled that role was working in the U.S. Marshal's office in Washington, D.C. After Kate was married and had someone else around to watch her back, he'd think more seriously about moving on. He would find a small town with a lake where he could cultivate his love of fishing and find an EMS job where he'd treat more bee stings and heart attacks than gunshot wounds. He liked the certainty of having that dream even if he didn't have a plan to act on yet.

His partner Ryan was towel drying his hair. The ambulance passenger door was open but Ryan stood outside. The heat built up inside the metal box fast.

"I'll drive," Stephen said. His new partner was still learning Chicago's streets.

Ryan tossed his towel across the hot leather seat. "Fine with me."

Dispatch assigned them to a code three run — a transport from Memorial Hospital to Lutheran General — so Stephen didn't bother with the lights and sirens. It was probably a high-risk pregnancy being moved to the specialized maternity unit. He'd almost rather deal with a gunshot victim than a woman in labor. They averaged two pregnancy runs a month where a lady mistimed the pace of her contractions and left going to the hospital a little too late. Infants were hard to handle in a moving vehicle that was never designed to be a delivery room. At least with pregnancy runs, one of the nurses from the maternity ward rode along to be safe.

Stephen pulled in to Memorial Hospital and looked around at the vehicles. He didn't see Meghan's jeep. There was family, there were girlfriends, and then there was Meghan. The ER nurse was in a class by herself.

"She must still be on night shifts," Ryan commented.

Stephen glanced over, his right eyebrow raised a fraction.

"Meghan. That *is* who you're looking for, isn't it?"

"She's just an old friend."

Ryan laughed. "If you say so, O'Malley." He tugged run sheets from the folder under the seat. "Let's go find our pregnant lady. I'm guessing triplets."

"Lunch says it's twins trying to come early."

"You're on. And if I'm right, I'm driving and you can ride the back bench with her."

Silverton, Illinois

Craig Fulton opened the door to Neil Coffer's jewelry store Friday afternoon and heard familiar chimes signal his entrance. He walked through the store past the display counters and the spin racks of postcards of famous jewelry to the door in the back of the store marked employees only. Ignoring the restriction, he walked through to the repair shop.

In a tourist town the size of Silverton, the jewelry Neil sold attracted more lookers than buyers. Not many farmers and small business owners could afford an antique bracelet that started in the thousands or a modern necklace that cost five figures. Fortunately, Neil also had a thriving jewelry repair business that paid the bills. Orders to jewelry stores around the state were stacked on the side counter, already prepared for Fed-Ex to pick up.

Craig waited until Neil looked up from the large magnifying glass and the piece he was working on. Neil hated to be interrupted while a repair was underway, and Craig had no desire to get on his bad side today. Hunched over the workbench the man looked more like ninety than seventy-five. He was a chain smoker and time had not been kind. How the man ever sold any jewelry was a mystery. He hadn't smiled since the Nixon era. When he did unwillingly part with a piece, he hardly offered much of a bargain.

Neil lifted the diamond from the ring with tweezers and placed it in a small ceramic dish inside a box labeled: Mrs. Heather Teal. Only one customer's piece was allowed on the repair bench at a time, and the smooth metal work area was lined with a ridge to prevent a stone from rolling off onto the floor. Rumors circulated that Neil had been a forger for the army during the cold war, making documents to allow soldiers to move around behind enemy lines, and Craig tended to believe it.

Neil finished his task and closed the box holding Mrs. Teal's work order. He walked to the east wall of the room and opened the door to the walk-in safe. When Neil had bought the old bank building, he turned its massive walk-in vault into a storage place for his jewelry.

Someone had robbed Neil two years ago, taking the pieces in the front room display cases. During the trial a year later, it had come out that the pieces in the display cases were actually excellent fakes of the real pieces Neil kept stored in the safe. When he went back to box a sold item, he retrieved the actual piece.

Some of the town residents had been impressed that he didn't leave out valuable pieces to be taken; others were embarrassed over raving about a fake diamond's size and clarity. The defense counsel had tried to argue that Neil was actually selling fakes and his client was wrongly charged. But the few pieces sold over the years to townspeople had all proven to be real diamonds, emeralds, and rubies, so the accusations didn't stick.

Craig had thought more than once about stealing Neil's real gems as a way to finance leaving town for good. He gave up that idea when he realized Neil kept the vault locked when he wasn't using it, had a loaded handgun under the counter, and had mirrors and cameras set around the rooms to let him see what went on at all times.

Neil brought back a small black box from the safe. Craig set his briefcase on the counter, opened it, then Neil put the box inside.

"You have Jonathan's directions?" Neil pulled an envelope from under the counter and added it to the briefcase.

Craig nodded. "I meet him at his hotel room in downtown Chicago at midnight. I'll be back here no later than 5 a.m."

Neil stared at him, and Craig felt sweat trickle down his back.

"The back door will be unlocked. I'll be waiting for you."

Craig nodded and closed the briefcase. He would consider double-crossing a lot of people, but Neil was not one of them. The man was just crazy enough to be unpredictable.

Chicago

The ambulance smelled like disinfectant by midafternoon. Stephen wiped down the gurney with warm water. It never failed to amaze him where blood ended up. The last transport had been a simple nosebleed, but neither ice nor pressure had stopped it. The doctors would have to pack it off. Now the ambulance was parked in Memorial Hospital's side parking lot while they cleaned the rig and restocked supplies.

Ryan closed drawers and locked the drug cabinet that held the morphine and Valium. Including those vials in the red medical case they carried with them to a scene just meant someone would inevitably grab the case and run. "We're in pretty good shape." Ryan passed over the clipboard. "Sign on page four and six and initial nine."

Stephen tugged a pen from his pocket, read the pages, then scrawled his signature. "Add another O_2 cylinder and a replacement nebulizer, and see about a dozen more biohazard bags. We've got a persistent sharps problem by the end of the shift." He'd nearly stuck himself with a used needle that had been slid into a discarded IV tubing for lack of something proper to encapsulate it.

Ryan nodded and took the pad. "I'll go sweet-talk Supply for us." He stepped down from the ambulance and headed toward the hospital.

Stephen wiped down the storage cabinets under the bench, then rubbed sweat off his face with the back of his sleeve.

"Maybe this will help."

He glanced to the back of the ambulance and set down the rag to take the large glass of ice water. "Thanks, Meghan." He wondered if she was working today. He leaned over to touch the sleeve of her uniform. The white fabric still had a pressed crease in it. "Air-conditioning. I'm jealous."

She laughed and perched on the bumper. "It's actually a bit chilly inside. Guys have an advantage — you look good sweaty."

He drained the entire glass then removed a piece of ice to rub on the back of his neck. She definitely did not look wilted. He flipped water from the melting ice at her and then set aside the glass.

It was nice having her back in his life. Her family had moved away from the Trevor House neighborhood when he was fifteen, and it wasn't until she was in nursing school that they'd been able to catch up on their old friendship.

She leaned into the ambulance to look at the roof, getting in his way and nearly dragging her hair in the dirty water. "Where is this bullet hole I heard about?"

He shifted her away from trouble and pointed toward the front of the ambulance. "The guys on last night's shift had an interesting time." They had been trying to treat a gunshot victim and had come under fire from shooters on the roof of a building across the street. It was a sad day when an ambulance wasn't considered an out-of-bounds target.

"If it rains tonight it's going to drip in here."

"Ryan is getting us some patching material. You think it's going to rain and break this heat?"

"Ken thinks so. He's predicting four

inches of rain, with heavy winds and unusually strong lightning."

Stephen hoped her cousin was at least partially right. They needed rain.

"According to his forecasts, it will probably blow in around 7 p.m. and last well into the night." Meghan reached for the lotion he kept in the cleaning supply case and rubbed it liberally into her hands. "I'm going storm chasing with him tomorrow. I want a tornado picture for my wall and am determined to get it this year."

"Quit wishing for trouble, Meghan, and drive carefully tonight. You'll be heading right into the rain."

"I get off at six. I'll either go before the rain arrives or wait until the worst of it passes."

"Just don't chase lightning when you can't find your tornado. I want you coming back as you are, not with lightning curled hair."

She laughed and tugged over the supply case to help him out.

Stephen was beginning to suspect she had a boyfriend in Silverton given how many trips home she made, but he drew the line at probing the subject. If he knew a name then he'd have to go check the guy out to make sure he was good enough for her, and that would cross the line into meddling. At least she was smart enough not to say yes to some of the doctors around here who asked her out. Meghan wasn't a city girl at heart, and it would do her good to find someone back in Silverton, move home, and work in her father's medical practice. She talked about it often enough. A house, babies, and working with her dad. The girl had good dreams.

His phone rang in his shirt pocket. He'd just plunged his hand into the bucket of water. He looked around for his towel and scowled when he saw it already pitched in the laundry bag.

Meghan solved the problem by reaching over and tugging out his phone. "Hi, you've reached Stephen's secretary." She grinned and leaned against the bench, lifting one foot up onto the bumper. "Hi there, Jennifer. Your brother is cleaning up the rig at the moment and making faces at me."

It was unusual to hear from Jennifer in the middle of the day. Stephen opened a new roll of paper towels. Meghan covered the phone. "Are you interested in a twenty-one-inch painting of a fish?"

He held out his hand. "Jack will love it for his birthday."

"Oh, that's awful and so perfect." Meghan passed him the phone.

"Hi, Jen. Yes, buy and ship it."

"It comes close to matching that set of painted eggshell salt and pepper shakers he gave you last year. I saw this and thought of you," Jennifer said.

"You're flea market shopping?"

"I'm making a house call on a fourteen-year-old who likes to paint. She's actually pretty good. The fish painting, however, was a joke for her brother, and in the end she couldn't go through with wrapping it."

"I love this kid. Trust me; I'll have no problem giving it to Jack."

The radio up front sounded dispatch tones. "Jen, I've gotta go."

Meghan scrambled off the bumper and grabbed the bucket of water. "I'll dump this for you."

"Thanks, Meg." Stephen shoved back supply cases and slammed doors. He piled into the driver's seat while Ryan ran out the ER doors and scrambled into the passenger seat.

Ryan called up the address and details. "A fire on Lexington Street. Better rush it. They've already gone to a second alarm so it must be big."

Stephen punched on the lights.

Meghan stood holding the bucket and

39

watched the ambulance pull out. The man needed a haircut. She had to think of *something* that could be improved on, for the bottom line was when Stephen smiled at her, her day turned over. That smile made it impossible to look away. Then he'd notice she was looking at him that way and his eyes would fill with laughter. He'd inevitably tease her about it.

He didn't see her as anything but a friend. It was for the best: Stephen wasn't interested in settling down. As far as she knew he had never set foot inside a church, and she couldn't imagine him ever being content to live in a small town that only had a volunteer EMS crew. She'd watched him grow into a tall strong handsome guy who inspired confidence by his presence. His years as a fireman had forged his muscles into an impressive build, and the last years as a paramedic had added a touch of gray now streaking through his brown hair. She watched him play basketball with his brothers and thought he was the best looking of the O'Malley guys. She was probably a bit prejudiced there.

Meghan washed out the bucket with the garden hose hidden by the planters and flipped it upside down to dry. She lifted a hand to the cop car pulling into the circular drive. She hoped Stephen's date with Paula Lewis fell through again. The doctor was nice and likely to turn Stephen's head, but she was heading to California in a couple months to take a position with a university medical group. Meghan didn't want to listen to Stephen's inevitable, "I miss her" remarks.

The guy was lonely. She knew him too well not to know that. He always kept dating relationships casual and short. Her mom said he wasn't yet ready to risk his heart — with people or with God. Maybe Mom was right and it was time to let go of her teenage crush. It just felt like a failure to give up on him.

"You know he likes you."

Meghan glanced at Kate O'Malley who was strolling over from the hospital side entrance. "I saw the ambulance heading out," Kate explained.

Meghan grimaced. "Stephen still sees me as a twelve-year-old."

"Not entirely. He just doesn't think about dating old friends." Kate draped an arm around her shoulders in a show of sympathy. "He notices when you're not at work, keeps tabs on your travels, comments when you are happy or sad. You're in a class by yourself. Think of Stephen as a tree that is

41

inevitably going to fall hard someday. He's looking for something without realizing it's right in front of him."

"Right now I just want him to notice me so I can turn him down."

Kate laughed. "That's my Meg."

"How's the hand?"

Kate moved her bruised fingers. "The ice helped. Next time a kid slams my hand in a door, I'm asking for hazard pay. Come on, let's get a late lunch."

Meghan took one last look at where the ambulance had disappeared and nodded. Stephen would be back after he rescued someone. He just didn't seem to realize how much he needed rescuing himself.

Silverton

Ken hung up the phone in his home office and jotted down Friday's temperature and humidity numbers called in from the barge floating down the Mississippi. The captain was a fellow amateur weatherman. The weather map on Ken's table showed isometric lines coming close together at Davenport. The coming storm tonight would be big. He had to get out there. His phone rang as he packed his camera bag.

The name on the caller ID urged him to answer. "Are we on, hon?"

"Two weeks in the Bahamas." His wife bubbled with the news. "Mom loved the idea of coming back to work for a couple weeks. I told you she was bored," JoAnne said. "She'll handle the store. You want me to call and confirm the tickets?"

"Absolutely. Neil said he'd buy the brooch himself if he couldn't find an immediate buyer for it. Book the tickets and I'll stop by to see Neil this afternoon then make the bank deposit."

"I'm so excited about this."

Ken folded the latest weather map and slid it in his case. "You found the locket and brooch, hon. You should get the vacation of your dreams as a reward. That and a new dishwasher."

"We might get more for the pieces if we waited a while to sell them."

"We weren't expecting to find real jewelry in that music box in the attic. There's no use being greedy. We'll keep the locket, sell the brooch, and enjoy the honeymoon we never had."

"Okay, I'm calling. Are you going storm chasing?"

"Just for an hour. I'll be back before you get home from work."

"Is Meghan coming home or should I call to tell her the news?"

"She's driving down tonight." His cousin and wife had been best friends since high school.

"I get her for shopping tomorrow. You'll have to take her storm chasing another day."

"How about a trip to Davenport to shop, then we can keep going to get some pictures?"

"If the sky looks interesting," JoAnne compromised. "I'll see you in a couple hours."

"Love ya, JoAnne. Drive careful."

Some things were too valuable to trust to the jewelry store vault. Neil returned the workbench to its original position and carried the hidden ledger over to his desk.

A brooch and a locket . . . He had to turn the pages back to 1982 to find the pieces. They had been stolen from a couple at the Wilshire hotel in Chicago during a false fire alarm, and excellent fakes were substituted for the genuine pieces. He vaguely remembered the theft . . . it had been so very long ago. There was no star by the line to indicate the theft had ever been discovered and a police report filed. The lady or her heirs probably still thought they had the real

44

stones. It was rare for one of his substitute pieces to hold up for twenty years, but it was possible if they were in an unopened jewelry box or a safe deposit box.

He never sold the originals until the thefts were at least a decade cold and never in the same state as they were taken from. Stashing the brooch and locket in the music box as a place to let them cool off had been a bad move. He didn't know when his wife gave away the music box, or to whom, but it eventually ended up in Ken and JoAnne's attic.

It was only the fourth time in years he'd had to buy back a piece he had originally stolen. He would have to do something about that locket. If JoAnne had taken a fancy to wearing it — He had best make another fake piece and recover the original from her. She wasn't the kind of woman to stay in a small town like Silverton when a few hours' drive could have her shopping in Chicago or in Davenport. Someone who knew jewelry would find the piece fascinating, and that locket was in a jewelry catalog as an interesting piece of work by a French artisan. He didn't want a chance question raised.

Neil flipped past pages of entries and wrote a new line for this purchase. Someday he would have to create a list of where exactly he had stashed all the pieces he had cooling off. It was getting rather hard to remember. For security reasons, he had never written down that information. It was one thing to record all he knew about a piece that had been stolen, another to admit he still possessed it. He refused to hide pieces at his store, and safe deposit boxes weren't worth the questions. Everyone in town knew he owned his own vault.

As friends in the business died off, he sold fewer and fewer pieces when they reached their decade cold mark. The new generation of young men willing to move a valuable piece such as those he acquired had no honor, and Neil refused to deal with a man whose word wasn't good for something. He was too old to spend a day in jail, and his wife needed someone around to take care of her.

He sold enough that they never lacked money, and he had enough pieces to last him through a comfortable retirement. But a man had to keep his hand in the game, and occasionally a collection was worth acquiring.

Tonight would be profitable.

He took the ledger back to its resting place. Where should he hide the pieces Craig was bringing back? He needed somewhere special for a special collection.

Two

Chicago

The house on Lexington collapsed on itself, flames raging against multiple streams of water from fire companies fighting it. Stephen watched the fire crews from the comfort of the ambulance left running to keep the air-conditioning on. He was a fireman before training as a paramedic. He knew the risks the guys were in from the flames, steam, and heatstroke. He watched for trouble but was content to be bored. Firemen rescued people; paramedics kept them alive. The profession change gave him the greater challenge.

When the fire was suppressed and they were finally released from the scene, rush hour traffic was well underway. Stephen and Ryan took up station in a grocery store parking lot on the south end of the district waiting for the next call. Stephen remembered why he hated the ambulance passenger seat. His knees were crammed against the dashboard, and he was ready to get out and yank the gray leather seat out of the vehicle to find the broken latch that wouldn't give him another two inches of legroom. Ken had been right about the storm. Heavy rain splattered against the windshield, the noise on the roof like crickets slamming into tin.

Stephen ate a burrito, trying not to mess up his new tie. His dinner with Paula was in two hours, and he was still trying to decide on what to wear. Ryan thought the tie he'd picked up was too upscale for the jeans. A 10-55 dispatch — car wreck with injuries — came as Stephen finished his late lunch. "There's construction on Cline. You'd better come in from the north on Lewis," Stephen recommended, picking up the radio to confirm their ETA with dispatch. "Unit 59, Roger code one to Cline and Lewis."

Ryan punched on the lights and siren and pulled out of the lot. By the time he parked behind cop cars and a fire engine blocking off the accident scene, Stephen's knuckles were white on the dash. His partner did not understand Chicago drivers and actually assumed they would get out of the way for an emergency vehicle. "Nice driving, ace."

Ryan grabbed his slicker. "I learned it from you."

Stephen barked out a laugh, set down his drink, which miraculously hadn't spilled all over his lap, and grabbed his own rain slicker.

A red Honda rested thirty feet across the interchange accordioned into a blue Toyota. A white van with Flowers and Finery painted on the side had come to a violent stop across the concrete median. Broken glass and a debris trail of headlight fragments and muffler parts marked the point of the three-vehicle collision. Stephen spotted two air bags in the Toyota still inflated from their explosive deployment.

Firefighters were clustered around the crushed red Honda and two EMTs were working at the van. Not enough ambulance crews had been dispatched. Stephen got on the radio to request two more.

Ryan opened the rear cabinet and grabbed the blue go-case with the airway supplies and trauma dressings. Stephen pulled out the red case packed with drug and IV supplies. The fire and rescue guys would already have collars, splints, and backboards out.

The fire captain met them. "The van driver had a rack of flower vases crash forward and he's covered in glass. We've got a mother and her young daughter trapped in the Honda — the mom is critical; the girl is stable. The Toyota driver walked away a bit dazed."

Stephen absorbed the information. No fatalities; that was a relief. "Two more ambulances are on the way."

"I'll make sure the cops clear a route out of here."

Stephen nodded and headed toward the crumpled Honda.

The fireman helping the driver made room for him. Thick black rubber mats had been draped over the jagged metal edges to make it possible to reach inside without being cut. As Stephen assessed the unconscious driver's condition, he tried to mentally re-create what would have happened to her during the accident.

Her car had been hit hard from the side. That impact would have caused her to hit the window and then would have flung her to her left. While she was in motion to her left, her car hit the Toyota head-on. He winced. That meant the lady's left side and rib cage would have been exposed when the steering column came back. He felt carefully where he predicted the worst impact. Broken ribs, internal bleeding, and from the sound of her breathing a partially collapsed lung. She was bleeding from a deep gash on her lower abdomen. She didn't respond to his touch — the most dangerous sign of all.

He looked over at the lady's daughter. She was maybe ten, terrified, and because of the way she was pinned, unable to turn her head away from her mom. He smiled, hoping to reassure the child. "My name is Stephen, and my partner Ryan is behind you. We're going to get you out of this car very soon."

"Mom's really hurt."

"And I'm a really good paramedic." He took a few precious seconds to reach across and touch her cheek. "Promise."

The first car accident victim arrived in the ER at 8:12 p.m., the stretcher pushed in by a paramedic wearing a rain slicker, her partner jogging alongside holding an IV bag up with one hand and steadying their small patient with his other. The sounds and smells from outside rushed in with them: An ambulance pulled out with sirens whooping like a huge bird to warn traffic, rain pounded, and a sweet oily smell hung in the air from the asphalt getting washed for the first time in weeks.

Meghan reached them first, taking the IV bag and scanning the ten-year-old girl's face. They had been warned she was coming in. She smiled at the child who didn't have much left of her hair because a rescue worker had been forced to cut it to extract her from the wreck. The remains of the braid rested like a crushed cord an inch above her left shoulder, the sliced golden strands working their way apart in a frayed mat. The girl had been crying, but she was silent now, her eyes wide, her fear growing.

Meghan leaned in close in order to be heard as they rushed toward exam area two. "Tracy, your mom is coming in the next ambulance. Relax and just listen to the doctor; he's nice. You're going to be fine." There was no time for anything more as the trauma team surrounded the girl.

By the time the lead paramedic was done giving his report, the little one was on oxygen, a warm blanket lay across her chest, and two doctors worked on the right leg splint placed at the scene, a portable X-ray machine moved in to capture an image of the shattered bone.

Another doctor worked on the child's facial lacerations and bruises, talking with her as he did so, the only man in the medley of people who seemed unhurried. The child wasn't dying on him, and Jim had a refined sense of when to expend extra energy. Meghan watched the doctor work and wished she understood how to duplicate that stillness. Her ER shifts felt like twelve hours on adrenaline.

She turned away from the group and shoved back the curtain on exam area four. From the early radioed warnings Tracy's mom had been driving without a seat belt, and it had cost her dearly. Ryan's voice on the call had been shaken. Paramedics saw *everything* in their job. It wouldn't be good. She doubled the amount of gauze set out.

Her shift had ended two hours ago but with the heavy rain she'd stayed where she could do some good. Now she was glad that she had. She heard the sound of the arriving ambulance moments before the doors crashed open. Ryan was pushing the gurney and Stephen was at its side. The water dripping from their jackets trailed back to the door, tinged red with blood. The resident took one look and hollered for Jim to join them.

Meghan pulled on fresh gloves and took up position a step behind Jim's right shoulder as Ryan swiftly gave details. Jim moved the packing to see what Ryan was describing. "Push that blood." His lead trauma nurse was a step ahead of him, already hanging another unit. He looked over at the chief resident. "How's her oxygen?"

"Horrible. Her lungs are collapsed on the left. I'm opening it up." The resident readied a deep needle to pull out the misplaced air. Meghan accepted handfuls of bloody pressure bandages from Jim as he worked, and fed him back clean packing.

A movement of blue caught her attention and Meghan glanced up. Stephen was leaning against the back wall watching them. The front of his shirt was covered with blood and he was still breathing hard. His hands were the only thing clean, for he'd stripped off his gloves. The man looked exhausted. Blue eyes met hers and held a moment, and she saw the depths of what he had seen at the scene.

The wall looked as though it was holding him up; he'd given everything he had. At times Stephen cared too much for his own good. She wished she had a free moment to give him a hug just to ease that look of hurt darkening his eyes.

She turned back to what Jim was doing, focusing on staying a step ahead of him. The odds that Tracy's mom would make it were already improving. Her heartbeat had steadied, her blood pressure was low but stable, and the oxygen in her blood was rising. Stabilize her, get her to surgery, and the specialists in ICU would keep her alive and give her a good chance to heal.

"Let's get her upstairs."

The nurse disconnected cardiac leads and transferred the IV to the hanging stand at the head of the stretcher. Stephen pushed away from the wall and touched a hand to the woman's bare foot as she was pushed by. "Where's her daughter?"

"Exam area two." Meghan bent to pick up one of the many bloody gauze squares that had fallen to the floor. Stephen nodded and walked down to see the child.

Meghan watched him go and hoped he remembered the blood on his shirt before he got there. He paused by a biohazard bag and the blue shirt came off, leaving a gray T-shirt that was wet with rainwater, sweat, or both. He tossed the bloody shirt into the bag and then turned into exam area two.

"He was the one who cut Tracy's hair," she murmured to Ryan.

"Yes. She was pinned looking at her mom. It was the only fast solution we had."

Most paramedics she had figured out pretty early on. They were white knights riding to the rescue, who enjoyed the adrenaline rush of a crisis. Stephen O'Malley was still a mystery. He was emotionally invested in rescuing people yet he was one of the best at the job she had ever met. But for all their history together, his past was at best opaque to her. Sometimes she thought he didn't want to do the job as much as he felt he *had* to do the job.

She tossed another bloody towel into a laundry hamper. Get this cleanup finished, get early word on how the woman's surgery was going, then she could head out. Right now more than anything she wanted to be sharing coffee at the kitchen table with her parents and be back in a world that was normal.

At least there she had the illusion of being safe.

A tap on the dressing room door interrupted his music. "Five minutes, Mr. Peters."

Jonathan didn't bother to answer. The music he would perform tonight was already playing in his mind, and in a brief time he would stride onto the stage and sit at the grand piano and let it spill out before the intimate audience of hundreds. He would prefer thousands but not every orchestra hall was perfect.

He smoothed his tux. The Chicago music critics were out there. He played like a genius and everyone knew it. They would write rave reviews. And tonight after the concert he would put on a world-class performance that no one would see.

He tucked a red rose into his lapel. The lady who had sent the huge bouquet would understand the message. She'd slip away to join him at his suite tonight. And he would do his best to ensure it was a night of romance worthy of good memories. It was the least he could do for one of his admirers.

He couldn't live on love alone and genius wasn't yet paying the bills. Before he left for Europe in the morning, he would acquire the jewels Marie wore. Neil had been pressing lately for a major theft and Jonathan would accommodate him. His cut for the stolen diamonds and emeralds would pay his expenses for the upcoming year. He stole a few gems each year to keep himself in the lifestyle he was accustomed to, and if he had to have a partner, Neil was the right choice. One didn't become an old thief without being smart about details.

If Marie realized the gems she put on tomorrow morning were exquisite fakes, she'd never admit the jewels had been taken at the hotel and by him. Her husband was an angry man and he most certainly would not approve.

"Two minutes, Mr. Peters."

He smiled at himself in the mirror. Yes,

tonight would be a golden performance. He could hear the music clearly, and the anticipation of and adrenaline for a night of crime was rising. It was time. He strode down the hall for the stage and toward the welcoming applause.

The surgical waiting room was a quiet place on a Friday night. Stephen nudged a sliver of wood from the disk he was whittling, adding ridges to the outside of the piece.

"You are going to be late for your date," Ryan commented, joining him.

Stephen glanced up from his work. "We're going to meet for a late coffee instead."

Ryan set the folder on the bench. "I handed the keys off to the next shift and the paperwork is filed."

Stephen nodded his thanks. "No need for you to stick around. Say hi to your wife for me."

Ryan settled on the bench. "It's Friday. I'll wait a bit."

Stephen looked at the clock. Tracy's mom wasn't going to make it, not if the surgery lasted much longer. She hadn't been that strong going in.

"Meghan is pacing the ER waiting room

watching the clock too. You could wander down that way."

"Meghan once told me she paces and prays — the harder she's pacing, the harder she prays. There's no need to interrupt. At this point I'd even rub a rabbit's foot if I thought it might help." He wasn't one to place much faith in a God who supposedly controlled things. From what he could see, life was hardly being controlled. But he wasn't going to tell Meghan her faith wasn't important. To her it was.

"Accidents happen."

"Yes." Stephen flipped the checker and caught it on the way down. Eagle she gets better. He looked at the image. An eagle. He turned over the disk. He'd carved two eagles in this one. He slipped it in his pocket and got to his feet. "I'm going to go say hi to Tracy for a minute." He'd carved the piece for her.

Three

Meghan walked out of the hospital shortly before eleven, shivering at the wind gusts. She slipped on her lavender windbreaker as she hurried across the parking lot to her white jeep. She didn't carry a purse and her cash and keys were in her jeans pockets. Tracy's mom was finally in the recovery room.

She saw Stephen's car still in the lot — she shouldn't have wished his date with Paula would fall through. He needed the distraction of a date tonight. She hesitated. Should she go find him? No. He knew where she was all evening if he wanted to talk.

She unlocked her jeep and used the towel from the passenger seat to dry her face. The rain was easing up, but it would still be an interesting trip. She headed to the highway.

She had the drive perfected so that she could listen to two audio books, stop at the truck stop on Route 39 for her midpoint fill-up, and in four hours be pulling into her parents' driveway.

Meghan drummed her hand on the wheel as she crept along at twenty miles per hour. What construction was snarling traffic this time? Getting out of Chicago was the longest part of the drive. She finally spotted an exit ramp and got off the highway. Even if the back roads added thirty miles to her trip, at least she would be going somewhere rather than sitting. She could cut through the forest preserve and over to the old two-lane county road that followed the railroad tracks across the state. It would eventually take her directly into Silverton.

The tall oak trees in the forest preserve were casting strange shadows across the hood of Craig's car as he sat in the public parking lot. It was posted as closed after six o'clock but had no gate or security to enforce the curfew. Craig studied the clock on the dashboard and listened to the rain on the roof. He had a little cocaine left, just enough for one more lift. He calculated the time and forced himself to seal up the drugs. He couldn't get too high before his meeting, or Jonathan would notice and not go through with the exchange.

Helping steal jewelry was the easiest

money he'd ever made, and he didn't want Jonathan to know what he was spending his extra income on. He was the courier, that was all, but it was steady income and someday . . . He had plans. Someday he would walk away with a few stones from what he transported and make himself a fortune.

Craig reached over and opened his briefcase then lifted the lid on the box inside. The jewels glittered even in the dim interior light. He ran his fingers across the stones. They were the fake ones, but he would have the real ones soon. And when he delivered them to Neil tonight, he would have enough money to party for a full month.

He closed the briefcase and looked up at the flash of lightning. He jolted as eyes looked back at him from outside. A deer. Craig giggled. He raised his hand to cover his mouth. It wouldn't do to show that giggle tonight; no, it really wouldn't do to show that. Getting high was his secret.

Oh, life is good.

He worked at his old man's general store and pharmacy during the week, and while his father inventoried the pharmacy drugs each week, suspecting something but never able to prove it, Craig borrowed the car on weekends and drove to Chicago to get away from the small town suffocating blanket of people who thought they had a right to know what he did every minute. Someday he would have enough cash to walk away from that "productive" and "honorable" job, and he didn't plan to give notice.

Craig started his car and gunned the engine, backing up and turning toward the exit. He loved the quiet solitude of this place. He could hear traffic but not see it, hear the sounds of the community around him but not have to show himself. His wheels spun on the wet pavement as he nearly plowed into the entrance sign and overcorrected back to the road. He thought hard. Go left to cross the bridge and head downtown? Jonathan would be annoyed if he was late.

Red lights flashed at him, but there wasn't a railroad crossing here. More construction? It would slow him down. The road began a rising incline and he relaxed, remembering the bridge. Cross the bridge and half a mile down the road he'd be back at the freeway.

White lights blinded him.

His foot slammed down on the accelerator as he tried to get out of the way. The white jeep already on the bridge nearly clipped him as it careened over the south side of the bridge and plunged into the gully below. The sound of the crash sobered him and Craig stopped his car, heart pounding. He looked back but didn't see anything.

It hadn't been real. No, it hadn't been real — he'd inhaled too much powder. His hand shook as he turned up the music. Lights in front of his eyes — the highs always made lights dance in front of his eyes. He drove on.

Jonathan was waiting for the soft knock on the hotel room door that came precisely at midnight. He opened it and stepped back to let Craig slip into the suite, frowning at the nervous way his friend rocked on his feet and looked behind him. "Something wrong?"

"I just heard the elevator."

"It's a hotel, Craig." Jonathan led the way into the sitting room. "Keep your voice down; she's asleep." He turned on a dim light. The jewelry was lined up on the side table: emerald earrings, a square-cut diamond ring, a bracelet and necklace with diamonds and emeralds set in gold. He had taken instant photographs of where Marie left the pieces around the suite so the replacements could be positioned where she remembered them. "Give me the stones."

Craig opened the briefcase and removed a box.

Jonathan laid the fakes beside the originals, comparing the pieces. Neil had made them in the last three months from photos Jonathan had sent him. Neil had a great cover owning and running a profitable jewelry shop. He could do all kinds of custom work quietly on the side. "These will work. I couldn't find her brooch, so you'll have to take that piece back." He returned the fake brooch to the case, then put the real gems into velvet pouches. "Tell Neil that taking all the pieces from a lady like this isn't worth the risk. She might not notice, but someone else bought them for her and *he* will eventually notice." If it had been his decision, he would have replaced only half the pieces with good quality fakes and left the others to help cover the theft.

"Neil wants to move to bigger but more infrequent thefts."

Jonathan looked at his friend. How could he be so naïve? "Neil will have me staking out marks in Europe and you flying over with replacement pieces, figuring if he steals in one country he can sell them sooner in another." The idea wasn't entirely unappealing. He'd like the income, but they just needed to take more care in what they stole. Jonathan closed the box. "Where's my first payment?"

Craig handed over an envelope. "Ten thousand."

"Stay here." Jonathan took the fake pieces and picked up the pictures. He left the earrings on the end table next to Marie's glass with its still-melting ice and carried the other pieces to the bedroom. He placed the ring on the bathroom counter next to the soap dish, the bracelet went on the bedside table, and the necklace inside the still-open hotel room safe.

He had ensured that she was too occupied to spin the dial on the safe last night. Jonathan walked back into the living room with the pictures and gave them to Craig. "Burn them."

"I know the drill." Craig stored the photographs in the briefcase.

"Don't even think about disappearing with those stones and reselling them." Craig's gaze shot up to his. Jonathan had gone to high school with Craig and he knew just how sticky his friend's fingers were.

"Five thousand to be a courier is fine. I'll be in Silverton by morning. These stones — The last thing I want to do is hold hot rocks one second longer than I have to."

Jonathan glanced back to the bedroom. "She does come from a rather interesting family . . . Get going."

★ ★ ★

Stephen drove on the edge of what was safe for the current road conditions as he headed to the restaurant. He had missed dinner; now he was late for midnight coffee. Paula understood about his job, but standing her up twice on the same night would stretch her patience too far.

The restaurant was one she had chosen near her home where apparently they had live music until 2 a.m. on weekends. He picked up his street map again. He didn't know this area and had already gotten lost twice. *"Go through the forest preserve and cross the one-way bridge. The restaurant is exactly one mile west on the left."* Her directions could use some help. *Go through the forest preserve* — she didn't mention four miles of forest preserve snaked through this area.

He'd stumbled into a stretch of trees so thick that at times they blocked all light. Homes in this area must run half a million dollars. If the restaurant was priced for its address, this was going to be expensive coffee. He finally found a road going west and saw a sign marking the upcoming scenic bridge. He had to squint to read the words. It really was one-way traffic. How old was this bridge? He waited for the flashing red lights to change and give him the right of way. He crossed the bridge as lightning cracked directly overhead.

A flash of white caught his eye.

He was done rescuing things. He was done . . . Stephen applied the brakes and backed up, peering through the rain. He'd seen something. Probably an animal. That was all he needed — a hurt animal putting him on pet patrol for the night. He lowered the window to see better.

It was the rear fender of a jeep. The vehicle was so far down into the gully it was visible only with the lightning.

He turned on his hazard lights and stepped out into the downpour.

The muddy bank crumbled under Stephen as he worked his way down, grasping tree trunks to help stay upright. There was the sound of rushing water down below and a squishing sound as he picked up his feet. His car headlights didn't shine much light downward leaving this area in dark shadows. He didn't dare risk using his flashlight until he reached the jeep for fear of dropping it.

Something had sent the jeep into the gully. Maybe a blown tire? So far he saw no signs that it had been struck from behind. His hand touched the bumper and Stephen leaned against the vehicle for balance, relieved to find it wedged into the ground so it wouldn't shift.

The jeep had been down here awhile. Leaves coated the vehicle and rainwater had filled the depressions on the roof. Stephen struggled the last few feet so he could lean in to see inside. His feet went out from under him and he grabbed the side mirror.

Meghan, what are you doing out here? He shoved the passenger door partially open and squeezed himself into the seat to reach her. This road at this time of night — She must have been taking the back roads home.

She was leaning forward against the steering wheel and her seat belt was pulled tight.

"Meghan, can you hear me?"

Her answer was slurred and unintelligible. He probed carefully but didn't find signs she had sustained an impact chest injury. The seat belt had done its job. He pushed aside part of a tree branch that had punctured the side window of the jeep and then snapped off. The blood in her hair had dried.

He spotted her cell phone near her feet and retrieved it, then saw her keys also on the floor near the gas pedal. She'd been conscious long enough to shut off the vehicle and pull out her phone. He started to reach for the keys, but his hand trembled too much to close around them. She'd been here long enough that conscious thought had turned to unintelligible sound. While he got himself lost trying to read a map, Meghan had been resting here slowly dying. The phone had a weak signal but he lost it as he dialed. He tried again and the call dropped a second time. He slid the phone into his shirt pocket.

"Meghan, try to wake up."

He carefully turned her head and shone his penlight in her eyes. Though her pupils reacted there was no indication in her blinking that she noticed the light. She showed all the signs of brain trauma with an intense and deadly result. The rest of her body just hadn't caught up with that fact yet. "I'm sorry I wasn't here earlier, Meghan. I got lost on my drive a couple times," he whispered, sliding his jacket around her, preparing to abandon her and head back up to the road to try to get a phone signal. He'd worked so hard to make sure no one died on him today. The bile in his throat threatened to come up.

He turned toward the open passenger door and got partway out before pausing there with his head down. Not this. The darkness grew for a few seconds until he pushed it away by strength of will. He took a deep breath. Meghan only had him right now. He couldn't afford the emotions.

He pulled the phone out to try again. He punched the redial button and this time the weak signal held. "Dispatch, this is Stephen O'Malley of Unit 59. I need a code one dispatch, and if they can get airborne in this weather, a med-life flight."

Four

"Keep her steady!" Stephen struggled against the mud and wet leaves as he and the other rescuers carried the stretcher up the bank to the road. The bank had turned into a mudslide under the foot traffic of so many people. A helicopter was nearby; he could hear the rotors. Vehicles crowded the road. He'd gotten the response he needed but feared it was too late.

Kate shoved people out of the way to reach his side as they carried the stretcher to the waiting ambulance that would take Meghan the short distance to the med-life flight. He'd put out an emergency page to the family. "She's alive, but it's going to be a fight! Find out what happened here, Kate."

She leaned in close to be heard above the noise. "I will. Jack's meeting you at the hospital."

"Meghan's parents?"

"On the way! Silverton's sheriff is driving them in."

Stephen pulled himself up into the ambulance. The doors slammed behind him and they were moving.

"You kept her alive." Aaron pushed up the oxygen flow. Stephen was glad this man was here to help him. Aaron had been his training officer years before.

Stephen swiftly slipped an IV line into a vein on Meghan's left arm. "It looks like her watch broke at 11:12 p.m. She is well over that critical hour." The survival stats for trauma victims dropped alarmingly after the first hour.

Meghan's face was darkening with bruises. Stephen wiped away mud that had splashed on her pale skin and wished she would open her eyes. If he thought it would help, he'd even pray to her God. Tears burned the back of his eyes but he refused to let them fall. *Hold on, Meghan.* Her breathing was so shallow.

The ambulance pulled near the waiting helicopter. Stephen shoved open the doors the instant they stopped. The helicopter had set down in the parking lot, the open spot in the midst of the trees barely large enough to give the rotors minimal clearance.

"It's a twelve-minute flight. She's heading to the best trauma unit in the state." Aaron grabbed the end of the stretcher and helped Stephen ease it down. They carried her to the helicopter and fit the gurney onto the track that pulled it in and locked it down.

"Do you have room for one more? I know her," Stephen pleaded.

"He's one of mine," Aaron added.

The trauma flight medic pointed to the jump seat. "Monitor her breathing and keep talking to her."

Stephen surged inside before the guy could change his mind, took the seat indicated, and clipped on the six-point restraint harness. Rotors began to spin.

"How's she doing?"

Stephen glanced up from the floor tiles to see his brother striding from the elevators. Jack must have come from a fire scene — his shirt was streaked with the stain of wet charcoal nearly inevitable during a fire cleanup. Stephen rested his head against the wall behind him. "The same. Alive." He was too tired to expand further. In a desperate attempt to keep Meghan alive, the doctors had lowered her body temperature and put her into an intentional coma. Her heart was beating. Everything else was an unknown. They wouldn't remove the respirator that was breathing for her until after the brain swelling came down. He'd been sitting in this chair since she arrived. If he left, he was afraid she'd die on him.

Jack dropped a sack on the seat beside him. "A change of clothes and a razor. Go clean up some of that face fuzz she teases you about. I'll pace for you while you change, see if I can wear a few more millimeters into your path on the floor."

Stephen smiled. Jack was the right kind of brother to have in a crisis, just enough humor to keep a situation in perspective and stop the drowning in despair. Stephen rose and picked up the sack. "Her parents are down in the cafeteria sharing a cup of coffee."

Jack squeezed his shoulder. "I'll find everyone if there's any change."

Stephen nodded and went to clean up. He'd changed shirts earlier, but there were still mud and bloodstains on his jeans, and it wouldn't do Meghan's mom any good to see it.

From the pocket of his jeans he pulled out the new checker he had been working on for Meghan. The quiet conversations between her mom and dad were beginning, *"If she's only blind . . ."* The other possibilities were too terrifying to plan for. No one knew what was coming, but the blow to her head worried those who saw the early CT scans. At least she would be able to feel checkers and tell by touch which ones were different.

Meghan had been alert for at least a few minutes after the crash. The doctors said that was promising. Stephen's hand tightened around the checker. She had to get better. In an undeclared way Meghan had joined the group of people he would always have in his life. He couldn't lose her.

She'd had a crush on him growing up; he wasn't so blind he missed that. Encouraging her then had seemed the wrong step when he knew he was averse to letting anyone be closer than a friend for the long haul. He'd been protecting her, but he could have been more kind about it. And later when she had come back for nursing school, worked at the hospital — what had he been waiting for? She'd been the best kind of friend, pleased to see him and kind with her words when he did great but also when he blew it. He should have seized the opportunity. In waiting, he had irreversibly lost.

Please, give me another chance. That's all I want. Another chance. Don't die on me, Meghan. I can't handle it.

Stephen pounded nails through the drywall, each blow a strike against time. They were slowly warming Meghan up and easing

76

her from the drugs. He couldn't take the waiting at the hospital anymore. He was too afraid. Her eyes were open, her hands were twitching, and she was responding to pain. But until the drugs were out of her system, they didn't know how far she was coming back. It had been four days since the accident. She might wake up and talk in an hour, tomorrow, a month from now . . . or never. It was terrifying.

When Stephen's dark emotions built, the best cure was work. He was remodeling this home, already having an idea of the couple who would best be the new owners. He rebuilt the kitchen with Sandy in mind. She loved to cook.

A knock on the back door interrupted him. He took three steps back, turned the lock without looking, and went back to hauling the next piece of drywall to the table to measure out the cut for the exhaust ductwork.

"You want help?"

He pointed Jack to the counter where extra gloves lay.

Jack grabbed the drywall and held it steady as Stephen started the saw. The noise stopped any conversation. The sawdust felt rough against his skin as it stuck to sweat-covered arms. Stephen shut off the saw and put it in a safety box so he didn't step on it.

"You know it's 2 a.m."

"I know."

Jack rolled up his sleeves and settled in for a few hours of work. It wouldn't be the first time they had spent a night waiting together. "Kate can't sleep either. She's on the way to the hospital."

Stephen hesitated. "Did she find out anything else at the scene?" He knew Kate had spent another day out there.

"She paced every inch of it with the investigating officers and came up with the same answer as before. Besides skid marks left by the other car, which show that the other driver likely accelerated onto the bridge, there's little to work with. So far no one has reported seeing anything. There is some evidence that the very end of the bridge railing might have been clipped, suggesting the other car has some damage, but rain washed away any trace of paint scrapes. Security tapes from the two gas stations in the area have fourteen cars on that road during the twenty minutes before 11:15, just in case Meghan's watch was fast. The cops are looking for them."

"Someone did this and left her there."

"They'll find him."

Stephen nearly drove the nail through

78

the wall. "They better."

"What's next?"

Stephen pointed behind him. "Flooring in the living room. I decided it should all come up."

Jack folded the two lawn chairs Stephen called his living room furniture and moved the two barrels he used as tables. "Meghan's a fighter, Stephen."

"I know."

The phone rang as they were losing the battle to force up a piece of flooring that had been nailed down forty-three years ago. Jack reached for the phone and Stephen waved him off. If this was bad news, he wouldn't ask Jack to take the call.

Mrs. Delhart was on the phone and she was crying. "Meghan's asking for you, Stephen."

Five

Meghan turned her head trying to find relief from the headache, but no matter which direction she looked the darkness was the same. She reached a shaky hand up to touch her left eye and felt the brush of eyelashes to reassure herself that her eyelid was open. It was so strange living in this world of darkness. It had no dimensions, no objects, no people . . . it was just a black hole where she had to feel her way around.

She jerked to the left as a squeaky wheel on a cart moved outside the hospital room door. She longed for earplugs. The sounds were overwhelming. There was never any warning of what was coming. *Jesus, it's like living in a body that is now just one raw nerve. How do I live trapped like this?*

She knew it was night. Her mom had tucked her in and her dad had kissed her good-night. She'd smiled as visiting hours ended and convinced them she was tired so they wouldn't worry so much about her. At least the confusion of voices had ceased with the coming of the night shift. This room was too near the nursing station. She spent her days listening to rushing feet and the sound of overlapping, urgent voices. All too often someone was beside her before he spoke to warn her he was nearby. *I want my privacy back. I hate living in a fishbowl.*

She struggled to sit up under the numerous blankets. The doctors said she would eventually get back her ability to regulate her body temperature, but it wasn't happening yet. Her mind was also doing its own thing with its sense of time. She was wide-awake. She swung her legs to the side of the bed and reached to the left to orient herself with the furnishings.

Mom left her clothes folded in the top drawer of the dresser. Meghan dressed, wishing she knew what color the clothes were. She felt for the chair beside the window, and once she found it, tugged over the blanket from the bed for her lap. It was such a small room. At least she didn't have to walk in the darkness but could move from point to point by touch.

She felt around the chair looking for the television remote. She found the water pitcher, a bowl of jelly beans, a stack of get-well cards, a folded newspaper, and two books. She turned and checked on the radiator, moving carefully so as not to knock over one of the flower vases. It smelled like she was living in a florist shop. She found the television remote and clicked on the late night news. It wasn't too bad, listening to the commentary. She tried to pretend she was doing something else and had the news on in the background so she wouldn't just sit here thinking about how she couldn't see it.

She picked up one of the books. From the weight and the raised lettering on the cover it felt like the book on John Adams she had bought her father last month. Tears welled in her eyes. Being blind was a miserable existence. She wanted to see the pages, to read for herself again. Having someone read to her was such a painful compromise.

She couldn't take her parents down with her into this sadness; it wasn't fair to them. *It's so hard to be brave, Lord. I just want a doctor to work a miracle and let me see again.* She slid the book back on the table. She'd find a way to read again, find a way to live her life. She had no choice.

A soft tap on the door was followed by the sound of it opening. The shoes sounded hard on the tile floor and that suggested it wasn't staff. She swiped at her eyes.

"Hi, Meghan."

Stephen. She desperately wanted to tell him to go away, but instead she jerkily nodded and heard him enter the room. He came by at least twice a day. She carefully touched her face and felt the soreness across her cheek and swelling around her jaw. Mom had told her that the bruises on her face had come in black and purple and were now fading to leave her skin with a yellow leathery tinge. She must look horrible. She lowered her hands, took a deep breath, and smiled toward where she thought he stood.

Stephen would be her friend, be generous with his time, help her cope. She had only to ask — no, she probably didn't even have to ask. He *wanted* to rescue her.

She wanted so badly to lean against him, to let him take that role. But she wasn't sure he was up to it. And she couldn't put that burden on him.

He was a good man, just not someone who could lead the way on the journey she faced. Learning to walk with a cane was the easy part; what she needed was someone who could help her accept. At best Stephen could only be temporary comfort. She was physically blind, but Stephen was spiritually blind. If she pitched forward and had to count on a friend to catch her, she knew her choice — it had to be Jesus.

She heard Stephen cross toward the bed and the springs give as he sat down. She tugged her sweater tighter and then lifted one hand to wipe her eyes again. She hated it when Stephen saw her tears. She purposely lightened her voice. "Just getting off your shift?"

"Yes. I have something for you."

He was always bringing her something. The feel of what he placed in her hand caught her interest. It was fuzzy, small, and the bottom was smooth and warm. She tried to figure it out by touch and when it hummed she smiled. "A Furby thing?"

"They call it a muffin. Your hand warms it up and the heat causes it to hum and then vibrate."

"It's cute." She held it in her palm until the vibration started. She carefully set it on the table and it went quiet.

The silence lengthened and became awkward, but she didn't know how to fill it.

"Meghan, I'm sorry —"

She nearly picked up the book and tossed it at him. "Don't! Don't apologize. I'm sick of people apologizing." Even the cops said they were sorry. They couldn't find the driver who caused this. It wasn't Stephen's fault he hadn't traveled that road thirty minutes earlier. It wasn't her fault for being on that road instead of the highway — it just was. She couldn't handle another apology. She looked down after the outburst and in frustration tugged at the blanket to get it around her cold feet.

Stephen sighed. "Here." His hand slid behind her ankles and lifted her feet, the blanket pulled under them to protect her from the cold floor. He squeezed her knee as he resumed his seat. "I was just going to say I was sorry for coming by so late. I got held up doing paperwork." She heard pillows thump against the headboard. "There's a good TV movie on tonight if you want a reason to fall asleep against me again like a bundled-up snail."

She knew he wasn't intending to say he was sorry for that, but at least he hadn't pursued the subject. A movie would be good. As long as it was a classic she could remember most of the scenes. She didn't want to have a conversation where she had to dance around avoiding answers to how she was feeling and what the doctors said.

"If you can get around here," she shifted back in the chair and pulled over the table, "let's play a game of checkers." He had whittled her a full set: red ones had ridged edges, black ones smooth. The checkerboard brought up from rehab therapy had slim wooden ridges marking off the squares so the checkers could be touched yet not moved out of their square. She'd played endless games with her father just to pass the time.

"Sure." Stephen moved over another chair.

He caught her hand as she set out her pieces, gently turned her wrist, and lifted her hand to his nose. "JoAnne has been by. Nice perfume."

"It's kind of soft. I liked yesterday's better. You smell a bit like soap and a lot like that cologne of Jack's."

"I grabbed a shower. I didn't figure you'd appreciate road oil and skunk."

"Really? What happened?"

"A car wreck when the driver swerved to avoid hitting the animal. It was a big, fat, old-timer of a skunk and the car ran over it. Guys were putting Vicks under their noses and wearing face masks if they had to spend any time near the vehicle."

Meghan laughed for the first time in days. "Oh my, that must have been a sight." She settled her hand on the checkerboard, selected a piece, and made her first move. Stephen took her hand and showed her his.

A game that would have normally taken

twenty minutes to play took them an hour. She was grateful Stephen didn't interrupt her concentration. She lost, but at least she'd been able to get a few pieces crowned this time.

"You're improving."

"It's still hard to hold more than two moves in my memory at a time." She picked up one of the pieces. "You did a really nice job with these. I can tell this is an eagle." She handed him her pieces.

He stacked them in the box. "Your dad said they're going to release you this weekend."

She tilted her head, wishing she knew what was behind the quiet statement. It was his work voice: calm and a bit detached. "They're talking about it. Dad can watch for any problems from the headaches."

"You're thinking about moving back to Silverton instead of staying in town for therapy?"

She had guessed right; he didn't like the idea. "I'll stay with my parents. Dad plans to hire someone so I won't feel like I'm imposing on them while I learn my way around." Back home everything from the post office to the church was familiar to her. It was time to go home. She needed desperately to be home.

Stephen caught her hand and squeezed it.

"I'm going to miss you, Meghan."

"I'll miss you too." She blinked tears back and started as Stephen reached past her.

"Kleenex."

"I'm sorry. It doesn't take much to make me cry anymore."

"The tears are good for you." He tugged the blanket on her lap tighter. "Your hands are still like ice."

His voice was husky behind the rough assertion and she laughed to try and lighten the mood. "Dad's been calling me his little iceberg." She leaned back in her chair, shredded the Kleenex, and her smile faded. "Stephen, do me a favor. Let this go, okay? You couldn't have changed things. I'll go home, get a Seeing Eye dog, and go on with my life. I need to know you will too. I'm going to be okay with Jesus' help."

She heard the subtle shift of his weight. Just the mention of Jesus' name made him uncomfortable. She'd been trying for years to get him to listen to the truth; and now . . . Jesus had to make this work or else her faith was misplaced. Maybe then Stephen would understand.

"I'll be fine, Meghan."

"Will you?"

He rubbed her wrist. "Now have I ever told you a fib?"

"I didn't look pretty yesterday."

"You did to me. Is it okay if I come to Silverton to see you occasionally?"

It really mattered that she show him she was okay, and that was not going to be a simple step. "You can call. But give me some time before you come by."

"I don't mind you being blind, Meghan. Please don't push me away."

She reached over and settled her hands against his face, her thumb finding the cleft in his chin and her palms the hard bone of his jaw. Her fingers lifted as a smile played at his mouth, her touch embarrassing him. "We've been friends for a lifetime. We'll always be friends." If she let him come, she'd lean against him, fall in love, and walk herself into a broken heart. "You can come visit in a year and buy me lunch."

His hands covered hers, callused and rough against her skin. "I'm going to hold you to that."

"I'm counting on it." She patted his cheeks. "I'll be fine. I promise."

His fingers entwined with hers. "Yes, you will be. You're stubborn that way."

Six

Present Day

Monday, June 25
Whitfield, Illinois

Meghan fixed tea for Stephen. His offer to come by and give her a lift back to Silverton surprised and pleased her. She was making a deliberate attempt during this trip to Chicago for Jennifer's visitation to renew old friendships. The teapot whistled. She turned off the burner and picked up the kettle with a hot pad. She hadn't wanted to intrude on the O'Malleys' grief, but it would be good to spend some time with Stephen rather than just talk on the phone, as they had done occasionally over the last few years.

The power went out with a snap — the TV she was listening to went dead and the appliances jolted to silence. Meghan froze. She was carrying a teapot full of hot water. The darkness didn't change for her, but she left the room lights on for her dog, and she had to figure out where he was before she moved. Blackie could lead her safely across a street with heavy traffic or around a crowded mall, but he couldn't handle cats, the smell of onions, which made him sneeze, or thunder.

She tried not to tease him about his weaknesses, at least not too much. He was okay with all three when he was in the harness working. Her collie gave her priceless freedom. "Where are you, Blackie?" The animal's tail slapped against her leg. "Why don't you go under the table for a minute, okay? I don't want to step on your tail."

She waited until she heard the sound of his movement before she carried the teapot to the counter to finish fixing the tea. Her grandparents were such creatures of habit that Meghan was able to find the cinnamon by first finding the glass jar of lemon drops and turning the spinning rack two items to the left. It had been that way when she could see, and years later it was still that way. Whoever said *new* was better was badly missing the value of predictability. She would like to strike new from her vocabulary now that she couldn't see.

The TV came back on as abruptly as it had gone off, the appliances resuming operation with a hum. She stirred honey in her tea.

Stephen had taken a leave of absence. She tossed her spoon toward the sink and heard the satisfying sound of metal striking stainless steel. If she were smart she would get over the anger before he got here, but then again maybe not. Maybe it would be better to just give him both barrels of her emotion so at least he'd have to deal with it. Running away. Repeating history. She thought she'd broken him of the habit when they were children.

She pulled out a chair, stopping her hand at the last moment to move the chair slowly until she figured out she wasn't going to give her dog a headache. Did Stephen really think leaving was going to help? She was an expert on running from unattractive realities in life, and it just meant he would inevitably crash into a wall and do it far from home and everybody who cared for him.

Meghan rested her elbows on the table and turned her cup around to grasp the handle. This was a lot more serious than the whispered words from Kate last night had made it out to be. Meghan adored family members that had the nerve to meddle, but had Kate whispered in the right person's ear? It had been over a year since she last talked to Stephen for more than a casual, "Hi, how are you?" and she was supposed to rescue him tonight?

Jesus, I'm no rescuer. Stephen has that title locked up in spades. As do You.

Thunder crashed overhead and she flinched. For years she had chased lightning and hail and tornadoes with Ken and laughed at nature's fury. Now thunder cracked without warning and her nerves couldn't handle it. The storm sounded as if it were directly overhead.

Jennifer's funeral had been this morning. Stephen needed to go out in this storm somewhere and cry his eyes out, release the emotions. But he wouldn't do it. Instead he'd run. And she knew for certain that if he ran, he would come to regret it. But she wouldn't push, not if his family had already decided to back off and let him go.

Lord, please help me figure out what to say tonight. At least blindness had clarified her sight in other ways. All of life was a spiritual battle on one level or another — acceptance, endurance, peace, joy. Trying to find those things without Christ was an exercise in futility. If he kept avoiding the subject of Jesus, Stephen wouldn't find the peace he sought.

Maybe she would have a chance to talk

with him about serious things during the drive. Her bags were by the front door, the bed was already stripped, the sheets washed and now in the dryer. She'd been planning to crash on the couch for the few hours before her father arrived. Since sleep wasn't going to happen in this storm, she'd much rather be on the road.

Meghan set down her cup of tea and stood. She walked through her grandparents' vacation home to turn on the outdoor lights.

Stephen needs to find some comfort tonight, Lord. Since he doesn't know You, I'll have to reflect to him how much You care about him. The sadness he's feeling about Jennifer must be incredible. I wish he understood that You're there for him. The man needs to find You. She knew it in her head and felt it in her heart, and she ached at the realization that he didn't. Years of praying for Stephen hadn't opened the door, but Meghan wasn't giving up on him. God hadn't. *Please remind him to drive carefully. There have been enough tragedies on nights like this.*

Outdoor lights came on next door.

Jonathan Peters froze. Meghan was blind and couldn't see him, but if she had company coming over . . . He finished unlocking the side door of the dark house. He'd like to give Neil another stroke for not hiding the gems that needed to cool off in something straightforward like a box buried under the woodpile or beneath attic insulation. Neil's wife, now deep in the confusion of Alzheimer's, had sold her china doll collection to her sister without asking her husband — and with it a hidden ruby bracelet worth a small fortune.

In the interwoven friendships of Silverton there was a certain logic to Meghan's grandparents buying a vacation home next door to Neil's wife's sister. Jonathan eased open the door. Neil had given him a key. With the owners traveling, the house was empty tonight, and the storm was good cover.

Jonathan had no choice but to be the one who tried to recover the bracelet. He couldn't trust Craig now that it was clear his friend was frying his common sense on drugs, and Neil wouldn't be going more than a hundred feet from his sitting chair for the foreseeable future. The stroke had partially paralyzed Neil's left side and ended his craftsman ability and thus their profitable sideline career. Future income would have to come from selling pieces they had already taken. Because of that, it was important not to let the ruby bracelet be lost or to have the cops called in and asking questions.

How many pieces over the years had disappeared by accident as Neil's wife lost her sense of the present and gave away items?

Jonathan turned on his flashlight and looked around the living room, careful not to let the light pass across the windows. Shelves had been emptied and tables cleared of pictures and knickknacks. They were having the rooms redone — the project of a retired lady with too much time on her hands. Would the dolls be out or tucked in some boxes somewhere?

He would have to pressure Neil to tell him where the remaining pieces were hidden. He had no leverage with the man and didn't expect the pressure to yield much, but if he had to go to Silverton after Neil died and rip up his house and jewelry store — it would be a headache creating the block of free time in his schedule. His manager was already demanding to know what was so urgent that he had to fly back to the States for a long weekend and miss an opportunity to rehearse with the London symphony.

In a way he was glad of Neil's stroke. The stealing had run its course. Find the pieces, consider the income from their sale his nest egg, and wrap this up for good.

Neil was a tough old man. He'd probably live another ten years, but if he didn't? Jonathan wasn't looking to change things as much as create some insurance. Would Neil have kept so many pieces on his own property, among his own things? Or had he spread them out tucked in spots around town? Maybe at Meghan's — the fact she couldn't see would have made her home an ideal stash site.

The mere thought of being in a race with Craig to find the stones Neil had hidden wasn't something Jonathan wanted to contemplate. It was definitely time to start thinking about how to handle his friend before the occasion arose.

The china cabinet was empty. Couldn't she have waited another two or three days to begin redecorating? He sighed and started looking through the boxes that weren't taped closed.

Time crawled by as Meghan waited for Stephen to arrive. She paced back and forth in the living room. The power was out again. The radio in the bathroom might still have good batteries. She walked with her hand trailing along the wall into the hallway

97

then to the stairway. Her dog bumped against her knee as she walked, pressing so close he interfered with her balance. She lowered her hand to stroke his head.

Meghan took the radio from the bathroom counter into the guest bedroom to try and find a location that got better reception. The local news crackled with static. A thunderbolt cracked overhead. Her dog yelped and she heard a door hit a wall.

"Blackie." He must have headed into his favorite hiding spot — the open walk-in closet. She tried to coax him out but he refused to come. She finally crawled in after him, shoving back the hanging coats to sit beside him. "I can't blame you, boy. It's loud enough to hurt your ears." She leaned her head against his warm coat.

Glass broke and Meghan flinched. Somewhere a tree limb had just pierced a window. She left Blackie to his temporary shelter, tossing a glove back at him to distract him. She followed the noise and realized it was the bathroom window. The rain was reaching her standing in the doorway, and she could tell from the wind it wasn't a little tap by a twig. Stepping on glass or cutting her hand was a bad idea. She gave up dealing with it herself and closed the bathroom door.

She thought there was plywood in the garage that could be used to patch the window for the night. Stephen was a good carpenter. Maybe it would help him out to have something to do tonight. She heard the potted fern in the bathroom shatter on the tiles. This was going to be a huge mess to clean up.

Jonathan found the china dolls wrapped in tissue paper in a box in the living room. He had unwrapped six before finding the one with painted black eyelashes, rosy cheeks, and a small red dimple on the right cheek. He opened up the base of the doll stand and the rubies tumbled out. The piece was gorgeous. He didn't remember who he had stolen it from. Had it really been that many years and that many pieces? He slipped the bracelet into his pocket. His percentage of the sale price would pay bills for a couple months.

Hearing a car slow, Jonathan clicked off his flashlight. Headlights crossed the windows. He walked over to the windows, staying back far enough from the curtains that his presence would remain unnoticed. The car pulled into Meghan's driveway. A man he didn't recognize with a baseball cap on his head dashed through the rain toward the house.

Jonathan wanted to check the other dolls and find out if Neil had tucked another piece in one of them and forgotten, but a guest noticing lights over here wasn't worth the risk. Tomorrow or the next day, he'd be back if necessary.

He walked through the room removing any signs of his presence. He slipped from the house. The entire subject of Neil and Craig needed to be thought through in detail.

Stephen wiped water off his face. He had gotten drenched from his run to the house. Meghan had left the door open as promised. He slipped off his wet jacket to hang on the coatrack, going off memory, for the kitchen was dark, the only illumination coming from lightning. "Meghan, where are you?"

"Up here. I left a flashlight on the stairs for you."

He hoped the power came on soon. He wasn't nearly as good at walking around in the dark as Meghan was. He found the flashlight and headed upstairs.

The first sight of her was one he would remember for quite a while. She was dragging a roll of heavy plastic from the spare bedroom. Her jeans were new and her sweatshirt was faded red. Her feet were bare, and her hair was blond. She'd been a brunette yesterday at Jennifer's visitation. She looked cute as a blonde.

"Watch the toolbox."

He spotted it in the hallway beside a piece of plywood and stopped on the top step to stay out of the way. "You're a trusting soul to leave the door unlocked."

"Who else is going to be out in this downpour? Your shoes are squishing."

"And my socks. It's a minor flood out there. Can I help?"

She settled the plastic against the wall. "The bathroom window got taken out by a tree limb. I'm going to let you do the hammering if you don't mind getting a little wetter."

"I doubt I'll notice more water. When did this happen?"

"Shortly after the power went out the second time." She took a step toward him and her hand found his chest. "I'm sorry about Jennifer."

He found it hard to look at eyes staring at his left shoulder. She couldn't see. It ripped his guts. He wanted — needed — to avoid the subject of Jennifer tonight. "Let's talk about it another day."

Her hand smoothed out the fabric of his

shirt. "I'm really going to miss her too." She nodded down the hall. "The bathroom is the second door on your right."

He heard it now, the close sound of wind and rain. He covered her hand with his, squeezed it, and then stepped away. He walked down the hall and opened the door, using the flashlight to inspect the damage. "The branch took out the top pane of glass and cracked the other panel. And the shower curtain has seen better days; the wind has it wrapped around the towel rack." He stepped into the room, careful of the glass shards and the plant, to see how long the branch was and if he could tug it completely inside to remove it.

"Did it damage the walls?"

"No. And I don't see any chipped floor tiles, although it's hard to tell with the fern and dirt. Stand in the doorway, Meghan, and hold the light for me." He took her hand and placed the flashlight in her palm, showing her how he'd like it positioned. "Right there."

She leaned her shoulder against the doorpost and held the light steady. "I'm sorry to put you to work as soon as you walked in the door."

"Don't be. I'm thinking seriously about becoming a carpenter in my new career."

He tugged the branch through the window, wishing he had brought gloves. He broke off smaller branches from the tree limb so he could set it sideways in the tub until he could carry it outside. Cleaning up the glass would be a challenge. He began taking down the ripped shower curtain. "Do you have a trash can or a box I can put these glass pieces in?"

"I've got a packing box that will work." Meghan held out the flashlight to him. "Be right back."

Her dog stayed in the doorway watching him rather than going with her. Stephen walked over to the doorway and without hurrying crouched down and held out his hand. The dog looked warily at him. "Blackie, how are you?"

Blackie wagged his tail and pushed against his hand.

Stephen warmed his hand in the canine's thick coat. "Taking good care of her, are you?" He pulled in the heavy plastic and began boarding up the window.

He stepped to the doorway when he heard Meghan coming back and turned the flashlight down the hallway to see if there was anything likely to trip her up. She ran her hand along the chair rail on the wall judging the distance. The box she carried was wide enough to take the larger glass pieces. "That should work, Meghan, thanks."

"I gather I should be glad I can't see that mess."

He looked back at the bathroom. "It's a mess all right. Give me twenty minutes. And maybe find something else to do so I can talk man-to-man with Blackie while I fight this."

She smiled at him as he'd hoped. "I'll find some dry towels to mop up the water."

"I appreciate it."

Stephen folded a towel for the side of the tub to give himself a place to sit. He picked up a piece of glass and dropped it in the box while Blackie lay in the doorway. Stephen angled his flashlight so it wouldn't shine in the animal's face. "I hear you don't like storms." Blackie wagged his tail. "Can't say I blame you. I'd rather see the storm blow over completely before we drive to Silverton."

Stephen picked up the destroyed fern and dumped it in the box. "Meghan's grandparents will need to buy another one, won't they, boy?" He was talking to a dog. *I miss you, Jennifer. You would have at least had something interesting to say about tonight.* He had to get a dog for his trip, or he'd be talking to *himself* before it was over.

When he was done with the repairs, Stephen carried the box of discarded pottery pieces and glass downstairs and out to the garage. He found Meghan in the kitchen wiping down the counter. "The patch should hold until the rain stops and someone can do something permanent. And the floor is once again safe for bare feet."

Her toes curled before she turned, drying her hands on the towel. "Thanks."

"You're very welcome." He leaned against the counter beside her.

"You smell like flowery soap. Sorry about that."

He lifted his hand and found she was right, then checked his shirtsleeve. "Better than smelling like sweat, smoke, or too much deodorant."

"Your shoes have finally stopped squeaking."

"But my socks are still wet." He reached up and brushed her hair behind her ear. She jolted at his touch.

"I like you as a blonde."

Her hand touched his. "I heard I was getting gray hair so it was time for some help."

"Not so I noticed. You look cute." She'd stopped wearing her sunglasses as a defensive shield at some point in the last year. Her eyes looked fine. He looked at them, haunted that there was no animation

105

backing them. The police had never found the driver who ran her off the road. The injustice of it made him so angry.

"Have a seat, Stephen, and I'll get the tea."

He set his flashlight on the table and pulled out a chair. Meghan poured the tea. He made no attempt to take the cup from her hand but let her slide it on the table in front of him. She was fine getting around as long as no one tried to be helpful and interrupted her movements.

"The honey should already be out."

"It's here. Thanks."

She settled on the chair across from him and picked up her cup. She'd lost some weight in the last few years, gotten a little more assertive with her words and more deliberate in her movements. Just looking at her made him tired — he was having a hard time handling *this* moment in his life, while she dealt well with so much more.

"Do you have plans for your travels?" Meghan asked.

"See some of the countryside, do some fishing, maybe some hiking. If money gets low, I'll pick up some carpentry work. Maybe I'll make a few items for wedding gifts."

"Kate introduced me to Shari last night. She seems nice."

"Marcus found a wonderful lady," he agreed. "I figure they'll set a wedding date soon, as will Rachel and Cole, and Jack and Cassie. There's no more reason for them to delay. No one wanted to make plans while Jennifer was so sick."

"Give yourself time to accept the loss, Stephen. Jennifer's death is a huge hole in the fabric of your family."

"It feels like an abyss."

She nudged the honey toward him. "Have some more tea. The second cup you can fix yourself."

He rose. "Would you like more too?"

"Sure."

He handed her the refilled cup, careful to wait until she had it steady in her hands before releasing it. The appliances kicked on with a shudder and hum, and the weather channel was on TV. Stephen glanced around. "Finish your tea; I'll reset the blinking clocks and such."

She nodded.

He walked through the downstairs rooms. When he returned to the living room, Meghan was there resting against the doorjamb.

"Your suitcases are packed?" Stephen asked.

"They're in the bedroom. I'll show you."

He walked beside her up the stairs. "I've just got one suitcase and a bag," Meghan said. "I'm glad you were here to deal with the window. The neighbor across the street was replacing one last month and cut himself rather badly. Blood was flowing and his wife was hysterical. I've never been so glad to hear the sound of ambulance sirens."

Stephen could feel his hands going cold as the memories returned — the drunk pinned in his car with his stomach opened up and his guts lying in his lap . . . the teenager shot for his new tennis shoes . . . the wife so battered her words slurred, who refused to admit her husband had beaten her up. He could see the blood. Smell it. "Change the subject, Meghan."

"Stephen?"

He'd left it too late. Her hand tightened on his arm as he wobbled, and he pushed her away to avoid taking her with him. The darkness deepened.

And then there was nothing.

Seven

He'd almost taken her down the stairs with him. The nausea that came with that fact overwhelmed him. "Are you okay?" Stephen whispered, struggling to focus.

"Lie still. I'm not the one who took the header down the stairs."

His head was in her lap and Blackie was resting his chin across Stephen's chest. He'd been here a while. He raised a shaky hand and rubbed his eyes. "How long was I out?"

"Two minutes, going on three." Her hand caught his and slid to his wrist to take his pulse. "Did you eat anything today?"

"Fed Ann's son Nathan M&M's, ate a few bites of dinner at Kate's. I bought a Polish sausage, but didn't get around to trying it."

"You passed out. Totally." She tightened her grip on his hand.

A nice headache was blooming and he didn't feel all that great, but it had nothing to do with the day. Meghan had been talking about her neighbor's accident, he saw it in his mind, and he felt himself mentally trying to step back from all the blood that was so near he could smell it. He'd fainted again — the second time in a week — at the description of blood. The realization made him cold.

Meghan rubbed his arm, chasing away the chill she felt. "Want to sit up?"

"Not particularly." It had been a long time since a woman held him in her arms and it was . . . nice.

She smiled down at him. "Since I can't see you, I want honest answers to the next questions. What hurts? And what happened?"

"I'm sorry I scared you."

"I admit that for a moment I forgot the storm."

He sighed. "I got light-headed and passed out. Hopefully I didn't do too much damage coming down the stairs." He slowly moved arms and legs, testing for broken bones.

"How many times have you passed out like that?"

He wanted to avoid the question. "A couple."

She checked for a fever. He thought about kissing her fingers as they passed by, anything to get that worry and fear off her face.

"You don't have a fever and your low pulse is improving." She lifted his head from her lap. "Up."

He reluctantly sat up and his head swam. This wasn't good.

She rubbed his neck. "Don't tense or you'll make it worse."

"I'm okay, Meghan."

She gave him a full minute sitting there. "Is it the memories? You asked me to change the subject."

He gave a rueful laugh. "I don't do blood very well anymore."

She rested her chin against his shoulder. "I'm sorry."

"So am I." He sighed. "It'll pass. I just need a vacation."

"You've needed a vacation for a long time." She got up behind him. "You want something to eat before we head out?"

"You're still okay riding with me?"

She smiled and offered a hand. "You'll do better behind the wheel than I will."

He stood, relieved to find the sense of weakness had passed. "Can you fix me a sandwich? Maybe food will help."

"Turkey and cheddar?"

"Please."

She oriented herself with a hand on the banister and turned toward the kitchen.

"How about two aspirin for the headache as well?"

"Sounds good." He bent to stroke Blackie's head and then went to get Meghan's suitcases.

Fainting. It seemed a fitting end for a day he hoped simply to forget.

Stephen's car was comfortable, very warm, and smelled a bit like leather cleaner. It was reassuring in a way to find that he took care of his car like he did his ambulance. Some habits died hard. Meghan settled deeper in the seat, debating the odds she would soon be asleep. Blackie was already snoring, stretched out in the backseat. Stephen had turned on the radio for her. She tilted her head toward him. "I remember the time you ran away when you were fourteen."

"Meghan."

She smiled at his discomfort. "I wanted to go with you and you wouldn't let me."

"There wasn't much reason to run away if I was taking someone along."

"Why are you running away this time?"

"I thought the point of running away was not to have a reason."

"You're an O'Malley. You've probably got reasons stacked on top of each other."

"I'm looking for some space, some peace, and that needed vacation."

She listened to the rhythm of the wipers. She could push or not. *Jesus, which is best?* She reached over and either he found her hand or she got reasonably lucky reaching out. She squeezed his fingers. "I'd like postcards from the various stops you make. Mom can read them to me." He was feeling cornered by so many pressures.

"I can probably manage that."

"You know you're worrying your family."

"I know."

She sighed. "I'm not going to change your mind, am I?"

"Were you trying to?"

"Apparently not hard enough."

"I need this, Meg. A trip with no destination and no clock governing my time."

"I hope you find what you're looking for." She was afraid he wouldn't. The peace he sought could only be found in what he was avoiding: faith. Jesus. She tried last night at the visitation to mention heaven and what Jennifer believed but had gotten the politest of brush-offs. She knew a stubborn will when she met one. She had herself as a model. The O'Malleys were right. It was best to let him go. *Lord, this journey needs to end with his finding You. Please. He's hurting.*

113

Maybe he'll be ready to listen this time. "Don't be gone too long, okay?"

He squeezed her hand. "Like I told Kate, I'll be back."

Meghan used the pillow she had brought along to cushion her head against the window. "Do you want help staying awake?"

"Go ahead and sleep while you can. I'm fine for now."

"I sleep more now that I'm blind. It's subtle but I've learned to love naps." She closed her eyes and let herself relax. Stephen was one of the few men she trusted to drive safely for the conditions.

She was going to help Stephen through the next few months, even if it meant postcards JoAnne helped her read and phone calls to keep him current on news at home. He wanted to leave, but what he really needed was to stay. He'd figure that out eventually.

Tiredness overwhelmed her and she didn't fight it. She slept.

"Meghan." Stephen rubbed her arm. "We're outside Silverton."

She awoke with a start, her dream filled with music. He'd changed the radio station she realized groggily. Whatever this station was, it was nice. "Do you need directions?

114

Dad said he'd leave the porch light on."

"I remember it's two right turns then watch for a huge rock."

"The rock moved a bit when someone ran into it, but it's still a safe marker. Are you getting tired? Should I find you a hotel room? Silverton has its first really nice tourist hotel and restaurant now."

"I've gotten a second wind; I'll be okay through the dawn." She heard the blinkers come on. "The night has cleared, the sky is full of stars, and there's a full moon over the western sky."

"It sounds like a good night to drive."

The car slowed. "There's the rock." The pavement changed to gravel in the long driveway to her parents' house. Stephen parked. "I'll bring your bag."

Meghan gathered up her water bottle and pillow, opened her door, and let Blackie out of the car. The gravel driveway had a distinct edge and a moderate downward slope. It took her only a few steps to place her position and walk confidently up to the house. She stepped inside, reaching back to hold the door open for Stephen. "Just set the bag by the stairs. Are you sure you wouldn't like some coffee?"

"I'm fine, Meg. Is there anything else I can do for you before I go?"

He was ready to move on. She smiled at him, determined to make it easy for him. "I'm home; this is comfortable terrain. Thanks for the ride."

"You're welcome."

She put out a hand to find Stephen's chest, then stepped forward to hug him. "Promise me, no heights until you stop with the fainting."

He laughed and ran his hand across her hair, ruffling it in a gesture that was as affectionate as it was simple. "No heights. It was nice having company tonight."

"You're welcome." She wanted to make the hurt of this day go away but couldn't. She rested her head against his chest. "It's going to be okay," she whispered and felt the emotions shake him. He was close to losing it and he wouldn't want her to witness that. She squeezed him and then let him go. She didn't try to put words to her good-bye; Stephen absolutely hated good-byes.

He stepped outside and she stood in the doorway, waving when she heard him put the car into gear. "Come back soon, Stephen," she whispered, listening to the car pull out of the drive.

Eight

Monday, December 17
Chicago

Kate tugged open her desk drawer, looked with longing at the chocolate bar and regretfully pushed it aside, knowing her queasy stomach would never handle it. She reached for the bag of crackers that came with the soup she'd had at lunch. She wanted the man currently in jail for kidnapping to catch a bad bout of the stomach flu as payback. He'd held a busload of children hostage because he wanted to kill himself and do it with media attention. At least one of the kids had the stomach flu. By the time Kate talked him into releasing them, she'd caught the bug and hadn't been able to shake it off for the last week.

"Try this." Her FBI agent husband set a bottle of Diet 7 Up in front of her and then perched on the edge of her desk. He didn't bother to tell her to go home. They'd already battled that out this morning before she left. One weekend in bed sick had convinced her she'd rather be on her feet. When she could stay standing, that was. The light-headedness hit at the most unfortunate times.

Dave didn't have to tell her she wasn't worth much on the job today. She'd voluntarily put herself on desk duty for the day. They had a deal: She would work as a hostage negotiator until they had a family, and then she would have to suffer a pedestrian career in homicide, robbery, or fraud. A child deserved to have both parents come home from work. And a hostage negotiator role was a bit too much risk to accept — even for her. This day of paperwork was turning her mind into mush and reminding her why she so disliked those safer options.

She twisted off the top and took a long drink then leaned back in her chair to look at him. The man looked fine, but he was smothering her with all his care. "I thought you had a day in court."

"It got bumped to tomorrow; the lawyers are arguing motions. It's kind of hard for a mob boss to get away with murdering his wife when it's obvious from the evidence that he did it. But he can stall the trial a bit."

The crime was four years old, or was it

five? She lost track of time. It was a case of Dave's from before she knew him. A mob boss killed his wife for having an affair — a pretty straightforward conviction assuming evidence didn't get tossed on a technicality. Dave and his team were too good at their jobs to have that happen. "What is this, his second or third trial?"

"He bribed a juror the first time. His lawyer died of a heart attack in the second one. He won't get so lucky a third time. What time did Marcus say he was coming into town?"

"I told him we'd pick him up at seven." Marcus was making a twenty-four-hour visit at her request so they could hash out plans — someone had to go after Stephen. It was one thing to be traveling to get some space, another to stay away over the Christmas holidays. She wanted him home.

"Would you like me to make myself scarce so you two can talk?"

"Stay around. I have a feeling I'm going to need the backup. Marcus has a different opinion than I do and it could be an interesting discussion."

"Stephen is okay." Dave nudged her hair back behind her ear and tipped up her chin. "He's an O'Malley. He may not often go this far afield, but it's not like he doesn't

119

have your phone number."

Would Dave tag along if she decided to go knock on Stephen's motel room door? He probably would, just so he could sympathize with her brother. "Some space is one thing; hurting and hiding is another. It's time to give him a shove back to the land of the living."

"I'll fix barbeque ribs on the grill for dinner to soften Marcus up, and we'll see if you can keep down a salad. You won't succeed in changing Marcus's mind, but for what it's worth, I'm on your side."

"You just don't want to spend the next couple weeks listening to me worry about Stephen."

Dave smiled. "You worry very nicely. It's kind of cute." He picked up the last cracker. "Eat; you need to keep something down today."

"I want my coffee back, and my sugar."

His eyes narrowed. "Still that rocky?"

She drank more of the Diet 7 Up. "This stuff is one step away from being medicine. Find me some goldfish crackers, okay? Those little yellow things."

Dave laughed. "It will ruin your image."

"Probably. But no one will dare say anything to my face."

He glanced around the open office

packed with desks and men. "Sure they will —" he looked back at her — "just not until you feel better."

Arizona

Stephen checked the straps tying down the cover on the fishing boat, confirming it was still tight and secured for the night. Arizona in December was an odd combination of cool weather, occasional rain, desert, and huge reservoirs that had some of the best fishing in the Southwest. He'd bought the boat and trailer last month from a couple at the nearby campground, and he planned to sell it next month when he was ready to move on. It was cheaper than renting a boat since he planned to use it each day.

He picked up the bucket of chicken from the front seat of his truck — a replacement for his car that had died in South Dakota. He lifted a hand to the motel owner, who was washing windows in the office, and walked down to room number eight. The motel wouldn't bankrupt him, so he'd put down semitemporary roots here.

The carpet was worn and the furniture old, but the linens were fresh, the bed neatly remade. The owner's wife had brought down his mail and set it on the round table along with a promised piece of her raspberry cobbler.

Stephen dropped his keys on the dresser and stepped out of his shoes, setting his dinner on the table, and out of habit turned on the TV. He didn't care much about local news, so he flipped to cable news to see what was going on in the world.

The national news wasn't interesting: a multicar pileup in Georgia, a line of ice and winter storms in Colorado, and a steady rain across Florida, causing some flooding. He clicked over to a rerun of *Quincy*.

Stephen fixed a plate for dinner. Chicken was a change from his own catch of fish, even if it was about the hundredth chicken meal he'd had since this trip began.

He still hadn't decided if he wanted to go back for the O'Malley Christmas gathering. The fact he was debating it when normally a family gathering was the highlight, told him the memories that had driven this journey were far from settled. He would be there for the weddings in June and July — Jack, Rachel, and Marcus in quick succession — then all of his family would be married except him.

It was time to make some decisions he'd been avoiding for months. He didn't want to go back to Chicago, back to being a para-medic. That life was distant now and he didn't miss it. But if not Chicago, then what? Keeping the O'Malleys out of trouble was a mission that had run its course.

He was getting tired of traveling. He'd visited national parks and Indian reservations, seen a lot of wildlife, walked through numerous art galleries, and studied beautiful homes. He'd met fishermen and hunters and retired couples and teens longing to head to the big city. He'd ridden horses, done some white-water rafting, tried his hand at skydiving, and got some practice at waterskiing. He had needed the downtime, but there had just been too much time to think during the long drives.

He could join a construction crew and earn some serious money for the summer, but what would he spend it on? He could buy a home in Chicago and fix it up to live in long term, but it would have him bouncing around a huge place alone. He could start a business of his own — carpentry, construction — but it just didn't spark any interest.

He was bored. And lonely.

No O'Malley handled bored very well. He set down his dinner plate and went to wax the truck.

He wished the loneliness had as easy a solution.

Chicago

Marcus O'Malley took his soda into the living room, impressed with the efforts Kate had gone to for this brief visit. She called; he came. He would have come anyway on Dave's word that Kate was still feeling pretty rocky after the bus hostage crisis. Children slid under her defenses like no other victims, and she bore the weight of those calls for months. And she had never been able to handle being sick.

He sat on the couch and looked across at Kate, curled up on one of the chairs. He'd been the guardian of the O'Malleys for over two decades. He'd walked through some very dark days with Kate and there was no one he trusted more. It had been hard since Jennifer died, for they both had been feeling their way through the weeks and months. "What's the family grapevine say?"

"That if Stephen isn't coming home, we skip Christmas as a family. No one wants to meet without him there."

He turned his glass in his hand, studying the ice. "Is that why you think we need to tug him back?" He looked up and caught an expression briefly crossing her face that he couldn't interpret. His eyes narrowed. Emotional control defined Kate and how she handled her life, her job, and that had been a very fascinating flash.

"It's time. His place is here, not miles away. Christmas will be miserable for him if he spends it alone."

"I know."

"I don't want that for him."

"He wants it for himself. He wants to feel again, Kate, and when he hits Christmas alone he's got an excuse to feel miserable. Tug him back here, and he'd just have to pretend he's okay."

"He doesn't need to rescue us from the hurt."

"Doesn't he?" Marcus set aside the glass. "He protects you and he always has. Protecting you from his grief — it matters to him."

He watched her rise. Kate had very few tells that gave away what she was thinking, but a break in eye contact, pacing — something more than a disrupted family gathering was behind her desire to have Stephen back in Chicago. "Something going on with Meghan?"

She glanced over, startled.

"She's the one other person he's been sending some letters to. I know the two of you have talked a few times. Did he say anything that has you concerned?"

"No."

"Then relax. Stephen was like this the year after his parents died, when he didn't want anyone close. Give him a year away. He'll be back for the weddings."

She leaned against the bookshelves, sipping a cup of tea Dave gave her, pensive in a way he didn't remember seeing in a long time. "Okay, Marcus. I won't chase him down."

"What else is going on?"

She looked over and shook her head. "Nothing."

"You sure?"

She came over to settle back in her seat. "Do you think he'll bring someone to Jack and Cassie's wedding?"

"Maybe Ann and the boys. It would be logical since she's already on the invitation list. Stephen will settle down when he's ready, when the desire for roots is larger than the fear of having them torn away by tragedy. Drink your tea," Marcus encouraged.

"Your flight is at ten tomorrow morning?"

"Yes."

"I'll drive you to the airport. Dave's got a court appearance."

"Let's talk more in the morning then. I'm ready for a few hours of sleep." He stood and picked up his glass, then paused by her chair to touch her shoulder. "I'm glad you called."

"So am I."

He'd figure out what was going on. He took his glass back to the kitchen and went to find Dave to start some quiet questioning.

Nine

Arizona didn't provide snow for Christmas. Stephen took a walk after breakfast on Christmas morning, and when he returned to the motel, he decided he would spend the day on the water fishing and reading a book from Lisa. It was a depressing day to spend alone, but he had chosen this over being with family. He had only himself to blame.

The phone rang as he unlocked his room. He reached it on the third ring. "Hello?"

"Stephen, Merry Christmas! I wasn't sure I'd catch you."

He rubbed his eyes. "Hey, lady." He didn't want to burst Meghan's happiness with his less-than-compelling company. "I'm just heading out, as a matter of fact."

"You sound down."

So much for keeping his voice steady. "I'm just tired." He pulled out a chair at the table.

"I won't keep you. I just wanted to thank you for the Christmas gift. The time you must have invested to carve an entire chess

128

set — I'm honored. The queen feels like an elegant lady. And the knights, I can feel their armor."

He sank back in the chair; he hadn't been sure how she would take the gift. "Finding time to whittle is easy given how many hours I've spent watching a bobber and hoping for a fish to come by. I remember you said you loved to play."

"There's no need to downplay the effort. I love the gift. I'll practice with Dad, so when you return I'll be able to give you a decent game."

"I'll enjoy that, Meg."

"Is your Christmas Day going okay?"

He looked at the remaining unwrapped gifts from his family still on the table. He was trying to avoid the bittersweet joy that would come with opening them. They could wait until tonight when his sadness had worn off. At least he hoped it would. "I'm going fishing. It's a sunny day here and nice weather to be on the water," he said, trying to convince himself.

"Have you opened my gift yet?"

He moved around the packages on the table. The shoebox-size gift from her had a big red bow on it. "I'll open it tonight. I'm saving it for last."

"Oh, that's sweet. Call me later when you

open it, okay? No matter what the time."

"It could be pretty late, Meg."

"That's okay. You'll understand later."

"All right. What are you doing with the rest of your day?"

"Thinking about furniture. I'm buying a house."

His hand stopped twisting the ribbon on her package. "When did this come about?"

Meghan laughed. "Suddenly. The current owners are moving to Nebraska for a job that starts January 1, and they have to sell quickly. We came to a fair price. It's the house I've dreamed about for years. It's in town, just off Main Street, so I can walk to work at the medical clinic. The house is small enough that I won't feel overwhelmed to maintain it, but the yard will be fine for Blackie. There's room for a craft area, an office, and a large bedroom suite. I'm not wild about the basement but I can use it for storage."

"I'm happy for you, Meg. Are your parents comfortable with the idea?"

"Not entirely, but it's time. You've got a standing invitation to see it when you come back to town."

"I'll take you up on that."

"Is there anything I can do to help make your day brighter?"

"You already have, Meghan. It was good to hear your voice. I'll call you later tonight."

"Then I'll let you go. Take care."

He hung up the phone, smiling, and picked up his keys. The day would pass peacefully if he didn't let himself think about what he'd lost. He had a conference call with his family arranged for this evening; he would look forward to that. *Jennifer, today I just miss your voice.*

Stephen opened the rest of the gifts from his family after dinner on Christmas Day, a cup of hot coffee on the table beside him, a piece of raspberry cobbler for dessert. It wasn't what they sent as much as the fact that they had plastered the wrapped gifts with stickers and all signed the funny Christmas card. He found his favorite salami, hot mustard, an assortment of cheeses, homemade cookies, new fishing lures, two new books, and a stack of prepaid phone cards. He smiled at the phone cards. He was missed. He was loved. And the gifts were comfort gifts.

Stephen picked up the large flat box from Jack. He tugged out a painting, and his laughter echoed around the room. Jack had sent him the fish painting. He should have predicted it; he'd given it to Jack five years ago. It had been passed around among the O'Malleys as the white elephant gift and had finally come full circle. Stephen took down a painting on the wall and hung the fish for its one day of the year on display.

He gathered up the wrapping paper and filled a garbage bag, then straightened the gifts on the table. Taking a couple home-made peanut butter cookies with him, he stretched out on the bed and picked up the phone. He dialed from memory. "Hello, Meghan. What am I interrupting?"

"I'm curled up in the chair between the fireplace and the Christmas tree, listening to the quiet house. I'll probably fall asleep here before I make it to bed."

He could see her there enjoying the fire. "A nice picture."

"Hmm, it is. Did your day turn out okay?"

"I had a good day fishing." He shifted to look at the shoebox beside him. "I opened your gift. I don't know what to say. I'm overwhelmed." The box was full of cassette tapes made by Meghan, recording her favorite songs and providing her own intros to the artists.

"I enjoyed being the deejay. I didn't want you falling asleep when you drove, so now you can have me for company."

"I wish I had been a better friend to you over the years."

"Would you stop? You're going to make me all teary tonight."

"The gift is great."

"You're very welcome." A comfortable silence stretched between them. "I wish I could take away the loneliness that comes with today, Stephen."

"Your voice helps."

"Has it helped, getting away for a while?"

He thought about the myriad ways he could answer that and couldn't put all the emotions into words. "Yes."

"Then I'm glad you went."

Life goes on. It was about the only thing he'd really learned, but it would do. "I think I might come home in the spring."

"Whenever you come I imagine you'll get quite an O'Malley welcome home party," Meghan finally replied.

She hadn't tried to lock him down on a return date. He relaxed. The idea had formed and been spoken in the same breath. "Will you come to the party?"

"Am I going to be jealous of a great tan, big fish tales, and generally wishing I could have seen all the sights you've seen?"

"Absolutely."

"Well in that case . . ."

It felt good to laugh with her. He thought of all the majestic sights he had seen and all the places he had visited. "Someday I'll take you to the Tetons. You'd love the way the wind blows through the canyons and words echo against the mountains. You need a vacation too." He'd probably have to haul her up the path when they got to the high altitudes, but she'd get a taste of a mountain so intense she'd almost be able to see it as she climbed those paths and encountered snow at the higher elevations.

"I'd like that."

"So would I." Silence stretched. "I should let you go. It's late there."

"If you can't sleep, try tape eight."

He leaned over the side of the bed and shifted cassettes. "I found it. Good night, beautiful."

"G'night."

She was the first to hang up. Stephen held the receiver, thinking a minute, smiling, then set it down. He'd been blessed in his friends.

He slipped the tape into the cassette player he carried with him when he went fishing and turned it on. "It was the night before Christmas and all through the house, not a single person was moving, except for a smart blind mouse." Stephen laughed and shut it off to listen to later. She was priceless. She'd known the silence of this place would get to him, and she solved it in a unique way.

There was one box yet to open. He glanced at it on the table occasionally as he prepared to turn in early. The box was square and heavy. It wasn't the desire to have one last package left that delayed him. The tag on the box said it was from Jennifer's husband Tom.

He finally sat at the table and picked up the accompanying envelope.

Stephen, Jennifer asked me to give you this after a year passed. After some thought, I decided you should have it for the holidays. — Tom

Stephen opened the envelope, his name written in Jennifer's familiar elegant script. The fragrance in the letter was faint but one he immediately associated with his sister. She loved lilacs.

Stephen, it's hard to write a note knowing it will be words from the grave. I love you. I know how hard this last year must have been for you. I'd like to help with a gentle nudge. You have so many facts about God, but you've never let yourself get to know Him. Please meet Him. Jesus is someone you can trust, and He's the only one who can help with the hurt you're feeling now. I miss you, my friend. With all my love, Jennifer.

The note was her voice.

His hand shook as he opened the box. After reading her words, he wasn't surprised at the contents. He picked up Jennifer's diary. It was dated in gold on the cover with last year's date. He remembered Tom had given her this new one at that last Christmas. Beneath the diary was her Bible. He carried the two items with him and stretched out on the bed. He couldn't open the diary, not yet. Whatever she had been feeling those last few weeks before she died would be so hard to read. He picked up the Bible instead. She'd left a bookmark in the fourth chapter of Luke.

Religion had always felt like false hope. He'd been disappointed too many times to want to put his faith in something tangible. But belief in God had become an important part of his siblings' lives. The topic would be there when he returned home whether he tried to run from it or not. He owed Jennifer. To ease the pain of how he'd disappointed her, he took her note to heart and accepted that he couldn't run anymore from the topic of God. He started reading at her bookmark.

Ten

Chicago

"This is the most depressing New Year's Eve party I've ever attended."

Kate glanced up from her Diet Coke, wondering if it was the crabmeat crackers or the lobster rolls that were making her queasy tonight. Great. She just got over the flu only to give herself food poisoning eating questionable hors d'oeuvres. She tugged out the chair beside her with her foot. "Sit, Jack. You're bored."

Her brother dropped into the chair, tugging at his tie. At the invitation of her captain, they were crashing a New Year's Eve party sponsored by the Police Retirement Association. She was on the job, but about the only crisis happening on New Year's Eve so far was an attempted shooting and barricade at a hotel down the block, which she'd settled in an hour. "Cassie will be here soon."

"I should have just gone to pick her up."

"Give her a chance to get beautiful. The night will be better when she arrives." Kate looked at her watch. Where was Dave? He got off at ten, and it was half an hour past when she thought he'd be here. She rubbed a headache growing worse with each hour. How much grief would Dave give her if she admitted red spots were dancing in the edge of her vision now? She was ready to go home.

"I heard Marcus is coming to town in a couple weeks. Maybe we can get a family basketball game in?"

How long had it been since they last gathered as a group to play some ball? The schedules for couples were never as easy to coordinate as the spur-of-the-moment games they used to have when everyone was single. They hadn't played in months. The night of Jennifer's funeral they had played a pick-up game, using it to wear off the stress of the day. But after Stephen left, it felt strange playing without him. Kate forced a smile, pretty sure she'd be flat on her face if she tried to run on a basketball court right now. "We'll do that."

She spotted Jack's fiancée walking across the hotel lobby. "There's Cassie."

He spun out of his chair before she finished the words.

Kate watched him reach Cassie and sweep her up in a greeting. It was good for the O'Malleys now to be couples. Jack and the others were happy; she was head over heels in love with her husband. But the price of their happiness was higher than she thought.

What was Stephen doing tonight? He was being left out as the family transformed itself. When he set out on his drive she should have gone with him, should have stopped him from leaving. She drank her Coke and brooded.

Kate shoved scrambled eggs onto two plates next to some toast. "Stephen spent New Year's Day helping a guy hang cabinets. We've got to get him, Marcus, and drag him back here. He isn't grieving; he's stuck in a hole and making a motel in Arizona his home. What does he think, that we don't want him here?" It was the middle of January, and she felt like she'd lost a brother as well as a sister. It had been wrong to let this go on so long.

Marcus took the plate she handed him and pulled out a chair across from hers. "It's more than grief over Jennifer and the memories from his past the funeral stirred. He absorbed the pressure of working in this town for years without a break. He needs some time to decide what he wants to do. That's not a crisis, Kate. It's just his way of figuring things out. You know he's a runner."

She scowled. "I remember." She had tried to tail him during one of his attempts to run away from Trevor House, and he intentionally lost her by doubling back through the school yard. Stephen had looked after her over the years; it was time she looked after him. "How much longer?"

"A few weeks."

She looked at Marcus and finally accepted it with a nod. She'd be one of those going after Stephen. She wanted so badly to get a hug from him and know they were okay. "Like some more coffee?"

"Sure."

Kate got up from the table and staggered.

Marcus shot out his hand to catch her arm. "Whoa, sit back down."

She sat and he pushed her head between her knees.

"Here." Marcus pressed her water glass into her hand.

She lifted clammy hands and gripped it hard.

"I saw what you didn't eat, so that's not what's causing this. Why didn't you let the doctor check you out last month when this started?"

She bobbled the glass and nearly spilled the water. "I don't want to hear I've got cancer like Jennifer."

His hand tightened on the back of her neck. "I wish you had said something to Dave." She looked up. Marcus looked like she'd punched him in the gut.

"Dave would have just taken me to see a doctor."

"What do you think I'm going to do?"

She lowered her head and tried to take deep breaths, knowing the day had just moved out of her control. She'd been trying so hard to keep Dave from seeing one of these spells. She should have known her luck would run out around Marcus.

"Seriously, can a doctor make you feel any worse?"

The light-headedness faded and she forced herself to sit up. "Call Meghan. Maybe she'll know the name of a good doctor who has a decent bedside manner." Between the headaches, the waves of light-headedness, and the recurring nausea, her symptoms were growing steadily worse. She couldn't avoid the reality any longer. She groaned and laid her head down on the table. "I feel awful."

"I'll be right back."

Meghan thanked JoAnne for the ride to Lake Forest, caught hold of Blackie's handle, and turned toward Dave and Kate's house. She was glad she'd already been in town when her mom passed along the call.

"Thanks for coming, Meghan."

"It's my pleasure." She walked toward Marcus's voice, grateful there was something she could do for the O'Malleys for a change. Blackie led her up two steps and into the house.

Marcus clasped her hand with his. "You look really good."

"Thank you. How's Kate doing?"

"I talked her into lying down upstairs."

"Take me to see her?"

"Sure. Can I get you a drink or something first?"

"I'm fine for now." She motioned Blackie to follow him and walked up the stairs, out of habit silently counting them. They reached the landing. "Let me see her alone."

Marcus hesitated. "Sure. Her room is the second door on your left."

Meghan squeezed his arm and walked down the hall, trailing a hand along the wall to the second doorway. She tapped on the

143

door. "I hear you're feeling pretty awful."

"Like someone is trying to take out my guts from the inside out," Kate replied. "The bed is six feet straight ahead, then there's a chair on your left."

Meghan let Blackie escort her to the chair as she smiled at her friend. "That symptom sounds descriptive. What time's your appointment?"

"One o'clock. And you don't need to make sure I actually get there."

"JoAnne and I were in town shopping. I was ready for a break." Meghan reached for Kate's wrist, checked her pulse, and then rubbed her arm.

"Don't bother. I'm dying."

Meghan settled back in the chair but kept her hand on Kate's. "You're not dying. I've seen a lot of the flu this year that is laying out grown men. You could be slightly allergic to the type of cologne Dave uses for all we know, but we'll eliminate the obvious things first — stomach flu, a reaction to your birth control pills, the start of an ulcer. Do you really think you've got cancer like Jennifer?"

"It crossed my mind a few times," Kate muttered.

Meghan squeezed Kate's hand, understanding just how hard it was to push away irrational thoughts when it came down to scary *what ifs*. "We'll let Sandy sort it out. I promise you'll feel better tomorrow, if only because you won't need to worry about it anymore."

"I'm scared, Meg. And I am never scared."

Meg turned Kate's wedding ring. "You're not going to lose everything you love just because for the first time you have happiness with Dave, a job you enjoy, and peace with God. It's not about to get ripped away from you. I promise you that."

"Jennifer died. Stephen left. And the fear eats at me because I'm never sick and something is wrong."

"Jennifer's waiting for you in heaven, and Stephen will come back. Depend on God, and the fear will find its right size. He's bigger than whatever is wrong."

"Dave's going to meet us at the doctor's office. He'll have to break the speed limit to get back in time, but he's determined."

"He loves you."

"I know, Meghan. I'm depending on that." Kate sighed. "I'd better change and get ready to go." She eased to the edge of the bed. "You'll keep Marcus company in the waiting room?"

"I will," Meg said. "He's worried about you."

"Good. It serves him right for telling on me to Dave."

Meg laughed.

Meghan sat beside Marcus and listened to the sounds in the waiting room. She could hear pages quickly turning in a magazine — Marcus wasn't pausing to read anything. "Would you relax? Kate's going to be fine."

"She looked awful."

Meghan patted his arm.

She missed this, the pace and flow of patients. She faintly heard Kate's voice saying good-bye to the doctor. "Marcus, call Dave again and tell him not to bother to park but to come around front to the circle drive. Kate and I will meet you in the lobby."

She heard him set down the magazine. "You're right; she's coming and her color is better."

"I think she would prefer talking with Dave downstairs rather than here in a crowded waiting room."

"A good assumption, Meg. I'll go intercept him. Meet you by the entrance downstairs."

A few moments later Kate collapsed into the seat Marcus just vacated. Meghan turned toward her. "What's the verdict?"

Kate struggled to get the words out. "I'm pregnant."

Meghan reached over and gripped her friend's hand. She'd been hoping that was the case. Kate's hand turned in hers and about cut off the circulation.

Kate sighed and then laughed. "Dave is going to be thrilled. World class thrilled."

"How far along did she think you are?"

"Eight weeks? Ten? I didn't hear much of what she said after the word *pregnant*." Kate leaned forward. "Am I going to be this sick the entire nine months?"

Meghan smiled as she rubbed Kate's back. "Cheer up. You've only got seven months to go."

Kate groaned.

"The first trimester is normally the worst of it. Are you happy about this?"

"Yeah. I think I'm going to start blubbering soon. What do I know about babies? I have no idea how to be a mom."

"You'll learn how just like everybody else. Marcus went to find Dave. He'll meet us at the entrance."

"He's going to pick me up, whirl me around, and I'm going to lose the crackers I had down the front of his shirt."

"Toast, hot tea, no caffeine. I'll take you through a whole list of things that will help."

Meghan got to her feet and offered her hand. Kate took it. "You're going to make a great mom."

"At least my son or daughter will have two parents who never leave."

Meghan wrapped her arm around Kate's waist and hugged her, hearing the absolute promise. "And I'm going to throw you the biggest baby shower you've ever seen."

"Meg, don't you dare."

Meghan laughed. "I bet your fellow cops would come. What are friends for, if not to embarrass you?"

Arizona

Stephen drove back to the motel Friday night, one hand on the wheel, the other rubbing a blister forming on the side of his left thumb. Next time he volunteered to help install a garage door opener, he would make sure he had on better gloves. Homemade bread still warm from the oven rested in a sack beside him, filling the cab with a wonderful aroma. He'd miss this barter system after he moved on to a more formal job in Texas. He pulled into the motel parking lot and felt a jolt. Marcus was leaning against a BMW waiting for him.

Stephen parked and shut off the truck. The solemn focus on his brother's face warned him.

"It's Kate," Stephen said, guessing what would send Marcus halfway across the country without a warning phone call.

Marcus just nodded.

Stephen picked up the sack and shut the door of the truck feeling like a very old man. He'd known a day like this would come when she walked into a crisis and got into serious trouble.

"She's pregnant, Stephen."

He stopped halfway across the parking lot at the quiet words. "Kate?"

An easy smile played at the corners of Marcus's mouth. "That was about her reaction too. Does this town have somewhere you can get a good meal?"

Stephen shifted the sack. "Grandy's down the road a bit."

"There's no close airport and I've been driving for hours. We need to talk."

Stephen drove him to Grandy's, taking along the homemade bread. They settled at the back table. "Is she doing okay?"

"She's sicker than I've ever seen a lady get and struggling to accept the change this will mean at work. She kept her promise to Dave — she's moving over to work robbery

149

and fraud. Her days as a hostage negotiator are over. She's hoping an opening in homicide will become available."

"Kate is going to be a mom." Stephen tried to get his thoughts around that new reality and found it a stretch. "I didn't even know she wanted to start a family right away."

Marcus smiled. "She came out of the doctor's office in a bit of shock. She didn't even suspect it."

"Dave is okay with it?"

"Walking on air and so proud you'd figure the baby was already born."

Stephen could see that; Dave was head over heels in love with Kate and the type of guy to celebrate the fact that he'd soon be a father. Stephen thought about Kate being pregnant and the image caused his smile to grow. "When's she due?"

"The doctor gave her a date in mid-July."

"I appreciate your coming to tell me in person, but you could have called."

"And miss out on seeing your expression when you heard the news?" Marcus opened the ketchup for his French fries. "I also figured I could talk you into showing me a good fishing spot so I could get a day out on the water before I fly back. I've seen those recent pictures you sent Jack."

"I can provide a great couple hours of fishing," Stephen promised, pleased to hear Marcus would be able to stay.

Marcus's smile turned serious as he started his meal. "This is me asking, not Kate: Did you get through Christmas okay?"

Stephen thought about it and shrugged. "The day passed. It was sadder than the day Jennifer died and so incredibly long. Every time I thought about past Christmases, she was always center in the memories. You?"

"Shari and I spent it with her family in Virginia, and I tried not to slow down long enough to think."

Stephen hesitated, then said quietly, "I went to church the Sunday after Christmas and sang a few songs. It seemed the thing to do."

Marcus looked over at him for a long moment and then nodded. "Thanks, it means a lot. And Jennifer would have really appreciated it too." Marcus picked up his sandwich. "I saw Meghan the other day. She asked about you."

"Is she doing okay?"

"She seems to be. She mentioned that Ken was teaching her to ski."

Stephen tore off a chunk of bread. "That's a nice way to break her neck."

"I told her that. She laughed and said when she *could* see she inevitably closed her eyes, so it wasn't much different."

"She mentioned at Christmas that she was buying a house."

"She's moved in. Kate saw the house and said it's wonderful. It's been good for Kate to have Meghan back in her life."

"Meg's a good friend to have."

"I wish you had gotten serious about her years ago. I like her."

"A few months ago you were hoping Ann and her boys would be the right fit."

"Ann's a great lady and her boys are priceless, but you dated her and settling down didn't cross your mind, which rather disappointed me as well as Jennifer," Marcus remarked. "You were restless then and you're *still* restless."

"I don't know what I'm looking for, Marcus. If I knew, I would have already found it." Stephen picked up his glass. "Ann seems pretty content the last couple times we've talked. I heard Gage was over at her place for Christmas, helping her boys with their new bikes." As surprised as he was at Gage's involvement, he knew it was a good development. Gage had lost his wife and son in a fire. For him to have found peace enough to spend time with Ann and her boys — Stephen knew his sister Rachel would be relieved at that turn of events. And surprisingly he thought it would be a good fit for both Ann and Gage.

"True enough." Marcus twirled ice in his water glass. "I'd like you to come home."

"I'll be there if I'm needed, you know that."

"That's the other reason I'm here. You're needed. Kate is worried about you, and that I would like to end."

Stephen winced. "I don't know that I ever planned to be gone this long. I'm sorry if it caused you problems."

Marcus shrugged. "It gives me something to do."

"I'll head home after I finish up a roofing job here."

"Thanks, Stephen." Marcus took a drink of his soda.

"Think I'll get a homecoming party?"

Marcus laughed. "With Jack around? You'll be lucky not to get a parade."

"So maybe I shouldn't advertise my return date . . ."

"You can try, but you'll never surprise him." Marcus finished his meal and tugged out his wallet to leave the tip. "Come on; let's get me a place to crash and plan to meet for an early morning of fishing."

They returned to the motel. Stephen saw his brother settled in a room near his, then said good-night.

He tossed his keys on the table in his room and looked around. He dug out his suitcase from the bottom of the closet and began to pack. It would take a couple weeks to finish the roofing job and sell the boat, but it was time.

He was going to be an uncle. Stephen couldn't hold back a smile. That was enough of a mission for the near future. He would go back to Chicago, rejoin his family, and spend the next couple years spoiling the next generation of O'Malleys. It felt like the right decision. For all the things Chicago lacked — good or bad — it was the place he thought of as home. He would be an exceptionally good uncle.

Eleven

Stephen drove north into Illinois the morning of February 15, the sun bright in his eyes and his sunglasses a welcome shield. Snow remained on the roadsides and in patches beneath trees where the sun couldn't reach. Fields lay dormant for the winter, the ground covered with rows of short brown stalks from corn harvests the fall before. He had left the state in the heat of summer and was returning with the merest hint of pending spring.

He slipped in the fourth tape Meghan had made, enjoying the sound of her voice introducing the songs. Occasionally he heard JoAnne on the tapes, laughing with Meghan in the background as the two of them selected songs.

No one knew he was coming today. It was a good tactical decision. He would open up his apartment, unload his groceries, do some laundry, then go make peace with Kate. Of all of his family, Kate was the one who read him best, who knew how close he was to not coming back.

He glanced at the huge rabbit in the passenger seat kept upright by a seat belt. It would get a laugh. Kate would probably hug him then playfully hit him, but it would at least break the ice.

Lisa and her husband Quinn were in Montana; Marcus was in Washington; Rachel — he wasn't sure where she was. The last he heard she was traveling in Georgia for the Red Cross. That left Jack as the only other O'Malley in Chicago, and finding him would only require a stop at the fire station. The time would let Stephen ease back into the flow with family.

And after that?

Stephen chewed on a toothpick. Two of his remodeled homes were nearing their closing dates to the couples currently renting them. He'd have to make a decision about what property to roll the income into next. The realtor had three properties she thought he might like to look at. It would do for a short-term answer.

A semi loaded with new cars rolled past. Stephen picked up the map. He would be home today. But before he got there, he had one stop to make.

Meghan scrubbed the skillet and the two pans she had used as she hummed along to the song on the radio. The kitchen was filled with the smell of baked lasagna and bubbling cheese. Dinner in exchange for Ken's help was a good deal. By nightfall her new home would be graced with a piano. Drying her hands, Meghan stopped to touch the timer and listen to the count-down. Five more minutes. She didn't want the lasagna to bake completely, so she could finish it when Ken and JoAnne arrived.

She ran a hand along the edge of the counter and walked from the kitchen into the living room. This was her home. After years of dreaming, it was now reality. Her things were on the counters, in the cup-boards, placed so she would know exactly where they were. The darkness was replaced with a certain knowledge of the rooms and where she had left items.

The spot on the wall for the upright piano was cleared. She sized up the opening again and took a step back to mark how far out the bench would come. She would still have three steps before she touched the side of the couch. Yes, this would work.

Furniture was always a hard thing to figure

out. A few inches one way or the other and she would find herself either brushing into things or losing her exact sense of position in the room. The more cues to give her perspective in a room the better.

She hated the reality of the darkness she now lived in and always walking forward on trust for what was ahead of her. No one who had a fear of falling could survive being blind. This home would be her sanctuary. She curled her bare toes into the warm carpet, able to tell the line in the room the sun had reached by the change in temperature. JoAnne said this room was white, bright, and lovely. Meghan loved that description.

Neil Coffer had blessed her by offering her the piano his wife had played for years. Live music would soon fill this house. Not very good music at first, but she made herself a long-term promise to learn to play.

Neil's wife had died this past September, succumbing to weakness in her lungs after a lingering case of pneumonia. Neil had been relieved his wife never reached the point that she needed to be placed in a nursing home. Her death was peaceful, and that was helping Neil cope with it more than anything else.

Over the past months Neil began slowly

giving away things his wife valued. It mattered to him that her piano be used, and Meghan had heard relief in his voice when she accepted his offer. Music was one of the few things his wife held on to until her death, and the piano was special.

Meghan touched her watch and listened to the spoken time. There was time to stop by the bank before she went back to work. She was going to do a round of home follow-ups with Ashley this afternoon, then make a point of stopping by the jewelry store to see Neil.

She opened the front door. "Blackie, are you ready to go?" He wasn't at the front door waiting to come back in, which was a bit of a surprise as he had a habit of begging whenever she cooked.

"Hello, Meghan."

Her hand tightened on the doorknob. "Stephen!" She leaned against the doorjamb and just let the pleasure of his presence settle inside. He was back. She knew this day was coming, but now that it was here . . . She laughed. "Where *are* you?"

She heard the sound of a jacket as he twisted. "Seated on the bottom step of your porch saying hello to your dog."

She moved that direction, putting out her hand and getting the reassuring grip of his

159

closing around hers. His hand was harder, stronger, and bigger than she remembered. Her memory had dulled with the passing of time. "Are you coming or going from Chicago?" she asked, wondering what else her memories had softened or forgotten about this man.

"I'm moseying that direction. I figured I would return via the same path I left."

He drew her down to sit on the step beside him. He had been only a voice at the end of a phone line for months, and now he was in the flesh and his presence had substance. She was aware of his broad shoulders as she shared the step.

Blackie pushed against her free hand, wiggling in between the two of them to share the joy. Stephen laughed. "You're speechless."

She smiled. "You didn't mention you were coming here."

"And miss this moment?" His shoulder leaned against hers. "It's great to see you, Meg."

She tried to remember what she was wearing, hoping she hadn't spilled lasagna fixings while making lunch, wishing like crazy that she'd at least had enough warning to brush her hair. "You'll have to take what you get then, because for the life of me, I don't know what I look like at the moment." He still held her hand. She suddenly realized she was sitting outside in February, and though there wasn't snow on the steps, it was still too close to winter. "And it's cold out here."

"You look as beautiful as ever, and the cold . . . I can help with that. I brought you something." He released her hand and turned away. "Here you go. I'll put it on your lap."

"You brought me a jacket?"

"Sheep's wool inside and a nice golden brown leather on the outside."

She stroked the coat, finding the pockets and then the collar. "It's so soft."

"I thought of you as soon as I saw it."

He took it and helped her put it on.

"Oh my." It was like slipping into a heated blanket.

Stephen turned up the collar. "It's a popular jacket in North Dakota for a reason. It gets really cold there."

"You shouldn't have."

"I know." She heard the smile in his voice. "I wanted to. There are matching gloves."

She slipped them on and they were a perfect fit. "Thank you, Stephen." She leaned over and hugged him hard, not only for the gift, but also for buying her mittens when he was fourteen. Hugging him hadn't been okay back then; she would have embarrassed him.

He rubbed her back. "You're very welcome. Ninety hours ago I was walking around in shirtsleeves in seventy-degree weather. I've been frozen since I crossed into the state. I'm remembering fast one of the reasons I left."

She laughed, hearing the old Stephen in his words and the tough edge of his humor. "Then why are we sitting out here?"

"The gift doesn't mean as much inside."

She looked around, feeling the slight breeze and the cold on her face. "We might be able to find enough snow to have a really brief snowball fight if you like, just to give you a taste of the winter you missed."

"Me? Toss a snowball at a blind lady?"

She shoved him off the step.

"On second thought . . ." She heard him sit back up. "I missed you, Meg."

"Someone has been pampering you while you were gone."

"I gained a few pounds from the pies, cakes, and cookies offered. Speaking of which, something smells good."

"Dinner!" Meghan surged to her feet.

She yanked open the door and rushed through the house into the kitchen. She

162

shut the oven off, then cracked the oven door to let the heat dissipate more quickly. Slipping off the jacket, she draped it over a chair, put the gloves on the table, and went to grab the hot pads.

"Everything okay?"

She set the hot dish down and closed the oven, aware her cheeks were flushed from the heat. "Ken and JoAnne are coming for dinner tonight. I thought I'd only partially bake it now, but it definitely smells done. Did the cheese overcook?"

"A nice golden brown on the edges. It will warm okay."

"Good. Thank you. You're welcome to stay for dinner if you like. As you can see, there's plenty." Blackie nudged her left knee, letting her know he had joined her. She held down her hand and stroked his fur. He offered more than just comfort, he was warm, furry, and affectionate.

"I'd enjoy dinner, Meg, but I'd best take a rain check. I need to be back in Chicago in time to see Kate tonight. I hear she turns in early these days."

Her smile softened. "I hear that too. Pregnancy was a huge change to her system the first few months, and she's had it pretty rough. It will be good for her to have you home."

"I'm looking forward to seeing her. I'm going to love being an uncle." She heard the floorboard creak as he moved away. "I like your new home."

She slipped her hands into her pockets, wishing she knew what he looked like after months away. Her memories were a mix of days of a teenage crush and from five years ago when he was a paramedic. His voice was different now . . . older maybe, though it was much more than that. "Speaking of which, how did you find my house?"

"I stopped by and saw your father at the clinic and he gave me directions. Would you give me a tour of your new house? Maybe take a walk and show me your town? I can linger a couple hours before I need to head to the city."

If he could give her a couple hours, she would take it. "Let me call the office and tell them I won't be in for a while."

"Already done. Ashley said she could handle the two urgent follow-up visits and move the others to tomorrow."

"Oh, okay," she said, surprised that he'd made the arrangements for her.

"You could also tell me to come back another day. We've been friends long enough I could probably take it."

She moved toward his voice, making a calculated guess where he was standing so she could invade his space but not run into him. She heard his half step back as she reached him, indicating she had guessed it right. She smiled privately as she lifted her hand to touch his jacket. Worn leather, aged, and comfortable to her touch. She had a feeling it was the same jacket she'd often tossed in the back of her car after he left it in the hospital employee lounge.

She wanted to grip it and hold on to that fleeting vivid flashback so she could see it. The memory shook her and her words didn't have the sassy fun tone she had planned but huskiness. "A brief tour of the house, and then we take a walk," she offered. "I've got one errand I need to do before I take the rest of the day off."

His hands settled on her shoulders. "Deal." He squeezed lightly then stepped back. She heard him pick up the jacket he had given her and the gloves. "You once called this your dream house. Why?"

She nodded toward the living room and he moved that direction. She followed him. "When I was in high school, I used to babysit for the people who lived here. I fell in love with the big bay windows and the sunlight in this room. They had a rocking chair . . . right here, and the sun during the summer months made it a cozy place to sit. When Jessie fussed I'd rock her in the chair and she'd always fall asleep. It was my chair, you know? My place. And I'd sit here rocking her, looking around the room, and think this place was so peaceful, the perfect home."

"Making it a dream."

She nodded. "I had it all planned when I was sixteen: married, kids, working for my dad, and living in this house." She thought of that dream, still wistful about how simple it was in those days, and turned to smile his direction. "I'll find the perfect rocking chair soon."

"What goes there on the east wall?"

Her joy fed her smile. "Ken is bringing my piano tonight."

"I didn't know you played."

"I'm taking piano lessons. Mrs. Teal sees me as a creative challenge. She's a great teacher. A few of her students have gone on to great things — Theresa is working in Hollywood composing original music for movies, and Jonathan is now in Europe playing with the London symphony and recording. I have a small goal, but the church needs a pianist next winter when the Carlsons go to Florida, and I want to know a few songs well enough to be able to play some Sundays."

"You will make a really good pianist; I already know it."

"I want to try. The music is mine, you know? That's the one thing that is the same before and after the blindness."

"I started to get that feeling as I listened to tape number six and realized you'd made it at about three in the morning. Those drumsticks you were tapping on the desk jarred the turntable, making the needle occasionally skip."

"JoAnne and I were crashed at her place going through a stack of old LPs she found. I liked making those tapes. That gift was something I didn't have to adapt because of my blindness."

"That's twice in the space of a few minutes you've drawn the line of before and after the accident. You're not compromising when you make life work, Meg."

"Sure I am."

"It's not 'good for someone who's blind'; it's just good."

She tilted her head, hearing under the quiet words a layer of steel. He'd taken her words personally and was offended at the idea on her behalf. "True. Maybe the compromises are more subtle. I don't try some things now that I once would have. The adjustments are too great."

"I hear you're learning to ski."

She laughed. "Two lessons and I about broke my leg." She smiled at him and tossed off the melancholy that came when she talked of unfulfilled dreams. "Come on, Stephen. Serious discussions can come later. Let's walk. I want to show you my town."

He helped her with the jacket. "Do you need to lock up the house?"

"Pull the door and it will lock. I've got keys in my pocket."

She snapped her fingers for Blackie. His harness was on a peg beside the door. He accepted it eagerly, his tail slapping against her jeans as she knelt beside him.

"He's been a good addition to your life."

"An excellent one. He's saved my life a few times when it comes to crazy drivers ignoring lights."

Stephen's hand touched her arm. "I hope he's not averse to working with a partner. There will be two of us watching for crazy drivers today."

She found the fact he was up front about it reassuring. "I think Blackie likes you. Just be careful not to confuse him and point left when I say right." He held the door and they stepped outside. She tightened her grip on the harness. "Let's walk toward Main Street; I need to stop by the bank."

"Sure."

The sidewalk wasn't wide enough to walk abreast without crowding Blackie. Stephen moved them to the street.

Meghan wasn't sure about it. "Walking on the street is dangerous."

"Silverton has how many cars total in the entire town?"

"Good point." She settled into a rhythm with Blackie, the dog's stride naturally fast. She liked heading somewhere with Blackie confidently leading the way. His assurance became hers, and she could move without worrying what was ahead of her.

"Tell me about your town."

She turned her head toward him and smiled. "I've decided there are three types of small towns: the sad ones that are dying because people are moving away; the confused ones formed by transplanted residents from big cities trying to learn to function in small communities; and the best kind, like Silverton."

She motioned to the houses on either side of the street. "Families have lived here for generations. The town is thriving but not trying to attract large numbers of new residents. The town has a heart to it in the library, post office, and restaurant. A center in its church. And functionality in its bank, general store, and pharmacy. The pace here is balanced between work and family."

"Silverton has always been part of your dream — a community that is part of your life."

"It's one of the reasons it was so hard to translate my dreams to a big city. I wanted this small-town background. And this place fits my nursing career so well. Working in the hospital was just about treating the sick or injured. Here I'm part of my patients' lives, and I know what's going on with their jobs and their families. I'm able to go with Ashley on her rounds and sit and talk with Dad's patients, have the follow-up conversations that can ferret out the small facts that can influence medication levels and recovery times."

"Ashley's been your father's head nurse for several years, right?"

"Forever it seems. She was the reason I wanted to be a nurse. I'd go hang out with Dad at the clinic, and Ashley would show me what she was doing and why. She's lived here for over twenty years; there are no secrets from her in this town. My blindness helps sometimes. Diabetes, age-related injuries, chronic pain — I understand the frustration of knowing what it's like to battle something day after day. People are more willing to listen to my suggestions because I've been there."

"You're happy back here, with your job, your house?"

"Yes. It's home, Stephen."

"I'm glad." He touched her arm. "The bank is just ahead."

"I'll be about ten minutes."

"No hurry. Why don't we meet at JoAnne's store?"

She nodded, wondering what her friend would think when Stephen walked in. At least JoAnne would be able to tell her what Stephen looked like after months away.

Meghan walked toward JoAnne's store, glad Stephen had offered to stay a while. Spending the next hour with him would be the highlight of her week.

"I'm right here, Meghan."

She paused at the words.

"The bench by the restaurant. I got sidetracked."

She heard the smile in Stephen's voice. With a small signal she had Blackie take her to join him. She sat on the bench beside him.

"Your friend was giving away samples of her muffins. Slip off your glove."

She did so and he handed her a still-warm muffin. "Mmm . . . blueberry and wonderful."

She stretched out her legs, settled back, and grinned as she broke off a piece. "I stop and get one of these every morning on my way to work."

"If she makes pies like this too, I can see why you claim the restaurant makes the best pies in the state."

"Good enough I've learned to take a lot of walks. This is another reason Silverton is special. It's kind of hard to do this in Chicago."

"True. Any more errands you need to run?"

"That was the only one." The bench was freezing. She got up and stomped her feet to get some warmth back in them. "Let's head back to my place and walk fast so I can warm up."

He laughed and let her pull him to his feet. He didn't release her hand.

She was glad she knew the streets, for it was hard to concentrate with her hand in his. She had so many questions for him, but at the core there was only one. "Tell me about your travels, Stephen. Did you find

172

what you were searching for?"

He didn't answer her for a long time. "No, I didn't. But the time away was the break I needed. For years life has been driven by my career, by close family ties. Both of those have changed now in permanent ways. I don't know yet what I want in their place."

"I'm an expert on building a new life. You start with the foundation, the things that matter the deepest in your heart. Everything else you fit in around them."

"A good perspective."

"Are you going to resume your paramedic job?"

"I don't think so, and that's a pretty hard pill to swallow. I don't want to walk away, and yet I don't want it back as it was."

"Give it time, Stephen. You'll make the right decision. I've known you for years and I haven't seen you make a strategic mistake yet."

"Oh, I think I've made a few."

He turned her direction — she heard in the change of his voice that he was looking at her. She squeezed his hand rather than say anything.

They were nearing her house. She took the lead, sitting on the top porch step to lean down and remove Blackie's harness. "I know you need to go soon if you're to get to Chicago to see Kate before it gets too late. I'm so glad you came."

He took a seat beside her. "I'm sorry I won't be here to help with your piano."

"Ken will bring at least a couple guys with him. Next time you're in town, you can hear it after it's tuned."

"I'll be back, Meghan. I've gotten pretty attached to the pace of small towns over the last few months."

"You'll find me at Dad's clinic, or here, and I would love to buy you a piece of that world famous pie." She folded Blackie's harness as he scampered away, free to roam the yard. "I have a favor to ask."

"Anything."

"Can I see what you've become while you were away?"

"What do you mean?"

"Let me see your face."

He stilled, which made her fear she'd asked that of him too soon. Then she heard his soft sigh and his hands clasped hers. He leaned over and lifted her hands to touch his face. "I'm older."

His smile wasn't perfect. It was a little bit higher on the right, but it leveled out as it grew to full breadth. She traced his mouth and that smile, ran her fingers across his cheekbones and around his eyes up to his forehead. "I like your face; it's solid with a little character added with your slightly crooked nose." She lifted her hands to trace the hairline around his face. "You haven't aged. My memory of what you look like is stuck in time from five years ago." She grinned as she lowered her hands. "I just thought you'd be flattered to know that."

"I'll take it. I've gone a bit gray, Meg, and the lines on my face are permanent now."

"Growing old isn't so bad." She liked the new image she had of him in her mind. "I'm more adventurous now that I can't see what my hair color looks like. I just go by the reactions I get from people to find out what works and what doesn't."

"Blond. I really like blond."

"It feels small to try to get your attention with my hair color."

"Nevertheless, a guy appreciates it." He took her hands and kissed her palms. "I have to leave." He stood.

Flustered by his actions, she tried to figure out where to set her hands without making it obvious she wanted to press them together to capture the kiss. "I know."

Blackie bounded up the stairs, pushed into her arms, and dropped a find in her lap. "Yuck." Stephen's kiss had just got slobbered. The baseball was nearly chewed up and it was cold all the way through. "I was really hoping you had lost this for good, Blackie."

He barked. She judged which direction her yard would be and tossed the ball. Blackie scrambled away. She wished she could see the chase she could hear.

"That dog loves you."

She smiled. Not only that, but he knew how to get her out of an awkward moment. "It's mutual. I hope you have a good welcome home. Call me tonight? Just to let me know you got there all right?"

"I will. Good-bye for now, Meg."

She listened to him leave, his footsteps growing fainter. She lifted her hand to wave as she heard his truck start, then got to her feet. *Jesus . . . thanks. I was worried about how he was doing.* Stephen would be back. Her life had just gotten a lot more interesting.

Blackie bounded up the stairs to join her. "Come on, friend. Company is coming for dinner."

Twelve

"Welcome home!"

Stephen stopped, one hand on the light switch and the other holding his duffle bag. People were three deep in his home: the O'Malleys, guys from the fire department, former coworkers from emergency services. "Should I go away for a few more minutes so you can try to fit another person in here?"

Jack laughed and caught his arm to tug him inside. "The dynamic duo is back together, brother. Bring on the food!"

Laughter rippled around the room and the sea of people parted to let Stephen in his own home. His sister Rachel was in the center of things, directing food, drink, and people crowding the kitchen. She pushed through to meet him, and he hugged her tight. "How did you know when I was coming?"

"Meghan called and offered to hold you there a bit longer; she guessed your drive time back. This was the crew that was free on short notice. A bigger group will celebrate your arrival this weekend."

I should have just kept driving.

Rachel laughed at his expression. "You know how many people dream about just taking off and driving around the country for several months? Everyone wants to hear the details."

"I'm staggered."

Jack slapped him on the back. "You were gone for months and managed to come back with only one bag?"

Stephen dug out his keys. "You have got to see the new wheels. The truck is in the drive. You might want to bring up what's in the passenger seat for me." Kate was sure to be in this crowd somewhere, and he was going to need that gift.

"You got it."

Jack looked so smugly happy that Stephen wanted to drop a headlock on him and ask why, but he had a good idea of the cause. His brother had gotten himself engaged. "Where's Cassie?"

"That way." Jack nodded down the hall toward the rooms Stephen had turned into an office and workshop. "I made sure we had at least one quiet spot in this medley so she could keep her sanity and not damage her sensitive hearing. You weren't around to help me pick out the ring. Cassie calls it excessive."

Stephen laughed. "A good beginning, Jack. I'll find her."

He moved through the crowd, greeting friends, his hand getting mangled in handshakes and his shoulder thumped in welcome. He spotted Kate coming toward him and his smile became a touch uncertain as he assessed her first reaction. "Hi, Kate." She was beginning to show, just a little. He knew her well enough to see the subtle signs. Her face was beautiful. His smile broadened. He was so proud of her.

She laughed as she hugged him. "You were gone a long time."

"I brought a stack of photos from every town I passed through." Stephen looked around the crowded rooms, then reached down and picked up Kate. "Coming through," he warned people, walking down the hallway.

Her arms strangled him. "Stephen, put me down!"

"Quiet." He caught Dave's attention and saw his surprise, then got a laugh and a thumbs-up.

The noise dropped as he left the main gathering. He heard Cassie's laughter from somewhere ahead and elbowed open the guest-room door. He sat Kate on the bed and then spun a chair around so he could sit facing her. "I understand you have news. I want to hear it firsthand."

Her face softened. "I'm pregnant."

He brushed her hair back, studying the changes in her face. "How do you feel about that?"

Her smile about burst from her face. "Thrilled. Terrified. Dave is doing some major hand-holding. I'm sicker than a dog most of the day, but it's fine. I can do this. I'm going to be an awesome mom, Stephen."

"What's your due date?"

"July 10."

"You'll be early," he predicted. Her pregnancy was good news, but also news with so many implications. "I heard you made some major changes at work. I'm sorry it was such an abrupt transition."

"I'm now a detective in robbery, fraud, and white-collar crimes. The first rule of parenting is to watch out for your kids, and I guess it starts now with a safer job. You know how much is stolen every year in this city? There is more stolen jewelry and equipment floating around this city than you could pick up in a lifetime."

"And I bet you try to find it all. I heard

you eventually want homicide."

"A dead body at least gives you a case with boundaries. Most robberies are nothing but paperwork, and the goods are easy to disperse."

"Homicide won't help the nausea any."

"A hurdle I'll cross when I get to it." She studied his face. "You look different, older. Was the trip okay?"

Stephen wasn't sure how to answer her. Every answer he gave to that question just suggested another. "Useful, but not everything I had hoped. Not having to wear a watch helped. The solitude made me realize how much I missed everyone." He smiled at her, not wanting to get into a deep discussion. "I came back as promised."

"Are you going to stay in Chicago now?"

He ran a knuckle along her chin. "A decision left for another day."

Jack tapped on the door. "If this family meeting is over, you might want to give her this thing."

"What in the world?" Kate said.

Stephen got up to take the huge rabbit. "I saw it and thought of you, Kate."

"You got that for *me?*"

Stephen laughed. "For my new niece or nephew. When are you going to know which it is, by the way?"

"I'm not telling. And I can't believe you bought that."

Stephen set it in her lap and it dwarfed his sister. "It's perfect."

"Come cut your cake, buddy," Jack said. "Oh, and priorities, man. We're playing basketball tonight. Anyone tell you that yet?"

Stephen looked around the rabbit to see Kate. "Are you providing the bleacher commentary?"

"Absolutely."

Stephen turned to Jack. "Can I plead out of practice now before the evidence becomes obvious?"

"As a homecoming gift I'll carry you this game," Jack offered. "Late night basketball will get you back in the swing of things fast."

The gym was hot and smelled of sweat and floor wax. Stephen couldn't get enough oxygen to his muscles to walk, let alone make a decent attempt at a jump shot. His legs, arms, and back muscles were quivering. It was a basketball game O'Malley style. The intensity over every point made it feel like a small war, nobly fought. The elbows and fouls were being tempered, but the pushing and shoving had an art to it.

He wasn't going to let Jack down. He

wasn't going to . . . Stephen took the basketball in a snap throw and forced his feet to move again.

"You're a bit rusty," Marcus said, sweat dripping off his face as he checked Stephen's forward progress with an outstretched hand and backed toward the basket. Marcus had flown back just to say welcome home and to join the game. Only he would think that a good use of time and money.

It would take breath to be able to answer. Stephen replied by faking out Marcus and going around him. Dave blocked him and Stephen passed off to Jack, relieved to have the ball out of his hands. Jack slammed it down in a dunk.

"When did he learn to do that?" Stephen tried not to trip over his feet as he moved backward.

"He's been floating on air ever since he and Cassie got engaged."

"Good shot." Stephen slapped Jack on the back as he went past. They'd been the dynamic duo since their teens, one heading into a skirmish and the other backing him up. He had missed this.

Jack stole the ball and raced down the court. Stephen grabbed a breath and ran too. He was going to kill his brother for being gung ho at midnight.

"You're limping."

"Be quiet, Kate." Stephen crossed the spacious kitchen in her home and pulled an ice pack from the freezer. Dawn light was coming in the window; just looking in that direction gave him a headache. They'd landed at Dave and Kate's after the basketball game, and somehow the night had never ended.

She laughed, pushed him toward a chair, and brought him aspirin. She kissed his forehead. "I'm glad you're home."

"Did we have to make the welcome home celebration into a twelve-hour event?"

"You're the one who said yes when Jack mentioned there was an all-night one-hour photo place down the street from the gym."

"I didn't think he meant right then and that we'd develop *every picture* I had taken on the trip. It cost me a fortune. I noticed you bailed at 2 a.m."

"I gave up my overnight tendencies when I got out of hostage rescue."

He flicked water from his glass at her. "I was practically waving a white flag and you were ignoring the signals."

"You could have just told Jack you were going home."

"Not in this lifetime. He would have shown up at my place at six o'clock to wake me up." Stephen ran his hand through his hair then rested his chin on his palm. He laughed. "It was fun. He won't be able to play an all-nighter once he's married."

"Marriage does change things a bit. Speaking of which, where is my husband?"

"Crashed in the living room, I think. I stumbled over him somewhere. I vaguely remember him saying something about the sun coming up, then the next thing I knew some fat orange cat was landing on my belly and digging in claws. I can't believe you still have that beast."

"I normally don't let Marvel inside. Dave is the soft touch."

Stephen debated the merits of falling asleep at his sister's kitchen table. "Thanks for being kind about the welcome home."

"Dave said I moped without you around."

He grinned. "Did you?"

"You don't have to look so pleased at the idea."

Stephen laughed and twirled his glass. "I'll tell you a secret, K. I'm going to spoil my niece or nephew something crazy."

"Niece. I'm really hoping for a little girl."

He blinked moisture out of his eyes as he lifted his glass. "A little girl. It will be great."

And he was going to be blubbering on her soon. "You'll find a good obstetrician and pediatrician?"

"Dave has already made sure of it."

"And follow their advice."

She kicked him under the table and he smiled back at her.

"Was your trip worth it, Stephen?"

His smile slowly faded. He was tired enough to be honest. "At least while I traveled I didn't have to face the sharpness of walking into places we had shared with Jennifer and dealing with the fact that she wasn't there anymore. Those first few weeks — my heart was bleeding. I'd sleep and see her face; I'd walk into a crowd of tourists and think I saw her. The ache of that doesn't go away, but at least it's not as sharp."

She rested her chin on her hand. "It was a double whammy for me. Jennifer was the one I'd call when I needed to know things were right with the world; she was always the optimist, while the rest of us are more realists. And then when you were gone too — I got used to your looking out for me and being there when I turned around. I missed you, Stephen. My days just weren't the same."

"I missed you too, more than I can put

into words. It was part of my daily routine too, that ritual of listening to the scanner so I could find out if you had gotten yourself into a jam somewhere. Can I ask you something?"

"Sure."

"How much is it going to bother you and the rest of the family if I don't end up here in Chicago?"

"I don't know about the others, but if you decide to settle in Arizona, you'll have problems with me."

Stephen smiled. He flexed his sore wrist. "It'll probably be around here somewhere. I want to swing a hammer for a bit this summer, and I'd prefer doing it where there isn't a traffic jam outside my window at 2 a.m. I did find out during my travels that I like the slower pace of small-town living."

"You'll make a good carpenter." Kate got up, reached over, and caught his hand. "Come on. I want to show you what I'm thinking for the nursery."

"You've got months yet, and it's bad luck to start planning a nursery this early."

"I'm doing this my own way. Besides, you need time to make the furniture."

His eyes narrowed at her pleased expression. "Just how much furniture are we talking about?"

Thirteen

Silverton

JoAnne and Ken had a nice place outside of Silverton. Stephen slowed to look at an old windmill as he drove past. It had been restored and appeared to be in perfect condition — freshly painted and built ages before to feed power to the well below. Two birds were swooping between the turning blades. There must be an awesome view of land all the way to the Mississippi River from up there. In the two weeks since his last drive into town, a promise of spring had come to the landscape. This was pretty country. He reached for the car phone and called Dr. Delhart's office. "Meghan Delhart please."

His call was transferred.

"This is Meghan. May I help you?"

Her voice was so businesslike and crisp; he grinned and made the turn into town. "Hey, beautiful. Can I take you to lunch?"

"Stephen! Sure, where are you?"

"Cruising up Main Street on the way to your office."

She laughed. "Stop at the restaurant and get a table. I'll finish up what I'm doing and be right down."

"I'm celebrating, so bring your appetite."

"Oh, really?"

"I'll tell you all about it over lunch."

Stephen found a place by the bank to park his truck. He locked the doors.

Main Street could be walked in its entirety in two minutes. He didn't hurry as he walked. It was a beautiful town with a budget that allowed the curbs to be kept in good repair, the public buildings painted, and the streets swept of clutter. Benches were set out and trees planted along Main Street, and numerous neatly painted signs marked parking and tourist stops. No wonder Meghan thought of it as a town with a good heart.

Stephen opened the door to Coffer's jewelry store. He'd met the owner twice during his walks with Meghan. She considered Neil a friend. The man was cleaning a glass display case. "There's a piece in the window, a bracelet," Stephen commented.

"I know the piece." Taking his time, Neil moved toward the front window and retrieved the piece. He set the velvet and the piece on the glass countertop.

Stephen picked it up. "It's beautiful." Each link was engraved with either a vine or a rose with starbursts holding the links together.

"I made it for my wife, but she passed away before I could finish it."

"Can you bear to part with it?"

"It's in the window, isn't it?"

There was no price on it. Stephen set the piece down on the velvet and ran his finger along the gold links. To have finished it after she had passed away . . . He could just imagine the memories. It might be in the window, but he bet Neil wasn't ready to let it go yet. "Thank you for showing it to me."

The man studied him, gave a curt nod, then carried it back to the window.

Stephen looked over the display cases. Numerous packing boxes were stacked by the door leading into the back of the store. "Are you moving?" Stephen asked, making conversation, liking the man even though he suspected it would take years to get a smile from him. The stroke had left Neil's left side weak and his walk a bit unsteady, but the man's thoughts were still sharp.

"Keeping the house now that my wife is

gone and that I'm limited in my movements isn't worth it. I figured I'd move permanently into the second-floor apartment here and sell the farm."

"Meghan mentioned your place during my last visit."

"It adjoins her parents' place. They're nice neighbors, the Delharts."

Stephen laid out the sketch of a bracelet he'd made on a napkin at dinner last night. "Could you make me something like this? Meghan's partial to silver."

Neil picked up the napkin. "It will take a few days. And I'm not so steady on the detail work any longer. I don't do much of this kind of work anymore."

"Your best effort. She'll love the fact that you made it." Stephen dug out a pen and jotted his cell phone number down. "I'll swing back to town when it's ready. And —" Stephen pointed to another bracelet in the case with a fine gold braided chain and a line of four linked hearts — "wrap that for me?"

Neil gave a rough bark of laughter. "You're either apologizing or courtin'."

"Celebrating." He pulled out his wallet.

"Same thing."

Neil wrapped the gift, added a bow to the box, and handed it over. "Come back anytime. I'll help you lighten more of that wallet."

Stephen laughed and nodded his thanks. He walked to the restaurant, the box in his hand, his finger curling the bow. Maybe it was a little much, but Meghan would like it and celebrations needed gifts.

Meghan was coming toward him, Blackie leading the way. Stephen slowed, enjoying the sight. She couldn't see, but she walked with a smile, head tilted up to enjoy the sun, her pace fast beside Blackie. He'd pretty much given up on lasting happiness — he'd seen too many people he loved get ripped away — but he wouldn't mind sharing Meghan's happiness on this day. She had a smile a man could get lost in. "I'm watching this really nice-looking lady out strolling without a jacket in February when it's only a few degrees above freezing out here."

She slowed as she heard his voice and then picked up her pace. She looked directly at him. It was a punch in the gut to have that gaze focused on him. For a moment it was as if she could see him. "I can feel spring in the air; whereas you've been traveling in all those warm places and forgotten this perfect moment that comes once a year."

"True. Hi there, Blackie."

"He loves the idea of spring too."

Stephen held the restaurant door for her. "Do you have a favorite table?"

"Third on the right." He settled her at the table and she double-checked that Blackie had his feet and tail tucked out of the way so he wouldn't get stepped on. "What are we celebrating?"

He pulled out a piece of paper from his pocket, looked at it, and then leaned over to hand her the check. "This. Across the top it says Stephen O'Malley. And on the next line is the sum of the proceeds of not only two home sales, but also a dining-room table I made. I should go away for a few months more often."

She traced her finger across the check and then offered it back to him. "That is so neat, Stephen. You deserve to have your carpentry skills recognized."

"Now comes the decision of what home to buy and fix up next. I want your opinion on some places."

He paused so they could order lunch. The waitress looked at the box with the bow he'd set on the table, then at Meghan, and then at him. The lady smiled and he smiled back. She didn't mention the box as she confirmed their order and went to get their drinks.

Stephen settled back in his chair, studying Meghan as her fingers skimmed the table-top, placing items into her mental map. "The realtor has already found three properties for me to consider. Two of them are single family homes; the other is a duplex."

"All of them are in the city? All need a lot of work?"

"Yes and yes."

"They sound right up your alley."

"That's why I want your advice. Kate asked me to make the furniture for the baby's room."

"Oh, you should! What a wonderful idea."

"It would be time consuming, and I'd need a workshop with some space. I don't think any of these properties would give that kind of space."

"You know you want to make Kate's furniture."

He smiled at her assertion. "You're right; I do. I'll pass on these properties and keep looking." Their lunch arrived and he paused as the waitress positioned plates and Meghan got her bearings. "That's my last two weeks. What have you been up to?"

Her smile faded a bit. "Breaking in my piano and getting accustomed to being a home owner."

"Something wrong, Meghan?"

She quickly shook her head. "It's just strange, learning the sounds of a new house. It was windy last night." She gave a rueful laugh. "I spook at the smallest things, thinking someone is there. Blackie is sleeping peacefully and I'm jumping at every creak of a board."

"You do look a little tired."

"In a few months I'll know this house as well as my parents' place, and it won't be that big a deal anymore."

"Call me next time you're lying there listening to strange sounds. You can describe them to me and I can guess along with you. It would be nice to have the phone ring in the middle of the night again. I kind of miss the pager interruptions in my life."

She tilted her head as she considered the offer. "Okay."

"Take me up on it. Meg —" he smiled at her and gently ran a finger along her cheek — "I'm glad you were free."

She smiled tentatively back at him, then nodded to her pie. "Do you have time for a walk after lunch?"

"I'd enjoy it."

When their meal was completed, Stephen paid the bill and tucked the jewelry box in his pocket as she gathered up Blackie's harness. They wandered down Main Street together. He thought she might turn toward her place and show him her new piano, but instead she motioned Blackie to stay on Main Street.

"The church is up ahead," Stephen commented.

"Do you mind if we stop in?"

He did, but he agreed to anyway. "We can stop."

The church was open, but the sanctuary was empty. Meghan released Blackie's harness and let him go off duty. "I love this place."

It was obvious she knew the church well, for she walked the aisle without thinking about her steps. Stephen trailed her. "Why?"

"My earliest memories are of the organ music. I was baptized here, and JoAnne and I met in the youth group."

Stephen looked around the room and saw comfortable pews, the worn carpet in the front of the sanctuary, the stained glass by the baptistery. He had been in churches like this as a child. His parents had gone to church on Sunday mornings no matter what town they were in, even during vacations. It felt strange, and kind of sad to be back in a place so similar to what he remembered from his childhood and to find it made him uncomfortable just being there.

Meghan slid into the second row from the front. "I prayed for you while you were gone."

"What did you pray?"

She rested her chin on the back of a pew in front of her. "That you'd come back."

"Nothing else?"

"Running away doesn't solve the hurt."

"It didn't. It just reminded me of what loneliness feels like."

She turned her head toward him. "You need a friend, Stephen."

"I've got you."

"Yes, you do. But Jesus wants to be your friend too. I wish you'd let Him."

"The idea of a personal relationship with someone you can't even know is there for certain —" He didn't finish the thought. He had no desire to hurt her with his words. "Is this where you came, the first year after you went blind, to find the ability to smile again? You came back with an enviable sense of peace about you."

"Yes. I'm partial to sitting under the big willow tree out back and remembering the view."

He looked out the window. The view she remembered had changed to a parking lot addition and a storage building. "What did you think about while you were sitting out there?"

She slid from the pew, hitting her hip on the end post. She rubbed the sore area as she walked forward to the piano. She pulled out the bench and sat down, picking out a few notes. He recognized the simple melody of "Jesus Loves Me."

"Mom often says that life is what you make of it. It took about a year, but I decided I would survive being blind. It's not the worst thing that could happen."

Stephen leaned against the grand piano, watching her expression soften and her eyes close as she played. "You've been practicing."

"Every day."

He sat beside her on the bench and it wobbled under both their weights. "Remind me to tighten these bench legs for you."

"This song is called 'Blessings.' " She shifted into a new song he'd not heard before.

"And I'm honestly not ducking your conversation about God. I'm just saving us from a disagreement."

"You were never a coward, Stephen. Why are you about this subject?"

"I've already made my decision. I know

what God expects of a man, and I'm not ready to meet my end of the deal."

"Well it's an honest answer at least. The basis of it is wrong, but it's honest. You can't earn your way to being okay with God — sin is too pervasive. And while God does expect a lot once you're a Christian, when you know Jesus the things you care about, the things you do, change. The changes God wants are a by-product of that friendship, not rules you have to meet in order to be accepted."

"Still, it's an agreement to follow and become like Him. That's a big promise."

"I know it's big. But it's worth it."

For her the agreement had been worth it, and over the last year the other O'Malleys had also decided it was a good deal. He just wasn't ready to take the same step. He put his hands on the keyboard and improvised notes over hers.

He risked asking a question he'd come back to Silverton to ask. "Are we ever going to be anything more than friends?"

Her fingers fumbled the song and then stilled on the piano keys. She tilted her head to look at him, and he knew her answer in the tension he saw before she spoke. "No."

She didn't even qualify it. That hurt, for he'd been letting himself hope that someday at least there was a possibility of more. She'd been the one he chose to stay in touch with, thought about the most, while he was away. She knew the most about his past outside of family, and there was comfort with Meghan he hadn't found elsewhere.

He'd hoped, maybe, that in coming home he could have a deeper relationship to help fill the void that was growing wider each day. He needed a place to belong. He'd decided that on the long drive back. "I'm sorry to hear that."

"I can't divide me, Stephen. God matters and we don't share that. It would rub a relationship raw over time. And my blindness is a pretty big hurdle too."

"Honest and direct, even if I don't like the answer." He'd been friends with her so long, and neither item was an insurmountable hurdle for him. But for Meghan, life didn't come with second chances very often. He rested his hands on the piano, considering her, and then set the wrapped box on the piano in front of her. "Don't take this the wrong way, but I got you something." He took her hand and lifted it to touch the box.

"Stephen . . ."

"No strings. I just wanted to share my day

of celebration, okay?" He kept the words light and smiled. No matter how much he regretted her answer, he wasn't going to let this moment damage the friendship he valued. She was simply too important.

He was afraid she wouldn't even open it, but she tugged at the ribbon. She opened the box and lifted out the bracelet, running her fingers over the links. Her eyes blinked fast at sudden moisture. "This is beautiful."

"I thought you'd like it." He fastened it around her slender wrist. "It looks good."

She leaned against him. "You might not be speaking to my Best Friend, which is a shame, but you do make an awfully nice friend yourself. Thank you."

"You're welcome."

"And I'm not going to give up on you or stop talking about Jesus; it's not my nature."

He hugged her. "I know. It's why you're a good friend." He leaned over and picked up a songbook from the stack. "Jennifer made arrangements for Tom to send me her diary and Bible for Christmas."

"Really?"

"I've been reading the Bible." He set the songbook on the stand. "How's your memory?"

"Not bad."

He picked out the melody. "Pay attention.

This lesson is going to cost you."

"How much?"

"It depends on how seriously you slaughter this tune."

She laughed. He patiently taught her the melody line of the song.

"What do you think about what you've read?"

"That I should read some more. It's something I'm doing for Jennifer — I owed her that — but I haven't found the courage to open the diary yet."

Her hand moved to cover his. "There's no hurry to open it."

"Listening to her words from her last days . . . I'm not ready." And he wasn't ready for this conversation either. He closed the songbook. "Come on; show me your willow tree, and then we'll walk back downtown. You're going to be late back to work if we don't head that direction."

"Will you surprise me for lunch and a walk again?"

He heard the uncertainty and tightened his hand on hers as he smiled. "You can count on it. If friends can't agree to disagree, what kind of friendship is that?" He tripped over Blackie and nearly took Meghan down with him. "Sorry about that."

"I need to put something on his collar to warn that Blackie is around. He's good at taking people by surprise." She clipped on Blackie's harness.

Stephen rubbed the dog's ears in apology. "More observant people would probably help too."

He walked with Meghan back to the clinic.

He would have stepped in to see her office, but the reception area was filling up with people. "There are patients waiting, and it looks like a full crowd."

"We're the place for everything from emergencies to earaches. It's too bad you aren't living here. We need a paramedic in this community."

He let the casual remark go by unanswered. "I'll call you, Meg. Thanks for today."

"I'm glad you came." She motioned her dog inside. He watched her enter the building, greet people, and then disappear from view. This day had not gone anything like he planned. He pushed his hands deep in his pockets as he walked back to his truck.

Disappointment didn't sit well with Stephen.

Half an hour later, he slowed his truck on

the road that passed by Meghan's parents' home. The Delhart land, adjacent to Neil's, ran as far as he could see. He pulled to the side of the road and got out. Hands on his hips, he looked his fill of the open land. This was the place Meghan had spent the last several years, and he could feel the peacefulness of it in the pond and the path around it, the open fields.

Her last comment about being a paramedic had struck a nerve. He wasn't going back to that profession in the foreseeable future. He would enjoy being a carpenter for the summer, and it was more than a small decision. What he needed most now was a sense of permanence and a place to belong that was his.

He could head back to Chicago and return to see Meghan in a few days. Or maybe . . . He turned and walked back to the truck.

Fourteen

Stephen entered Neil's jewelry store. The store was empty and the sound of a radio came from a door in the back that was open a few inches. "Mr. Coffer?"

Neil came from the back work area. "Meghan didn't like the bracelet."

"Are you kidding? She loved it." Stephen knew of no way to lead into the conversation but simply to ask. "You mentioned you were considering selling your place next to the Delharts'."

Neil leaned against the counter, considering him. "I've been thinking on it."

"Would it be possible to see it? At your convenience?"

Neil crossed over to the window and turned the sign to say closed. "It's time for a break. Let's take a drive now."

Stephen knew enough about land to know that what he was seeing was roots, generations of roots in one place. "Are you sure you want to sell this place, Neil?

There's history here."

They walked slowly along the rock driveway from the barn back toward the house. The place was so much more than Stephen had expected. He no longer wondered what he was doing but rather how he could possibly make this work. The barn would be a perfect workshop — there were outbuildings for supplies and equipment — and he'd have so much land to use for future projects. The potential here was overwhelming.

"My wife and I had good years here. I married her down there by the pond, and we had our twenty-fifth anniversary out at the barn with a good old-fashioned square dance. She started to lose her memory, but she never forgot the dance or the pond or how much she loved to pick blackberries from that patch down the way. For me . . . I'm not growing any younger, and since my stroke this place is more work than I can manage. It's not like I have family to inherit it.

"I'll spend my last years quite comfortable living above the store. I've already been staying there during the winter when the weather is bad. It's even got an elevator from when it was a bank. I'll be selling this place. The only real question is whether the house and land need to be divided in order to find buyers."

Stephen looked around the grounds. "What are your boundaries?"

"The pond is all on my property, Bill Delhart's place comes to that line of trees near the other bank, and the homestead plot goes south to the line of trees. I own the acres across the road down to the corn Nelson had planted. There's just over a hundred acres total. There are five buildings on the property between the house, barn, garage, and two storage buildings. It would probably be better to simply tear down the house and start over than try to rebuild it."

Stephen didn't know much about living in the country. He knew less about farming. But today neither mattered. "Neil, I'd like to buy your place."

"You feel like haggling the price over a cup of coffee?"

Stephen smiled. "It's been a long time since I haggled over anything more than fish bait, but I'll go a few rounds."

"Once you see inside the house, you'll change your mind about this place."

"The house is the one thing I'm capable of restoring. There's no sagging and settling with age; that says whoever built it did a good job."

"Come on; I'll show you. I've already taken the furniture that mattered to me out and the last of my personal bits and pieces. Everything that's left can either go with the property or be sold at auction. Some items in the house go back to my parents, and the farm equipment in the storage barns runs, but it's old enough I don't know who would be interested in buying it."

Stephen followed him up the porch and into the house. The heat was turned down and there was the feel of a place that had been unoccupied, despite rugs on the hardwood floors, aged curtains, and plants on the windowsill still soaking up the sun. It was a simple house, but the ceilings were tall, the doorways narrow, and the windows larger than he expected. Stephen saw past the first layers to the potential. "I just sold two remodeled homes in Chicago and I've got the proceeds to work with. The land will secure a loan for the rest."

"We'll haggle a price and handshake on a deal. Give me a lift back to the store, and then come back and walk the place. My wife would be pleased to know it was going to be a home again."

"This is a lot of place for just a handshake."

"I never did a deal with a man whose

word I couldn't trust," Neil replied. "My banker and lawyer will make it work. I'm old enough I'd rather have a few years to enjoy the proceeds than make this a drawn-out sale."

Stephen looked around the house and smiled. "Let's go get that coffee."

Craig froze at the sound of people moving around inside the old house. The insulation in the attic was scratching his skin, and just the idea that he had to be still immediately started driving him crazy. He was hot, tired, and hadn't found anything, but Neil was not a man to make this easy.

Craig knew there were gems hidden somewhere on this property or at the store, and he had to start the hunt somewhere. How many pieces were still stashed to cool off was hard to figure out, but he thought it had to be at least forty. He figured Neil wouldn't have been able to recover any pieces hidden in hard-to-reach places since his stroke. The attic had seemed logical, but so far Craig had come up dry. He moved farther back from the attic trapdoor that went down into the utility room. He'd have to wait them out.

Another few weeks to search this place and he'd have what was here. He couldn't believe Neil was moving so fast to sell the property.

Once voices faded and he heard the sound of a vehicle leaving, Craig lowered himself down through the trapdoor. He would come back when it was dark. There was no use being seen out here. He was too well known in town that if someone saw him, even briefly, they would recognize him. If Neil got wind that he was out here, he didn't want to predict what Neil would do. The man didn't like being double-crossed.

Knowing his luck, the pieces had probably been moved to the store and Craig would have to wait for the man's next stroke. He had to do something to get cash soon. Steal from the pharmacy, something. He was desperate for another fix, and he could only stretch out what he had for so long.

Stephen waited as Neil went into the back of his store and then came back with a ring of keys. "That barn will make you a good workshop. I had them run extra power circuits and breakers for the building."

The banker had been more than willing to accept the endorsed cashier's check, the lawyer a one-page agreement, and with a handshake Stephen found himself the owner of the homestead. A loan for the sale of the sixty acres of farmland would process at its own speed, but as of now he was the tenant on record. He had to admire the efficiency of men who already had their ducks in a row. All the banker and lawyer had been waiting on was a name and price to add to the paperwork.

Stephen accepted the keys from Neil and offered his hand. "Thank you."

"You wanted a challenge; now you have one."

Stephen walked the property. It was a huge place, and he would have to learn the art of caring for grounds that had everything from grapevines to blackberries and several dozen types of trees in the orchard. The yard would take a huge mower, and he'd have to sort out the condition of the equipment acquired from Neil. The man had taken good care of this place, but as his wife's health slipped and he'd had less time and energy to give it, the years of neglect showed as nature reclaimed its territory. Several seasons of work would be needed to prune and trim it back under control.

The gravel driveway extended from the main road to a detached garage behind and to the left of the house. A long walkway connected the garage to the house. To his left a fenced pasture hailed back to the days when livestock roamed the property. The huge barn was close to the house, and farther out were two storage buildings. He'd bought the property without an appraisal, bought the contents of the barn and storage buildings with merely a glance inside, and did the same with the house. He would have to go through each to see what he would keep and what he would sell. Stephen wasn't worried about the speed of his decision; he knew how to read a man, and the price arrived at had been fair to them both.

This was his new home.

He took a deep breath as the depth of that hit him and leaned back against the front bumper of his truck. Home. He had no thought of ever selling this land.

Mom, Dad, I wish you were here to see this.

At the thought he pulled out his phone to call the family he had. "Jack? What are you doing at the moment?"

"Debating the merits of which movie to see with Cassie."

"If you two have a couple days free in your work rotations, want to see my new place?"

"You picked one of the homes to fix up?"

Stephen grinned. "Nope — a house and a

hundred acres of land. I'm looking at something I think is a sundial beside an ancient well, and I own them both."

"Where are you?"

"Silverton."

"You bought a farm? What do you know about farms?"

"That's what I said, then I shrugged and shook the man's hand. You want to come help me out here?"

"You'll have to give precise directions. I don't drive outside of concrete and pavement."

"Bring your phone along. I'll get you here."

"Do I need to pack a sleeping bag?"

Stephen laughed. "It's not *that* rural. The town has a nice hotel and also a bed-and-breakfast. See if Cassie wants to come and I'll get you both rooms. I need help moving furniture from the house out to the storage buildings. I'm going to gut the house back to its frame."

"Do you want me to bring your basic move-in gear, or are you coming back into town tonight?"

"I'd appreciate it if you could bring what you can."

Jack checked with Cassie. "We'll be there Friday afternoon. Have you told the others yet?"

"I'm making the calls now."

"I think this is great, Stephen."

He looked around his property as the sun was beginning to set. His new niece or nephew should have a chance to explore the country life, ride a horse, pet a chicken, and feed a cow. This was the perfect place. "So do I. Call when you get near town and I'll give you directions."

He understood why his siblings were all getting married, why they wanted to make relationships permanent. This was his own definition of permanence — a place that would show his sweat equity and maybe a future business, if he loved the carpentry work as much as he thought he would.

He considered calling Meghan but didn't. The speed of this decision, the unexpected-ness of it, would make her cautious. His arrival into her community might feel like pressure, and he didn't want that. Their friendship would have to find new footing with the addition of the word *neighbor.*

He wanted the same peace she had in her life, and part of that had come from having a permanent home. He might have selected Silverton because she was here, but he'd made the decision on the land for reasons that had little to do with her.

He needed to make peace with life, and

he would begin that process here. Stephen O'Malley, landowner. It was a good feeling.

Stephen elected to take a hotel room for the night rather than stay at the farmhouse, if only to allow himself a good night's sleep and a chance to think through a plan for the next days. He stretched out on the bed and listened to the evening news while he thought about sleeping. Would Meghan understand? He thought about calling her several times during the course of the evening but never reached for the phone. There was time to tell her he was now her neighbor, but he didn't know yet what the ramifications were for the two of them. In a small town they would be seeing each other often.

He rubbed his eyes and reached over to the nightstand. He'd brought Jennifer's diary with him. For the first time since Tom had sent it to him, Stephen opened the book. He had settled down to one place and given himself roots. Jennifer wasn't around to call and tell about his new home. Every milestone in his life for the last two decades had been marked by Jennifer's quiet words. He missed her tonight. He turned pages and randomly chose an entry.

Tom's up already; I can hear him in the

hotel living room. I can't help but smile, listening to a man try to reason with a less-than-year-old puppy about the difference between shoes and toys. Tom's patience continues to be the most fascinating part of his character. I'm blessed. We're going to join Marcus and Shari for lunch if I have the energy, and I'm trying to be good and rest to conserve my energy. I'm oddly restless and wanting to get the day started, feeling each day now that time is getting short. May Tom's patience extend to a strong-willed wife. He loves me, and I fear I take unfair advantage of that some days.

I heard through the family grapevine that Stephen had a bad run last night. A two-year-old in a car seat didn't survive a car crash. It hurts to think about it. I'd have been bawling, doctor or not. I've cared for too many children. Knowing Stephen, he'd be the one comforting me.

Kate said he was at the gym shooting baskets late last night and not in the mood to talk about it. Oh, I wish I'd been there just to hug the big guy.

I know the feelings that resonate for him when a child dies, when he has to relive the stress of Peg dying and being unable to help his own sister. Losing a child brings back that pain. Maybe the fact he has seen so much is what keeps him sane and able to keep helping. I'm going to find him before this day is done. If he's not working a double shift, he'll be working on some house. I'd page him, but to see my number would just worry him needlessly. I wish I could send him a reason to smile today. I worry about him because he's kind enough to let me.

Tom just sent the puppy in to wake me up. My toes are kind of numb and the pain in my side is growing. He'll be forced to help me walk today. I get so tired of being ill. My mind still has me fit and mobile and reality is annoying. I need to send Stephen my puppy for a visit — Butterball is always good for a smile and a laugh.

Stephen paused after reading the two-page entry. The straightforwardness of the entry was a relief. Jennifer had never been one to focus inward, and the entry didn't trigger the emotional reaction he had feared. He remembered the child.

I got through the days because I had to. He

wasn't sure what had triggered his breaking point, what had brought the fainting at the sight of blood to the forefront. All those emergency calls had built inside until he finally cracked.

He thought about turning the page but instead closed the diary. He had a strong suspicion that as Jennifer's days drew to the end, not all the entries would be so easy to read.

He was rebuilding his life. Reading Jennifer's diary would help him let go of the emotions. But it would best be done slowly. He put the book back on the bedside table and turned off the light.

Fifteen

Meghan set down a coffee cup next to her mom. She shifted fabric samples for her new drapes to one side so she could take a seat on the piano bench. After the finishing touches were done on the living room and bedroom, she planned to tackle remodeling the bathroom. The decisions were never ending, but it was one of the best things about having a place of her own. Everywhere would eventually be touched by her decisions.

"So what do you think?" Mom asked.

Meghan didn't have to ask about the subject. It was all she had heard about over the last four days as patients flowed through the office.

"I'm surprised," Meghan replied, trying not to let herself get sucked too far into the speculation going on. She wasn't sure what to think about Stephen becoming a permanent resident of Silverton. He had never settled down before. Why now? Why here? Stephen just liked to complicate her life.

"You can do better than that, Meghan."

"What am I supposed to say?"

"Take him a pie as a welcome gift."

"And walk my heart back into a mess?"

"Do the safe thing — accept that he's part of the community, welcome him, then establish the relationship on the terms you want."

"I've already told him we'll only be friends."

"You might have mentioned that to him, but it wouldn't hurt to remind yourself again." Her mom touched her hand. "Stephen's a nice guy, and I know this will be hard for you. You had a crush on him as a teenager for a reason."

"I wish he hadn't put that kind of cash down."

"I've known Stephen since he was twelve. The man didn't buy a place in Silverton just so he could stop by and say hi to you. That was just an extra bonus. Invite him to church and over for lunch with us on Sunday. Your dad wants to talk with him. Of anyone who could have moved in and become our new neighbor, I can't think of a more interesting person than Stephen."

"I'll ask him." Meghan thought it was likely he'd say yes. And if he came to her parents' place for lunch, her mom could ask Stephen some of the questions Meghan would love to have answered but wasn't sure she'd have the nerve to ask.

He hadn't even called her to mention that he was buying Neil's place. Was he that upset about the no she had given him? Or was he changing tactics? He was moving in next door to her parents, and it wasn't the kind of place to be bought and sold quickly. This was a long-term decision. He already had her off balance enough that she wasn't sure what to think. This was so confusing.

She set aside the fabric samples. She wasn't going to rush over to deliver that welcome gift. Let him wonder a bit how she was reacting to the news. Maybe in a few days she'd have figured out the answer.

"Coming over." Stephen tossed another bale of hay to Jack. It landed at the end of the flatbed trailer, tossing up a cloud of dust and hay bits. Jack got his hands around the baling wire and hoisted the bale onto the stack he was building. They'd figured out from trial and error that the tractor pulling the flatbed could handle the weight of about a hundred bales per load. Stephen lifted an arm and wiped sweat away from his eyes. Three hours of hauling hay, and he still couldn't see the floor and walls of the first storage building. His neighbor Nelson would buy all the hay they could haul and store it in his barn. It was a good offer; Stephen hoped they could get the job done today.

"This will help."

Stephen looked back over his shoulder. Cassie carried a huge pitcher of ice water. Walking beside her were Meghan and Blackie.

"Break time," Jack said, vaulting from the trailer bed to the ground and striding over to join his fiancée. "Hello, Meghan. You're looking good."

"Hi, Jack. I heard you answered the call to help Stephen out."

"It's the novelty factor. Although a few hours of pitching hay already seems like a lifetime, we're making good progress."

Stephen steadied himself on the stacked hay bales he stood on and carefully climbed down. He tugged off his work gloves, shoved them in his back pocket, and accepted a glass of water from Cassie. "Thanks. Welcome to my new place, Meg. You're out visiting your parents?"

"Yes."

He'd wondered when he would hear from her or see her. The news had passed around town the same evening he bought the place, and the visits of neighbors and town folks stopping by to welcome him and offer a hand had been steady. The fact that she'd waited until midweek to get in touch was interesting.

"We'll leave you two big guys to get back to work. We just wanted to bring down the pitcher and see how you were doing," Cassie said.

Stephen wasn't letting Meghan get away that quickly. "I'll walk back to the house with you. Jack can drive this load up to the road then we'll take it over to unload."

Jack nodded, and Stephen fell into step beside the ladies. "How's the kitchen coming, Cassie?"

"I'm starting on the dishes and pans. It's going fast since you said to just pack it."

"Once the remodeling is done, I'll figure out what I want back in the house. For now we'll box everything in the house and store it in the second storage building. I'm hoping Jack and I can take out the kitchen cabinets tomorrow morning."

"Speaking of packing, I'll need more tape soon," Cassie said.

Stephen dug keys to his truck out of his pocket. "Sorry, I forgot to carry in the supplies I picked up this morning. Check the passenger seat. There's tape there and in the bed of the truck are more boxes."

Cassie accepted the keys and headed toward the truck.

"I wasn't sure you were going to come by," Stephen said to Meghan.

"It wasn't that simple to arrange. And I was planning to bring you a pie as a welcome gift, but my two attempts flopped. I should have just picked one up at the diner. Why this place, Stephen? You could have knocked me over with a feather when I heard the news."

"I had the cash and Neil wanted to sell. The timing was right. I fell in love with the idea of having a big workshop, a place my niece or nephew can come spend summer vacations, and a home with no traffic outside the window."

"You move fast when you make a decision."

"Yes, I do."

Meghan laughed and Stephen let himself relax. She stopped walking to turn and listen to the sound of the tractor coming to life. "This will be a good place for you, big and spacious and full of projects that will never be done."

"It has potential. The barn is great. I want a huge workbench that I can walk around with all the tools out and easy to access, and cubbyholes for everything I need to store. The floor is in good shape and the lighting is good. I'm hoping in a month to have it set up."

"Can I come and watch some days when you're making Kate's furniture?"

"You're welcome anytime. I'll even put you to work helping me if you like."

"I'd enjoy that." She scuffed her shoe in the dirt, then looked toward him. "Mom would like you to come to lunch this Sunday, if you're available."

"Sure. I'd love to stop by."

"Say around quarter till noon for lunch? Unless you'd like to come to church with us. You can meet the rest of your neighbors."

"Another Sunday, Meghan. Let's start with lunch." The tractor came up to the road. "There's Jack; I need to go help him unload the hay at Nelson's."

"I'll stay and help Cassie a bit if you don't mind."

He touched her hand. "Stay and help as long as you like. I'm glad you came."

"So am I." Meghan motioned Blackie toward the house.

Stephen watched her walk away.

He went to join his brother. A hay bale had fallen off the stack and Jack sat on it, chewing on a piece of hay. "If I wasn't happily engaged . . ."

Stephen pushed him off the hay bale.

His brother laughed, picked himself up, dusted off his jeans, and pulled out his gloves. He tossed the bale back up with the others. "I'll drive the tractor; you can ride the stack."

Stephen climbed up to make sure everything stayed steady during the short drive. He'd bought the right place — close enough that family would be over often from Chicago, near enough that Meghan would once again be part of his world. Family, friends, a permanent place . . . He wouldn't be bored, and at least the loneliness was at bay.

Stephen grabbed a hay bale. "Jack! Watch where you're driving! I'd rather not end up in the ditch."

The sun shone through the big bay windows into the Delhart dining room, sending rainbows dancing on the table as the light passed through the crystal water glasses. Stephen turned his glass a fraction and directed one of the rainbows toward Meghan. Still dressed in her church finery, she looked gorgeous. His first formal meal in Silverton, and it was at the table of Meghan's parents. It didn't get better than this. "Thank you, Mrs. Delhart. It was a wonderful meal."

"You're welcome to join us any Sunday."

Meghan's mom began gathering the dessert plates. Meghan rose and helped her mom clear the table, her touch steady and smooth across the tabletop as she searched and found pieces to pick up. He would have offered a hand, but Dr. Delhart nodded toward his office and Stephen didn't feel he had much option but to accept the silent invitation. "It's good to have you here, Stephen."

"Thank you, sir."

Dr. Delhart moved around to have a seat at his desk. "Are you thinking about settling down here long term? Or are you just fixing up the place to sell later?"

Stephen took a seat across from him. He didn't mind the direct question. The subject had been raised during lunch but only briefly. Meghan's mom kept the conversation focused on his travels and the places he had seen. "I plan to stay, Dr. Delhart. I've got another generation of family to think about, and the land is a good investment."

"I'm not faulting your judgment. It's good land and you made a fair deal for it. And please, make it Bill. We've known each other a long time."

"It's a friendship I've appreciated." Stephen set down his glass and stood, feeling more at ease on his feet. He walked over to

227

study the bookshelves. Dr. Delhart had a good medical library.

"We could use your skills, Stephen. EMS for this town is provided by the county, and right now the ambulance and crew comes from the next town over. With another paramedic in the mix, we could fix that and have an ambulance stationed here at the clinic, effectively cutting down response times by fifteen to twenty minutes."

Stephen hadn't seen that coming. He rubbed the back of his neck before turning to look at Meghan's father. "I'm going to be occupied with the house for the summer at least. And to be honest, I haven't thought about picking up that EMS jacket again."

"I know the profession nearly chewed you up and spit you out. I've watched you with some concern the last few years. But I know you pretty well, Stephen. You're going to miss it." Bill leaned back in his chair and held his gaze. "I won't pretend it's easier work out here. We may get fewer emergencies per day, but Silverton is a long way from any hospital. What happens if you put that EMS jacket back on and have a really nasty loss like five-year-old twins in a car accident, or a heart attack in the grocery store, and you can't keep them alive during the long drive to the hospital? Here, you're it. But you're a good paramedic, and someday you have to find peace with the profession you poured your heart and soul into for a decade. Being a paramedic is more than a job; it's part of who you are. Walking away may not be the right answer."

Stephen listened to the advice and nodded. Bill was offering him a way back to the work if he wanted it. "I'll think about it."

"If I get shorthanded in a crisis, will you help me out? Strictly volunteer; the pay is expenses. I'll get you a pager and put you on insurance coverage with the county so you don't need to worry about that. I'll only call if it's life and death."

Stephen smiled. "No pressure." The idea of someone dying because EMS support was too far away — he'd been in the profession too long not to feel the responsibility. And bottom line, in a situation like that it would be Meghan trying to help her father out if it wasn't him. "If you need me in a crisis, I'll be there."

Bill got to his feet and shook Stephen's hand to seal the deal, his grip firm. "Thank you." Bill smiled. "Now you've got an excuse to drop by and see Meghan at the clinic if you need one."

"I'm pretty good at creating reasons to stop by on my own."

"I hope you do."

They moved to rejoin the ladies.

They found Meghan and Elizabeth had moved into the living room. Meghan was sitting on the floor by the fireplace, sorting through a basket of supplies. She snapped her fingers for her dog to join her. "I've got the brush. Come on, Blackie." Stephen watched her dog move somewhat warily to her side. Meghan laughed and ruffled his ears. "You love having this done, you fraud." She started working out the tangles in his fur.

"I found the photo album I told you about," Elizabeth mentioned, reaching for it on the corner table. Stephen crossed over to the couch and took a seat beside her. "I knew I had a picture of you. Here it is." She turned the album toward him. "You must have been about thirteen."

He looked at the photo. "I was so skinny — I was a stick."

"You and Jack started hanging out together that year. I remember that's the bike the two of you shared."

"Meghan, there's one here with you in braids."

Her mouth twisted wryly. "Don't remind me."

She looked so incredibly young. He wanted to laugh at the era, but there were too many pictures of him in this album to risk it. He hadn't realized how much he and Jack hung out with Meghan in those days. She had certainly loved books. In many pictures there was one set down near her. He'd seen stacks of books on tape at her home — so the love was still there. If he could figure out how to make the offer without sounding stupid, he'd offer to read for her.

"I'm glad you kept these, Elizabeth."

"So am I."

Stephen turned pages. There were several photos of JoAnne and Meghan together through high school, most of them with Ken making up the threesome. He paused when he found a picture of Meghan in a rocking chair with a baby nestled on her shoulder. She looked about sixteen, and if he wasn't mistaken, the photo had been taken in the home she now owned. "May I borrow this?" Stephen asked her mom, turning the picture to show her.

"If you like."

He'd add a rocking chair for Meghan to the list of furniture he was making for Kate. He'd get the photo blown up and figure out what he could of the chair from the picture. It would make a perfect housewarming gift.

He eventually came to the end of the pages. "Thanks for digging this album out. It brings back memories. You were cute, Meghan."

"Please, don't remind me of the braces and bell-bottom jeans."

Stephen glanced at the clock. "Ken was going to bring over a load of lumber this afternoon. I need to be going in case he's early."

"I hope you'll consider joining us again," Elizabeth offered.

"I hope I can return the favor soon."

"Meghan, why don't you walk Stephen home," Elizabeth suggested.

Stephen looked over at Meghan to see that she'd stilled in her brushing of Blackie's coat. "If you have the time."

She glanced at her mom and then back toward him. "I've got the time."

He waited as she gathered her items together and held the door for her. The sun warmed his shirt as they walked along the path that ran between the two properties. "It's a blue sky today with a few white clouds. I like this arrival of spring."

Meghan leaned her head back as she walked, seeking the direction of the sun. "Beautiful. I love lazy days where you can curl up and enjoy the warmth of the sun and take a nap."

He reached to take her hand, felt her start, and smiled as he waited for her to get comfortable. "It was nice of your mom to invite me over. She's one incredible cook and a great hostess. You've got great parents."

"I think so." She shifted her hand on Blackie's harness. "What were you and Dad talking about for so long?"

"He wants me to take an EMS job with the county."

Her steps slowed. "I'm sorry he pushed, Stephen."

He stroked his thumb across the back of her hand. "Don't be. This town needs a paramedic on call who actually lives here rather than the next town over. He was right to ask. I said I'd think about it, and I agreed to be a backup in a crisis. I like the work, Meg. A lot of the problem in the past was the fact that the job consumed every hour of my life. There was never any margin."

"If you're sure. There have been a few close calls in the last year where it would have really helped to have you around."

"You'll add my phone number to your speed dial?"

She laughed. "Yes."

He led the way around the pond.

"Any buyer's remorse for having locked

yourself in to this place?"

"None. In fact Kate is already wondering if she'll ever get me back to Chicago. I don't miss it at all." Stephen pulled out his keys. "Why don't you and I take a drive after I help Ken unload this lumber?"

"Can we make it another time? JoAnne and I are looking at options for my bathroom wallpaper this afternoon."

Schedule collisions . . . "I can see our respective fix-up projects are going to be a challenge to manage so they don't step on higher priorities."

"If you're going to live here for the next decade, I'm sure we'll eventually have time free at the same time." She turned to walk back along the path to her parents' home. "I'll see you later."

"Count on it," Stephen called after her. He might have to settle for a friendship, but he still wanted the groundwork laid for something more.

She waved back at him and kept going.

In the shadow of Ken's windmill, Stephen leaned down and retied his shoelaces before beginning his climb. Above him Ken was already at work. He had done Stephen a favor bringing the shipment of lumber over two weeks ago; now he was returning the favor.

He climbed, careful to get a good grasp on the rungs. Stephen could make out the Mississippi River through the hazy humidity on the horizon. He clipped his safety line to the top crossbar and moved from the ladder to the narrow walkway. "Do you ever do things halfway, Ken?"

"Not if I can help it. When you grow up in a small town, sometimes you have to make your own excitement."

Stephen reached for the rope, which stretched down to the ground, and tied it to the crossbar. He'd secured the case at the other end before beginning his climb. He began hand over hand pulling the case and its well-cushioned microphone up to their perch. He held the equipment in place while Ken bolted it down.

"If I could talk JoAnne into moving to Oklahoma, I'd study the big storms and twisters. But since it's doubtful I'd ever get her to move from Silverton, I'll settle for figuring out how to predict where rain will fall." Ken ran a test strip on the humidity gauge. "Everyone should have a hobby that lasts a lifetime."

"Does Meghan still go out with you on storm chases?"

"We get out at least once a month. She can hear the hail long before I can. Come along on our next storm chase. You'd enjoy it."

"I'm game to try it once. Give me a call."

"You got it." Ken climbed up two more rungs on the ladder to check the rain gauges. "I hear you're stocking your pond next week."

"I'm thinking sunfish and some bass. Bill suggested I expand the pond into his land and the two of us would make it a real fishing attraction. Maybe co-op the costs for those who want to fish in it and have them pay based on how much they catch and take out so we can keep it restocked."

"I'll take a charter membership in that co-op," Ken offered. "When you fish, it's nice to actually catch something."

Stephen swung around to the other side of the equipment platform and started work on securing the wind gauges. "Any idea where I can find someone who has sheep?"

Ken leaned around to see him. "I thought you were planning for some cattle."

"Actually, I'm leaning toward a petting zoo. Meghan would enjoy it."

Ken laughed. "Nice idea. I'll ask around for you." He mounted the protective hood on the microphone. "I admit I'm a bit curious about the two of you. Back in the days when she first moved here, Meghan used to talk about you. It was Stephen this, Stephen that. Then one day she didn't mention you anymore."

Stephen was glad the safety harness had him securely held in place. He didn't need any surprises, like a former boyfriend. "When was that?"

"About the time you started going out with someone named Caitlyn? JoAnne fixed Meghan up with Jonathan that summer, and we were a foursome until he moved on to study his music with more prestigious musicians."

Stephen had heard the name before. "Jonathan's the piano player?"

"Concert pianist, if you please. I've heard him play. He's good, if a bit arrogant now that he's famous."

"What's his full name?"

"Jonathan Peters."

"You know, I think Meghan sent me some of his stuff on one of those tapes at Christmas. He is good. Isn't Meghan taking piano lessons from the person who taught him?"

"Mrs. Teal. You'll like her; she's basically the town grandmother."

Stephen finished his task and slipped his hammer back on his belt. "Was Meghan serious about Jonathan?"

"For a while. He was more serious about his music. I never did understand that priority, but you can't argue with his success. Mrs. Teal says he's playing in Chicago this summer. If JoAnne and I can get tickets, do you and Meghan want to come?"

Stephen liked the way that was phrased. "Sure."

Meghan had dated Jonathan Peters, yet she never mentioned the name to him. What else had been going on in her life that he didn't know about? As far as he knew he was the only guy interested in dating Meghan who happened to still be in Silverton. He needed to press that advantage before it was too late. He moved over to the ladder to descend to the ground. What would be his next best move?

Sixteen

Friday, April 12
Silverton

Stephen picked up a piece of pine Ken had brought over. Maybe use it for a display case? He moved it to the stack of wood being set aside for furniture. A month of hard work had finally made it possible to turn his attention from clearing the outbuildings and gutting the house to getting his workshop put together. Stephen brushed away a bug. The barn doors were open and the midday sun made it comfortable working out there. The stacks of wood barely made a dent in the work space; this barn was huge.

Once the wood was sorted, he started to look at what he wanted to do for a workbench and shelving. Neil had built up one area of the barn under the loft with a wooden floor, workbench, and good electrical connections and lights. By raising the wooden floor from the concrete, Neil had taken the first steps to make this a year-round workroom.

Stephen tugged on the shelving to see how sturdy the joints were and could barely nudge it. This unit was not going to be taken apart. And it would be best used over by the door. He thought about the weight to move, accepted that it had to be done, and went to get the dolly. *Jack, where are you when I need a helping hand?* The shelves weighed enough, even with the straps and wheels providing leverage, that it still took everything he had to move it to the door.

The wall behind where the shelves had stood was coated with cobwebs and dust. Stephen batted them away with a paper towel as he struggled to catch his breath. He used a hammer to rip out the two nails exposed and bent to see what shape the electrical outlets were in.

He found a couple spots on the wooden floor that gave under his weight. The board looked solid enough until he stepped down and realized the joist beneath it must have worn away. Probably mice, termites, or both. He tapped with the hammer to see where flooring might have to be replaced. He pulled up the floorboard, expecting dirt, decayed wood, and sawdust. He found that — and more. Stephen tugged out a leather pouch nestled between floor joists.

The leather, dry and stiff with age, cracked at his touch. The brittle drawstring broke as he loosened it. It must have been down there over a decade. He tipped the pouch and out slid a ring. The gold band and the stones had dulled. He carried it to the door to look at it in the afternoon light. It was a square-cut diamond of good size with two smaller diamonds and an emerald in a rather ornate setting. The band itself was etched. He lifted it to try to read what was engraved inside. The initials *T. R.*

Why had Neil hidden an expensive ring under the floor in his barn? Stephen polished it with the corner of his shirt. The stones looked real. Why hadn't it been in the safe at Neil's store? It would spend tonight in that bank vault, for Neil owned it. Stephen slipped the ring back into the leather pouch and zipped it inside his pocket.

His pager went off. Stephen unclipped it to read the number. Bill needed him. It had been silent for so long he'd begun to wonder if the pager worked.

He called the dispatcher as he dug out the keys to his truck. "I'm on my way." He had a possible heart attack at Neil's jewelry store.

Meghan picked up the clinic mail as she

241

passed through the reception area. Blackie nearly tripped her as they wedged through the doorway into her back office. "Easy, boy."

She would have to get him in to see a vet. She was afraid his bruised back leg was still causing him problems. He'd stopped her from falling into a ditch Wednesday, and as a thank-you she managed to fall on him. Blackie curled up on his big pillow, and she knelt beside him to tug out several biscuits from the box in the cabinet. "How are you doing?" He licked her hand in answer. She laughed and gave him a back rub.

She squeezed between the corner of the desk and file cabinet to reach her chair. They would have to move the clinic to a larger facility soon. Meghan placed the first letter on the scanner and the software read the return address aloud. She filed it with bills to be paid that month. Dad was making rounds today, and it was her chance to get caught up on the office paperwork.

The door chimes rang.

"Meghan?" JoAnne sounded out of breath.

"In the office."

"Your dad needs you at Coffer's jewelry store. It looks as if Neil is having a heart attack. Bill said to make sure it's been called

242

in and to bring the blue and red cases."

Meghan reached for the radio behind her and requested the county EMS to send the ambulance. "The cases are in the cabinet by the door in the receptionist area." Meghan snapped her fingers for Blackie and swiftly slipped on his harness. She joined JoAnne and pulled on her jacket. "Who found him?"

"The Fed-Ex driver brought packages and saw Neil in the front of the shop on the floor."

That didn't help much to narrow down the time of onset. Neil would have had nitroglycerin tablets with him. If he'd been able to take them, maybe the attack had been arrested in time. "Was he conscious?"

"Yes."

Meghan took JoAnne's arm and they hurried down Main Street to the store. "Let us through," JoAnne urged. Meghan heard several voices she recognized among the gathering crowd.

"Thanks, Meg." Her dad opened the cases. She knelt at Neil's left side as her dad worked and listened as he attached the heart monitor and started an IV to give the first round of drugs. Neil's hand felt clammy, and the sound of his breathing told her he was in a lot of pain.

"Meg, come along . . ."

She rubbed the back of Neil's hand. "You know I will."

"The workbench . . ." He tried to say something but his voice tapered off.

"Save your breath, Neil," her dad cautioned. "You're going to come through this okay. Meghan, lift his head and let's slip on oxygen."

Meghan gently raised Neil's head. If he came through this, he'd probably need to be on oxygen full time. Just another tug-of-war she'd have with him when he started to feel better. She adjusted the mask for him. "JoAnne will make sure everything's locked up here, and the deputy will watch the place while you're gone. We'll make sure everything is as you left it."

His hand tightened on hers. She couldn't do much, but she could ensure he didn't have to worry about his business. She heard people near the doorway shuffle back.

"JoAnne, ask around. Let's get vehicles parked at the street moved so the ambulance crew has easier access." Meghan turned her head, hearing Stephen's voice, intensely relieved. Moments later a hand squeezed her shoulder. "How you doing here?"

"Glad you're around. I called dispatch, and the ambulance is on its way."

"Good. Bill, you ready for me to brace his knee?"

"Yes. He's got as much painkiller in him as he can handle."

"Meg, Neil twisted his left knee when he fell. It's swelling fast," Stephen said. "I need some scissors."

She reached for the blue case and found them by touch.

"Got it; thanks. Find me something we can use to immobilize the leg."

She heard fabric tear. "There are collapsible splints in the bottom of the red case."

"Neil, how bad is the burn in your knee?" Stephen asked.

"Bad," he gasped from under the oxygen mask.

"You may have dislocated part of your kneecap. Hold on; this will make it better. Meg, hold here." Her hands were pressed into position below the knee injury. She could feel the muscle and bone and the heat of the swelling above her hands.

"I'm going to splint above your hands."

She nodded and Stephen leaned past her to get supplies. She used her fingers to hold the edge of the brace as he put it in position. The heart monitor printer hummed as a strip of paper was pushed out. "What's it look like, Dad?"

"Decent. Neil, you're doing fine."

She turned her head. "EMS is here; I hear the sirens coming."

"About time. You were right, Bill," Stephen said. "Twenty minutes from the page."

"Let's get him ready to transport."

Meghan moved out of the way as two paramedics came in. She listened to Stephen working with them and her dad, fitting in as if he had been part of the team for years. Neil was moved to a stretcher.

"Would you ride along with him, Stephen? I'll follow in a car with Meghan."

"Sure."

"Neil, just relax and let the drugs work," her dad encouraged.

"Better already."

"I'll get you there comfortably," Stephen promised.

Meghan started as Stephen's hand squeezed her shoulder. "I'll see you there." She nodded, and he moved past her. Moments later she heard doors slam and the ambulance pull away.

Meghan helped her father repack the two cases. "What do you think, Dad?"

"His color is bad. He was down for at least half an hour before he got help. There's going to be some lasting heart damage from this one."

"Will he make it?"

"He's a tough man. He's got a good chance." Her dad dropped his arm around her shoulders. "There was nothing more you could have done to prevent this. Neil has to stop smoking if he wants to have a chance."

"Maybe this time he'll listen."

"I hope so. Come on; my car's at the clinic."

Meghan paced the hospital hallway, one finger running along the wall to keep her place. She hated that she wasn't able to bring Blackie to this floor. Neil had been at the hospital for over two hours now, and still there wasn't word from Stephen or her dad about Neil's prognosis. She reached the elevator and turned, then retraced her steps. The cane felt odd in her hand, but it was better than nothing.

"Meghan."

She turned at Stephen's voice and knew what he was going to say just by the tone of his voice. His hand settled on her shoulder and the warmth of it relaxed her muscles.

"I'm sorry. They were setting him up for an emergency angioplasty when he had another heart attack. It was massive."

"Oh no." Neil had been a friend despite

the gruff personality that didn't let someone get close. And he'd liked her too; she knew it from the treats he always had for Blackie when she stopped by.

Elevator doors opened and the hall filled with the noise of other conversations, making her wish Blackie were with her now. The situation was disheartening. She wanted to lean against Stephen but used the wall instead. "He'd done so well surviving the challenge of losing his wife and his first heart attack."

"This was sudden. Maybe for him that was best. He wouldn't have enjoyed living with the restrictions that would have been inevitable."

"Did you see my father?"

"I'm right here, Meg." Her dad's voice came from her right. "Stephen is correct. Nothing else could have been done to pull him out of this one." His hand touched her arm. "There's nothing more we can do here. Let's go home. Stephen, can we give you a ride back to Silverton?"

"I'll help Joseph get the ambulance re-stocked and stay in town for the evening to see family. Jack will give me a lift out tomorrow with more stuff from my place here."

Meghan wished he would come with

them, but she understood his desire to stay and see family while he was in town. If they were more than just friends, maybe he'd invite her to join him . . . She pushed aside the disquieting thought and forced herself to smile. "Thanks for what you did, Stephen. It helped having you there."

"Anytime. See you around, Meg."

Stephen asked around the police central building until someone could direct him to the robbery and fraud group. He finally located Kate's new office on the third floor down the hall from the water fountain.

Stephen paused at a door that had Kate's name stenciled on the glass and smiled. His sister had arrived. He knew she must already hate the bureaucracy of it. He tapped on the door and opened it. She looked up from some paperwork. Her concentration turned into an instant grin. "This is a surprise."

The speed at which she dropped the papers had him laughing. "A pleasant one I hope."

"Always."

"You look really good." He entered her office and did a 360-degree turn to study it. "I'm impressed. Four walls with actual artwork and not a lot of paper clutter. A calendar turned to the correct month. And if

I'm not mistaken, that plant is not plastic. Are you sure you're not borrowing someone else's office?"

"Dave helped me decorate. I drew the line at accepting an autographed football from Dave's famous brother-in-law for the credenza. What brings you back to town? Not that I'm not thrilled, but I figured we would have to drag you back."

"Neil Coffer, the jeweler in Silverton, had a heart attack. He died a short while ago at the hospital."

"I'm sorry to hear that."

Stephen pushed his hands into his pockets, not sure what he thought about the loss other than disappointment that it happened. His first time back as a paramedic and his patient died after arriving at the hospital. At least the time away from his profession had given back a sense of perspective — he wasn't carrying the weight of this loss home with him. "He was a long-term smoker and had already had one heart attack last year. It wasn't likely that he'd die getting hit by a bus."

"Without meaning to downplay his death, will it complicate your life and the property sale?"

"It shouldn't. All the paperwork is signed and the land sale is contingent only on the final loan approval, and that's in process with the bank." Stephen finally stopped walking and took a seat in the chair across from her. "You're looking good, Kate."

"I'm feeling better." She swiveled her chair back and forth with her foot as she studied him. "You didn't go to the trouble to find my office because you were at loose ends for the afternoon."

"No." Stephen thought about what it would mean for the reputation of a man not able to defend himself if he answered Kate's question. He sighed and did what he had to. He unzipped his jacket pocket and pulled out the pouch. "I've got a mystery for you. I found this under a floorboard in the barn. Neil has owned that farm for over thirty years; he owns a jewelry store with a walk-in bank vault. Somehow I don't think this was in the barn by accident."

Kate took the pouch, opened it, and let the ring fall into her hand. She studied it and then looked back up at him. "Is it real?"

"You tell me. The man had a heart attack before I could even mention it to him."

"Did you find anything else?"

He started to say, "not so far" but stopped himself. "No. As an honest jeweler, realizing someone he knew sold him something stolen, he hid it and hoped to bury the incident rather than report it. The man just died, Kate. From everything I hear, he was a decent guy."

"Yet you didn't go to the local sheriff."

Stephen inclined his head, conceding. He wanted for now to keep this in the family. He had a suspicion he knew what would be found, and he didn't want the news spreading around Silverton until the implications were fully understood. "I don't know him. I know you."

"I'll look into it. Quietly," Kate promised.

"Thanks." He thought about staying to chat but his mission for the moment was over. Besides, Kate would start to look into that ring as soon as he left. He got to his feet.

"Are you in town for the evening?"

"I'm heading to the house to pack up another load. But I'll take an hour of your time tonight to look over some furniture sketches if you're free."

"I'm free. In this job the pager rarely goes off. Say about seven?"

"Perfect." He pulled out his keys.

"Stephen."

He stopped at the door to look back at her.

"Neil just died. If this isn't a one-time innocent thing, if there are more pieces, someone else may know that and try to find them. Watch yourself, okay?"

"I don't like the way you think."

"Sometimes I don't either."

He jiggled his keys and nodded. "I'll take care."

Craig searched carefully through the desk drawers in Meghan's home and found many receipts but not what he sought. She kept a neat house. Where were her credit cards, her checkbook? She hadn't had a purse with her when she left with her father for the hospital — he'd slipped quickly into her office at the clinic, and it hadn't been there. She might not carry a purse because she wanted her hands free for the dog harness, but she would still have the contents of a purse around.

He moved into the living room to check the path she would take when she came home, looking for the natural place she would set a bag. He found a large coin purse set beside the cookie jar on his second walk-through and unzipped it. Bingo. He sorted credit cards and chose the one with the longest expiration date. A stolen credit card would sell for some instant cash, and he needed fast cash.

He'd lifted forty dollars from the cash in

the cigar box on her desk, and one of the two diamond earrings she left on the dresser. He had to be careful in his choices. He couldn't risk taking something so obvious she noticed the theft right away, and he had to make sure she had reasonable doubt that there really had been a theft. Having a blind lady move into town was a gift; he didn't want to spook her into installing an alarm. He planned to be back.

Craig needed to get into Neil's store, but a cop was watching the place for the night. And Craig had to have a fix to calm the jitters before he tried to rob the place. He didn't have long — a few days, a week — before Jonathan would hear that Neil was dead and came looking for jewels too. Craig would make sure he had them first.

Maybe during the funeral there would be a window of time to slip into the store. If the stones were in the vault, he was out of luck. But he suspected Neil had simply moved the hidden gems from his house to the second-floor apartment. The cop probably wouldn't think to check the apartment, so if Craig could get in, he'd find what he was after. With the number of gems stolen over the years, it would pile up into a fortune.

"Blackie, are you coming in?"

Craig froze. Meghan was home early. He looked toward the back door but couldn't get to it in time. He eased a step back toward the living room as the front door opened, reaching out for something to use as a weapon. His hand closed over a tall thin statue.

He hated dogs. He slid a hand across his mouth to quiet his breathing as she turned in the doorway less than twenty feet away and waved to someone at the street. She closed the door and moved into the room, humming softly. She paused at the closet to hang up her jacket and disappeared into the kitchen, sorting the mail she had carried in with her.

He took a breath. No dog — she'd left Blackie outside. He relaxed his grip on the statue and placed it silently back on the piano. He eased toward the back door at a snail's pace, wanting to run but not able to afford so much as a board creaking.

She turned on the faucet, and he turned the doorknob and eased open the back door. He slipped through and closed it slowly. That had been too close. He took two steps away from the house and let himself breathe again.

He'd have his fix tonight, he'd plan the robbery, and in a few days he would leave this town rich, and set for years to come.

The pesky dog growled at him as he walked around the side of the house. It began barking furiously and lunging at the fence. Craig walked away. Next time he'd bring something to handle the mutt.

Meghan opened her closet and sorted through her clothes to find the dress she would wear for Neil's funeral tomorrow at 10 a.m. She had a simple black dress that would be perfect with her pearls. She located the dress, relieved to find she had sent it to be dry cleaned before putting it away. She laid the dress out and looked for her shoes.

She picked up her pearls and felt around for her diamond earrings. She found one but as she kept searching she wasn't finding the second one. She knew she had put it here in the jewelry box. Meghan took the box over to the bed and carefully emptied it. She felt along the lining and every compartment. How did she lose just one earring?

She checked the other jewelry to see if it had become stuck in a brooch or tangled with a necklace but didn't find anything. If she'd snagged the back of the post on her clothing and lost the earring, she would have noticed when she removed them. She had put two earrings in the box but there was only one here.

Meghan went through the box again.

She was misplacing things; it had to be that simple. She lifted her head as Blackie rambled down the hall, trailing something of interest to him. The random noises in the house were suddenly not innocuous. She went to the dresser and opened the first drawer, systematically beginning a more thorough search.

Seventeen

Stephen leaned against the door to the clinic office and watched Meghan work, her concentration on the document in front of her complete. She wore earphones, moving the cursor around on the screen and typing in spurts at a furious pace. She was so incredibly pretty . . . He wished life wasn't so complicated.

Taking her to dinner, inviting her to the next O'Malley basketball game — in the past he would have done so without a second thought. Now his actions would be clouded with how it would be interpreted. How did you just be friends when you wanted to be something so much more? The puzzle had no easy answer. She leaned over and replaced something on the scanner, then hit the button to activate the scan.

Stephen knelt and greeted her dog.

"Who's there?"

He looked up, startled to realize she'd slipped off the earphones and heard him.

The anger and fear in her voice shook him. "I'm sorry, Meghan. You were working or I would have said something."

Her gaze dropped to focus toward him next to Blackie.

She was pale. He rose slowly. "Are you okay?"

She turned back to her work. "You just surprised me."

Meghan wasn't normally so spooked about being surprised by someone. And she had never been very good at lying. "I came to ask if I could take you to the funeral."

She took a deep breath and paused what she was doing, then glanced back at him. "Sure, just give me a moment and I'll be ready to go."

He leaned against the door again and waited as she shut down her equipment and reached for her bag. "Okay."

She was wearing the bracelet he had given her. With the elegant black dress and pearls, it looked good. He would have to buy her earrings to match. "You can leave Blackie off duty and walk with me to the church if you trust me for the details."

"I'd like that." She came around the desk.

He guided her hand to his arm and felt how cold her hand was. "Is there anything I

259

can do to help you out today? Funerals aren't easy."

She glanced his way as they walked. "I was just about to ask you the same thing. This will resonate with Jennifer's funeral."

"And Peg's . . . and my parents'." Stephen set his hand above hers and squeezed it. "It's okay. I'm getting pretty good at knowing what funerals are like. I didn't know Neil more than casually. I'm sorry he didn't make it, but at least he had a full life before he died."

"I'm likely to need some Kleenex. I've known him all my life, and I'm going to miss his gruffness even if I didn't know him all that well."

Stephen patted her hand. "I came prepared."

Meghan moved around her mother's kitchen loading the dishwasher after dinner, thinking about the funeral. It had been so hard to listen to them lower Neil into the ground and wonder what else she could have done. Her hand touched something sharp and she jerked back. *Don't get distracted when handling knives.*

She finished loading the dishwasher and looked out where she knew the window was toward Stephen's property. What was he

260

doing tonight? He'd been quiet after the funeral. The pastor had been talking about heaven and she picked up on Stephen's discomfort. He had walked her back to the office, then left to go back to work on his house. "What's the time, Mom?"

"Ten till seven."

Meghan dried her hands. She wanted to see the changes Stephen had made to the house. He invited her to stop by, but it looked like it would have to be a late visit. Neil's lawyer had asked to see both her and Dad tonight. There would inevitably be final items for the estate to settle up surrounding how he died. Meghan wished it could have been put off for another night.

"Walter's here, honey. Could you bring in the coffee?"

"I'll get it, Mom."

They settled in the living room, and Meghan listened politely to Walter as he talked over business items with her father. Meghan picked up the baby blanket squares her mom was putting together to make a quilt for Kate's baby shower. A teddy bear embroidered in each fourth square was within her skill level. The outline was already made and she simply needed to count stitches to fill the circles.

"Let me get to the reason I'm here,"

Walter said. "As you know, Neil had no surviving family members. I asked him what he would like to do with his estate, and he wanted the proceeds to go toward expanding the health care clinic of Silverton."

"That was generous of him," Dad remarked.

"He appreciated your help through the years, Bill. Since you already have the clinic structured as a nonprofit, it won't be that difficult to arrange in terms of complying with the trust bequest. After talking about a number of ways to make that wish happen, Neil went for simplicity. Meghan, Neil left you in charge of the jewelry store."

She stopped counting stitches. "He what?"

"The business and property are now in trust for the clinic, and they're yours to liquidate. The sale of the house and grounds to Stephen will go through, for the contracts are valid, but the proceeds will simply flow into the estate at settlement."

She couldn't get past the simple fact that he'd entrusted his jewelry business to a blind lady. "Why me?"

"Several reasons," she heard Walter smile as he explained. "He liked you, and he knew you'd care that it was done right and that you'd oversee the funds to get the best return possible. He also knew you would have the time this was going to take."

"But what do I know about jewelry?"

"Enough to ask good questions," Walter replied. "The problem won't be getting offers of help but in choosing the right people. Neil empowered his banker and me to help you with the details. He kept his own books, and from what I've seen they are meticulously maintained. You should have no problem following them. It is a very simple business at its heart.

"The trust provides for the immediate needs of the business, the chief one security. You may notice there have already been private security officers stationed at the store, taking over for the deputy who watched the store the first day. Neil had that already arranged and he hired a good firm. You'll have no worries there.

"The business will have to be closed and pieces that were on consignment for sale or for repair returned to their owners. That's the immediate concern. For the inventory owned outright by the business, you can either hold onto the pieces, reopen the store under your own name to facilitate their sale, or you may wish to sell the pieces to other dealers and accept the discount prices you'll get. Then you'll have to decide on the building and whether to sell the property or maintain it and rent it out."

"Did Neil use an accountant?" Meghan asked.

"A tax accountant. I have copies of the last several years of filings. I know this sounds overwhelming, Meghan, but it won't be. I have the keys at my office, and I can walk you through bank accounts and such. Come down when you feel ready. Feel free to bring along anyone you like to hear the details."

"When this estate is wrapped up, how much money are we talking about, Walter?" her father asked.

"I'm guessing a million, a million plus."

"Oh, my," her mother said into the silence.

Meghan felt shock to her toes at those kinds of numbers. And she was responsible for it?

"Neil had simple tastes, he reinvested in the stones he bought, and he did it for decades." Walter got to his feet. "I'll leave you to talk among yourselves. Meghan, call me when you're ready and I'll answer any questions you might have."

"What happens if I say no, if I don't want the responsibility?"

"He asked Stephen to do it."

264

She slowly nodded. Her third surprise of the night. "I'll call you."

Stephen left his workshop in the barn and strode back to the house, unable to focus on the task at hand. The funeral had been for someone he only casually knew, but it had been enough to make the memories return. Jennifer's funeral was too fresh in his mind. Stephen changed his shirt to one that didn't smell of varnish and set aside his work shirt to be laundered.

He sat on the bed and picked up the liniment he was using on a new blister. He applied it and a new Band-Aid. The funeral remarks had been close to a sermon on heaven. He sighed and picked up Jennifer's Bible from the bedside table. *Jenny, I wish you hadn't sent me this.* He had read the book of Luke from beginning to end, then had started the book of John. The more he read, the heavier his heart became.

He was willing to accept all of it, that God existed, that Jesus was His son and had risen from the dead, but it didn't change the problem he wrestled with the most — the life that came after the words 'I'm a Christian.' The idea of God having a personal relationship with people here on earth, for that relationship to continue for eternity simply didn't seem reasonable. God was well . . . God. A relationship of any real intimacy seemed far-fetched. And when it came right down to it, if he couldn't sort out what being a Christian meant after he said the words, it didn't make sense to take that step.

Meghan was one of those who came right out and called it a friendship.

It felt like a contradiction. Most Christians didn't live like they were best friends with God. Yet that relationship was described as the norm of what Christianity would be like. Maybe for a Moses who got the Ten Commandments or a King David who led Israel the word fit. But even if Stephen accepted it might be the norm for others, it didn't fit what he thought Christianity would be like for him. He was lousy at playing by team rules. And no matter how he cut it, Christianity came with a significant amount of expectations. Maybe it was cowardly to say he didn't want to try, but he didn't want to fail. And this looked like a failure waiting to happen.

He took the Bible with him out to the front porch and sat in the rocking chair, fulfilling his silent promise to Jennifer to keep reading until either his questions were addressed or he finished the book. He glanced at his watch. Meghan should be here within the hour. The meeting at her parents' had to be breaking up soon. He'd invited her to stop by, and he promised Bill he'd see her safely home. He hoped she could come.

Jenny, I'm not sure how I'm doing with Meghan. The last thing I want to do is ruin a good friendship; she's just so . . . I don't know . . . together with her life. I envy her the peace she's found. And you always liked her. I wish you were around to give me some personal advice.

He set his chair to rocking. He missed his sister. Maybe that was why Meghan had agreed to come by tonight. She had sensed how the funeral was lingering in his mind. She was able to read his mood better than he could read hers. *Why can't life be simple, Meg?*

"I'm sitting on the front porch, Meg." Stephen saw her coming around the path by the pond, walking at such a slow pace he knew she was lost in thought, depending on Blackie to take her safely where she was going.

She lifted her head and looked his direction. "Say where again?"

"Twenty some feet ahead and angle two to your left. Blackie is getting distracted by the flower garden I just planted."

Stephen lifted a hand to Bill, watching his daughter from the edge of his property. If Meghan knew silent angels often watched her, she never commented on it. She might live in a world of darkness where it was the same day or night, but for those who loved her, it helped to know she got safely from place to place. "There's a second chair on the porch free, we can go inside, or we can share the steps."

"Direct me to the chair. I'll let Blackie loose to get some exercise."

Stephen reached out a hand as she came up the stairs. "Here you go."

He waited until she was settled and comfortable. She rested her head against the back of the chair and sighed. He handed her a glass of iced tea. "Problems?"

"Neil left me in charge of the jewelry store, with the proceeds to be used to expand the clinic."

He stopped in the process of setting down the book in his lap. "That's a very generous bequest *and* a big job."

She smiled. "My first reaction was 'wow,' my second, 'what in the world am I going to do?' "

He picked up his glass. "You'll do fine."

"You better hope so, because if I say no,

he left it to you to handle."

Stephen choked on his drink.

Meghan reached over and slapped him on the back.

Stephen alternated between coughing and laughing as he looked at her. "I am not letting you say no."

Meghan slid her hand down to his and squeezed his hand. "I may need some of your help."

"Whatever you need," Stephen said. "Just as long as you keep the project." There was nothing Meghan couldn't figure out given some time. He set his chair in motion, rocking as he watched Blackie roam around the yard.

"Is the sky clear?"

"Hmm. There's a big bright band of stars that mark the Milky Way, and the moon is very bright tonight."

"That fits with the image in my mind."

"I could never see stars like this in the city. I didn't know what I was missing."

She drank the iced tea and rocked her chair in rhythm with his. Stephen let the quiet between them linger, just enjoying her presence. "Blackie's wearing down, Meg. Come on inside and let me show you my home."

"I was here many times visiting Neil's wife."

He stood and smiled. "Somehow I don't think your memory of this place will be much help." He opened the door, offered his arm, and led her inside. "The four walls and the windows are the same, but that's about it. Jack and I removed the kitchen cabinets the first week. Since then we took down one interior wall between the kitchen and the living room. Until I figure out the layout I want, there is now one huge open room with a hallway going back to the bedrooms." He described his plans, somewhat nervous about what she might think.

She turned in a quarter circle as she tried to mentally visualize what he described. "No furniture?"

"Just whatever's in your imagination. Plus one sofa brought from my home, a stereo, and my ever-present lawn chairs for comfort. Jack still has my barrel tables for some shindig at the fire district."

"You can't be serious."

He smiled. "Absolutely. I can recommend the couch for sitting a spell. Other than that . . . well at least there isn't much you can trip over."

She stamped her foot on the wooden floor and listened to the echo. "I like it. Which direction to the couch?"

He took her shoulders and turned her a

little more east. "Fifteen of your little paces, ten of my strides."

"Show off." She smiled and moved forward to sit down. "You've got big plans for this place."

"I do. I want my nephew or niece to spend a few weeks of his or her summers in the country. I've got in mind to become one very doting uncle."

"You'll make a good one, Stephen."

"I plan to."

She laughed. "Nothing like a huge dose of self-confidence."

"You want some more of that iced tea? Your mom taught me how to make it with a jar in the sun and the whole bit."

"You're falling in love with my mom."

"I've had a crush on your mom since I was twelve. You're just now catching on?" He came back with a refill on the tea. "I need a favor."

"What's that?"

"When you decide details for what to do with the jewelry store, can you keep me in mind for Neil's workbench? He built that one to last, and I'd hate to see it not find a good home."

"Sure."

He took a seat on the chair across from her, not wanting to push his luck with sharing the couch. "I'm glad you came."

She smiled back at him. "Me too."

He started his chair rocking again.

"Where do we start?" JoAnne asked.

Meghan set down the handheld tape player she'd used to record the conversation with Walter as he went over the business accounts. In the days since the funeral, she'd slowly been putting together a plan for where to begin. It was going to be a long Saturday.

"Let's locate the business records and paperwork first, inventory items second, appraise and evaluate third." With JoAnne's help, this job was doable. "We can tackle Neil's apartment and his personal effects later. Since we know he kept some fake pieces in his display cases and the real pieces in the vault, we'll need to have a gemologist make sure we don't misclassify a piece."

Meghan trailed her hand along the countertop, mentally putting a picture together of the store. "Let's find a place we can bring in a couple tables and set up a workstation and scanner and bring in a couple file cabinets to hold the records as we sort them out. I'd like you to photograph everything. We'll need a numbering system for the jewelry so they can be uniquely tagged."

"I've got an extra case of those clear plastic bags with closure tabs," JoAnne said. "We can use them and both slip tags around the pieces and number the bags as we take the pictures."

"Good. I have a feeling there will be several hundred pieces by the time we're done with this inventory. Are you ready for this?"

"I'm surrounded by jewelry. This is going to be fun."

Meghan laughed. "Let's see what you think in about six hours. Tell me about the layout in here."

Neil had placed an incredible trust in her, and she was determined to do her very best job. The time it would take to do the job right — maybe it was best.

Besides, if she was busy, she wouldn't be spending her evenings rocking on Stephen's porch and wondering where their relationship would go over the coming years. She'd enjoyed the evening almost too much for her peace of mind. *You're such a good guy, Stephen. Why did you have to land in my backyard? No one else compares anymore. And you're still out of reach.*

Eighteen

A week after Neil's funeral, Jonathan Peters checked into the hotel on Broadway Street in Silverton making a point to chat with the front desk clerk. He remembered her from high school and even back then she had been a gossip. He wanted the news that he had arrived spread around town before he could finish unpacking. There was no hiding the fact a famous son had returned to town, and it would be worth using that to his advantage. Before long there would be a few people seeking autographs and asking about living in Europe, and the conversations would allow him to ask some questions in return and probe recent events in town.

He took the room key he was handed, nodded to the couple getting off the elevator, and carried his two bags up to the second floor. He would have normally let the hotel staff carry his bags, but there were some items he was carrying he would rather keep in his possession.

Neil had sold his farm. Jonathan hoped

that was the last surprise of this trip. He had figured they would have to bury Neil there, that the man would never leave the land that had been in his family for decades. The stolen jewels must not be there anymore. That left the store or the strange places Neil had hidden gems in the past among his possessions. At least the heart attack would have given Neil no time to dispose of the jewels to buyers. They were still here somewhere.

Jonathan opened his bag and shook out his shirts and hung them up in the closet. The flight back from Europe had been a dash through airports on whatever seat he could get. He was going to kill Craig for not contacting him about Neil's death. The news had come from Mrs. Teal, calling to congratulate him for a splendid concert performance the week before in London. He sent her the recordings as a way to ensure he regularly heard news of what was happening in Silverton. She'd mentioned it in passing, a few days after Neil's funeral.

Mrs. Teal had been eager to pass on what she knew. Neil had left his estate for the new medical clinic, had put Meghan in charge of the liquidation. Jonathan was grateful to the man for that fact. It would be easy enough for him to stay in the loop, for

Meghan was too open for her own good at times. If there had been anything out of the ordinary found in the estate thus far, it would have been on the town grapevine. It was what he wasn't hearing that was reassuring: No stolen pieces had been found and the sheriff wasn't investigating Neil for suspicious sales.

He had to find the recently stolen European pieces; the older pieces couldn't as easily be tied back to him. The diamond choker stolen in Germany led the list of gems to find. The replacement piece had been damaged less than forty-eight hours after the exchange had been made and the piece discovered to be a fake. A search for the stolen choker was underway in Europe. If that choker showed up here in his hometown, his name would be written all over the theft.

He wanted ten hours of sleep to fight the jet lag but couldn't afford the delay. He glanced at his watch. He bet he could find Meghan at the clinic or the store. He wanted to time his visit so he could invite her to dinner. She was his access to the hidden jewels; she just didn't know it.

He also had to find Craig. The man would be desperately searching for the stones. Craig acting rashly and getting caught was the real threat. If he thought it would help his own situation out, he'd talk about the years of stealing.

Jonathan had stolen the stones over the years. If they were going to fall to anyone now that Neil was dead, it would be to him. He had already been in contact with two buyers who had dealt with Neil in the past. They were interested in buying whatever he would care to pass on. He would take them up on it. Jonathan planned to return to Europe with a fortune tucked safely away. He slipped the key in his pocket and went to scope out the situation.

Craig could be handled. Jonathan had had a few months since his last trip to Silverton to figure out how. Craig *would* be handled.

Chicago

Kate picked up the ring Stephen had left with her: gold band, three diamonds and an emerald, the stones real. The initials T. R. inside. And the report had just come back verifying the piece as stolen.

Dave pushed a salad across the desk. "Eat, love."

"I'm not hungry," she replied, absently

turning the ring. She pushed the open file toward her husband. "Five years ago a lady is having her ring cleaned before her thirty-fifth anniversary and learns it's actually an excellent fake. Last month the real ring is discovered hidden in Stephen's barn."

"And you said working robbery was boring." He stabbed an olive in his salad and used his other hand to flip open the file.

"The ring is worth a small fortune and Neil had it hidden in his barn. If he was the fence for the piece, surely he would have sold it by now. I don't want to wrongly accuse a dead man. He acquired the piece, realized it was stolen, and tried to make sure it disappeared for a lifetime. He wouldn't be the first honest shopkeeper to find out he had been sold stolen goods or end up in a quandary about what to do."

He turned pages in the file. "Maybe. But he didn't turn it in to the sheriff communicating his suspicions. Was that the only item recovered in a strange location?"

"So far." She compared the ring she held with the photo of the fake ring. They looked identical. "How many thieves go to the trouble of replacing a ring with a high-quality fake?"

"A thief who steals a lot and is covering his tracks. You don't go to all that trouble and cost if you intend to snatch only one or two pieces. How many good-quality fakes have shown up over the last few years?"

Kate flipped open her notepad. "I went back ten years and found two other local cases; those original pieces have never turned up. I'm still trying to get any national information."

"Stay with the case you have — that diamond ring. If the others are connected, they'll fall into place."

"Who made the fake? How did he know how to design the piece? Who pulled off the swap? When? And where?"

Dave smiled at her. "I'd say you've got an interesting case."

"One that may quickly become a quagmire. It's old, and from the filed report, the owner won't be much help identifying where and when it was swapped."

"Stay with where it was found; that's the opening."

"If he's deeply involved in this, Neil might have been the one making the fake pieces."

"A good possibility. There's only one way to find out, and it's not sitting here in an office. Let's go check out that bed-and-breakfast in Silverton. You can nose around this case for Stephen quietly as promised."

"As long as you're coming along off duty. No offense, but I'd rather do this investigation without FBI help."

Dave slid the file back across her desk. "You'd rather, but you won't because I have one similar national case for you. My mob boss case where he murdered his wife Marie? Her emerald earrings, a square-cut diamond ring, and a diamond and emerald bracelet and necklace were all discovered to be excellent fakes. Only her brooch was real. Her husband thought she had been having an affair and was selling the jewelry he bought her to make a nest egg for herself before she bolted."

Kate stared at her husband. "Let's try to keep the mob out of this one, okay?"

He smiled. "It could be a coincidence."

"Right." The ring in her hand felt warm now. "I may have a lead on a thief who stole from a mob boss's wife."

"One step at a time, Kate. We need to know if there's more than just that one ring among Neil's things before we speculate on how far this might go."

She handed him the phone. "Make us reservations in Silverton. The last thing I need is for Stephen to be in the dark on this. If there are more pieces, he may be the first to stumble on them. And if not Ste-

280

phen, then Meghan. Neil put her in charge of wrapping up the jewelry store."

Silverton

Meghan stretched her hands high over her head, flexing her stiff back. "JoAnne, you about ready to go?" They'd been working on cataloging the gems for a week, and it felt like they had barely made a dent in the project. She couldn't concentrate any longer tonight.

"Just about."

Meghan shut down the computer and scanner and pushed her chair back under the table.

"Anything you need me to store in the vault?"

"No. Go ahead and lock it up." Meghan knelt and slipped on Blackie's harness.

She followed JoAnne through the showroom to the front door. "Good night, Lou."

"Miss Delhart. Have a good evening. I'll get the door."

"Thanks." It helped, knowing there was a security guard present around the clock. She didn't have to worry about getting accustomed to the sounds in the building. Security made sure the store and valuable contents stayed safe.

"Neil bought a lot of jewelry."

"Little by little, we'll get it done," JoAnne reassured. "I'm going to stop by and order that pizza. Do you want to come with me or should I pick you up in about forty minutes?"

Ken was tracking an incoming storm, and a night sharing a meal and debating weather data with her friends beat returning home alone to listen to the storm come in. "Blackie needs to stretch his legs, and I could use a good walk. Why don't you pick me up at the church after you pick up the pizza?"

"Sure. Pepperoni and mushrooms okay with you?"

"Excellent." Meghan turned to walk Main Street and let Blackie set the pace. The heat of the store and her slight headache faded as the fresh air revived her.

The church doors were open as Meghan expected. She entered the sanctuary and walked toward the front. Someday she'd play the piano for Sunday services. The dream felt so far off. She pulled out the bench and sat, picking her way through two songs she had memorized. She turned her attention to playing scales. It felt clumsy. She frowned in concentration and slowly the B-flat scale smoothed out.

"You're improving, Meg."

She tilted her head, vaguely recognizing the voice.

"It's Jonathan. I was wondering if I might find you here."

She smiled and finished the scale. "I have a piano at home to practice on now, but I love hearing the sound of the baby grand. I heard you were back in town, Jon." It had been a long time since she had been sixteen and going out with him, but the comfort level was still there. She'd come to really appreciate music since she had gone blind, and he'd been one of the few friends who hadn't let the change in her eyesight change how he acted around her. "I didn't think you'd be back until after the London recording sessions were finished."

"Mrs. Teal's birthday is this weekend. There are some things a man should honor in his life, and the teacher who opened doors to the world is one of them."

She finished the scale and dropped her hands to her lap as she heard Jonathan move up the aisle.

"Please, don't stop playing on my account."

"I'm finished. Have you come down to the church to practice?"

"I try to get in my four hours a day even when I'm traveling," he replied, and she heard him lean against the piano. "We can play duets if you like."

"Why don't you start your practice time, and I'll just sit in a pew and listen."

"I'd love an audience. So what have you been doing with your life since I last saw you? Getting more beautiful, I see. I like you as a blonde."

"So does Stephen."

"The guy who bought Neil's place the month before he died?"

She laughed. "The grapevine is working fine I see."

She moved to the second pew and rested her hands on the back of the first pew, listening as the music began. "You make that sound so easy."

"It is." He added a flourish to a melody. "Mrs. Teal mentioned Neil had passed away. I was sorry to hear that. He was a fixture in town even when I lived here. I understand you are working on settling some of his estate?"

"The jewelry store. He left his estate to the medical clinic so it could be expanded."

"That must be a challenge."

"JoAnne's helping me. We've been working on it about a week, and we're making slow but steady progress. Will you be in town for long?"

"Four or five days. Since I was making a trip back, I said yes to a concert in Chicago and then I have a music clinic to teach. I'll be back in June to do a series of performances in Chicago."

"I know Mrs. Teal will be thrilled to have you back for a visit."

He switched to playing scales. "I'm trying to keep it a surprise for tomorrow morning, but the odds of that happening are slim. Would you be interested in joining me for dinner tonight, Meghan?"

"I'm afraid I have plans. A storm is coming through tonight and I'm helping Ken with his research."

Jonathan laughed. "Ken always was thrilled by a good storm. Another day for dinner perhaps?"

"I would like that."

He shifted to a sonata.

"You did well with your gift. You turned it into everything it could be."

"Thanks, Meg. I've tried."

She stayed and listened to him practice until JoAnne arrived, then gathered up Blackie's harness. "It was good to see you, Jon."

"For me as well. I'll look forward to that dinner."

"So will I."

He began playing a jazz piece as she left.

Stephen rubbed an aching shoulder as he walked through his rather sparsely furnished house listening to Meghan's phone keep ringing. Her machine finally answered. So much for suggesting he would see her today. He left a second message and hung up. It was getting depressing how hard it was to coordinate schedules. She spent her days at the jewelry store; he spent his tied up with deliveries for the remodeling work. Shingles had arrived today. He'd call her parents to see if she was there, but he figured she would have called to say hi if she was so close by.

She'd be at church in the morning. He sat on the couch, willing to consider going to church if only to have a chance to see Meghan and maybe get invited to lunch afterward. What a lousy reason to go. He was faintly ashamed for being so crass about it but he was getting squeezed. Kate and Dave were coming tomorrow afternoon, which meant he had to scratch the idea of seeing Meghan then. Kate must finally have some news about the ring, or else Dave was trying

286

to get her away for the weekend. At six months pregnant, Kate needed to start taking more weekends off.

His new guest butted his ankles. Stephen looked down. "Would you relax and think about getting some sleep?"

The baby goat chewed at his bootlaces. Stephen had the fenced-in area finished and the covered pens done, but the kid would be the only living thing out there tonight. Stephen listened to the wind whip outside and wondered what Ken's equipment was registering. The storm was blowing in fast. Surely Meghan wouldn't sit at home alone tonight listening to this storm come in.

"I wish you were a baby lamb or at least something soft. You're all knobby knees and shedding hair." He scratched the animal's back anyway. The utility room would work for the night. There wasn't anything the goat could butt in there that wasn't already slated to come out during the remodeling.

His phone rang and he leaned over for it.

"Is there hail by you?"

"Meghan?"

"Yes, sorry. Is there hail by you? Or rain?"

He was thinking about romance and she was thinking about the weather. He couldn't catch a break tonight. But he had to smile at the contrast — at least she would never be predictable. "Where are you?"

"With Ken tracking this storm data. The rain is coming. He thinks it will hit your place in four minutes."

Stephen carried the phone with him to the door off the kitchen and stepped outside under the overhang. "There's wind, a lot of wind, but no rain."

"Wait for it."

"You sound like you're having fun."

"I am. You should be here. JoAnne and I brought a pizza back for dinner and started helping Ken plot his numbers. The new equipment is working out great. You should see the data streaming in from the windmill."

He wished he was with her. He heard something in the trees growing louder as it approached. "Here comes the hail." It started slapping the ground, small white chunks bouncing on the grass showing in the lights from the house.

"Ken called that within five minutes. Not too bad. We need another data station on the west side of town. The small set of equipment he has at his parents' isn't as good as what he has on the windmill. I've got to go. I need to call Mrs. Teal and see if the rain has reached her place yet. Thanks for the news."

"No problem. Talk to you later, Meg." He set down the phone and thumped his hand against the wall before walking into the kitchen. She was blissfully unaware of any romantic undercurrents as she called and started talking about storm data. It was time to get with reality. From the casualness in her voice, she wasn't even thinking of something more than friendship. And if he was smart, he'd let it remain that way.

Out the window a light flickered in the distance. He stopped and watched.

Someone was in the barn.

Stephen hunched his shoulders, his jacket lifted high to protect his head from the pounding hail and rain. Mud clung to his boots. A small river now ran across the yard, covering the walkway. Wind buffeted his back. The light, if that was what he had seen, was gone. He walked down to the barn, convinced he had probably seen headlights from the road.

He reached the barn as the first lightning flashed and thunder rolled instantaneously overhead. He pulled the door open. A man slammed into him. They tumbled back, hitting the ground with a splash. Stephen grabbed at coarse fabric of the coat smashed into his face and tried to shove the intruder off him. The smell of sweat and desperation clung to the man, and a weight pressed against Stephen's chest trying to keep him down on the ground.

Coming from the barn . . . the thought that it must be a vagrant flashed by as Stephen grabbed an arm and twisted it away. He had to put this man down, or one of them was going to really get hurt. It had been too long since he was in a knock-down-drag-out fight. Stephen threw the man off him like a stubborn bale of hay and got leverage to rise to his knees. He blocked the coming blow and charged from his kneeling position, knocking the guy back through the doors and into the barn. It was like slamming into a steer, the impact numbing his arm.

He ducked a fist thrown at his face and threw a punch back, sending the guy into the shelves he had moved beside the door. There was barely time to get his hands up before the handle of the rake connected, catching him across the face. Stephen rolled with the force of it and scrambled back up. The barn door swung wildly in the wind.

The man was gone.

Stephen staggered to the door and caught it, wrestling to hold it. The thick tree branches whipped back and forth in the wind, darker moving shadows in a dark night. He couldn't see anyone out there. Stephen wiped his bleeding nose; leaned over, his hands resting against his knees; and sucked in air. Fading adrenaline left white spots in front of his eyes. He heard a car start somewhere far down the road. The idea to give chase lasted only as long as it took for the thought to form. Stephen instead reentered the barn and turned on the lights.

Holes had been punched into the walls and a few places in the floor. Stephen kicked wood out of his way. Had a sledgehammer been swung with great delight at the walls? What had the guy been doing? The floorboard where the pouch had been found now rested upright in the empty crevice. Stephen saw an empty bottle of whisky on the floor and several tossed beer cans. That hadn't been a kid, and it hadn't been an old vagrant. It had been a man with at least a bit of muscle on him.

The ring.

If he'd been searching for it, there was some comfort in knowing it wasn't there to be found. But had something else been here? Stephen had searched this portion of the barn with care, but he hadn't ripped into the walls.

He went to check his workbench and equipment. At least it appeared to have been left undamaged. The far end of the barn he'd yet to clear of equipment didn't look disturbed.

Stephen sat on the pile of lumber and looked around. What else had Neil hidden? And who was looking for it?

Puzzles. The others in his family loved them; he hated them. He touched his sore face. Puzzles left people getting hurt.

Meghan. If tonight was related to the jewelry, that meant the store was also a prime target. She was with JoAnne and Ken for the evening, would be at church with her family in the morning, and Kate and Dave would be here by the afternoon. They'd help him figure out what to do.

Stephen wearily pushed himself to his feet. What a way to end a miserable day. He dug out a padlock for the barn doors. He would call the sheriff, but with this weather the man probably had his hands full with accidents. Stephen expected his own pager to sound before long. The morning would be early enough to investigate this.

He needed an ice pack.

Nineteen

Stephen worked his way across the barn roof carrying another bundle of shingles, taking care to find good footing. The breeze still carried a fine drizzle in it. The bundle of shingles weighed eighty pounds, and they were as likely to send him crashing through a soft spot in the roof as tumbling off of it. It would be another month before he wanted to risk replacing the roof. His repairs would hold that long, assuming they didn't get another burst of sixty-mile-per-hour winds coming through. A vandal damaged the inside of the barn; the storm damaged the outside. His first look in daylight hadn't been promising.

There had to be an easier definition of home ownership. He wiped sweat and water off his face with the back of his hand and then pulled on his gloves. He ripped open the package of shingles. The staple gun was battery powered, and years of practice meant it took less time to line up and place three rows of shingles than it took to haul them up to the roof.

A blue Lexus came down the road and slowed. Stephen paused to watch as the car pulled into his drive. He picked up his tools. The ladder sank deeper into the ground as he descended. "Welcome to my place," he called, watching Kate get out of the car. She moved slowly, the six months of pregnancy no longer something that could be hidden.

"Hi, Dave."

Kate's husband nodded toward the barn. "How much damage did you get last night?"

"Wind, a little hail, enough to leave its mark."

Kate walked over to join him and her smile disappeared as she neared him. "Who'd you get into a fight with?" she asked softly; a dangerous softness that hardened her eyes.

He touched his face. Between his left eye and his jaw his face was simply sore. "It looks as black as that?"

"Be glad Meghan can't see."

"I had some unwelcome company last night." He pulled the tarp over the supplies so the packaging wouldn't turn into a wet lump of paper mess. "You've had a long drive. Before you hit me with the questions, why don't I get you two something to drink while you stretch your legs and look around? It's not like the details will change."

Kate looked over at Dave then back at him. "Give me the CliffsNotes first then."

Stephen touched her determined chin, smiled, and pointed to the barn. "Come on in; I'll show you. I didn't fix anything inside yet, figuring you'd want to see it for yourself. My guest was looking for something."

He reached around her and turned on lights as she entered the barn.

"What a mess," Dave said.

"I'll say." Stephen walked over to look at one of the deepest strikes against the wall. "He punched holes but didn't come back around to try and pry off the drywall. I'm guessing he was pretty drunk or high, maybe both, and I interrupted him."

"Any idea who it was?"

Stephen shrugged. "Male, medium height, medium build. He hadn't had a bath recently. I never got a good look at him. There were beer cans and a whisky bottle left tossed about so there may be prints." Stephen pointed to the box he'd put them into.

"I'll have the lab take a look. Does it seem like he found anything?" Kate asked.

Stephen looked around at the dozen or so holes. "Not that I can tell."

"I'm glad he wasn't swinging that sledge-hammer at *you*."

"The rake handle was enough. He ran, and I heard a car start shortly thereafter down by the east pasture, but in the rain I never got a look at the make or model."

"I'll go check the area," Dave suggested. "If he was drinking here, he may have been also drinking and pitching beer bottles while he waited for it to get late enough to start snooping. Maybe he left more trash behind that will help us identify him."

"Good idea."

Dave left the barn.

Kate settled on the stool by Stephen's workbench. "Where did you find the pouch with the ring?"

Stephen pointed. "That floorboard was pried up. He either knew about that spot or saw where I'd recently pulled it up."

"The ring was stolen."

"As I nursed my aching jaw last night, I figured that was probably the case," Stephen agreed. "Who was it stolen from? And when?"

"Five years ago a lady was having her ring cleaned before her thirty-fifth anniversary. She found out then that it was a fake. A really good counterfeit of the piece you handed me. When and where the swap had

296

been made?" Kate shook her head. "It could have been years before. We've got no good way to tell."

"Was it a ring she wore often?"

"Yes. What are you thinking?"

"So the fake was durable." Stephen rested a boot against the stacked lumber. "I've heard about the fake pieces Neil displayed in the front of his store while he kept the real pieces in the safe. They're so good that Meghan had to bring in two appraisers to help with the store inventory to figure out what is real and what's a brilliant copy."

"I pulled Neil's records and he's clean," Kate said. "Nothing shows up for receiving or dealing stolen property. There were no financial or tax problems, no suggestions of anything criminal."

"He wouldn't get to be an old thief by making mistakes."

"Have you found any more pieces?" Kate asked.

"No."

"Any indication more pieces were hidden here that Neil removed before he sold this place? Maybe he simply forgot the piece you found in the barn?"

Stephen started to shake his head then stopped.

"What?"

"Before I started ripping into the house and barn, I did a pretty thorough assessment of what needed to be repaired or replaced. The attic insulation in the house was disturbed. I remember wondering if a squirrel had gotten trapped up there and panicked before finding a way out."

"Could something still be hidden up there that you didn't find?"

"Most of the insulation came up when I looked at the wiring. I would have found something."

"Show me," Kate said.

"The trapdoor to the attic is in the utility room. You don't need to be crawling around up there pregnant. I'll show Dave and he can check it out."

"That's fine with me. Let's walk up to the house now. I could use a drink and a chance to stretch my legs."

He closed up the barn and slipped on the padlock. They walked to the house.

"You need security out here," Kate said. "Word gets out that there is a treasure hunt underway and you'll have more than just one unwanted guest."

"That's one of the reasons I didn't call the sheriff — nothing in this town stays quiet. Word may already be out for all I know. The guy was drunk enough he probably talked about it before he came out here. At least it shouldn't be that hard to find who around town has an eye to match mine. What we need to do is talk with Meghan. If Neil has more pieces hidden, the probable place he put them isn't here but at the store or the apartment over it. She's the one most likely to find something."

"I agree it's better we keep this quiet. I'm afraid you may be sitting on a cache site, Stephen, and that more pieces are here even more valuable than that ring. I don't want to add more worry, but you need to know this could get complex fast. Dave had a case that could factor in: A mob boss killed his wife when he found out she was having an affair. Since he went at her in the master bedroom and bashed in her head, it was open and shut. But one of the things that turned up was that some of her rather priceless jewelry were elegant fakes. If one of those stolen pieces shows up here . . ."

"A thief that messed with a mob boss? Now living in Silverton?" Stephen shook his head. "I thought I left behind big city crime when I got out of Chicago. You just described it being in my backyard."

"We need to figure out what's going on here. If there are more pieces found, if word leaks back to the jail system . . . In that scenario, we don't catch a thief; we end up finding a body."

"Miss Delhart, there's a Stephen O'Malley to see you," the security guard said. Meghan leaned back from her intense focus tracing numbers through the inventory books. She was not in any shape for company, but it wasn't polite to say no. "Please send him back."

She heard footsteps coming and keyed the software to record her place on the page, then turned on her stool. "Hi, Stephen."

"I brought along a surprise guest."

"Hi, Meg."

"Kate!" Meghan spun her stool the rest of the way around. "Stephen, find her a chair somewhere."

Kate laughed and Meghan heard rollers on a chair move. "I brought Dave along too."

"Hey, Meghan."

"Oh, it's great to see you both." She struggled to sort out sounds as the three of them came into the room. "How are you feeling Kate? You're at . . . six months?"

"I'm doing lovely. I'm still sick every morning, tired in the afternoon, and walking on swollen ankles —"

"Fussing at being pampered, craving

pickles and black walnut ice cream, already rearranging the house to start nesting —" Dave added.

Meghan laughed. She loved it. "Oh, I'm so glad you came for a visit."

"I heard about your project," Kate said. "It looks like you are making good progress."

Meghan gestured to her worktable. "Jo-Anne and I have cataloged every piece of jewelry in the store and had them appraised. Now it's a matter of tracking down every piece here through Neil's paperwork so I know what he owns and what was on consignment. So far his paperwork is holding up."

"No surprises?"

"Only one. Would you like to see what a million dollars in jewelry looks like?" She stood and crossed over to the walk-in vault. She had changed the combination so it stopped on only major digits, and on the old huge dial it was easy to check by touch. She centered the last number and pulled open the large door.

The jewelry pieces, numbered and sealed in plastic bags, rested on platters lined in velvet. She counted down to the fourth tray and pulled it out. "These are a few of the expensive pieces he had collected."

"Wow," Stephen breathed to her left. His reaction made her smile. She couldn't see the pieces, but she'd noted JoAnne's reaction, the appraisers', and her touch told her a lot.

"May I?" Dave asked.

She stepped back to let him access the pieces.

Kate beside her hadn't said anything. "What do you think, Dave?"

"The pieces he bought — he was a collector. That explains a lot."

"What do you mean?"

"They're all chokers or necklaces, all emeralds, rubies, or diamonds. He liked a particular look. I wish you could see them, Meg. They are quite spectacular."

"I've got a good imagination."

"How much progress have you made identifying these pieces?" Kate asked.

"The bags that have red tags on them have been located in the paperwork. Neil kept a registry. When he bought a piece he wrote down a line in the book. When he sold a piece he wrote it in the book and made a notation back on the purchase line to show that the piece had passed out of his inventory. It's pretty basic, but it matches up — one line in, one line out throughout the book."

"Is the registry complete?"

Meghan shook her head. "I'm not sure yet, Dave. I know Neil handled a few pieces for which I haven't been able to find a record: JoAnne's brooch for example. Neil bought a piece from JoAnne a few years back; it's what let them be able to afford a vacation cruise. Ken and JoAnne had found a brooch and a locket in an old music box stored in their attic. They kept the locket and sold Neil the brooch. We didn't find the brooch in his inventory, and I can't find lines in the registry recording its purchase or sale. It's possible he handled a few pieces like those as favors and was buying them out of his own pocket."

"I hate to ask this question so bluntly, but I'll explain in a moment. Was Neil honest?" Kate asked.

Meghan frowned. She had been Kate's friend for a very long time. It sounded like the cop in Kate asking the question. She was looking for something. "I've found no indication he cheated in his cash flow or on his taxes. Nor are there more pieces here than he has records for. The value he placed on pieces is in line with what the other appraisers judged them to be. The repair shop records are more nebulous, for he often bought gold and silver, even loose stones, to

303

repair another piece. There are some records where a piece was taken apart and its diamonds reused. What's going on, Kate?"

"Stephen found a ring hidden under the floor of Neil's barn. It's a diamond ring, and we've confirmed it was stolen."

Stolen. Meghan leaned against the wall, absorbing that hurt. The suggestion that Neil had handled stolen gems didn't fit what she knew about him. "There's no indication within the store that any stolen goods flowed through here, either in the inventory or the records."

"Was the business in the black? Was it generating good cash flow?"

"It was generating more cash than he could spend. The checking account and savings accounts for the business are very healthy."

"How well have you searched this store to locate any pieces that might be here?" Stephen asked.

She looked his direction. "We weren't trying to find something hidden, but we've been through every display case, drawer, box, and file cabinet while doing the inventory. JoAnne put white dots on the furniture as we went through them."

"Has security been here every day since Neil's death?" Kate asked.

"Around the clock. It was part of the arrangements Neil had made in his will and with his attorney. It's a good security firm." Meghan hated where this was leading. "What do you want to do, Kate?"

"Find out if that ring recovered in the barn was a one-of-a-kind incident or the first of several stolen items. We need to do another search of Neil's possessions with an eye toward finding something concealed. Have you started working through his personal belongings upstairs?"

"Just the basics of disposing of perishables, finding paperwork to close out bills, and the like." Meghan rubbed her forehead. "I don't believe he could have been involved in something like you're suggesting, Kate. So let's prove it one way or the other. I'm responsible for everything in this building, and Stephen owns Neil's former land. You've got full access. How do you want to start the search?"

"I'm not interested in trashing Neil's reputation. We can do the search ourselves, and there's no time like the present to get started," Kate suggested.

"You don't want to bring in the sheriff?"

"Not yet, Meghan. We're worried that this might be bigger than just Neil. Someone tried to search Stephen's barn last night and took a sledgehammer to the walls and floors. Someone local is involved in this, and we'd rather not tip him off until we know who that is."

Meghan spun toward Stephen.

"I had a bit of a tussle and acquired a black eye that I'm very glad you are not able to see," Stephen said, answering her unspoken question.

"You should tell the sheriff."

"No. It's important that word not get out and trigger the start of a treasure hunt," Stephen replied. "We know there's one person out there to worry about — the guy who searched the barn. I'd rather not add a layer of idiots trying to find jewelry we only suspect might be out there."

"What about your place, Stephen? Who's watching it while you're in town?"

"Marcus is coming to help out," Kate replied for him.

"He's what?" Stephen protested.

"Marcus and Shari will be here Monday. Shari's going to assist with your new kitchen while Marcus helps us conduct a complete search."

"When was *this* decided?"

"A 2 a.m. phone call," Kate said.

Before Stephen could protest the fact his family was stepping in, Meghan settled her hand on his arm. "Kate, I suggest we divide and conquer. Why don't you and I work down here, and Dave and Stephen can take the upstairs."

Jonathan tugged out another of Craig's dresser drawers and rifled through it. This place was a dump. Craig hadn't been seen this weekend, and Jonathan had run out of patience tracking him down. The man was likely bingeing somewhere on drugs, booze, or both, assuming he had scrounged up enough cash or stolen anything of value. The barkeeper told him Craig had been rambling on about cobwebs, bugs, and barns. There was enough truth in that drunken babbling to suggest Craig had been exploring for the jewelry on his own since Neil's death.

Jonathan stepped over piles of trash to shove open the closet door. The odds Craig had actually destroyed all the pictures of the jewelry taken over the years as he was ordered were nil. The man took his money and got high. It was a wonder he hadn't had a head-on car wreck, leaving real jewels and evidence of a robbery lying around to be picked up. It was the price of small-town crime that he ended up with an excellent partner in Neil and a nearly incompetent partner in his friend Craig.

Jonathan heard the sound of a car that badly needed a tune-up approaching. He left the bedroom and strode through the rooms. He shoved open the front door and walked outside as the car went off the driveway and came to a stop half over a bush.

Craig got out of the car while Jonathan waited. He caught hold of the man's shirt, spun him around, and slammed him against the car. "What have you been doing, Craig? Acting on your own?" His friend's bruised face and knuckles told their own story. "You've been out to the farm searching? Getting yourself spotted?"

"The pieces are out there," Craig said, his mouth swollen and his words nearly impossible to make out. His eyes were still wild with whatever drug he was on.

"And if we're going to retrieve them, it's necessary that the authorities not know we're looking for them! You think Stephen won't react to you prowling around his land? There will probably be dogs and every kind of hassle to get past now."

"You can't stop me. I earned the right to those jewels just as much as you."

"Well you're not looking for them anymore. You are going back to Chicago or wherever you crawled home from and cool your heels. If you so much as think about looking for the gems again, you'll be sporting more than bruises."

Craig tried to wrestle away from Jonathan's grasp.

He pressed against Craig's chest so he couldn't draw a breath. "You listen to me, punk. We don't want a *single* piece found; we want *them all.* I'll get them my own way. You push me on this and you will regret it."

He waited until Craig stuttered an agreement.

Jonathan shoved an envelope into Craig's shirt pocket. "Go get high somewhere. Just stay out of my way."

Twenty

Stephen lowered his frame into one of the lawn chairs that along with the couch comprised the extent of his living room furniture. A long frustrating day of searching had led to nothing of substance. "It's good that we didn't find anything."

Kate swung her feet up onto the couch and reached to rub her ankle. "Maybe. Neil either had no other pieces to hide or he had a very cautious plan for hiding them. Meghan and I didn't get very far in our search. If we go two more days without finding anything else, then I'll start to relax." She moved around the pillows. "I'm impressed with your home. This is going to be a great place."

Stephen set down his iced tea. "Where the walls will go is marked on the floor in chalk, and the furniture locations are marked out in squares on the carpet. You have to use a lot of imagination."

"The plan is there." Kate settled back on the couch. "And Dave really likes that baby goat you bought. He was calling his office to check in, but he was walking toward the barn as he dialed. I bet he's gotten lost playing with the goat again."

"That animal does kind of grow on you. The kid will have company soon; I've got feelers out for some lambs."

"You couldn't just buy a dog?"

Stephen laughed. "It's called freedom to do stuff I couldn't contemplate in the city. I'm thinking a llama might be a nice addition at some point."

"Stick to raising fish in your pond."

"Meghan will enjoy the petting zoo more."

Kate studied him. "Any movement on that front?"

"We're both so busy it's hard to get time together." He couldn't hold back a sigh. "We're friends. She's made it pretty clear that's all it will be until I'm a Christian."

"Good. She's not offering you false hope that she's going to change her mind."

"Thanks a lot, sis."

"She's right. A compromise wouldn't last. You might respect what she believes and the importance of church in her life, but inevitably you'd feel left out. She can't love Jesus and you too without eventually being forced to choose between you. She won't walk into that quicksand."

He didn't want to have this conversation, but maybe it would be better to simply get it over with. He'd been reading Jennifer's Bible, and his questions were still much the same. "Why does it feel like God has conditions on loving me?"

"He doesn't. You're projecting your own list of what you think He should expect. It gets pretty intense when you realize He accepts you despite the fact you're a mess at the moment."

He scowled at her. "I appreciate the endorsement."

"Face it, Stephen, you are. You took off after Jennifer died and left in chaos. You came back and you're still in chaos. Jesus is the kind who moves in, says I love you anyway, and then starts helping repair the mess. He means it when He says He loves you as you are, not based on what you've done. But He loves you too much to leave you in that chaos once you know Him."

"Just like that."

"Pretty much. Stephen, there are not many times in life when we get a chance to hear 'I love you and it has nothing to do with what you can do for me.' Don't let wrong assumptions cause you to mishandle the most important decision of your life."

"All the O'Malleys believe but me; therefore, I'm missing something."

"We just went first and figured out the ground on this side of believing is safe."

"Is it really?"

"Yes, it is. Jesus is a good friend. I don't regret for a moment the decision I made to believe." Kate reached for her iced tea. "You and I have been friends for ages. If I tell you I'm going to do something, you don't waste a lot of time wondering if I'm going to keep my word. Because we're friends, you trust my word to be good. And when I suggest to Marcus that he come and help out, when I push you to talk about a bad day at work, you take it in the spirit it's intended. I do it because I care an enormous amount about how you're doing and I want to help."

Kate relaxed her head back against the pillows. "That's the kind of friendship I have with Jesus. He keeps His word, and He cares about my welfare. You're so tense around the subject of religion and God that you can't envision what a friendship with Him is like. You're waiting to be let down, don't you see? You can't have both. You either trust His word and the fact that He cares about you or you don't. Until you approach Jesus with the intention of finding a trustworthy friend waiting to respond, you'll never be able to

313

connect and get to know Him."

Stephen turned his empty glass in his hand and sighed, then set it on the floor. "I appreciate how real this is for you. I really do. It just doesn't ring true for me."

Kate tried hard to hide her disappointment. He was grateful for that as she smiled at him. "Well when it finally does ring true, will you at least promise me you'll act on it? It's tough watching you stuck there with all your questions and no answer resonating." She tugged one of the pillows out from behind her. "I know it's not an easy step, Stephen, to believe. It took Dave months to help me figure out answers to my questions. Please, keep searching for the answers instead of pushing aside the questions. When family keeps coming back to this subject, please understand — it's not because we think less of you. It's because we're convinced life is better this way. We want you to have that peace and assurance too."

"I promise I'm still listening."

"Good enough." Kate smiled. "What are the odds I might be able to talk you into finding me some ice cream?"

"Decent, assuming I can move to get out of this chair."

"You really look like someone bopped you one."

"It's been too long since I was in a street fight." Stephen pushed himself to his feet. "I'll get you some ice cream and myself an ice pack. I'm glad you came, Kate."

"So am I."

Stephen followed Kate and Dave to the bed-and-breakfast where they were staying, lifted a hand in farewell, and drove to the pharmacy. He didn't immediately need the bottle of aspirin and new ice packs he bought, but it gave him an excuse to come into town.

He drove by the jewelry store to check that all was quiet, and then he went around an extra block to check on Meghan's place. He was surprised to see her lights still on and Blackie sitting on the front porch. Stephen pulled over to the curb and stopped.

He walked up the sidewalk. Stephen held out his hand to Blackie, rubbed the dog's head, and leaned past him to knock on the door. "Meghan, it's Stephen," he called, wanting to avoid her worrying about who was knocking on her door at this time of night.

"Stephen?" He heard movement inside, then the door opened. "Is something wrong?"

"Everything's fine. I happened to be in

315

town and saw your lights were still on."

"I was just listening to a book on tape. Would you like to come in?"

He wanted her advice on what he was thinking about Kate's comments. He knew Meghan would listen and not take offense if he asked some tough questions. He shifted his hands in his pockets. "It's a pretty night. Why don't you get a jacket and sit out on the porch with me."

She hesitated and then nodded. "Give me a minute."

Stephen settled on the top step of the porch. Blackie moved over to join him.

Meghan sat beside him a few minutes later, offering a cup of coffee. "I don't want you getting chilled sitting out here this time of night."

"Thanks. The moon is about half full right now, very white, and hanging low in the eastern sky."

She closed her eyes and smiled. "I can see it." She took a sip of tea. "Did you have a good evening with Dave and Kate?"

"I always have a good time with them," Stephen said, switching the mug to warm both hands. "Kate's happy. When they got married I wondered how smoothly she could make the adjustment to being half of a couple. Dave's good with her — he's figured out the right mix of giving her space and taking care of her without being smothering."

"She's trying hard to put on a good front, but she's nervous about the idea of being a mom."

"Kate gets very quiet when she's trying to figure out an unknown. She never had a mom around as a role model. I figure her confidence will go through the roof and she'll get a bit smug after she's figured out what she's doing. Kate feeling smug — it just begs for me to tease her a bit."

Meghan laughed. "Still glad you're going to be an uncle?"

"The idea of a child trailing me around expecting me to know answers to life's questions — like why caterpillars crawl, the sunset turns color, and raindrops don't collide with each other — I'm going to enjoy it." Just thinking about it caused him to relax. "There's going to be a second generation of O'Malleys. That's a good feeling." He set down his coffee mug. "The conversation tonight turned serious with Kate. She pretty much gave me both barrels about why I push away God."

Meghan rested her chin on her up-drawn knees. "Sorry about that."

"It's okay. We dance around the subject of

religion every few months. I should have predicted the conversation." He sighed and nudged back Blackie so he could rest his hands behind him on the porch to take his weight. "I don't know if I'll ever believe, Meg. I wish I could say it would be different, but I may never make that step my family has." The reality of that decision was hurting him and his family. It was why they were after him, why Jennifer had left the gift she had. He didn't know what to do.

"I know Jennifer's primary goal near the end of her life was to help each of you come to believe. I hope her death hasn't been a stumbling block."

"I miss her, and it is part of this. Jennifer's Bible is marked up with underlines and dates and scribbled-in notes."

"Mine is too; those underlined verses and notes are memories of conversations."

"What do you mean?"

"The Bible is a living book, and her notes are records of an ongoing dialogue between her and the Lord. She'd start reading having a question or with something going on in her life that concerned her, then as she read, verses would stand out that brought answers, comfort, or insight. It's a friendship. God provides His side of the conversation through His written words. I know God enjoys my company and I enjoy His. That's what Jennifer found too."

"You talk as if it's a day-to-day friendship. I don't understand how you get to that point. I've read parts of the Bible, and it's like reading history and a kind of daily journal of Jesus as He traveled through towns around Jerusalem."

Her expression softened. "You keep reading. You listen. You hold onto what you do understand and continue to pursue what's still confusing. God then steps in and makes that dialogue alive. There's no secret; it's not intended to be hard. The Bible reassures us on that point — those who seek God will find Him." She reached over and touched his knee. "Why don't you want Jesus as a friend?"

She was breaking his heart pushing against that question. "He's not always there, Meg. Not when you really need Him."

"Yes, He is," she whispered. "He was there when Jennifer died, when Peg died, when they came to tell you your parents had been killed. Jesus was there." He looked over and caught a glimpse of deep emotion before her expression became calm. "Just like He was there the night I went blind. I know He's good and that He loves me. He

319

didn't give me back my sight, but He gave me something more precious — a full and joyous life in the midst of this. I would have chosen my sight, but that decision was His to make. I trust Him, even in this."

"I wish I had that peace in spite of circumstances."

"You can't find the happiness you want and the peace you seek by borrowing from mine. It doesn't work that way. As much as you know about Jesus, you've never let yourself accept Him. Please, stop hiding behind the fear that you might be let down. You won't be."

She pushed her hands into her pockets. "I'll always be your friend, Stephen. Whether you believe or not, that isn't going to change. But if you don't believe, you limit our relationship to friends only. And I'll be forced to spend eternity without you. That grieves me."

"I know it does. I often wonder what I'm holding out for, but I'm not sure."

"When you can answer that, you'll have this resolved." She smiled at him. "Let it go for tonight."

Stephen smiled back. "For a day or two." He nudged Blackie away from his coffee cup. "Would you like to come out to the farm this week? Maybe Wednesday, after we do another round of searching the jewelry store? I have something to show you."

"I'd enjoy that."

"I think I'll invite JoAnne and Ken, whichever O'Malley's can make it, your parents and have my first open house."

"Oh, this sounds like fun. Let me know if I can help with food or such."

"You got it."

Neil had turned the second bedroom in the apartment into a storage room. Stephen steadied a stack of boxes and lifted off the top three. He carried the boxes into the living room where Dave had set up a worktable. Neil could have hidden jewelry in practically anything from the flour canister to a box buried behind dozens of other boxes. The only way to make sure they didn't miss something was to look through everything.

"If Neil was deeply involved in these thefts, he'd have pictures of the pieces he was duplicating, someplace to store the stolen jewels until they cooled off, and a buyer. Can we also work this problem by figuring out if he traveled? Who his regular customers were?"

"When did he have his first stroke?" Dave asked.

"A little over a year ago. I know the paralysis he was suffering on his left side made it difficult for him to do the jewelry repair work any longer."

"So that first stroke would have basically ended the creation of fakes. If Neil was dealing with stolen gems, he had a year to plan how he would close it down."

"We still don't know if Neil ever took more than the one piece I found in the barn, Dave."

"We know that diamond ring was stolen and replaced with a high-quality fake. And we know the guy who blackened your eye had an idea something was there to find. That's enough to suggest we're on the right track."

Stephen looked around the room. "He's had a stroke, he has decided he's going to move, and he knows he basically wants to shut down whatever he'd been involved with. He could either sell the stolen pieces at a big discount and move them all on to buyers or wrap them up and put them away somewhere he would consider safe."

"He didn't need money," Dave said. "What if he decided to keep the last pieces rather than sell them? His wife is dead, his health is fading, and he's got one interest left in his life: the jewelry. If he decided to keep them just because they were beautiful pieces, he's going to keep them somewhere he can see them occasionally."

"If he went to the trouble of making a final place to hide them, he'd design it to be exactly what he needed."

Dave stopped his search. "If he's got several pieces, he'd have them stored together."

"It's what I would do."

Dave sighed. "I agree with you. I'm just not sure what we do next. Searching in boxes, cupboards, behind furniture, and in walls is doable. Getting inside Neil's head is not."

Stephen circled the room. "How many pieces of jewelry would you suspect might be stashed?"

"Rings, bracelets, a couple necklaces, maybe a few really expensive pieces like he had in the vault."

"So they could fit in something about the size of a shoebox? Maybe flatter and longer?"

"That sounds about right."

"Maybe inside a piece of furniture then." Stephen picked up cushions from the couch. He tipped up the couch to check the framing to see if it looked like anything had been modified. Stephen turned over the chair by the window. The fabric had been taped to the frame in a couple places. He pulled aside the tape and used his small pocketknife to pry up a couple staples holding the fabric. "It's got to be inside something."

"Try this one," Dave tossed over his pocketknife.

"What is this, the Boy Scout special deluxe model?"

"You never know with Kate what you're going to need."

Stephen thought about that a moment and laughed. "You're right." He used the pinchers to tug up the edge of the cushion. "This works." He didn't find the box he sought, but he picked up a penny. "Nineteen forty-two. It's still got a shine. Meghan loves old coins."

"Does she?"

"Something about the idea of holding something really old." Stephen tucked the penny in his pocket. "I'm having a gathering out at the farm Wednesday afternoon, a kind of house warming party. Could you and Kate stay over another night and come?"

"We'll be there. I'm worried her blood pressure is a little high, and that job of hers isn't helping. She could use another day or two here."

"What's going on? I thought it was a pretty low-key job."

"She's not in control anymore. She hears her friends on the SWAT team and the emergency response group are out on a tough call and she's listening to hear if they're okay. I think it would be easier on her to be at the scene in the communication van making suggestions than being so far out of the loop."

"They're comrades on the front line and it feels like she's abandoned them."

"Something like that. She doesn't want an emergency response job and those risks now that we're having a family, but I don't think either one of us thought through the ramifications of it."

"She's trying for homicide."

"I know." Dave sighed. "I'm praying she doesn't get it, Stephen, and you may not tell her that. She was a great hostage negotiator because she walked right up to the line between life and death and put herself between death and the innocents caught up in events. She survived her job because she won and people walked out alive. For Kate to be working homicides — I'd give her about six months before she brought the job home with her, unable to shut it off."

Dave shook his head. "I don't know what

might be best right now. Robbery is burying her in bureaucracy and cases so old and numerous that she can't solve enough of them to feel like she is successful and contributing something worthwhile."

Stephen tipped over another chair. "She isn't supervisor material."

"What she is, is one of the best hostage negotiators I've ever seen. I think she would make a brilliant teacher. I want her working at FBI and teaching at Quantico."

Stephen burst out laughing. "Kate, a Fed?"

"I haven't figured out how to approach her with the idea."

"My suggestion: stand far across the room when you do."

"She's not going to like the idea of working for a federal bureaucracy?" Dave teased.

"It will never happen. She's not good at working according to anyone else's script."

"Well Kate and I have got to figure out a solution."

Stephen moved from inspecting the furniture to checking the walls for any signs of construction in the last few years. He lifted down the wall clock. "We need to find at least one more hidden gem; then you'll have part of your solution. Kate can stay here a few more days to give you more time to think."

"How about four square diamonds and three emeralds set in a silver and gold starburst brooch?"

Stephen turned.

Dave had a piece of jewelry about the size of a small sand dollar resting in the palm of his hand.

"He had it wrapped in velvet and slid into a closed case along with his wife's diary. This one was sentimental."

Twenty-one

Stephen watched from his hammock as Meghan walked the path from her parents' home toward the pond and the path that led to his house. He reached down and lazily moved a piece on the chessboard resting on an overturned shipping case. "Check."

Jack scowled.

"It's the bishops. You keep forgetting I like to go deep," Stephen remarked. "We're over this direction, Meg."

She paused Blackie.

"I hung a hammock under the oak trees beside the pond."

Blackie led her toward them.

"Do you have a fishing line in the water?" she asked, drawing closer.

He glanced over at the pond. "The bobber is getting poked a few times as baby fish check out my worm. I can cast while lying in my hammock. It doesn't get better than this." He nudged his fishing pole a little more upright in the holder driven into the ground to tighten the slack in the line created by the light breeze.

"This is going to be his hiding place, or so he says," Jack added, moving his rook.

Stephen looked at the board. "Do you really want to do that?"

"Just move."

Stephen moved his pawn. "Checkmate."

Jack sat back and studied the board. "I'm not playing you again until we figure out an adequate handicap."

"Hey, I gave you a queen."

"And decimated me before I could ever use mine," Jack replied.

Blackie stopped to check out the board. "Am I early? Or are the party plans already done?" Meghan asked.

Stephen smiled. "I've got the grill ready, the chicken marinating, the salad, rolls, and pies from the restaurant now in the refrigerator. I know how to arrange a party in an hour."

"I'm impressed."

"There are two chairs about three feet straight ahead, and a blanket spread out on the bank of the pond. Take your pick."

"I smell freshly cut grass." She took a seat on the blanket and unclipped Blackie's harness to let him go off duty.

"Jack helped me get the big mower going. We only managed to knock over a couple posts and about five feet of fencing while we figured out how to execute turns." Stephen touched her shoulder and offered her a soda from the cooler. "We're relaxing after hard labor."

"Sweaty hard labor," Jack added, greeting Blackie.

"I'm glad you came over, Jack."

"Cassie and I had a rare scheduling agreement to have the same day off. And I'm for starting up that grill. I'm getting hungry."

Stephen checked his watch. "Yes, it would be good to at least head that direction." He reeled in his fishing line.

"I'll take the chairs back to the house."

"Thanks, Jack."

Meghan folded up the blanket. "We're going to have to break in that chess set you made for me. I've been practicing with Dad."

"I'd like that. If you want to take my arm, Blackie can keep wandering." She complied and he led her to the house.

"Do you know if Kate heard anything yet about the brooch Dave found?" Meghan asked.

"She hasn't mentioned anything."

"I hope it's not stolen."

"It could have been a gift Neil made for

his wife, Meg. Don't borrow trouble until we know something for sure."

"I'm trying not to. It's just unsettling to realize I didn't know Neil like I thought I did. And as executor it gets strange, knowing some of the jewels he has might be stolen."

"The sheriff was out to the house this morning, and he's agreed it's best to keep news about these pieces quiet. There is no benefit to having it discussed at the diner. Kate will stay a few more days and help us with the search. Once there are more facts to work with, they'll decide the next course of action."

"Good. I'd really like to keep this quiet."

"Meg, remember that I'm listed in Neil's trust document. If this becomes public knowledge and you need me to finish wrapping up the work at the store, I'd be glad to step in and help you out."

"Would you?"

"You bet."

She relaxed. "I've known Neil all my life, been in his home, helped care for his wife. I don't want to learn he was a felon through all those years."

"Then you have my promise. If you need to step back, just ask."

"I will."

Stephen opened the gate for them.

"Have Marcus and Shari arrived yet?"

"They'll be here anytime. They flew into Chicago this morning and are driving out." He paused her before she could turn toward the house. "Leave the blanket here on the gate. What I want to show you is down by the barn."

She left the folded blanket over the top railing.

"This way." He led with her hand tucked in his arm.

"Do you have your carpentry shop up and running?"

"Yes. I'm starting my first piece for Kate, a cubbyhole storage unit she wants for beside the crib. You're welcome to come over and keep me company as I work anytime."

"I'll do that."

Stephen stopped by the fenced-in area he had repaired and completed. "Why don't you wait here? I'll be right back." The sounds would give him away soon and he would prefer to have this be a surprise. He walked over to the enclosed pen and brought back his surprise.

"Hold out your arms, about a foot apart."

She did so and he smiled. She was a trusting lady.

He handed her the surprise. "Stephen?"

Her whispered delight was worth every bit of the effort to make the moment happen. She sat on the ground where she had stood, cradling the animal. "You got a lamb."

"Three, and their mothers."

Her hands gently ran across the animal. "Keep Blackie away so he won't scare this baby."

"Blackie is over by the pen getting acquainted with the others. It looks like a calm greeting session all around."

"You bought lambs — I'm delighted, but why?"

He laughed at the stunned way she repeated it. "I also bought a baby goat. I'm creating a petting zoo."

She leaned her head back to look at him. "You aren't."

He crouched beside her. "Yep, I am. And the answer to your question is easy: Why not?"

She laughed. "Good point. Fish . . . animals. You're making good use of this place."

"It's fun, Meg. I don't think I've done enough fun things in my life."

"Well this is a good start."

"The goat is a rambunctious little guy. I'll take you to meet him next."

She buried her face in the soft coat of the lamb. "I'm glad you came to Silverton."

"So am I." He reached over and brushed back her hair, slipping her sunglasses up on top of her head. "So am I," he whispered. "It's a good place to find some peace in life, not that you're helping that much." He let his thumb trace her smile. "I'd love to kiss you right now."

She blinked at him.

"Stephen, where's the charcoal for the grill?" Dave called.

Meghan averted her face. He was going to murder his brother-in-law. Stephen let his hand drop. "I'd better go help him. You want me to take you down to the enclosure to meet the other animals?"

She looked up at him, a smile playing around her mouth again. "Yes, please. And there's no need to spill blood over Dave's timing."

"The moment he interrupted is indelibly printed in my memory as another of my life's unfortunate *if onlys* . . ." Blackie about tripped him as he darted back to Meghan's side. Stephen caught himself before he stumbled into Meghan. "I'm going to get the party started now before something else untimely happens."

She patted his chest. "Go."

Like her mom, Meghan made a wonderful hostess. Stephen watched her mingle with his family and stop to talk with Shari. The group had moved inside as darkness fell. Marcus rested his arm around Shari's shoulders, and something he said had Meghan tipping her head back as she laughed. She had relaxed after a comprehensive walk-through of the large room and how he had set up chairs for the party. She paused to touch the corner of the couch, orient herself, and then walked toward where he had put the table with drinks. He'd have to remember to provide more location cues for her next time he had a gathering.

Meghan's parents joined him. "It's been a great evening, Stephen."

"Thank you, Bill."

"We're going to head on home. Would you stop by the office tomorrow? The new extraction gear arrived. We're going to load it so it will be available on the ambulance. I'd like your opinion."

"I'll be there about nine," Stephen said, pleased Bill made the request. When the nights were quiet and long, he was beginning to miss the paramedic work. Maybe part-time wouldn't be such a bad idea, just to keep his skills up-to-date. He walked Elizabeth and Bill to their car and thought about sounding Bill out tomorrow about the idea.

The night was gorgeous. As soon as he could reasonably slip away from his own party, he would have to talk Meghan into walking with him. Going back to work as a paramedic even part time had some risks with it. Was he ready to be responsible for someone's life or death? Before he pursued the idea, he wanted to know Meghan's reaction. If she had reservations, she'd be a good enough friend to be honest about it.

Stephen looked around the party. Kate and Dave were down by the fire ring where a few logs had been tossed together so marshmallows could be toasted. Stephen picked up two glasses left on the picnic table and walked their direction. Dave leaned over and kissed Kate. Stephen stopped, quietly turned, and went back toward the house.

He found the group inside had moved to the living room where Jack was telling some story and gesturing to a chorus of laughter. Smiling, Stephen turned into the kitchen area to return the glasses. Meghan was ahead of him, walking over to the cooler filled with ice and pop cans.

The barrier he had put around the cutout flooring where the sink and dishwasher used to be had slipped forward and her hand held palm out would pass over it.

"Stop, Meg!" He could see her catching her foot on that opening and pitching into the cut-off pipes sticking up into the air, impaling herself. He caught her around the waist and swung her away from the danger. For a moment, all he could hear was the sound of his own heartbeat. "Sorry. The barrier had moved. There was a hole."

She rested her head against his chest and his heart came out of his throat. The image of blood flowing made him cold.

Her hands came up to settle around his. "I knew the pipes were there, Stephen. I'm okay. You can let me go now." Her words finally registered. He eased his grip and she stepped back.

The glass had spilled, staining her top. Her hand touched the wet fabric. "Thanks for stopping me."

She hadn't needed his help. He'd overreacted. And he'd been the one to embarrass her. "I'm sorry, Meg."

She looked up and gave him a rueful smile. "It's fine. It will dry."

"I'll get you a towel."

"That would be good." She put out her hand and felt for the wall, reorienting herself.

She accepted the hand towel he brought her. Her hand reached out and touched his chest. "Go get me a Diet Pepsi please, and I was getting Kate a 7 Up."

"Sure."

She walked back into the living room, only a slight hesitation to her first steps until she reached the change in flooring marking where the wall used to be. She moved to the couch and took a seat beside Shari, who leaned over to ask Meghan something and got a small shake of the head in reply.

Stephen sighed. It wasn't the first time he'd embarrassed her; it wouldn't be the last. It just wasn't a great lead-in for asking her to go for a moonlit walk.

He got her soda and Kate's then went to join them.

The party broke up shortly after ten. In the sorting out of people heading to both the bed-and-breakfast and the hotel, Meghan accepted an offer from Marcus and Shari to drop her off at home. Stephen ended up saying good-night to her in a snatched moment between the three of them stepping outside and the ringing phone pulling him back inside.

It wasn't how he wanted the evening to end.

Later Stephen walked the property one last time, checking his animals, confirming the barn was padlocked, and the alarm system installed with Jack's help was turned on. He wanted the pager he wore to go off so he would have an excuse to drive into town. After the emergency was done, he'd drive by to see if Meghan was still up and ask her what she'd think of his being a paramedic again part-time. He wanted a full life back — with the job he had run from and with something that was more than just a friendship with Meghan.

It was a night for wishful thinking. The clock didn't turn back easily. And just the thought of seeing Meghan bleeding had been enough to make him cold. The sight of anyone bleeding like that . . . He wasn't sure he'd be able to handle it. She'd come so close to stumbling into an accident.

He kicked at a fence post. He knew why he overreacted. Would his past never leave him alone?

He could have at least apologized better for the spilled drink. Stephen pushed his hand through his hair. He could walk around deciding on what he should have said and done, or he could see if she was still up and tell her. He wouldn't get much sleep tonight while he pondered the issues of his future.

Stephen walked back to the house, picked up his keys, and took the truck into town. He drove down her street, expecting her to have already turned in but hoping luck was with him.

Meghan was sitting on her front steps, Blackie beside her.

He parked the truck and stepped out, closing the door and pocketing the keys. "Meghan? Is something wrong?"

"No, I was just hoping you might stop by." She was still nursing the soda she had taken with her an hour before. "This is one of the few times I really hate the fact I can no longer drive. I really miss it."

His steps slowed as he reached her. He'd known her for a long time. His eyes narrowed as he studied her. "You were praying for me to show up."

She gave him a small smile. "It worked didn't it? If I need something, I find it makes life easier to pray and give God a chance to intervene if He'd like to. I bet you started thinking about me? I love how that just happens."

"In this case I don't think it takes God to make me think of you. Maybe to make me not think about you . . ."

She laughed at that gentle rejoinder and

patted the step beside her. "I need to talk to you and was hoping to do it face-to-face. Another half hour and I would have just called you."

He sat down beside her. "Okay. I'm here. What's going on?"

"I'm sorry I embarrassed you."

He about slid off the step turning toward her. "You didn't —"

Her hand on his arm stopped him. "It was nice that you acted like you did. You don't know how many people hesitate when they should say something, and I end up walking around with two different-colored socks or with a twisted ankle or a jammed finger. I'm glad you acted, even if it was un-necessary."

"And I was coming over to apologize for how many things I didn't think through be-fore tonight — the room cues, the moved furniture, the path down to the barn. You had to do several saves just to be able to enjoy the party."

Her hand on his arm tightened. "Let's call it even."

Her smile settled deep inside his heart where it made him feel like a knight in shining armor, saving her with his fumbled attempt to help her. He laughed softly as he relaxed. "You've got a deal, Meg."

He stretched out his legs and settled back leaning against his elbows. Should he tell her why he had acted as he did, or simply close the subject? Honesty on a night like this mattered. And the one thing he'd rarely let himself talk about with Meghan was the past.

"I'll apologize in advance for the next time I embarrass you because I overreact, Meg. It's instinct to watch out for you. It's got nothing to do with whether or not you can take care of yourself. I spent years watching out for Kate too, and it's got nothing to do with her skills as a cop. If you get in trouble, I just need to be near enough so I can help."

"I truly appreciate the sentiment, but why?"

He should have said something years ago. "Peg."

"Tell me about what happened. You've never talked much about that day."

"I was nine, my sister was just six. I was watching her that day for an hour while Mom went grocery shopping and Dad worked in the garage." The sounds of that afternoon still echoed in his mind like yesterday. Why, oh why, did he have to remember so well? "She was playing with her dolls in the living room, the dolls lined up in front of the couch, using the one I gave her for Christmas to direct her choir while Peg sang some made-up song. The phone rang. I remember the phone rang and I yelled at Peg to quiet down so I could hear."

Meghan's grip began to hurt and he rubbed the back of her hand with his. He was okay . . . he had to be. He couldn't change the memory. "Mom called checking on something I wanted her to get at the grocery store for a sleepover I was having with friends from school. Peg slipped outside while I was on the phone."

He sighed and the overwhelming emotions quieted. The rest just was. He didn't let himself feel it. "She was always fascinated with our neighbor's swimming pool. She could swim like a fish. But on that day, something went wrong. When I found her Peg was facedown in the water. I didn't know CPR."

He smiled at the pain that her grip caused, for it kept him in the present. "Ease up a bit, honey."

Meg opened her hand so fast he was pretty sure she hadn't even been aware she'd tightened her grip again. Her silence helped. Meg cared more about listening than trying to soothe with premature words.

"The paramedics that came worked on

Peg forever and never gave up, even as they took her to the ambulance. They were still working on her when they reached the hospital. I never forgot that. They got her breathing again, but it wasn't enough to save her life. She died three days later."

Meg leaned her head against his shoulder. "You were nine. And you know CPR now."

"No one ever blamed me — Mom reassured me and hugged me so much it was embarrassing. She tried so hard to convince me it wasn't my fault, that Peg had had an accident. Of course it was my fault. We all knew it. An accident, but my negligence."

"I'm not six years old. I can holler with the best of them, and I've got Blackie who can bark up a storm and get help."

"I know that, Meg. It's not that. You were up on the ladder helping Kate get boxes down at the store the other day. I watched you and I was nine again inside. It's not that I think you might fall; it's more subtle than that. But if you fall, what will I do and where will I be. The more someone matters, the more intense the emotion that I have to be there. To back off, I have to care less, and that's a vicious line to try to walk."

She smiled. "That's so romantic."

"Quit changing the subject."

She laughed and leaned against him.

"Thank you. The close attention and your choice to eventually be a paramedic are starting to make sense. You can't not hover over Kate unless you love her less. And you're starting to hover over me because I'm slipping into your heart too."

It was more like a full invasion, but he would let her think it was something softer. Neither of them knew what to do with this emotion pushing them beyond just being friends. She didn't want it, and he didn't know what to do with the feelings that kept getting stronger. "I just wanted to make sure you knew that your being blind has nothing to do with it. I don't think in any way that you can't handle yourself. I didn't hover in the first years after you went blind."

"You didn't care what happened to me?" she teased.

"Not so much my heart was in my throat at the thought of not being there. And I see that smile you're trying to hide."

"So what are we going to do about this new development?"

"You'll be kind enough to pat my arm, smile, and let me hover. And I'll see what I can do about shoving my heart out of my throat when you get yourself close to trouble."

"Why don't you just trust Jesus to take care of me?"

"I don't think He cares as much about you as I do."

"He loves me more actually."

"Then maybe it's the fact that it just doesn't feel like He does. We've already established the feeling in my gut is driving this."

"Would you just relax your grip and let God be God? Jesus is the one person you'll never have to rescue. If He wants the weather still, He makes it still. He wants the dead to come to life, He raises them. He wants to feed a multitude, He does it. That nine-year-old's sense of panic in your gut will never ease unless you accept there is someone bigger and more comforting in control. Jesus can watch out for me just fine."

Her eloquence had never been the problem; his doubts were, and he had no answer left to give her. He wanted to lean over and kiss her just to change the subject, then was ashamed of that thought. His struggle over religion wasn't going to be answered with logic. His parents had believed, all the O'Malleys believed, Meghan did — Logic said he should listen and come to the same conclusion they did, for his respect ran deep for each one of them. But the resistance ran deeper into his emotions and memories, and he did not want to go back into those memories again tonight. He leaned his head against hers. Her hand crept around his waist and she leaned back. And for once Blackie didn't interrupt.

He let himself kiss her, felt the jolt of her surprise, and deepened the kiss, drawing her closer. Years of history with Meghan and he'd never imagined something this sweet.

Meghan broke off their kiss and pressed her hand against his chest. "You're going to break my heart," she whispered. "Don't do this. I already made my choice. If I had to make it again, I'm sorry but you'd lose."

"I know." He eased back. "And I'm not going to put you in that position. I'll give us both some space." He watched her touch her lips, and the softness in her smile was enough to become a priceless memory of this night. "Could I ask a favor?"

"Sure."

He asked it fast, while he thought she might say yes. "I'd like you to remove yourself from the jewelry search. I don't want to worry about your getting into trouble with the same idiot who broke into my barn. My heart can't take it, Meg."

She stilled.

"Please. I know it's a big favor, but do it for me. Put your focus back on the nursing work at the clinic and let Kate and Dave deal with the search."

She rubbed his arm. "I can't. Someone was in my house last week."

Twenty-two

Stephen studied all the doors from the kitchen to the garage, looking for any signs of tampering. He tightened the doorknob screws until the Phillips head screwdriver began to strip the metal, his anger simmering just below the surface. "Why didn't you say something earlier?"

Meghan circled her finger around the coaster on the kitchen table, not looking over at him. "I thought it was my just misplacing things."

Someone in her place . . . He had felt guilty about keeping a secret from her about what had happened when he was nine years old and she'd been hiding *this*. "What else besides the earring is missing?"

"A bag of chips I bought. I checked: It was on my grocery receipt, I know I put the bag away in the cupboard, and it's gone." She shifted in her chair and leaned down to rub Blackie's back. "And I think some cash is missing, but it's hard to tell how much. It's probably a kid. I could have lost the earring, but why take only one earring and not two?"

Stephen didn't want to scare her to death, but what if she really had someone watching her, someone feeling comfortable coming and going from her house, taking items to keep as mementos and putting her off balance . . . ? Stephen looked at the dog. Blackie would take a man down if he thought Meghan was threatened. That was the one point of comfort in this.

Maybe it was a kid; the chips would suggest that. Maybe she had simply lost one of the earrings. Maybe she had miscounted the cash. There were a lot of maybes . . . "Has Blackie ever acted unusual when you got home?"

"No. And you know he would if anyone was here. He's very territorial. When we get home I let him run around the yard or he prowls through the house. At a minimum he's going to bark like mad when he senses something is wrong, get his back up, and stand between potential danger and me. He's trained for it, and it's also his nature."

Stephen walked past Meghan into the living room. He checked the front door. There was no sign of tampering. If someone was stealing from her, how were they getting in? He checked the windows. The alarm system was good — it would catch a door or window opening. "What's down in the basement?"

"Darkness." She smiled. "It's a place I rarely go because the stairs are narrow and steep. It's also concrete with a lot of odd things to touch such as the furnace and the hot-water heater. The door is by the utility room."

"Any windows down there?"

"Just two small eight-inch half windows at ground level."

Stephen opened the door to the basement, turned on the light switch, and found the bulb had good wattage. "I'll take a look."

"I'm staying right here."

He found the basement sparse; the water heater, furnace, and sump pump were in the east corner. The windows had a reassuring layer of cobwebs and accumulated dirt on the panes. The lighting was good, and he inspected the stairs while he was there, looking for any signs they were weakening or that the banister had loosened in case Meghan ever needed to come down here. He walked back upstairs, shut off the light, and closed the door. "The basement looks fine. How do you get into the attic?"

"Stephen, that's not necessary."

"Then it will just take a couple minutes to confirm it."

She led the way down the hall and stopped by the linen closet, then pointed up. "The ladder tugs down."

He opened the access panel and went up to check the attic. There wasn't much clearance and one glance told him based on the layer of dust that nothing around the access door had been disturbed in months if not years.

"Everything okay?"

"It's okay." He closed the access door. Meghan stood in the hallway, arms crossed, leaning against the wall, a combination of weariness and uncertainty in her expression. "I'm adding my phone number to that list of automatic dials the alarm system makes."

She nodded.

"I want your word you'll let Blackie go into the house ahead of you, and if there's anything at all you question that is missing, moved, or just doesn't feel right, you'll call me."

"You've got my word."

He reached out and ran his hand down her arm. "Then I'll let this rest."

"The alarm system is good, and I've got Blackie. There's Mace in the bedside table, a phone in the bathroom, and good locks on

that door if I decide I have to bolt somewhere. I'm not letting a possibility drive me
out of my own home."

"I'll worry about you anyway."

She half smiled. "At least I didn't acquire
a black eye."

He leaned over and planted a quick kiss
on her lips, unable to resist that smile. "I'm
going home."

Stephen walked his land, not bothering to
try to sleep for the remaining hours of the
night. *The precious idiot.* She didn't think it
was worth mentioning that something felt
wrong at her home. She was blind, but she
had moved so far beyond it in how she
structured her life that it took nights like tonight to remind him just how vulnerable she
was to trouble. At least with Blackie and
that alarm system this was contained. She
really was invading his heart. What was he
going to do now?

I'm in over my head.

It wasn't his job this time; it was his personal life, or lack thereof. And what he had
to do now was intensely more complex. He
wanted what was best for Meghan. Her
faith had allowed her to survive being blind
and was the foundation of the peace in her
life. She felt incredibly loved by her God,

but he wasn't on speaking terms with her best friend.

The bind he put Meghan in because of that was huge. He wanted to deny it was that big of a deal. God was spirit, and it shouldn't be that big a deal if he knew Him or not, but Stephen was kidding himself. She'd made the right choice by saying it was an insurmountable problem. She wouldn't be able to talk freely about God and share that bond with him. If he fell in love with a lady who wasn't on speaking terms with one of the O'Malleys, it would have ripped him apart trying to choose between them.

He was already feeling the stress of being the only holdout in a family of Christians. There was a growing sense of a distance because he just didn't get it. He hated that void. They were working so hard not to let the relationship change, and yet it was happening. He wanted to belong. He'd been searching for that his whole life — in his profession, his family — and all he knew for certain was that he hadn't found the perfect answer yet. Maybe it was God who filled that void. The other O'Malleys thought so.

He looked at the land he called home and the stars displayed overhead.

"I don't know what to say to You."

He stopped walking. He'd just acknowledged that there was someone there to listen to his words, whom he expected to respond. He'd spoken without thinking, and now it was out there lingering as if there was someone listening. Maybe a relationship with God might be personal, even for him.

He couldn't think of anything to say.

He started walking again.

Meghan and his family all had personal relationships with God that were enviable for their closeness. He had friends whom he knew in a distant kind of way, enough to call them friends even if he didn't hang out with them twenty-four/seven. And he had friends like the O'Malleys whom he could count on with absolute confidence they would always be there if he needed anything.

"Which kind of friendship is this going to be, God? I can't make the choice on Your side. Distant or close? For years I've avoided knowing You for the simple reason that I don't want a distant relationship, struggling to meet Your expectations and never quite feeling accepted. My family expects a lot of me, but they give me plenty in return. You are a high expectations God. I've read the verses: 'Be holy, for I am holy,' and 'Love your enemies.' "

Stephen hesitated. Was it okay to be bluntly honest with God? Or were you supposed to be polite for a while and diplomatic? This was not as straightforward as Meghan claimed. All he really knew how to be was himself, and that meant blunt honesty. "I'm afraid to take the step to be a Christian. I know what is expected of me, but I don't know if I can meet it. So what do we do now?"

It felt odd to talk aloud, alone, as he walked the property, but he remembered his mom praying aloud at dinner, and he'd feel even sillier stopping and closing his eyes. "Kate says she figured out the ground on the other side of believing is safe, that it's the relationship that makes believing work. I'll admit I'd like to understand what she means."

He stopped at the fenced-in area where his sheep were lying down for the night and leaned against the railing, finding peace just looking at the animals. He had come to love them. The baby goat was a splotch of gray with a white streak curled up, sleeping and dreaming if that was what baby goats did at night.

Either he found peace with the God Meghan called her best friend or . . . what? To stay and let the emotions grow between them when they were at an impasse would just hurt them both. And he couldn't handle being the one to hurt Meghan. He was falling in love with her.

There were no good options.

He walked back to the house, not sure what he should do next. The house was quiet, and he went through the rooms turning off lights and checking locks, then headed back to his bedroom.

He pushed off his boots and stretched out atop the bedspread and out of habit reached for Jennifer's Bible. He turned pages in it absently, having already read through Luke. He felt as though he were eavesdropping at times as he read Jennifer's notes and what she had underlined. Meghan was right. They were echoes of a conversation Jennifer had been having with God.

He turned to where he had left the bookmark in the book of John. He'd spoken his piece tonight, and Meghan said God did His talking primarily through His Word. He didn't understand what she meant when she said the Bible was a living book, that the words "came alive." What he'd read so far was interesting, but it was ancient history. Since the New Testament was Jesus' biography, he started reading in John.

As the father has loved me, so have I loved you; abide in my love. If you keep my commandments, you will abide in my love, just as I have kept my Father's commandments and abide in his love. These things I have spoken to you, that my joy may be in you, and that your joy may be full. This is my commandment, that you love one another as I have loved you. Greater love has no man than this, that a man lay down his life for his friends. You are my friends if you do what I command you. No longer do I call you servants, for the servant does not know what his master is doing; but I have called you friends, for all that I have heard from my Father I have made known to you.

Stephen turned the Bible to read Jennifer's note written in the margin in her flowing handwriting. The great love relationship for eternity; mine; so much joy!

She'd lived her last year with a joy that he'd had a hard time understanding given the cancer she fought. Her note was dated a month before she died. Jennifer's joy had come from within.

He read again the verse she'd underlined. *Greater love has no man than this, that a man lay down his life for his friends.* He knew what that verse meant, and more than just theoretically. Of all the emergency calls he had answered as a paramedic, the most heartbreaking were those where someone had died trying to rescue a friend. It spoke of a love so deep that person's own safety no longer mattered, of a will to help so strong that no obstacle would stop them even if it meant rushing into a burning building or a collapsing structure. It was an absolute love that had no limits. Did Jesus offer to be a friend like that?

Hope stirred.

He rolled onto his back and looked toward the ceiling, imagining the stars above the house and the vastness of that vista he'd been walking under a few minutes ago. "Jesus, I didn't understand why You would come to the earth, die on a cross, and then walk out of a tomb. But maybe now I'm beginning to. The laying down Your life for another — I understand that. I know in my gut what it takes to put it all on the line to rescue someone else.

"I know for a fact I'm a sinner: I live with me; I know how many times I blow it every day. Was dying for me the only way You could save me? Did You make that ultimate sacrifice on just the hope that we would one day be friends?

"It speaks volumes about Your character if You did, and it blows me away with its generosity. If You're willing to die for me, I should be able to trust You." He flexed his fingers and watched the veins move on the back of his hand. "You know trust is not something I easily give, but this feels real.

"My family and Meghan have been trying so hard to get me to see the truth. And I think I just saw a bit of it. But what now, Jesus? I don't have much to offer You in return." He thought about the last decades of his life. "Not much at all. I'm a burned-out paramedic who's a decent carpenter." He picked up the Bible and tried to read through the rest of the page where the bookmark rested but couldn't concentrate on the words. He closed the Bible.

He didn't have much to offer at all. And the baggage of his past was still there. A tear built in the corner of his eye. So much baggage. "Is Peg happy in heaven?"

Twenty-three

Meghan shifted pharmacy sacks in her satchel Friday afternoon. The number of holes in the attached punch card was her system for identifying them. She made rounds with Ashley delivering medicines and doing follow-up care visits, but errands like this to drop off supplies like gauze strips or diabetic blood sugar test strips was something Meghan could do on her own.

Craig Fulton was a borderline diabetic. Add to that the fact he had a drug addiction he didn't want to beat, and his health was fading fast. He'd missed his last two appointments with her dad, and the supplies were an excuse to stop by, check on him, and encourage him to make a third appointment. If she let him give up, there would never be a recovery.

She walked up his porch steps and opened the screen door. She knocked on the main door, startled when it moved under her hand. "Craig? It's Meghan. I brought you more supplies."

Blackie lunged forward in his harness, whining. She held him back and raised her voice. "Craig, are you home?"

Blackie came close to pulling her off balance. "Okay, boy, okay. Take me to a person," she urged, opening the door wider. He tugged her inside.

The smell of oil, burnt toast, and rotting garbage came from all directions. Blackie pulled her forward to her right. Under her feet she could feel places where the carpet was worn and frayed. Blackie sat and whined.

"Craig?"

Her searching hands found no furniture turned over. Blackie pushed at her knee nearly buckling her. Her foot touched something hard that gave. She reached down and her hand hit flannel and warmth and . . . deadweight. She jerked back and her elbow collided with the side of Blackie's head. The dog yelped. Her hands searched in front of her and encountered rough denim, and she struggled to figure out how Craig had fallen. "Craig!" His body began to shake — he must be having a seizure.

She grabbed for her phone and scrambled to push the right buttons.

Stephen pushed through the narrow doorway into Craig's apartment, carrying the gray medical supply case. The weight of the case rubbed against jeans still muddy from work rebuilding the water piping from the old well on his farm. He'd managed an eight-minute response to get here, and from the look on Meghan's face it hadn't been fast enough. "I've got the backup kit, Bill."

"Bring it over."

Stephen shoved a card table out of his way and stepped over Blackie to squeeze in beside Meghan's father. Stephen looked at their patient, then turned startled eyes toward Bill, who shook his head. It was hopeless. Craig's eyes were still open, but life was gone. Bill was doing CPR, but it wasn't for the patient he was attempting to treat.

No . . . not this. Stephen closed his eyes, took a deep breath, and steadied himself. He reached over to rub Meghan's shoulder. "You need a hand?" She was rhythmically squeezing the air bag.

"I've got it. I found him on the floor where he had fallen. His pulse was racing; he was still breathing. Seizures, three of them, hard."

"Okay. Slow down, honey. We're here now."

He tugged on latex gloves and studied Craig. There were signs of seizure-induced

363

bleeding: muscles locked and blood vessels ruptured behind his eyes. Stephen scanned the room. The drugs on the dresser and the trace on the floorboards marked the cause. He didn't need a chemical test to tell him the powder was cocaine and overly pure. He'd seen this death before — the overdose had exploded his heart. Craig was a dead man the moment he inhaled the drug, taking it straight through the back of the nasal cavity and rapidly into the brain. Even a doctor with the full suite of drugs available couldn't have stopped it.

A terrible death. And Meghan had been here when those death rattles came.

Stephen pushed aside the footstool and stepped around to get closer to Meghan. He nodded to her father.

"Craig overdosed, honey," Bill said softly. "We can stop now." He discontinued his compressions and reached over to still her hands on the air bag. "There's no way to bring him back."

"No. Do something! He was alive when I got here, when Blackie found him."

Stephen moved her back and nearly got his chin clipped with the top of her head when she tried to ward him off. He turned her head into his shoulder. Meghan was shaking. "He overdosed, Meg. There was nothing you could have done," he murmured, trying to comfort her.

She'd seen death before as an ER nurse. But this time — unable to see what was happening and why, with no medical equipment available, and Craig dying — those minutes alone must have felt like an eternity.

He stood, lifting her with him.

The sheriff came in with the county paramedic. Stephen looked over at her father. "We'll be outside."

Bill looked at his daughter, then back at him, and nodded. "I'll need to be here a while. Why don't you take her home?"

"If I've got any questions, I'll come by later," the sheriff said.

"Thanks, guys. Come on, Meg."

She didn't want to go, but he insisted and led her out of the room. Blackie pushed against her leg and she reached a hand down, seeking his reassurance. Stephen opened the door and her dog led the way outside.

Meghan pulled away from him and sat on the top step. She wrapped her arms around Blackie and buried her face in his fur. Stephen hoped she would cry, but she just clenched her hands in that warm fur. Slowly the shakes stilled. Blackie whined and pushed at her. "What did he take?"

"It looks like cocaine."

Stephen tugged over the small medical kit the paramedic had left on the porch and found wet wipes. He ripped three open and cleaned the blood from her hands. "You came to see Craig?"

"To drop off supplies," she said tiredly. "And Jonathan left Craig tickets for the benefit. Not that it was likely he would have come to the symphony but maybe to the gathering afterward. The two were friends since high school . . . You hope for the best of a friend. Jonathan thought he might come. I offered to drop the tickets off."

"Was he in seizures when you arrived?"

"Yes."

"He probably ingested the drugs in the hour before. Seizures like you described mark the final moments." He wrapped his arm around her and hugged her. "At least he didn't die alone. You were there with him."

Her tears finally came. He wiped them away as they ran down her cheeks.

"I wish I'd been able to help him more than that."

"If he'd wanted help with his drug problem, he would have let you help months ago." Stephen got to his feet.

"Come on. I'm taking you home."

"I'd rather not go home," she whispered. "I don't want to take this with me."

"My place then. You can walk for a while."

Stephen stirred the chili and put it back in the microwave, then got out dishes from the cabinet. Meghan might not feel like eating but it would distract her. He saw the sheriff's car turn into the drive. Meghan didn't need more hard information hitting her tonight, or questions. Stephen set down the dishes, stopped the microwave, and went outside to meet the man.

The sheriff leaned against the side of the squad car and waited for him. "Whoever sold him that packet might as well have shot him. It was 90 percent pure, not cut down much at all. I sure hope it was only a small batch and the dealer figures it out soon, or we're going to learn the hard way just how many in this community he's selling to."

"I was afraid of that."

"I wish I had more to tell you, Stephen. We're inventorying Craig's things, looking for whatever leads that indicate where he's been and who he's been dealing with. Craig's been acquiring cash to feed his habit from somewhere, and if he's turned to dealing, I figure we'll find a trail. I would have never placed him as a dealer, but then I also didn't see him as stupid enough to die from it."

"He's been getting cash from somewhere, Sheriff. Do you think he's connected to the stolen jewelry we found?"

"Maybe. The one thing Craig did a lot of was spend his weekends away from here, often driving to Chicago and Davenport. He could have been couriering pieces and getting cash that way." The sheriff pointed to Stephen's barn. "Now that damage fits what I would expect of Craig."

"He fits the general size and build of the guy who gave me the shiner."

"And if you look below the overdose, it's pretty obvious he's been in a fight recently."

"I saw the bruises." Stephen pushed his hands into his pockets. "Does it end here if Craig was the one searching my barn and the courier for stolen pieces Neil was fencing? Both of them are now dead and we're finding the remaining jewels."

The sheriff pushed back his hat. "I'd be relieved if it was just the two of them. The barn suggests Craig knew about the jewelry, and Neil had to be the one creating those excellent replicas. Maybe it does end here. We'll see what the investigation turns up to further connect them."

"You'll let me know what you find?"

"Sure thing. How is Meghan?"

Stephen glanced back to the house. "She doesn't like people dying."

"I've got no questions that can't wait for another day." He opened the squad car door.

Stephen saw the sheriff off, then turned and went back to the house. He could also see Craig going through Meghan's house while she was away, lifting things he could use to pay for his habit. As tragic as this day had been, it may have just removed a few serious worries.

Stephen let the door close softly behind him and walked through the house. Meghan had shifted on the sofa and her eyes were closed, her hand resting down to curl in Blackie's coat. The dog was watching her, a vigil that hadn't changed since they arrived. He stood watching the two of them for a moment, then grinned.

He was jealous of a dog.

He tugged her sock to wake her. "How you doing?"

She moved her feet to let him have a seat on the couch. "Do I need to go home?"

"What?"

"I lost track of time. Do I need to go home?"

"It's only about eight."

She sighed. "Okay."

She slid the pillow up over her face. Dwelling on the memories was the last thing she needed, and sleep wouldn't come without images to disturb it. He wouldn't be shaking Meghan out of this silent depression easily.

"Still chilly?"

"A little."

He added the blanket the baby goat had been playing with on top of the throw she was already using. The dust might make Meghan sneeze, but it was better than letting her end up with a chill.

"This is what you dealt with for years in Chicago — overdoses, guys splattered in car wrecks, and images like it," she observed, her voice heavy.

"Yes."

"No wonder your system said enough and forced you to take that vacation. I thought I understood what it was like to deal with trauma from working in the ER. I didn't even have a taste of it. Not the frontline weight of being first on the scene."

"You'll notice I'm now raising fish and pretending to be a farmer." Stephen reached over and clicked on the music, put the CDs on random play, then turned the volume down. "When I walked away from days like this as a paramedic, I'd go play basketball to wear away the memories. What would you like to do?"

She shrugged.

Letting her rest here wasn't going to help her get over it. "Come on down to my shop. I'm working on a chest of drawers for Kate."

"Can I do something to help?"

"Want to help make the knobs for me? It's a little work with a whittling knife and a lot of work with sandpaper."

She opened her eyes and moved her head, making the effort to look toward him. "Do you have something warm I could borrow to wear?"

"I've still got my North Dakota jacket around here somewhere. It's bigger than yours, but it'll keep you snuggly warm. I'll get it for you."

She offered her hand. "Put me to work."

Stephen tightened a piece of wood in the vice and then reached for his measuring tape and a pencil. "I like having you down here keeping me company, but if you fall asleep at that workbench, you'll fall off the stool and give us both a scare. What do you say I take you home now?"

Meghan ran her hand across the round drawer knobs she had sorted, sanded, measured, and confirmed were identical. "I like being here. How come you're not getting tired?"

"Because I like working on a piece until late into the night. It's therapy; gives me time to think. You on the other hand stop moving and the thinking stops; then you start nodding off to sleep."

She smiled at him. He was falling in love with that smile, and it had taken its time to finally reappear tonight. He didn't really want to take her home, but it was getting late.

"Did you know Jesus was a carpenter?"

Stephen opened the vice and nudged the piece of wood farther down. "Jennifer mentioned it." The sadness that came just with saying her name didn't hit with its normal intensity. It was progress. "I bet He was a good one."

"I wish you were comfortable with the fact Jesus loves you."

"I'm working on it. I'm comfortable that Jesus loves *you*." He knew she'd be overjoyed to learn he had crossed the line to believe in Jesus, but that conversation would inevitably lead to his mentioning his revelation about Peg and the tears that had ended his night. He wasn't ready for that yet, and Meghan had already absorbed too much emotion today. A peaceful conversation tomorrow would do just fine.

Stephen walked over and got out the cushion foams from his cabinet of supplies. "Why don't you toss your towel over this cushion, and you'll have yourself a pillow so you can close your eyes and rest them a moment."

"Thanks."

"Hold still a minute." He knelt and used his tape to measure the distance from her shoe soles to the back of her knee.

She reached down and touched his hand. "What are you doing?"

"You're about Kate's height. It helps if custom chairs are at least within the ballpark of the right height for comfort."

He walked back over to his workbench and jotted down the figures. "I was thinking I might pick you up next Sunday and go to services with you."

He glanced over, hoping it might catch her speechless, but that small smile appeared and she just rested her chin on her hand as she looked at him. "I'm thinking I would like it if you did."

She'd been praying for him again; he was starting to recognize that small smile. Stephen softly whistled as he measured a piece of wood to Meghan's height. Yes, he could certainly get used to more nights like this one. "Would you like to come to Chicago with me next month for two weddings? Cole and Rachel are having a quiet ceremony on Friday afternoon, the twenty-eighth, and Jack and Cassie are getting married the next day. I'd enjoy your company for the weekend."

"Can I think about the invitation for a few days?"

"Sure. As long as you say yes."

"I like the changes you're making out here," Bill commented, walking along the new fence Stephen built.

"Thanks."

Stephen followed Meghan's father, watching the man as he reached out to touch a post, shake a board, confirming just how solid the work had been done then nod with approval.

Stephen pulled his hand from his pocket and pointed ahead to where the walk to the pond joined their two properties. "I'm thinking about making the path to the pond into something more defined, with woodchips and edging and the occasional post with a different pattern to each top knob, so Meghan doesn't have to wonder about her location on the path. If I do, would you like me to extend it over to your orchard fence?"

"Please. Come over anytime and I'll help you mark it out." Bill paused to watch the sheep. "I appreciate what you did yesterday. I knew it was hopeless as soon as I saw Craig, but I saw how invested she was in saving him —" Bill shook his head.

"You did the right thing. When an infant died of SIDS, we'd often do the same attempts to resuscitate even though it was useless effort just to give the parents a little more time to accept what was happening. You treat the living, and the shock they are experiencing. Meghan did what she could, but nothing could have saved Craig's life. Accepting that doesn't come easy, not when she's blind and having to take our word for it."

"I shared coffee with her this morning. She's dealing with it."

Stephen leaned against the fence, watching the baby goat race through the grazing sheep, running off energy. "I've been thinking about picking up that paramedic's jacket, returning to the job part-time. It wouldn't solve all the response-time problems given just the sheer distances out here, but it would help."

"It would let us get one of the county ambulances stationed at the clinic in Silverton, if not as its permanent hub then as a rotating one. Are you sure you're ready, Stephen? The job chewed you up the last time."

"I don't know if I'll ever be really ready. But the last two pages — they've felt right. I'm a good paramedic and I'm comfortable with the pressure of being the one who's responsible. It's not my job to determine the outcome; it's God's. I can live with that."

Bill looked over at him thoughtfully and nodded. "I'm glad you found that perspective. You sound at peace with it."

"I am."

Bill held out his hand. "I'd be honored to have you on the team. We can do the paperwork with the county EMS this afternoon and make it official."

Stephen appreciated the confidence offered, but he wasn't sure he had earned it yet. "I won't let you down."

"I don't expect you will."

As momentous as the change, it was finalized in merely a minute. Stephen kicked at a fence post and figured he'd better get himself a phone to carry with him, maybe get that jacket of his repaired so the emblem didn't pull away. "I haven't told Meghan yet; I'd appreciate if you let me break the news."

"Sure. She'll be glad to have you coming in and out of the office occasionally."

"Will she?"

Bill smiled and patted him on the back. "You're going to settle your questions about God, find the peace you're after, and start making my life havoc by asking Meghan out. I'm an old man, but I still notice the obvious. Ever since you bought this place, you've begun setting down roots."

"I'm well on my way to being there. I'll make her happy, Bill."

"I know you will. Would you like to come over for lunch Sunday?"

"I'm planning to give Meg a lift to church; I'll be glad to join you for lunch afterward. Your wife makes a great pie."

"That she does. How's the remodeling coming along?"

"Good. Come on up to the house and I'll show you around. I could use your opinion on my future office. I want to build shelves like those you have."

Twenty-four

Meghan agreed to a picnic lunch on Saturday, and Stephen chose a place over by the river, hoping even the few miles of distance would help her shake the sadness of the last few days.

The quilt covered the grass and the ground wasn't that uncomfortable for an hour. At least the ants had yet to appear. Stephen finished his second croissant sandwich and speared one of the olives in the relish tray.

Meghan nibbled her way around the last of a pear. "You make a nice lunch."

"Thanks." He leaned over and nudged Blackie, offering him the last piece of cheese. The dog was doing his best not to beg but this had to be tough — the food was spread out to one side of the blanket in front of him. The pepper cheese disappeared in one bite.

"He's a mooch, and you're just going to make him sick."

Stephen rubbed Blackie's ears. "Hard

work deserves a reward occasionally."

He packed away the remains of their lunch and placed them in the picnic basket. "I told your father I'd start working more formally as one of the county paramedics. It won't prevent days like yesterday, but maybe in the next crisis I'll be able to help you more."

"You're comfortable doing that?"

"It's time, Meg. And I'm not as queasy at the sight of blood anymore."

"I'm glad. You'll do a wonderful job, and the town residents will welcome you to the job with open arms."

"Think you can handle me wandering in and out of the clinic when I'm in town?"

"Are you going to make a point of letting me know you're around?"

"Hmm."

She smiled. "I was afraid of that."

He rolled onto his back. He was in the mood to close his eyes and catch a nap.

"Something is different today, Stephen. I can hear it in your voice. You sound . . . I don't know the right word. Calm."

"I'm falling asleep," he clarified. "It's good to have the decision made. And I made another big one just before it." He turned his head to look at her, interested in watching her face. "The Bible is starting to make sense, Meg. I understand now how you know Jesus as a friend."

The pear juice got ahead of her and had to be rubbed off her chin. He watched the emotions on her face — joy, curiosity, hesitancy to make too much of his words. "You believe."

He smiled at her caution. "Yes, what I understand so far. I was reading through John and it started to come alive as you described, and the pieces began to make sense. Your description of it as a conversation — it fit. The fact Jesus would come and die on a cross for me, when it began to click that He could love me that much — There's something powerful in that, Meg, that overrides so many of the questions that still linger."

"He loves completely, and every time I think I've figured that out, I find I've barely scratched the surface. On the questions, a suggestion? Take your time and keep searching for answers. He's not bothered by honest conversation when we hurt."

"It was the first time I thought about Peg being in heaven where I would get to see her again. It got pretty emotional."

"Peg's there and it will be a good reunion. She's going to be everything you remember, and more. Only her body died. And Jesus promised a new one for heaven and eternity."

"You'll see again in heaven."

"Heaven is described as being so beautiful. A few years without sight here on earth will make the joy of seeing heaven so incredible." She lifted a sleeve to wipe at her eyes. "Oh, I'm going to cry, and that's not fair."

He rolled toward her. "Here, I've got more napkins. And your happy tears aren't so bad."

She took a handful of the napkins. "I've been praying for you so long." She scrubbed at her face and then just buried her head in her hands. "Oh, look somewhere else will you? My nose is going red; I can tell."

He laughed. "It's kind of endearing, but it's not like all that many people are out here to notice." He waited until she pushed her hair back and looked up. "I'm glad you kept praying."

"I figured the O'Malleys were trying to do enough of the explaining." She mopped her eyes and gave him a smile. "Did you bring dessert? I could use a distraction."

"First-class dessert: cheesecake." He pulled over the picnic basket. "How about we rent a movie tonight? Something you remember well and hopefully not too mushy.

We can see if Ken and JoAnne are free. I need his help with the new kitchen cabinets."

He watched her relax.

"Could I feed your sheep?"

"Sure. You'll have to watch out for the baby goat; he loves shoelaces." Stephen touched her hand and offered a plate. "Dessert is served."

Jonathan sat in the diner at a corner table near the front window, watching people coming and going along Main Street. Craig was no longer a threat. Jonathan had to swallow hard to eat without choking. He'd done what he had to do. It cost him seven thousand to buy that envelope and its contents. He'd given Craig a chance; he hadn't forced his friend to open the envelope and use what it contained . . . but Jonathan had known he would do it. Craig had betrayed him and tried to take the jewelry for himself. There had been no other choice.

He'd never killed before.

He wasn't sure he liked how it felt.

He pushed the emotions aside, for it was over and done. He had a decision to make, and it was his own life on the line this time. The stolen gems were still out there somewhere.

If the jewels were not going to be found, then the correct tactical decision was to walk away and leave them behind — unsold, unfound, and the knowledge of them buried with Neil and Craig. But if Meghan or the cops had a chance of finding the gems, then recovering them had to be his top priority and would be worth any risk short of being discovered.

Neil, where did you put them?

The owner of some of those pieces might — He should have never let Neil talk him into stealing them from the wife of a mob boss. Rumor had it the man liked his victims to bleed to death. Slowly.

The jewelry could never be found. He would have to ensure that. So far they had been hidden well enough, even though in the last few days several people were looking for them. The authorities didn't have tangible proof yet that more pieces existed, so eventually they'd give up and figure they had already found everything. If he tried to search and revealed that someone else was involved beyond Neil and Craig, it would create trouble and keep the search going.

Maybe Neil had done one thing right and hidden them well enough they would never be found. Maybe it was better to do nothing. Jonathan pushed his coffee cup aside. He was taking a nasty risk no matter which he chose. Was this over?

He left the restaurant and walked back to the hotel, then stopped at the desk to ask for messages and that his bill be prepared.

If he did come back to Silverton, it would be because trouble had arrived and the jewels had been found. He'd be forced again to act to protect himself.

They said the second murder was easier than the first. He didn't want to have to find out . . .

Twenty-five

Monday, June 10
Silverton

Meghan curled her bare feet into the living-room carpet, enjoying the warmth of the sun. In the last few weeks as summer arrived, this room had become her favorite place to spend her afternoons. She walked over and nudged out her piano bench with her foot, reached forward to search the piano top to find her coaster, and carefully set down her glass of ice water. She turned on the cassette player and listened to Mrs. Teal's last lesson in order to hear the song played correctly. Mrs. Teal made this sound so easy.

Meghan found the opening chords and began her hour of practice. Someday she'd be able to play the song without jarring mistakes. She loved "Amazing Grace." And the fact Stephen had mentioned it had been a favorite of his mom's, she so wanted to be able to play it smoothly.

He likes me . . . he likes me a lot . . . he loves me . . . She paused to run a scale. *Jesus, where's this heading? Stephen has got me so off balance.* She loved her job, her home, and the hope for a husband and family was a lifelong dream. Maybe it was finally drawing near . . . she sure hoped so.

Blackie barked. Meghan pushed back the bench and shut off the cassette player. JoAnne was coming over this morning to help her hang pictures. She knocked over the water glass. Meghan instinctively shoved her arm across the top of the piano to push the water off the piano top before it flowed down and into the keyboard. She knocked the metronome, the empty cassette box, her little bear, and the photo she kept there of Jonathan and Mrs. Teal from a high school concert to the floor.

She hurried into the kitchen and grabbed the roll of paper towels. She tore off squares to dry the spill. Accidents happened, even to people who could see. It just *had* to be the piano, the one thing she treasured most in her house.

As she came back into the living room she missed her location cues and struck her knee hard on the piano bench, then yelped as it tumbled over and struck her foot. She pulled back and stepped on something.

Meghan froze. Wanting to kick something in frustration, she forced herself to stand still and absorb the wave of emotion that came at such blindness-caused clumsiness. She eased back from the disaster, knelt to see what she had just destroyed, hoping it wasn't the picture frame, and reached out toward broken glass fragments.

She had broken the metronome. The wood had cracked at the base. She tried to sort out how badly the wood had separated and if the metronome would still keep time. The bar that swung back and forth wouldn't move. She pushed at it and felt the device come apart in her hands. Something that landed in her palm felt wrong. *What in the world?*

Velvet. She closed her hand around the unexpected item and set the rest of the broken device on the floor. The velvet was taped and when she opened it, she found herself holding a ring. It felt like a woman's ring — slender, a big stone, and what felt like a modern setting. A ring, in her metronome. Neil's piano . . . Neil's metronome.

She was holding a stolen ring.

Neil, no. Why did you have to be a thief?

She had thought it was over, the searches having turned up only the ring in the barn and the brooch in Neil's apartment. Dave and Kate had gone back to Chicago weeks ago, comfortable they had found everything.

Should she call Stephen? The sheriff?

She tucked the ring in her pocket, carefully stood, and walked into the kitchen. She dialed from memory. Dave would be back in town this weekend to do her a favor regarding the jewelry store as she prepared to complete her work with the estate. "Kate, I've got a ring in my hand that is likely another of Neil's stashed pieces. Could you come with Dave this weekend and take a look?"

Joseph looked over the edge of the ravine and shook his head as he stepped back.

"The boy just had to break his leg when he was all the way down there, instead of tripping at the top of the trail."

Stephen hoisted the ropes to his shoulder and smiled at his new partner. "Want me to lead the way to break your fall, or shall I hold the safety rope so you don't crash to the bottom like he did?"

"The kid is my nephew, so I guess I should do the honors. I'll take the lead. You would figure he'd have listened when I warned him. This loose shale will do it to you every time."

"What's down there that's so fascinating?"

"An old coal mine. It's kind of like Silverton's equivalent to a haunted house. A couple miners died down there in the 1930s, and their ghosts are the legend behind all kinds of stories the kids tell to spook each other."

Stephen accepted the water bottle from Joseph.

"I've got the splints and litter. Let's go get him." Joseph moved over to the start of the steep trail and began his descent. Stephen watched his footing and followed. A cop and two other teens were already down there with the boy. It was good to be back working as a paramedic. And his partner had been doing the job for decades. Stephen liked being the junior man on the team for a change.

Splint the boy's leg, carry him out, transport him to the hospital to get his leg x-rayed and set — They'd be done with this run by two. That left plenty of time to stop by and see Meghan and tease a smile out of her when he turned in paperwork.

He started whistling as he slid down a particularly steep six feet of the path. Meg liked to hear about the job runs and he enjoyed talking to her about his day. He slapped at a mosquito and scowled at the swarm of them ahead of him. He'd forgotten the bug spray again.

★ ★ ★

Kate pushed open the door to the jewelry store Saturday morning, smiling as she caught Meghan and Stephen standing a step closer than just friends, Stephen's hand idly rubbing Meghan's shoulder as they talked. Her brother looked . . . content. Kate hadn't seen that relaxed expression and stance since before Jennifer died. She nearly stepped back outside rather than interrupt them.

Stephen half turned. "Hi, Kate." He reached for a spot below his shoulder. "Right about there." Meghan scratched his back. "Oh . . . perfect, now down a bit to the left." He sighed. "I walked through a swarm of mosquitoes this week and the bites are driving me crazy."

"He forgot to use repellant and now he's paying for it. But I think he just wants to be pampered a bit," Meghan added, leaning against Stephen's back to rest her chin on his shoulder. "You made good time, Kate. Was the drive okay?"

Kate looked from Meg to Stephen and walked over to the table and set down her coffee. "Dave and I left early so we could stop often. Are we the first ones here, or has Jack arrived?"

"He's measuring the truck now to figure

out how to load the workbench. I'd better go help him out." Stephen reached back and held Meg's hand. "You've got everything you need?"

"Yes. Don't drop that thing on someone's foot when you haul it out."

"We won't."

Stephen shook his finger in silent caution as he went by and Kate smiled back, planning to ignore the warning. Something had definitely changed here in the last few weeks, and Stephen wasn't talking.

Meghan touched the counter and oriented herself. "Kate, I've got the ring back in the vault. Would you like to see it now or does Dave need me to do paperwork?"

"He's still making a couple calls squaring away details, so we've got time. How does Stephen like being a paramedic again?"

Meg laughed. "He loves it, even though he takes every opportunity to make a big deal about the calls." She led the way through the jewelry store to the back repair room. The shelves were about empty and the worktables cleared.

Meghan opened the vault door and retrieved the box from the second shelf. "Here's the ring I found."

Kate turned on the powerful lighted magnifying glass and Meghan brought her the ring. Kate turned it slowly, studying every detail. "It's gold with the inscription: *I have, I hold.* The words don't strike me as a particularly romantic phrase. The diamond is nice size though."

"It didn't show up anywhere in Neil's registry. Do you think it was stolen?"

"It's a more modern setting than the last stone, and the inscription should be easy enough to track down if a report was filed. I'll take it with me, if that's okay."

"Of course. Given this is the third piece found, I have to figure there will be more pieces turning up in random places. We never stopped to think about the number of items Neil gave away over the years."

"It's hard to know when these discoveries will end. Thanks for calling me." Kate carefully put the ring away.

Jack strode into the workroom, followed by Stephen. Jack leaned over the massive workbench in the center of the room to see how the brace was secured. "Do you really have to have this workbench?" He shoved it and barely moved the bench a few inches.

"It will be perfect at the barn," Stephen said.

"And I need the floor space," Meghan added. "I can't sell this building with that thing still here."

"Well if we do get it to the barn, it's going to stay there," Jack declared. "This is a monster. How do we do this?"

"Tip it on its side and shove it through the door?"

"Getting it on the truck will be the tricky part." Jack put his entire weight against one end of the bench to get it to tip. "Meg, you might want to keep Blackie back. I'd hate to step on a foot or a tail."

She snapped her fingers and the dog moved to her side.

Stephen shoved and the bench began to move. They walked it toward the doorway.

"Watch the door frame," Jack cautioned.

"I'm watching it. There's no clearance for fingers." Stephen heaved to get it over the rise.

Kate leaned back against the wall. "Guys look good flexing muscles and sweating," she commented for Meghan's benefit. "I've got good-looking brothers."

"Thanks for the visual."

Kate laughed.

"Hold it, Jack. This isn't going to work. We can't clear the display case."

"Let me see." He shoved the workbench back. "We can fix this. Meg, where's the power screwdriver?" Jack called. "I need to take out a glass door and two handles."

"The toolbox is behind the counter."

"Thanks."

The security guard squeezed around the guys. "Miss Delhart, the armored truck is here."

"Thanks, Lou. Kate, JoAnne left the tally sheets in the top drawer of the file cabinet."

Kate pushed away from the wall to stand straight. She would be so glad when she delivered this child. She couldn't see her feet and her balance was off. She felt great for the first time in months; she just couldn't walk without thinking about her balance. She found the documents and flipped to the final page. "Wow. You weren't kidding about the appraisals."

"Neil had some good pieces."

Kate looked up as her husband came in. "It's a good thing they sent two security guards."

Dave accepted the list. "Are you sure you're ready to do this, Meghan?"

"I'll be incredibly relieved to have it over. You'll need to check each piece against the list, make sure we didn't miss anything." Meghan opened the vault door and picked up two black hard-sided cases stored inside. "Thank you for this."

"I'm riding back to Chicago with my wife and following an armored truck with a million dollars in jewels. I can think of harder ways to spend an afternoon. We'll sign them over to the wholesale buyer and call you when the delivery is complete."

"It's a huge load off my shoulders to have this done."

"Have you decided on the next step here?" Dave asked.

"Dad has decided to use some of the estate gift to expand the clinic. We'll start looking for a doctor to join the practice."

"That sounds like a good plan. Kate, hold on to the list and I'll take these cases outside."

Meghan used a brick to brace open the vault door so it would air out. "Would you check to make sure I haven't missed anything?"

"Sure." Kate found a flashlight and checked the back corners of the drawers and edges of the shelves. "I think you were smart to work with one dealer to take all the pieces."

"It ends it at least. It's awful to say after all Neil's years of effort that I'll be relieved to have his business liquidated, but I will. The realtor already has a possible buyer for the property."

Kate looked around to make sure Stephen was still outside. "Have you decided if you'll come with Stephen to Jack's wedding?"

"I'm still thinking about it."

"Come, please. We'd love for you to be there."

"It's a big deal, Kate."

"I know. I need you to come, Meg. Stephen will be the last O'Malley not married, and I don't want him to be there alone. I don't know how he'll be feeling at the end of the weekend when he leaves to drive back here. I'd rather he had someone with him."

"When you put it that way — yes, I'll talk to Stephen and come."

Meghan pushed a broom across the now open floor area, finishing the cleanup. She was amazed that Jack and Stephen had been able to move the workbench in one piece. She was sure they'd have to take it apart to have any chance of getting it out of the room.

The problem with going to the O'Malley weddings was the drive to town and back with Stephen, being the focus of his attention for the weekend. That amount of time would either move them a huge step closer together or something would happen that brought out just how hard it really was to have a relationship with a blind lady. She bit her bottom lip and shoved at the broom.

It was one thing to dream, another to realize a dream might be coming true. What had been easy to dismiss earlier now had to be dealt with. She'd be on unfamiliar territory and would have to depend on Stephen for so many details just to get around.

Her broom caught on an uneven point in the floor. Meghan stepped forward to see if a nail had worked upwards or if it was a loose board. The board moved on her.

She leaned down and found a board was more than loose; it sat slightly below the floor level. She tried to remove it only to find it was actually pivoting. She felt under the board, expecting cobwebs, sawdust, and concrete but touched a hard-sided book.

She lifted it out, realizing as she rubbed off the dust that the dimensions and the heavy weight of the paper were similar to a book she'd been handling every day for the last few weeks. She laughed. Neil had kept a second registry. He has kept meticulous records for the store; it made sense that he'd do the same for the pieces he was forging.

She carried it over to the table with the computer and scanner she had used as she went through his first registry. She turned on the equipment. As she waited impatiently for it to warm up, she found her phone and dialed.

"Stephen! You have to come back to the store. I found it. Neil's registry of stolen goods, at least that's what I think it is. It was under a floorboard where the workbench used to be and it feels like a similar ledger. I haven't scanned it yet, but I can tell it's been well-used over the years."

"I'll be there just as soon as Jack and I get this workbench off the back of the truck."

"Thanks."

She opened the registry, laid it on the glass, and scanned the first page.

Neil must have printed in a tight hand because the software had a hard time deciphering every letter, but it could read enough of each line to let her fill in the blanks. She listened as the software read dates, descriptions of pieces, and dollar amounts. Occasionally there was a second line with an annotated reference about the piece.

Neil had been stealing and forging pieces for years. She started jumping forward to pages at random, looking for the year Neil would have bought the brooch from JoAnne. Had it been a stolen piece that her friend had found in that music box years ago?

Stephen parked the truck in front of the

jewelry store and grabbed his keys. The front door was locked. "Meghan?" He knocked, surprised the security guard was no longer on duty.

Blackie began to bark inside.

"I'm coming!"

He opened the door and his greeting died. Tears traced down Meghan's cheeks. "What's wrong?"

She shook her head and trailed a hand along the display cases that headed to the back room. "Come back and see the registry."

Stephen locked the front door behind him and followed her. "Where's the security guard?"

"There's nothing else here of value now that the vault is empty. Today was his last day."

Those didn't look like her happy tears. "Meghan, why are you crying?"

"Tell me about the ledger first." The floorboard piece she'd found was propped open. She was right. The bench would have concealed it, and it was heavy enough that no one would have looked underneath it. Meghan lifted the lid on the scanner and picked up the registry and offered it to him.

He tugged a Kleenex from his pocket and pressed it into her hand, then looked at what she'd found. "The ledger is black leather binding, legal-size pages with the light green guide lines. There are about sixty pages, the first ten pages or so with entries." She wiped at her eyes. "What's wrong, Meghan? Is it this book?"

"Read the line for Friday, August 16, 1996."

He ran his hand down the page to find the entry.

August 16, Wilshire Hotel, Chicago, midnight. Three pieces switched: emerald earrings, a square-cut diamond ring, a bracelet and necklace with diamonds and emeralds in twenty-four carat gold. Fakes. 18 hours labor.

Two columns labeled simply E and T respectively showed the words advance 10,000. The next line in the ledger was a note.

Advance Craig additional 2,000 — clipped bridge railing, bumper damage on father's car.

Neil had known a great deal about the robbery — he listed when and where the stones were taken, the specifics of the pieces taken, the time it took him to create the replicas. Did *T* stand for *transport?* Maybe *E* for who had made the exchange? "The ledger proves Craig had been the courier Neil used for the robberies." He looked over lines in the registry. No other names were mentioned on the page. He didn't understand.

Stephen rubbed Meghan's back, for she was still wiping away tears. "You're breaking my heart, honey. What is it?"

"Friday, August 16, 1996, is the night I went blind."

Twenty-six

Stephen felt as though he'd taken another punch as her words registered.

"Craig had to be at the Wilshire Hotel in Chicago at midnight," Meghan said. "He would have been coming from Silverton. Sometime during that trip he damaged his dad's car on a bridge railing. You want to figure the odds of two people traveling to and from Silverton on a Friday night six years ago, who both have accidents on a bridge, and have it be two different bridges?"

She wrapped her arms tight across her waist. "The other car accelerated at me. Craig was probably high; even back then he was a heavy user. He ran me off the bridge and left me blind."

Stephen set down the ledger, his gaze never leaving her. "What do you want to do? Throw something? I'll get out of the way. Scream? I'll hold my ears. Just please do something with that anger but stand there rocking on your feet. You're going to have a coronary on me here." Stephen reached out to grip her arm. She'd begun to tremble.

Her hand clung to his and cut into the circulation. And rather than speak she just moved into his arms. Stephen winced at the sobs that shook her. "It's okay. Shh." There was nothing that made this better. She'd gone blind because of a robbery. "Don't, Meg."

He closed his eyes against his own tears and rocked with her where they stood. *Jesus, how do You heal this pain she's in? Couldn't You have sent Craig into that ditch instead of Meghan?* There were some events that simply didn't square up and make sense. *You could have but You didn't. And Meg lives blind. That's hard to accept.* "You're worrying Blackie, honey, crying this hard. Let's go sit down." He led her toward a chair and wished he knew what to do that would help.

A storm wasn't much of a distraction, but it was all Stephen could come up with to get Meghan away from Silverton and the topic of the stolen jewelry. He was relieved Ken was going storm chasing today. Kate could sort out the ledger for them. He had a more pressing problem helping Meghan shake the depression.

He tended to run when life overwhelmed him; she just got quiet, and it wasn't easy to shift her out of that sad place. He couldn't remember the last time he ate lunch literally at the side of the road, sitting on lawn chairs and eating sandwiches. The wind blowing toward them was brisk. He watched her and was glad they came.

"The sound in the trees is changing," Meghan commented.

Ken lowered his camera. "The front is coming against blue sky and it's vast, with thunderheads blowing upward for tens of thousands of feet."

"Are we going to get hail?"

Ken studied the laptop screen beside him. "Probably. There's a big humidity and temperature change as the front crosses the Mississippi River. It looks as if the front is already beginning to generate its own wind. By the time it reaches Silverton we're going to have a serious storm on our hands."

Stephen tossed a tennis ball into the field for Blackie to chase. "I can see why you like to spend Saturdays out doing this, Ken. What got you started?"

"Where else can you watch something this magnificent, enjoy it for several hours, and it's free? It was great in college when I wanted JoAnne's time for several hours but didn't have more than a couple bucks in my pocket."

The wind began to pick up pieces of roadside gravel. Stephen shielded his eyes.

"Are the clouds beginning to roll at the leading edge of the storm?" Meghan asked, holding down the papers on the makeshift table.

Ken snapped more pictures. "Oh yeah. The front edge is beginning to lead the main storm like a pressure wave."

"Let's head for the Lookout," JoAnne suggested.

"Good idea. Pile back in the van; let's move before we get wet."

Ken and Stephen quickly collapsed lawn chairs. JoAnne laughed and chased the cooler as the wind blew it toward the field.

Meghan slid into the backseat and Blackie scrambled in with her. "Don't you love this?"

Stephen slid in beside her. "It's memorable, I'll give you."

Ken turned the van around and they drove away from the storm front. He pulled into the Lookout Restaurant west of Davenport. Stephen understood the name when he saw the layout of the restaurant. Windows stretched along the west wall and gave a panoramic view of the incoming storm.

Their presence doubled the number of patrons in the restaurant.

"Is our table free?" Meghan asked.

"Yes," JoAnne confirmed.

Meghan and Blackie set off across the restaurant for the center booth by the windows.

"I gather you come here often?" Stephen asked Ken.

"It's the halfway point for most storm chasing trips," Ken explained. "That's one of my photographs, taken from this parking lot in '98."

Stephen walked over to see. The sky was a roiling gray and green with a clear funnel cloud beginning to drop at the south end of the photo.

"It came in fast and furious and about took the roof of the restaurant off when it dropped to the ground. You can still see some of its path where it decimated trees across the interstate. It ripped up and tossed eighty-year-old oaks around like they were twigs."

Stephen glanced back outside. "Any chance this storm front will be that violent?"

"It's generating its own wind; the cumulus clouds are rising into the low edges of the jet stream. All it needs now is energy

406

to feed on, and the humid air held in place by the high pressure over Ohio fits the bill. They might get some twister action a state or two over tonight."

"You sound regretful."

"It's hard to chase storms after sunset and get decent photos; otherwise I'd be planning to go after it. Once you've been close to a twister, you'll understand the pull." He and Ken ordered for the group then carried trays over to the booth.

Stephen slid in beside Meghan and shared a milkshake with her as they watched the storm come in. In half an hour, rain began to thump against the roof. "I vote we get back to Silverton so you can babysit your windmill, Ken."

"Agreed. This is going to be a good test."

Jonathan drove toward Silverton, rain and wind buffeting his van. He'd gambled and lost. They had found a ring. Mrs. Teal had only known the most cursory of details and about the inscription on the ring, but it was enough to know he was in serious trouble.

That ring was his death warrant.

He wiped sweaty hands and turned the windshield wipers up on high to push away the rain faster.

The mob boss would murder him for

having an affair with Marie and would make it painfully slow for also having robbed from him. Somehow Jonathan had to get the ring back and locate the other items from that robbery — earrings, a bracelet, and a necklace.

Why did it have to be Meghan who found it, someone he knew and liked? The idea of hurting her . . . He had to get that ring back, and somehow he doubted she would give it to him and not tell anyone he had it. She was blind; there had to be a way to use that to his advantage. She probably had it stored in the bank vault. If he could get Meghan to open the vault for some reason, maybe he could slide the ring into his pocket and she'd never be the wiser.

And if the ring had already been turned over to the cops? He'd have to somehow force them to return it without revealing his identity. He couldn't send someone else to get the ring, and there was no one else alive who knew the truth. The cops would have to bring the ring to him . . . and he had no idea how to make that happen.

It would be better all around if Meghan still had the ring.

If it had been in the metronome, there was a good chance the other pieces would be nearby. Maybe somewhere in Neil's piano. He'd start there. He didn't have much time to get this done.

Kate shifted in the front car seat, trying to find a comfortable position.

"Are you sure you don't want me to stop and let you have a chance to walk around for a few minutes?" Dave asked.

Her back ached, her feet were swollen, she was eight months and four days pregnant, and she was ready to have this over. She hadn't been comfortable in weeks. "I'm okay. I'd rather get to Silverton before this storm does." She made a notation on the enlarged copies of the registry pages she had been working on since Meg found the book.

"What are you planning to tell Meghan?"

"Something other than the fact the ring was stolen from a mob boss. But we have to find the other stones, even if we have to break up every piece of furniture Neil ever owned."

"Agreed."

Stephen turned up the radio to try to drown out the noise outside as the rain reached the barn. Meghan, smoothing the edges of the baby cradle he had made for Kate, set aside the sandpaper and looked up at the roof. "It sounds nasty out there."

"We can go up to the house if you like. If we go now we can probably make it before the heaviest rain arrives."

"I'm okay out here. As long as the barn roof stays on."

"It will. Your dog is not very happy right now though; he just disappeared underneath the table."

"Blackie hates thunder, and I can't blame him."

Stephen rubbed a soft cloth over the piece of furniture on the workbench, checking that the glue had dried, then set it on the ground. "Come over here a minute. I'd like you to try something."

Meghan got up, her hand trailing along the worktable. "What do you have?"

Stephen took her hand and set it on the back of the chair. She rubbed her hand along the edges trying to figure out what it was. She smiled. "You made Kate a rocking chair."

He guided her into the chair. "Actually . . . I made *you* a rocking chair."

She stopped rocking. "Me?"

"Your mom gave me a photo of the rocking chair you used when you were a teen and babysat in the house you now own."

Meghan ran her hands along the armrests and the spokes, then she laughed. "It's an incredible rocking chair."

"The wood is unpainted right now, a light oak. I can either varnish it or paint it for you."

"Maybe a light varnish. Why did you decide to make this?"

He rested his hands on the arms of the rocking chair. "Your smile." Stephen leaned down and kissed her, enjoying the blush. "There are times I like the fact you're blind," he whispered.

Her hand curled in his shirt as her smile grew. "There are times I like being surprised."

He eased back. "You're dangerous."

"Hmm." She released his shirt and smoothed the wrinkles out. "What else do we have to work on tonight? I'm about done with the cradle."

His thoughts were too muddled with ideas of kissing her again to think about work, and at his long pause she laughed. "Focus, Stephen."

"I'm trying, but you're intoxicating." He took a deep breath and took a full step back. "I need the slats sanded for the display case, and I've got a couple repair projects to work on."

"Let me work on the slats."

"Sure." He looked away to get his thoughts back to the work at hand. "Sanding. You'll need more sandpaper."

"I love it when you're flustered."

He glanced over at her. "It's nice to have your smile back."

"It's hard to stay sad around you. Thanks, Stephen. Today meant a lot."

"You're very welcome."

He set her up at the workbench and then moved to pick up the first repair project. He'd brought her damaged piano bench back with him to the workshop to tighten the legs and remove the wobble. He turned it upside down on the worktable and got out the wood glue, working with small shims to tighten the joints. The fabric was worn through around the staples and had begun to tear. He studied the fabric and realized the original staples had been inserted over a double fold of material. He could move the staples and give the bench another few years of life.

He found a pair of needle-nose pliers and tugged up the staples.

The wood underneath the staples shifted. He stopped. If he removed these staples the bench was so old it might come apart. Better to fix it than have it give way on

412

Meghan someday. He pulled up the staples and rather than a solid piece of wood supporting the seat cushion found a flat piece of wood covering a hollow space.

Intrigued, he pulled the wood back. "Meghan, set down what you're doing and come over here. I just found something."

He tugged out a backgammon-sized case secured inside the bench.

Meghan joined him.

"Inside the piano bench there was a slim compartment and a case." He used a knife to force the clasp open. "Oh, my."

"What is it?"

He reached inside the box. "It's not everything we've been searching for, but it's quite a sight. Three pieces — emerald earrings and a diamond-and-emerald bracelet and necklace. Assuming these are real, compared to the pieces you had appraised, these would be in the exceptional category."

"I doubt Neil would hide fakes." Meghan reached out and Stephen took her hand, showed her the pieces. "Is it too late to call Kate?"

"For this she'll appreciate a call. I'll get my phone."

The pager he wore went off.

"There's been an accident caused by the storm," Meghan predicted. He squeezed her hand as he dialed the dispatch center instead of his sister. It was a car wreck on the highway, police were responding, but he was the only one available for EMS. He confirmed he was on his way and closed the phone. "The jewels have been here for a long time; they can wait a little longer. Come with me. I can drop you at the clinic." He didn't want to leave her here alone.

"Why don't I take the case and you can drop me at the store on the way to the clinic to get the ambulance. This barn doesn't have a good track record for storing valuables and the wind here is scary."

The store was brick and originally built to be a bank. It was a better place on a stormy night than this barn. "Agreed." He closed the box clasp. "I'm afraid you're about to get somewhat wet."

She snapped her fingers for Blackie. "I won't melt, and I can run. Let's go."

Stephen stepped on the truck brakes as his headlights picked out a huge limb of a fallen tree. It stretched across the road. Meghan tightened her arms draped around her dog sitting on the seat between them, and Stephen reached over to steady him too.

"What is it?"

414

"The road's blocked." There was not enough clearance around either end to drive around the fallen tree. "This is going to be a longer trip than I planned." He backed up and found a place he could turn the truck around. "I'll have to get to the accident scene the long way around. I'm sorry, Meghan. You'll have to come with me."

"Do it. Blackie and I will survive."

Stephen called the dispatcher to find out if Joseph could get through to Silverton to bring the ambulance and to ask if there was any chance of fire and rescue being available. He didn't want to think about having to transport victims in the back of a police car. Wind pummeled the truck. Lightning snapped overhead and the thunder sounded like it was right over them. Meghan flinched. "The worst has to pass over us soon," Stephen reassured. If not for the jewels in the case at her feet, he would have left her at his house.

"I'd say there is a bit of hail in that rain."

"I think you could be right."

Stephen finally saw the flashing lights ahead in the rain. "At least one cop car has made it here. Stay in the truck, Meg. If I can use your help, I'll send someone to get you." He parked off the side of the road as far as he could get and wished there were at least a few drivers out tonight who might stop and render assistance. He wanted Meghan to stay with someone rather than sit here on her own.

"I'll be fine. Go do your job."

Stephen squeezed her hand, grabbed his powerful torchlight, his EMS jacket, and slipped out of the truck.

The rain beat at him, the wind tried to blow him over, and Meghan had been right about the hail. He was getting a few strikes harder than just rain.

Two cars had clipped each other in an off-center head-on collision. "Over here!" The cop shouted from the car off the west side of the road.

The officer came around the back of the car to meet him. "This driver is trapped with a broken left leg; the driver of the other car looks more like straight shock and a broken wrist when the air bag went off. I moved him over here to keep him dry and watch him since I couldn't be two places at the same time."

"Good thinking. Trees are down; the ambulance may not be able to get here, and fire and rescue is currently committed to other accidents. For now it's just us. Let's get this driver freed, then we can transport one in my truck and one in your car. My date has some medical training, so she can ride with you."

"Fine. Anything is better than drowning out here."

Stephen circled the wreck. With a broken leg, they needed options that didn't involve twisting the driver around. "While I check their conditions, head back to your squad car and get on the radio. See if you can raise another driver, a semi truck, anybody out on the roads to give us a hand. Once we get the injured moved, we need to push these cars off the highway. And I need a tire iron, a jack, and whatever you might have in your squad car that won't bend when we use it as a wedge to force that metal."

"I'll get on it."

Stephen opened the driver-side door and slid in to check the conditions of one of the two drivers. Both drivers were now his responsibility.

Meghan hunched in the front seat of the truck, using the length of the seat to stretch out her legs and give Blackie room to lie down. He still whined when thunder rumbled and about exhausted himself shaking.

God, I know You made the lightning, thunder, rain, and hail, but this is awful. Please tone it down.

Stephen had been gone half an hour — in this weather it seemed like an eternity. The wreck and the injuries must be bad or he would have been back by now. She wished she could go offer to help without being in his way.

She jerked as a brisk rap on the window behind her seized her breathing and scared a decade off her life.

"Meghan! I'm parked nearby and the ambulance is arriving behind me. Let's get you out of here!"

Relieved to hear a familiar voice, she turned and opened the door.

Stephen headed back down the road to get Meghan, fighting the wind and rubbing a bruised wrist, relieved to have Joseph here with the ambulance. His two patients were loaded and ready to head to the hospital. She could ride in the passenger seat of the ambulance with Blackie while he rode in back.

The truck passenger door was open, the overhead light on, and the dashboard chime was dinging a warning for an open door with the truck running.

The vehicle was empty. "Meghan!" He turned in a full circle, only to see nothing but night. "Meghan!" The wind blew his shout back to him. Where had she gone? Why? How long had she been gone? He leaned into the door of the truck and found the seat wet but that told him little. Blackie was gone and she'd taken the jewelry case with her.

He looked around for any other cars that had stopped, anyone else she might have gone to help. The wreck had blocked both lanes of traffic. A car was completing a three-point turn on the road in order to turn around and go back the way they had come; another car pulled to the side, the driver waiting his turn to make the same maneuver. Stephen hurried toward it.

The girl on the passenger side lowered the window. "Is the wreck bad?"

"The ambulance crew has it covered. Have you seen a lady walking this direction with a collie?"

"We haven't seen anything but the cop lights ahead and the cars turning around. The ambulance came around us, but everyone else has been turning around."

"Did you see anyone get out of a car, walk around, go to see the wreck?"

She shook her head. "Sorry. Nothing."

Stephen stepped back from the car and went to ask the next driver. He couldn't believe Meghan would leave the scene to go back to town with another driver without coming to let him know.

No one had seen Meghan or Blackie. Stephen walked back toward his truck and the accident scene, his torch sweeping both sides of the road. She'd left the door open. Had Blackie darted out ahead of her when she intended to slip on his harness? "Meghan!" The dog was having a rough time in the storm, maybe that was it.

Maybe she'd heard something? Thought someone else needed help?

He reached his truck and searched it again, looking to see what was missing — her jacket, and a cursory look under the seats and in the glove box didn't turn up the jewelry case. He headed toward the accident scene. She got worried and must have left the truck to come and help him. He shone his light back and forth to both sides of the road searching as he headed toward the wreck. The noise would have been enough to help her go the right direction. "Meghan!"

She couldn't have just disappeared.

Blackie appeared through the rain running toward him, barking ferociously.

"What's going on?"
"An accident of some sort." Dave slowed

the car. Traffic wasn't getting past. "That looks like a county cop car and ambulance lights." He pulled to the shoulder and activated the hazard lights. "I'll go see if they need help."

"I'd help but . . ."

Dave squeezed her hand. "Eight-month pregnant ladies can leave helping at accidents to their husbands. I love you. Stay put."

"Go."

Dave grabbed his jacket and climbed out into the wind and rain.

Twenty-seven

"What do you mean Meghan's missing?" Kate demanded as Dave leaned in the passenger window of their car.

"Exactly that. She was in Stephen's truck; now she's missing. Blackie bolted, she went after the dog and got lost off the side of the road or in the field. Something." Dave reached in past her and opened the glove box and pulled out the extra package of batteries and the flashlight inside.

Kate reached around to the backseat for her jacket. The ambulance doing a point-by-point turn shone lights into her eyes. "Help me out of the car."

"Just a minute," Dave said. "As soon as the ambulance clears I'll drive us up next to Stephen's truck. The cop is going to drive the ambulance while Joseph rides in back with the two patients, so Stephen and I can set up a search to find Meghan."

"We need more help."

"It's coming, but we're in the middle of nowhere and trees are down. Getting here isn't easy. Sit tight, Kate. I'll be right back."

Dave disappeared back into the rain.

Meghan was missing. Kate fought the nausea that now came in overwhelming speed when she was under stress. *Jesus, I don't know what's going on, but Meghan . . . Please help us find her quickly.*

The radio broke in with another weather alert: a severe storm warning with heavy rain, hail, and tornado watch continuing until 11 p.m.

We need lightning, Lord, as much of it as You can send. We need to be able to see.

The driver's door pulled open and Dave slid into the seat. He drove the car forward to beside Stephen's truck.

The rear driver's side door opened and Stephen tossed a blanket on the seat and lifted in Meghan's wet and shivering dog. Kate leaned over to help hold Blackie.

"Stephen, get in too, please." Kate caught his wet sleeve and tugged him in. "You're as wet as Blackie is." She spent her life negotiating her way through emotionally charged situations, and one glance told her Stephen needed her skills. "So many people are coming there will be an army here soon to help," she promised, knowing Dave would call in favors to make it happen. If he didn't calm down soon, he wouldn't be thinking clearly and might leave out details that would make the difference between their finding Meghan or not.

"She's been gone at least an hour now."

"Tell me what happened."

"I left her in the truck with Blackie and went to help the cop at the wreck. I told her I would send someone back if I needed her. The ambulance arrived about a half hour later. I went back to get Meghan." Stephen took a deep breath. "The passenger side door was open, the truck was still running, the seat was wet. Meghan and Blackie were gone. Blackie came running from the direction of the wreck, barking furiously. There's no sign of Meghan, Kate."

"The likely reality is she opened the truck door, Blackie bolted, she went after him and got farther than she realized, and is sitting waiting for someone to find her. She may have even sent Blackie back to get us. She'll be okay, Stephen." Kate held his gaze until she saw him accept that and relax just a bit. "We'll start a systematic search outward from your truck as soon as enough help arrives."

They needed ideas for how to direct the search. "Or a second possibility: She went with someone back to town and she left a note for you. Someone else coming onto the scene found the truck abandoned, opened the door, and the note was blown away by the wind. For that matter, maybe they decided to steal the truck and got interrupted."

"Meghan wouldn't leave here without Blackie. Even if he bolted in the thunder, she would not leave without him."

"Okay. Third option: If she did go with someone else and it wasn't voluntary, why?"

"The jewels." Stephen leaned his head down against the front seat. "We found a case hidden in the lining of the piano bench Neil gave her. It's the reason Meghan was traveling with me to begin with. The page came in and she didn't want to stay out at my place with them. I was going to drop her off at the jewelry store on the way to the clinic to get the ambulance so she could put them in the vault. That case is not in the truck."

"Who knew she had them?" Dave asked.

"No one. We found them literally minutes before the page for the wreck came in."

"What were the stones?"

"Emerald earrings, a diamond-and-emerald bracelet and necklace."

Kate looked over at Dave, her own alarm hard to check. Those pieces went with the ring Meghan had given her to check out.

They'd been stolen from the wife of a mob boss. Had he heard about the ring being discovered? That inscription *I have, I hold* — he would have known immediately it was the real piece. Kate could just hear the simple direct order: *Find that blind lady and get my ring.* And as they had discovered tonight, the only road into Silverton was this one.

Headlights shone across them as several cars arrived. "Let's get this search underway." She didn't want to explain the implications of option number three to Stephen.

Jonathan parked the car in the alley behind the jewelry store, waiting until lightning showed they were alone before shutting off the car. "Come on."

Meghan didn't move.

He circled the car, opened the door, and pulled her out. "The passive aggression isn't going to help so I suggest you start cooperating. Give me your keys."

He tugged around her jacket to get to the pocket and she pulled out her hand to give them to him. "Why are you doing this?"

He ignored the question. He opened the door to the store and pushed her inside. He shook rain off his jacket.

Without the dog, controlling her was simple. She couldn't see him, so she couldn't fight him, and she couldn't run. And so far they had been on territory she didn't know. This store she knew and he saw the change as she reached out one hand behind her to touch the wall, feel the door frame, and get her bearings.

"The faster I get what I want, the faster this is over." He caught her elbow and led her into the back room. "Since the security guard is gone and you have pretty much cleared this room of furniture, I gather the vault is also empty?"

"It's empty."

"Then you won't mind showing me. Open it."

She tugged against his hand.

"Don't push me, Meghan. You don't know what's going on here tonight. If the vault is empty, just show me. It makes no sense to resist on principle when there is nothing to protect."

She moved to the vault and began turning the tumblers.

He set the case she had with her in the truck on the worktable next to a computer she must have brought in, for Neil had never owned one. He opened the clasp on the case.

The luck of the evening was with him — he had three of the four pieces. Marie's earrings, necklace, and bracelet. Five years had dulled his memory of their beauty. He picked up the necklace. Now that he had the pieces, what was he going to do with them? Dump them in the river, bury them, somehow make them disappear.

He needed the ring.

He sat down and turned on her computer. While it booted, he looked through the papers on the table. Anything incriminating he was going to burn. And given the rain, he couldn't just torch the store and be confident that everything would burn before the rain extinguished the fire. The computer came on and he set it to not just delete files but also to wipe the data.

He pulled over the two registries Neil kept. He was startled to see in one the stolen pieces over the years. He scanned for his name and didn't see it, but someone matching his itinerary to this list would see too many similarities for comfort. Burn it.

Meghan opened the vault door.

Jonathan joined her. "Ladies first." He didn't want her closing him inside the vault; she'd do it if given a chance. He kept a hand on her arm as he pulled trays out and confirmed they were empty.

"Not even a loose clasp left in here . . . you did a thorough job." He steered her out

428

of the vault and walked her over to a chair. "Who has the ring you found? You know the one; the inscription says: *I Have, I Hold.*"

She set her jaw and didn't answer.

He left her sitting in the chair. The electrical box in the corner of the room gave him water and fire alarm circuits. He cut both. He tugged the metal garbage can into the center of the room. Jonathan tossed a match onto the pages in the trash can, and while it burned, he ripped pages from the ledger and tossed them into the flames.

She shoved the chair back as she smelled smoke.

"Where's the ring, Meghan? Or should I just leave you in this building?"

"I don't have the ring. Stephen's sister Kate has it."

"But you can get it." He picked up the phone, walked over, and handed it to her. "Call Kate and tell her to bring the ring."

"What?"

"It's a simple deal; the ring for your location."

"You wouldn't —"

"I'm dead if that ring is left out there. Get me the ring, Meghan. Or you're not going to see tomorrow."

Kate shoved maps to the side and arched

her back as best she could in the car seat to ease the ache that had become nearly a cramp. The problem with being this pregnant was everything in her body protested being in the same position for more than ten minutes at a time.

The radio crackled as another searcher called back his grid number. She marked off another square on her hand-drawn map of the road, the wreck, and the area they needed to search. Dave and Stephen were out with Blackie, and nine others had now arrived to help with the search. They would find Meghan. They wouldn't stop looking until they did, but it was taking longer than expected. She wished the sheriff would call and say Meghan was in Silverton and this was a mix up.

Radio tones sounded and the updated weather warnings were read. Kate grabbed the knob and turned up the volume as the town list was read again. She found the map and struggled to read the fine print of town names. She closed her eyes and wanted to swear, but instead put her hand on the car horn and gave a fifteen-second-long blast, paused for five seconds, and gave another long blast. She forced her arms into her coat and wrestled open the door. The wind slammed the door back at her. The nearest officer coming her way had a radio. "There's hail coming, quarter of an inch. Get everyone back in!"

Blackie pawed at the car door. Stephen wrapped his arms around the wet animal and pulled him back. "I know you want to go out there and find her, but you can't go, boy."

The dog shook water off his coat and rested his head on Stephen's arm. "I know." Stephen shared the dog's depression. The hail on the roof was deafening. "If she's out in this —" Stephen couldn't finish that thought.

"We pray," Kate said from the front seat. "We pray, we hope, and when it eases up, I'm joining the search too."

Stephen buried his head in the dog's fur. *Jesus, Meghan loves You, and I love her. I failed to keep her safe. Please, help me rescue her. Wherever she is, help me find her.*

Car lights swept across the rear window. Stephen looked back to see if it was more help arriving, but the car drove past.

"We've got another theory beyond she got lost and is out there somewhere in this," Kate offered.

He turned toward his sister. Anything was better than the image of Meghan out there

431

getting pounded by this hail. "I'm listening."

"The ring Meghan found, the pieces you found in the piano bench — they're from the same robbery. If the original owner heard about the ring, he may have sent someone to retrieve his property. He'll be after the four pieces, and Meghan has three of them with her. She knows I've got the fourth."

Dave nodded. "Or another possibility: The ledger had a column of payments to someone who made the exchange. The person who originally swapped the pieces could have heard the jewelry had been found and is trying to get hold of them."

Kate looked at her husband. "Good point."

"I know you're making up these hypothetical scenarios to help me out," Stephen said, "but why would the ring be so important to justify snatching Meghan?"

"Steal something from a mob boss, you kind of hope it never reappears in your lifetime. The guy who made the exchange needs the pieces back no matter what the cost. Jail is an easier alternative than death. And if the mob boss wants them back, I don't think he's going to wait for the cops to return them."

"I don't care who or why, we just have to

get Meghan back safe."

The car phone rang and they all froze. It had been a hypothetical idea to keep his mind off the fact Meghan was out getting bloodied by this hail, but suddenly he wasn't sure, and neither were they.

Dave looked at Kate. "You're the negotiator."

Surprise crossed her face as Dave offered her the lead in this, and then her expression smoothed out and became impassive as Kate mentally shifted to work mode. No matter what happened, she'd try to calmly shape events. She picked up the phone and answered in a smooth and cheerful voice, "This is Kate."

"Let's go, Meghan. We've got an exchange to make." Jonathan pulled her to her feet. The smoke was choking them now as it settled in the room. The pieces he had taken recently in Europe were marked on that ledger page as sold. A surprise, but Neil apparently had been moving pieces taken on other continents as soon as they came in. It was his second lucky break of the night. That left the ring and its chilling inscription as the final piece to find before he could safely disappear.

He opened the driver's door and pushed

Meghan's head down to put her into the car. "Slide over." He wouldn't put it past her to try to bolt on him into the darkness.

"No matter where you run, they'll find you."

"You're the only one who knows my identity, and you won't be talking."

"I won't cover for you."

He started the car. "Stephen will be dead if you don't. These stones were stolen from a man who would think nothing of murdering to get them back. You try to suggest I'm involved, and I'll make sure one of those pieces in that case is delivered to the owner by courier, and I'll point at Stephen as the thief. He'll kill Stephen slowly and ask questions later. Do you understand me?"

"I hear you."

He drove north. There was one good thing about having known Craig. If this town had a shadier side and hiding places, Craig had known them. Jonathan knew where they could wait without risk of being found.

The sheriff's office was crowded. Kate rested her hip against the desk and sipped at the 7 Up Dave had gotten her for the nausea. "He knows this town. Look at directions to the drop-off point: *'Leave the ring east end of the bridge, in a briefcase on the concrete bench honoring the flood victims of 1913.'* This has got to be the guy who worked with Craig and Neil. Meghan didn't give any indication she knew the person who took her, but I bet she's got an idea. With this weather, we can't track him from the air, and on country roads we'll have a very hard time staying with his car without revealing our presence. You can't be stealthy in a downpour."

"Meghan's location and safety is the only thing that matters," Stephen insisted. Kate reached over and squeezed his arm. "It's the first thing that matters. He's got every incentive to make this trade and make it fast. He'll want to get away under cover of the storm. I doubt Meghan will be close to the exchange site. He'll want to use the fact we have to go get her as a way to buy himself more time to get away. Lying to us and taking her with him — it would only add to the intensity of the manhunt. It's in his best interests to tell us where she is. Stephen, do you want to stay here, and we call the location in so you can go with the cops to get her, or do you want to go out to the drop site?"

"I'm going with you," Stephen said. "Where are Meg's parents?"

"On their way back from Chicago. Bill was at the hospital with a patient when we got word to him. Elizabeth had gone along to help the patient's wife. I sent an officer to drive them back," the sheriff replied.

"Can you divert them to their home? After this is over Meghan will need a safe place to decompress, and I'd rather take her to her parents' home than back here for the debriefing. Anything short of serious medical needs, her father can best handle."

"Done."

"Who do you suggest should leave the briefcase with the ring at the bench?" Kate asked.

The sheriff nodded to his deputy. "Tom. He knows that area well. He can leave the briefcase, drive away, and find the nearest secluded spot to stop and observe. My guess is the guy will try to cross the Mississippi and head into Iowa. This weather is going to cut off a lot of his options. We've got power lines down and numerous trees. We can get resources on the most likely crossing points."

"What if this guy goes to ground somewhere around here after he picks up the ring? Just sits and waits for the search to cool off?" Stephen asked.

"He'd be risking Meghan being able to

tell us who he is."

The front door of the sheriff's office slammed open. "The jewelry store is on fire!"

Stephen surged outside with the officers. The store . . . the vault. If the guy had locked Meghan in the vault and tossed a match on some gasoline . . . Meghan's dog bolted away from him and into the night, heading in the direction of Meghan's house.

"Blackie!"

He couldn't go after the animal but couldn't lose him either. Meghan would need Blackie when they found her.

The wind whipped around and smoke blanketed the street. He choked and raised his arm to breathe through his sleeve. The inferno inside the jewelry store flashed over, and windows in the upper apartment exploded. An interior wall collapsed. Stephen tried to get near the building but was forced back by officers. The volunteer firemen began to arrive.

Anyone inside that building was dead.

Kate wrapped her arm around him. "She's not in there."

"You don't know that."

"We have to believe it." She tugged at his arm. "Come on; let's go. We'll leave the ring at the bench and wait for the call."

Twenty-eight

"Don't leave me here," Meghan pleaded against being abandoned. As much as she wanted to be away from Jonathan, she didn't want it happening like this. The cues from the trip, how long the car ride was, the road surfaces, nothing gave her a clue for where she was. She couldn't hear traffic or the sounds of town life. Just the whistle of the wind and the intense crack of thunder.

"Sit down."

Her hand felt a quilt and the edge of a bed; she touched an old iron headboard.

"The place just smells musty from lack of use. It's dry and there are no bugs or mice. The refrigerator is still running; you can hear its hum. There are plenty of sodas still in it, and there are peanut butter and tubes of crackers on the top shelf of the refrigerator. Craig used this place all the time."

"Where are we? Please, I need to know."

"You are safer if you don't know, if you simply stay here. Don't try to get yourself home, Meghan. On a night like this you'll break your neck in those woods. When I have the ring and am away from here, I'll let them know where you are." He walked away. The fury of the storm whipped inside when he opened the door. "I'm sorry about this."

"If you were sorry about it, you wouldn't be doing this."

The door closed. Meghan sat frozen, listening to the unknown stillness around her. She drew her feet up on the bed and wrapped her arms around her knees. The shaking started and then the tears. *Oh, Lord, what am I going to do?*

She tasted blood as she bit her lower lip. Gulping air, she forced herself to calm down. *Jesus* . . . She rubbed her arms to try and stop the shaking. Jonathan was gone. She was alone, but she was okay.

Kate was somewhere in Silverton. Stephen must have called his family for help as soon as he realized she wasn't in the truck. They'd find her. Stephen wouldn't stop searching until he found her.

She had to get up and explore this place. If there was power for a refrigerator then someone was paying utility bills. There might be a phone. Stephen and her parents had to be nearly frantic by now. She cautiously moved a foot down to the floor. A wind gust rattled a plane of glass so hard it sounded as if it cracked.

"Did he take the ring or not?" Stephen demanded, feeling every minute past midnight tick by as an eternity. "The briefcase and ring were left as ordered. Why hasn't he taken it and called?"

Dave focused his binoculars out the open driver's side window. "I can't tell if the case is still there or not. The rain is too heavy to see with night vision goggles any better than straight binoculars. Kate?"

"Nothing."

Dave picked up the radio. "Tom, do you see anything?"

"Negative."

Stephen leaned across from the backseat, peering into the rain. "One of us needs to go down there to see if he already took the case and left us sitting here without a lead on Meghan."

Kate squeezed his hand. "We wait."

Stephen leaned his head down against the front seat. Five hours. Meghan had been missing close to five hours. *Jesus, I can't stand this wait. Where is she?* He was trying hard to trust God to be a faithful friend and help him. It wasn't easy.

440

The phone rang and Kate grabbed it. "Yes, this is Kate."

She dropped the phone and grabbed the radio. "Tom, she's at the old mill house! Where is that?"

"The northeast side of town, near the old water tower."

"We'll go. You've got this scene. Don't move in to check that bench until we know for sure we have Meghan."

"Roger."

Dave put the car in reverse, leaving the headlights off until he had slowly moved away from their lookout spot. Then he turned around, switched on the headlights, and put his foot down on the gas. Kate scrambled to search the map.

"Okay. Go east at this next interchange," Kate pointed out.

"What exactly did he say?" Stephen asked.

"Just the location and he hung up. There wasn't enough for me to be able to recognize the voice."

The car hit a pothole and Kate shifted uncomfortably. Stephen put his hand down on her shoulder, silently sympathizing with the discomfort she was in.

"When we get there, you and Dave go on ahead and rescue her. Just don't rush forward until you have a feel for what the situation is."

"We'll be careful," Stephen promised. *Meghan, we're coming. Just hold on.*

The radio broke in for a weather update. A tornado watch and flash flood warning were added to the severe storm warning. Meghan hated storms. And without Blackie available to help her . . . They had to find her soon.

"There it is!" Stephen spotted the old water tower first. "The gravel road has to be just ahead."

Dave slowed the car. The car rocked in the powerful wind gusts. Stephen strained to look through the darkness and rain. There were few visual clues to mark the area — no homes, few side roads. The sheriff described the old mill house as a one-room hunting lodge rarely used by its owners.

Kate pointed. "On your left. There's the private drive."

It was narrow gravel and disappeared into the trees. Dave turned down the road. "How far back in these woods do you guess it is?"

"A hunting lodge could be a mile back," Stephen guessed. The road began to head up a steep incline.

"This is far enough, Dave," Kate warned. "Look at the phone poles. Power and phone lines just joined together. It's probably not that far ahead."

"Agreed. From here we walk." Dave pulled to the side and stopped the car. He turned off the headlights. The howling wind immediately dominated every sound. Dave tried his phone. "I've still got a signal. I'll call you, Kate, and you can drive up once we know what we're dealing with."

Stephen picked up the extra torchlight and the medical kit backpack. He pushed open the door and the wind about ripped the door off its hinges. To the left of the road was an open field and the tall grass was whipping first east and then flattening to the west. Gravel was beginning to stir on the road.

A tree crashed nearby in an explosion of wood. Stephen had been out in a lot of bad weather but this was scary. "Kate, we need to park the car elsewhere." A tree would land on her if they left it here.

Kate opened her door. "Take me with you. When we find Meghan, we'd best be prepared to hunker down and stay put until this blows over."

Dave looked around and nodded. "I don't like it but yes, come with us. If we drive up to the house, we risk getting shot at. If I leave you here, it may be very hard to get back to you later. I don't want you sitting in a car for the rest of the night. Just stay back when the fun starts."

They set off along the road, Kate walking between them. If the mill house was set back in those trees there were no lights on. The only sign something was there was the road and the power lines. Meghan alone, in a place she didn't know . . . "I can't believe he just left her out here."

"We'll find her, Stephen," Kate promised.

"I hope she didn't try to get to help on her own."

"She's a wise lady, even when scared to death. She will sit and wait for us."

Stephen wasn't so sure. If Meghan thought the man might come back, she'd get away while she could.

Stephen felt a sudden updraft. Seconds passed and it did not dissipate. He looked up at the sky hearing a faint rumble of distant thunder and something else. The updraft intensified.

Kate stopped. "What is *that?*"

Dave shoved his wife toward the open field as a tree ahead of them snapped. "We are not moving to the country!"

Stephen heard it then, the sound of a

freight train coming. He grabbed Kate and swung her over the roadside ditch as Dave jumped it. Dave picked Kate up and ran. Stephen spotted the culvert and pushed Dave toward it. They hit the ground as the wind started lifting anything it could. Stephen pushed Kate's head down and prayed the depression was deep enough. He grabbed his phone from his pocket and felt like swearing when he couldn't get a signal. Then he reached across and grabbed Dave's and had better luck getting through to the sheriff's office. "There's a tornado on the ground north of the water tower! Sound the sirens, warn people!"

The noise turned deafening. Trees lifted from the ground. Dave sheltered Kate's body as debris began to rain down. The tornado tore through ahead of them, cutting apart the land. Stephen put his face into the wet earth.

Meghan. Oh, God, please, keep her safe.

Meghan hit a table hard, bruising her thigh. She pushed the table aside, grabbed the chair and shoved it ahead of her, using it to clear her way. She knew that frightening sound.

The roof groaned above her. It would be ripped away any moment. Under the bed was no protection. Outside would be worse as trees came down.

Lord, what do I do?

She was a sitting duck.

Her hand touched brick.

A fireplace. She searched frantically to find out if there was a built-in wood box or something strong and sturdy near this wall of bricks.

The roof peeled up and began breaking apart. Meghan covered her head with one arm as she tried to protect herself. Water cascaded inside. She whimpered and struggled with the only thing she could find. She tipped the heavy couch over and shoved it near the brick wall. She crawled beneath it for shelter, hoping it was heavy enough it would be buried in the rubble and not lifted away in the wind. Glass exploded.

"Meghan! Where are you?!" Stephen's torchlight lit up a broken bedroom door leaning drunkenly against an oak tree. Curtains wrapped around a fallen tree branch fluttered. The kitchen table was twenty yards ahead sitting among the grass as if set up there in a normal place for a meal. Stephen helped Kate over a tree trunk.

Kate's torchlight illuminated a shattered lamp resting ten feet up in a tree. The old mill house was now pieces of wood and brick and furniture strewn on the ground through the trees.

"There!" Dave focused his light ahead of them. The skeleton of the house was still there — two outside walls were still standing and part of the roof tipped in on its side. Stephen released Kate's arm, looked to make sure she was steady, and then surged ahead of her to join Dave.

He picked his way around the foundation of the house. "Meghan!"

"Is there a basement or a shelter somewhere she would have dove for cover?" Dave asked, his light running across the building remains.

Stephen wedged his light in a crevice. "Dig!" He started tossing drywall and broken furniture away. Tears tracked down his face. *She was in this!* A nail on a board pierced his glove and drew blood. He tossed the board away. He climbed over the remains of the refrigerator and with Dave's help shoved it off the debris pile. They needed more help, light, time. Minutes counted when someone was hurt. Dawn was still hours away, and he was afraid there would be no extra hands to help them. Destruction marked the path of the tornado as it cut toward town.

Meghan pushed her hand against the fabric of the couch, her head aching, nearly deaf from the noise. "Here." Someone was out there. She tried to call and could barely whisper. She tried to get a deeper breath but it made her dizzy. Something was covering the opening she had used when she slipped under the sofa. Bricks. Those were bricks. The fireplace had come down over the couch.

She was getting hot. She lifted her head a few inches from the floor and realized her mouth was bleeding again. "Over here." Her hand felt the cool metal of the fire poker near the couch arm. She couldn't lift it, but she could wiggle it. She moved it as much as she could, trying to dislodge what it had struck. She heard something fall.

"Meghan!"

The voices were getting louder. She pushed the poker again and realized she could move the bricks. She rested her head back down on the floor and put her energy into moving out bricks.

"She's under here!"

Stephen. She let her head rest back against the floorboard. He'd come. She gulped air around the tears of relief, then she reached a hand toward where she could hear them digging. She waited for her rescuer to reach her.

Stephen tugged his sweater over Meghan's head, turning her into a mummy of wool. "Better?" He wiped at the remaining traces of tears.

"Much." She wrapped her arms around the warmth. They sat in the shelter of the remaining wall, out of the wind and the tapering-off rain. Stephen checked her pulse again and this time she didn't try to push his hand away. She had a cut on her lip, a few bruises, and he was still worried about her hearing, but she'd come through this night in better shape than he could have hoped.

He dug through his pockets looking for anything else that might help, or at least bring comfort. He found a piece of gum, not sure how old it was. It wouldn't do her sore jaw any good. He set it aside.

She laughed weakly. "I wish I'd been able to see the tornado. Ken has been trying to get near one for years and I ended up under one."

"A little too close for my comfort." He ran his finger along her hairline, pushing back her dripping bangs and wishing he had a hat to offer her. "That couch is about the only piece of furniture still actually left in the house. We passed the mattress stuck up in a tree and the bed frame wrapped around a snapped telephone pole."

"I prayed for an angel to sit on it for me to keep it from moving."

Stephen leaned down and kissed her forehead. "I'll take it, however it happened. I did a lot of praying too."

She smiled toward him, and then her expression turned distant. "Did they catch him?"

Stephen didn't let himself dwell on what he would like to do to the man who had kidnapped her. "I don't know. I was coming to rescue you."

"I appreciate your priorities." She leaned against his chest and wrapped her arms around him. "I knew you would come."

He rubbed his hand across her back. "You wanna talk about it?"

She instantly shook her head.

He leaned down to see her face. The separation from Blackie, the storm, being snatched, going through it blind — they had to talk about it sometime soon, or the memories would just mess with her head. Now wasn't the right time to push. "Maybe later," he offered and she didn't reject the idea.

"Where's Blackie?"

"I had him with me at the sheriff's office when word came in the jewelry store was on fire. He bolted on me, heading toward your house. He's been frantically looking for you."

"He'll crawl under the porch — he's got a blanket pulled under there — or if he can get into the house and head under my bed, he'll be there."

"I'll find him as soon as we get to town," he promised. The weight of the day was catching up with him. He hugged her and sighed. "Let's not do this again, okay?"

"I'm exhausted enough to fall asleep right here. I don't think I'll worry about hearing just a little wind and thunder anymore."

"I agree with that."

Dave's torchlight appeared as he helped Kate over the uneven ground.

"Kate is pretty wiped out too. She's coming over with Dave now."

"You let her out in this?"

"Saying no wasn't an option."

Meghan struggled to sit up. "The couch was upside down; it will still be pretty dry. Dig it out and give us somewhere more comfortable to sit than the ground."

It was a good idea. Stephen squeezed Meghan's hand and stood. He tugged the couch out of the remaining rubble of the fireplace. Kate joined Meghan and Dave came over to help him.

"What are the odds we'll find the car still drivable?" Stephen asked Dave as he flipped over the couch cushions to find the driest side.

"I'll hike back to the road and find out," Dave said. "I'll drive in as close as I can. I'd rather not spend the rest of the night out here."

"Take the extra batteries for the flashlight."

"Will do." Dave stopped and hugged Kate, then headed for the road.

"Meghan, let's move you to the couch." Stephen helped her up. She held onto his hand and Kate's arm and picked her way through the debris. She gripped the arm of the couch and moved to sit down. "Okay, this is good."

Meghan tugged Kate down to sit beside her. "Swing your feet up on the couch and breathe deeply. Stephen, can you find the throw pillows? They were near the couch earlier. And we need a blanket."

"What's wrong?"

Kate groaned and started to pant.

Meghan laughed. "She's in labor."

Twenty-nine

Dave pushed the car keys into his pocket and walked through the trees back to the destroyed hunting lodge. They had transportation out of here. Meghan needed to get back on familiar turf, and he had to get Kate somewhere she could get some rest. Ahead of him Meghan and Stephen both hovered over Kate. He broke into a jog over the rough ground.

"What's wrong?" He looked from Stephen to Meghan and then at his wife, and he forgot everything else going on around him. Her face was bunched in a tight grimace, her eyes closed, the strain showing in her body. "She's in labor!"

"Yes."

The contraction shook his wife. "Kate —" Dave knelt beside the couch, his hand gripping hers tight. He was going to be a dad too early, and far from the hospital where he had her preregistered. "Breathe, love, like they showed you."

The contraction eased off and her eyes

opened as she sucked in a deep breath. "I'm having this baby. Now!"

His hand shook as he pushed back her hair. "And you're going to be fine; I'm right here, just like I promised. Why didn't you say something earlier?"

"I didn't know. My back ached, but then the contractions just started."

"The car survived; we've got transportation to get us back to Silverton."

"That would be good," she whispered, breathing out. "Assuming Stephen doesn't want to deliver his niece or nephew right here."

Stephen paled. "Dave, give me the keys to the car. I'll check how much gas we've got left and see if phones still work, find out which roads are passable. We either try for Silverton, or we head the extra miles to Ridgefield. Don't move her until I get back and can help."

Dave dug out his keys and handed them to Stephen. "Just getting back to the highway is going to be the biggest challenge."

"I'm willing to shove aside a downed tree if you are. Meghan, come with me. Let's see what we can do about getting the backseat cleared for Kate to recline."

"Guys, relax. She's got plenty of time."

Meghan hugged Kate. "I'll be back." She reached for Stephen's hand. "Let's go."

Dave watched Stephen and Meghan walk toward the car. "They make a nice couple."

"It's about time he settled down."

Dave turned back to his wife, leaned forward and kissed her. "No chance this is a false alarm and the little one is just making sure we're paying attention?"

"None."

"I was afraid of that." He leaned his head forward against hers. His wife handled a kidnapping first and pushed aside the fact she was in labor until after the job was done. "Good job, Kate." He laughed. "Just think of the story we'll have to tell at birthdays."

"I want a little girl."

"As long as she is just like you, that would be okay with me."

She looked around. "I really do not want to have this baby here."

"I'll carry you back to town if I have to. Lie back and relax while you can. The car ride will be tough."

The tornado had hit the town. Stephen drove slowly through the debris-filled main street, easing the car over bricks and boards and stripped tree limbs. The smoke rising from the jewelry store added to the sense of its being a war zone. Two bulldozers were literally pushing debris out of the roadway. "It's bad, Meghan." There wasn't panic among those directing the cleanup. Men would be digging by hand through that rubble if someone was thought buried under there. The tornado sirens must have given the residents just enough warning to get to cover.

"Get us as close to the side door of the clinic as you can," Meghan urged.

"I'll try. The road is crowded with cars, and deputies are bringing what looks like the walking injured into the clinic," Stephen said. "The building is in good shape, just a couple toppled trees. Ahh, here we go. Joseph has triage set up in the parking lot. He can help us get Kate inside."

Kate arched her back to ease a contraction. "It's good timing. We don't have much time!"

"Dave, support her back. Breathe, Kate. Pant. Stay ahead of it," Meghan said.

"I'm trying."

Stephen didn't dare look back. He concentrated on getting through the vehicles.

"That's good. Keep with it. It's going to ease off," Meghan encouraged.

Kate groaned. "It is not. And I want to push."

"Not yet!" Dave ordered. "Just squeeze my hand and don't push."

"Kate, it's early yet. The sensation is just the baby moving. You've still got several hours of labor ahead of you, I'm afraid."

"Oh, don't say that, Meg. I won't survive it."

Stephen threw the car in park and rushed around to open the back door. "Okay, sis, we're here." She was panting as the contraction faded away.

"We've got a couple minutes before the next one hits. Let's get you comfortable inside, love," Dave encouraged. Stephen helped Dave ease her out of the car. Dave swept her up into his arms.

Stephen rushed ahead of him to open the door.

"This way." Meghan directed them through the back hall of the clinic. "I'll get Dad. He's wonderful at delivering babies."

Stephen caught her hand to pause her at the doorway. "I'm needed out there with Joseph. I hate to leave you here, but . . ." His lips brushed against hers. "Remember I love you."

Her hands framed his face and she kissed him back. "I love you too. Now go to work."

Stephen struggled to get around the downed trees and power lines to reach Meghan's street. She desperately needed Blackie with her.

Her house was gone. He stood and stared at the destruction, feeling sick. All that remained was the fireplace, an interior wall, and part of the roof bracing. There were no discernable rooms, no sign of her piano. The flooring had gone into the basement area. The next house on the street was merely a smooth foundation. She'd loved this house and all the dreams it represented.

"Blackie!" Meghan had suggested under the porch or under her bed. Stephen didn't have much hope for either.

The answering bark was faint but joyous. And it was somewhere from the far left side of this mess. "Blackie, where are you?"

Stephen climbed over the debris and got down on his belly as he realized the sound was coming from below him in what had once been the basement. He shoved aside loose boards. The dog was down there in two feet of water. Blackie desperately tried to jump and get a foothold on the debris only to slide back into the water with a splash.

"Easy, boy. Let me come to you." A beam

had protected the dog from being buried in the debris. He was behind what looked like the hot-water heater, the white metal giving the animal no traction. Plaster pieces floated in the water around him.

Stephen locked his feet around a beam and wiggled another six inches over the edge. He got a hand around the dog's front leg and another in the fur behind his neck and he did the only thing he could — hauling the animal out even as he yelped. "Sorry, boy, sorry."

He got a drenching as the wet animal slammed against him and then a hot bath as the dog licked every inch of his face he could reach. Stephen held the dog off his chest and heaved a deep breath as he laughed. "I'm glad you're alive too. And there's someone who is going to be very happy to see you."

The sun rose into a pink dawn. Stephen held a towel against a lady's badly gashed arm as he walked with her into the clinic, grateful the sight of blood was no longer causing him problems. A nurse met them before they had even crossed the waiting room. Doctors and nurses from surrounding towns poured into Silverton to help, and for the first time since this had begun, Stephen felt as though they were getting ahead of the rescue efforts.

"Thank you, Stephen."

"My pleasure, Mrs. Heath. They'll have you fixed up in no time." He handed his patient off.

He saw Meghan step out of an exam room at the end of the hall and he whistled as he headed her direction. Her head came up and she swiveled her head to locate the direction of the sound, and then a private smile appeared just for him.

"Hey there, beautiful." Blackie was pressed so tight against her left knee she had to take cautious steps.

She pushed back her hair with both hands. "Hardly beautiful after this night, but I'll take the kind words."

"How's Kate doing?"

Her face lit up with her smile. "Good. Ashley is coaching her, and she's the expert. Maybe in the next half hour. If the ambulances weren't so urgently needed for the injured, Dad would have transferred Kate to the hospital, but I think the plan now is to let her deliver here. Two obstetricians are among the medical teams helping out, so she'll be in good hands when the time comes. Dave's with her. Would you like to see them?"

"In a bit. Can you take a couple minutes and share the back steps and a cup of coffee?"

"I would love to."

Volunteers had set up coffee, tea, toast, and donuts on the table in the receptionist area. Stephen got them coffee and walked Meghan out through the back of the clinic. "I'm glad you can't see this damage. The town took a direct hit."

She pushed off her tennis shoes and worked a rock out. "There were no casualties, so it could have been much worse. Dad said their place and yours are pretty much untouched."

Stephen rested a hand against her face to turn her toward him. "I'm sorry about your house."

"So am I. Everything I dreamed about from the curtains over the kitchen sink to the wind chimes by the front door. It was a house kept alive in my memories all these years. I can't believe it's just gone."

"I'll rebuild it for you. Every detail."

Her eyes filled with tears. "You would do that for me?"

"You bet." He would love to have her one day sharing his farm, but he wasn't going to use this timing to even suggest she think that direction.

Her smile appeared. "I'll think about it some. Maybe the next house shouldn't have a basement. Or that step into the garage I kept missing."

He wiped away her tears. "We'll make it right, okay? Of everything you have to be sad about right now, the loss of the house is one thing we can fix." Stephen picked up her hand and looked at how the scrapes were healing. She'd been wearing latex gloves and the powder had irritated the scrapes. He soothed his thumb across them and made a note to get some lotion. "How else are you doing?"

"I'm okay, just very tired."

An understatement if he'd ever heard one. She looked exhausted.

A car door in the parking lot slammed and her coffee sloshed. She was still very nervous under that fatigue. "Would you tell me about what happened?"

"I'd rather not."

He let her drink her coffee. "Why?"

"I was so scared . . ." she whispered.

"Then share it, let me at least soften the memories."

"I hate being blind. There was no reference point for where I was, what the surroundings were like. Without Blackie — I was petrified to move. And when I heard

462

that sound of the wind . . . I just want to forget."

He rubbed her arm. "Did you know your abductor?"

She didn't answer him.

Stephen turned her face toward him and brushed his hand along her cheek. "You can trust me with whatever that answer is."

"I trust you. I just don't want to talk about it."

Someone she knew. It must be someone she knew. And if he pushed, he'd be adding to the pressure she felt. "We'll talk later, then. I may be gone a good part of this morning. I'll be going up soon with the police helicopter to comb the area for others who need help. Jack is part of that area search team and he needs another paramedic out there. If you get done here, would you head out to your parents and I'll meet you there later?"

"Yes. I'll stop by with Mom and take care of your animals if you like."

"I'd appreciate that. Maybe I'll just say a brief hi to Kate from the doorway. Labor is hard to watch."

Meghan laughed and got to her feet. "It's hard to endure too. Come on; I'll hold your hand."

Because her smile had returned, Stephen

463

took her up on the offer. They went back into the clinic and walked through to a comfortable room at the back.

Dave was sitting by Kate's side, feeding her ice chips. Both looked like they had been through a battle. Uncertain about this, wishing he hadn't asked, Stephen walked over to Kate. He gently touched her sweaty hand. "Hi."

She opened her eyes enough to smile at him. "I'm having a baby, not dying. This is just tiring work."

Dave fed her more ice. "We have a baby who has decided to take her time in coming."

Kate groaned as another contraction hit.

Meghan slipped her hand in his and Stephen squeezed it, appreciating the comfort.

Ashley timed the latest contraction. "Why don't you go find your dad, Meg? I think this little one is finally ready to make an appearance."

"About time," Kate panted.

Dave wiped her forehead. "Tomorrow you'll be saying it wasn't so bad."

"Then I'd be lying."

Dave laughed and kissed her forehead.

Thirty

The police helicopter landed east of the bank and Stephen hurried toward it. Jack shoved open the door for him. "We've got to rush it — they've only got fuel for another forty minutes before they have to divert to the airport, and there's a lot of territory to cover."

Stephen clipped on the seat restraints. "I'm good."

The pilot lifted off.

Jack handed over a map. "We've been searching the tornado path west along the highway and it's a wide swath. They think a couple secondary twisters in the storm front added to the damage. Teams of searchers are fanning out along the roads to check damaged structures, but some of the remote homes can only be reached by air."

"How many injuries so far?"

"Twelve, nothing serious. We're transporting to the nearest ground team if it's not life threatening."

Stephen found a place to store the extra

gloves he'd brought. "Where's Tom working?"

"South of here, at a collapsed silo. Two teams are trying to reach a trapped man."

"Did Tom have anything to pass on regarding last night?"

"Tom spotted a car leaving the area where the ring was left, but he lost it right about here in this cloverleaf of roads. I'm betting the guy headed toward the river. But that road, at that time of night — he was driving across the path of the twister. He would have been hit with the brunt of this storm front."

"Do we know anything about the make and model of the car?"

"Tom saw enough to place it as a late model tan Toyota."

"Keep your eyes peeled for it just in case we get lucky and the guy had a flat tire or drove himself into a ditch." The odds they would find the car eight hours later were slim, but Stephen couldn't stand the idea of Meghan's abductor getting away.

"Will do." Jack dug out a second pair of binoculars and handed them over.

The helicopter passed over the path of the tornado. The ground had been stripped down to the dirt, and a long trail of debris adorned the path. Stephen started searching the area for signs of anyone needing help.

"Jack, down there!" Stephen slapped his brother's shoulder and pointed to the country road to their east. From the air the vehicle was a shiny reflection in the sun against the water. It rested upside down on the banks of an overflowing stream, shoved there during the night by a powerful flow of water. "It's not tagged."

Searchers had been leaving bright fluorescent stickers on structures and vehicles they checked to mark them as cleared. Stephen was pretty sure even at these angles that the vehicle had tan paint.

"Let's check it out."

The helicopter pilot nodded and banked them toward the stream. Stephen reached for a couple fluorescent tags. As soon as the helicopter touched ground, Jack shoved open the door. Stephen unclipped his restraints and followed his brother. They jogged toward the crash.

"The car isn't stable," Jack warned, seeing the water rock it.

"Help me down over there. I can get near enough to check if it's empty." Stephen pulled on his gloves. It was a tan Toyota. He wanted to check this vehicle for more reasons than just an injured driver. Jack tested how secure the tree was at the top of the incline and nodded, then got a good hold and offered Stephen a hand to help ease his way down.

Stephen scrambled not to topple into the water as his feet hit the stream bank. "This water is freezing." He picked his way downstream to reach the car and knelt to peer through the broken-out side window. "It's empty!"

"He probably abandoned the vehicle before the worst of the storm came through."

"Maybe. The river water did a number on the inside — there's nothing in the car not fastened down." He tried to reach in and open the glove box but it was jammed. Stephen pushed himself away from the car, disappointed. If this was the car Meghan had been in, there was nothing here to help him. He slapped the fluorescent tags on so they could be seen from the air.

Stephen elected to pass the car and go up the bank farther downstream. He saw the case as he reached for a low-lying tree limb. Open, wedged against the tree roots, the velvet was destroyed by the water. It was the case he'd held last night, found in the piano bench. He reached for it.

The hinge had broken and the top of the case had cracked. Beyond water and mud it was empty. He searched the stream bank and nothing caught his attention. If the jewelry was anywhere here to be found, it would take a miracle to find it.

"This is the car." Stephen held up the box. "This is the jewelry box."

"There isn't going to be much forensic evidence worth finding. The river ran through the car for the night." Jack leaned down to help him out of the ravine. "Stay and search?" Jack asked. "The guy may be around here."

"If a driver's injured out here, we'll have better luck spotting him from the air," Stephen said. "Call Tom so he can mark the car and have it hauled in for evidence. Maybe they can trace the license plate. I bet the guy had another vehicle waiting and this car was abandoned here. There'd be no need to take an empty box along when he could stuff the jewels in his pocket."

"At least it's a solid lead."

Stephen had the feeling that it was the last clue they would get. The guy was gone.

Thirty-one

Stephen cradled his two-and-a-half-week-old niece against his chest and walked around the hotel banquet room, lulling Holly back to sleep. Jennifer had asked that he be happy, settled, and at peace with life. He couldn't get more content than this. Holly was perfection. Dark hair like Kate's, perfect eyelashes, cute fingers. Her skin was so incredibly soft.

He was an uncle.

Cole and Rachel's wedding this afternoon had been perfect in its simplicity and Jack and Cassie's tomorrow would be a day-long party. Tonight Kate, Dave, and their new daughter were stealing the show.

"Stephen, come over here."

He turned. Kate patted the open spot on the couch beside her. "I think Holly already has you wrapped around her little finger. I've never seen you so relaxed."

"Your daughter might have something to do with it." He smiled at Meghan seated beside Kate. She had a lot more to do with it.

"Want to hold Holly, Meg?"

"Please."

He carefully transferred the sleeping infant and then sat on the couch beside Meghan. He stretched out his arm and rested it along the back of the couch and around her shoulders. He idly twirled a lock of Meghan's hair around his finger. "Jack wants to go shoot a few baskets tonight to run off some nerves. Do you think you'll be okay here with Blackie for an hour? I'd better go along to keep him out of trouble." The dog lifted his head at the sound of his name, and Stephen reached down to rub his ears. Blackie was still showing the after-effects of having lost Meghan. He did not let her leave a room without going after her.

"I'll be fine here; you don't have to hurry back."

He smiled at her. "You just want to tug more stories out of Kate." Stephen leaned over and kissed her. "I'll be back in an hour."

Stephen slapped the basketball away from Jack, took off for the basket, and made a layup. "That's sixteen."

Jack chased down the ball. "Lucky grab." Jack tossed him the ball and Stephen tossed it back, putting it in play. This was the way they had formed their friendship decades ago, doing friendly battle over a basketball court.

"So are you ready to get married to-morrow?"

"Past ready." Jack cut around him and tried to dunk the ball. "I was pleased to see Meghan came with you."

"You'll forgive me if my attention as best man tomorrow is not entirely on my duties."

The gym door opened. Marcus walked in but not dressed to play ball; he was still in a suit from the party. "Hey, guys. Stephen, I need you a minute."

Stephen offered his hand to Jack. "Call it a draw?"

"Deal." Jack headed over to the bench where Cassie sat watching the game.

Stephen jogged over to Marcus. "What's happening?"

"Maybe a few answers." Marcus offered a file he held. "Kate wants to know if you happen to recognize these. They were couri-ered over tonight."

Stephen took the file. He was looking at a photo of the jewelry that had nearly cost him Meghan's life. The emerald earrings in particular were brilliant. His gaze shot up to hold Marcus's.

"You recognize them?"

Stephen closed the file and handed it to Marcus. "Those are the pieces we found in the piano bench, that Meghan was carrying the night she was snatched."

"Someone tried to resell them in St. Louis."

"Who was it?"

"The recovered car was rented to Jonathan Peters, and the description of the guy in St. Louis fits him."

"The pianist?" Stephen said.

"Yes. He's using his credit cards, but we haven't been able to put our hands on him yet."

"Meghan is going to be horrified."

Marcus gave a small smile. "Nice standing up for your lady. You know she already knows it was him."

"She'll never testify against him."

"That's pretty obvious." Marcus tucked the file under his arm.

Meghan was trying so hard to keep it quiet rather than say it had been a friend. "Does she have to know the stones were recovered?"

"For now the photos become part of the file. If we catch Jonathan, then we'll see what kind of case can be made."

Stephen relaxed. "Thanks."

"Don't mention it." Marcus nodded to Jack. "Letting him win as a wedding present?"

Stephen looked over at his brother. "Now would I do that?"

Marcus laughed and strolled toward Cassie. "I think I'll stick around and watch the end of this game."

Stephen stopped by his hotel room to clean up and retrieve a package from his suitcase before returning to the gathering. Kate looked to be asleep. Stephen paused by the couch to look down at her and then over at Dave sitting in the chair just watching his wife sleep. He shared a smile with him. Stephen looked around for Holly. Meghan had her, strolling back and forth in front of the windows as she rocked the infant. Stephen moved to join them, whistling softly.

Her head came up and she gave a half turn toward him.

"You look very comfortable."

She smiled as she rested her head against Holly. "I am. How was the game?"

"I let Jack win, but don't tell him that." He hesitated, but knew it was only a matter of time before the police apprehended Jonathan. "They found the jewelry, Meg. They know it was Jonathan."

Her sudden tension woke Holly and Stephen rested a hand on Meghan's shoulder to ease the reaction.

"They picked him up?"

"Not yet, but they likely will soon."

Meghan sighed and rocked Holly to calm the infant. "He threatened to use the jewels he did have to point the mob boss toward you as the thief. I've known Jonathan a long time. He was desperate, and I couldn't figure what he might do. And I didn't want to be the one to turn him in for kidnapping. He was a friend, even if he'd forgotten that fact. I wish I had been able to talk him into giving himself up."

"Don't, honey. You can't protect him from the results of his own choices."

"Will I have to testify against him?"

He stroked her shoulder with his thumb. "If you do, I'll be there with you. At least this ends it. The theft ring was Neil and Craig and Jonathan. It's finally over."

"Yes." Meghan smiled slightly. "I'm glad. I want my peaceful life back."

"So do I, as long as I get to be part of your peaceful future." He touched his niece's little hand. "I have something for you, but you'll have to trade me Holly."

"That's going to have to be something pretty special."

"Hmm, it is."

She carefully handed him the infant and Stephen settled his niece against his chest. "I'm in love with this little lady." He tucked the blanket snugly around the child. "Months ago, I had Neil make me something."

"I remember the receipt in the register. He just noted it was a customized piece."

"Don't look so flustered; I sketched it in the first days I came back. I just wanted it for a night we had something to celebrate. I wish Neil had done more of this kind of creating pieces than getting involved in what he did. He had a lot of talent." He half turned. "Slip your hand into my left jacket pocket."

She retrieved the tissue-paper-wrapped gift.

"I asked Neil to do it in silver."

"Oh, Stephen." The heart pendant was swirled in silver, with a script *M* inside.

He leaned over and kissed her forehead. "I would have added an *S* if it wouldn't have seemed too forward at the time." Stephen nudged her arm. "Hey, I've got my hands full. You can't cry on me."

She blinked back the tears even as she laughed. "I'm thinking I'll add it as a superman *S*, right behind my heart."

"Really?"

She slid her hand around his arm. "Did I just fluster you?"

"A bit." It was hard to think coherently when she was invading his space. "You rescued me, Meg, by leading me to the ultimate Rescuer. I thought we'd celebrate that tonight. I wish I'd figured out you were what I was searching for years ago." He bent to tenderly kiss her. "I wasted so much time."

"I love you, Stephen."

He smiled and wiped one of her tears, then shifted Holly so he could hug Meghan. He was tired of waiting when he finally found what he wanted. "When we get home, what do you say you come walk through the farmhouse and decide on a place for a new piano? What would you say about marrying me someday, Meghan?"

She about hugged the breath out of him. "I'd say yes."

He laughed and caught her close. The night was complete, and nearly perfect. "I wish Jennifer were here so I could tell her first."

"She knows," Meghan whispered against his shirt, then leaned back. "What do you say we wake up Kate to tell her next? Then call my parents."

Stephen looked over at his sister and smiled. "Yes, let's do that. This should be an O'Malley family celebration."

Dear Reader,

Thank you for reading this story. Stephen opened the O'Malley series with Kate in *The Negotiator*, and now in *The Rescuer* brings this set of books to a close. He's the last O'Malley to settle down, and his loneliness after the death of Jennifer is intense. His friendship with Meghan was the thing he turned to, and as I got to know Meghan, I understood why Stephen chose her. She's been through hard times and found the peace he seeks.

Stephen is the last O'Malley to believe. He knows who God is, knows what religion asks of a man, and his struggle is a matter of will. What Stephen needs most to hear is that Jesus wants to be his friend. He has to see the truth become personal: That Jesus wants to rescue him because God wants more than a servant; He wants a friendship. Is God trustworthy to be our deepest, closest Friend? Exploring that question with Stephen made this one of the richest

O'Malley books to write.

Thank you for reading the O'Malley series and getting to know this special family.

As always, I love to hear from my readers. Feel free to write me at:

Dee Henderson
c/o Multnomah Fiction
P.O. Box 1720
Sisters, Oregon 97759
E-mail: dee@deehenderson.com
or on-line: http://www.deehenderson.com

First chapters of all my books are on-line. I invite you to stop by and check them out. God bless,

Dee Henderson